This omnibus gathers together the novels of Jaime Clarke featuring Charlie Martens, who is desperate for stability in an otherwise peripatetic life. An explosion that killed his parents when he was young robbed him of any chance for normalcy and he was shuttled from relative to relative, left alone to decipher the world he encountered in order to cobble together an answer as to how he would live.

In *Vernon Downs* (2014), Charlie recognizes in Olivia, an international student from London, the sense of otherness he feels and their relationship seems to promise salvation. But when Olivia abandons him, his desperate mind fixates on her favorite writer, Vernon Downs, who becomes an emblem for reunion with Olivia. Charlie's quest takes him from Phoenix to New York City and when chance brings him into proximity to Vernon Downs, he quickly ingratiates himself into Downs's world. Proximity invites certain temptations, though, and it isn't long before Charlie moves dangerously from fandom to apprentice to outright possession.

World Gone Water (2015) enlarges the portrait of Charlie Martens. Set in Phoenix, seven years before the events of *Vernon Downs*, Charlie finds himself released from a voluntary stay at a behavioral clinic in the Sonoran desert, the result of an incident with a woman he met while tending bar in Florida where Charlie had fled to forget his high school sweetheart, whose sudden marriage to someone else devastates him. But Charlie's homecoming launches him into a chain of events with a cast of characters that assault his fragile state and further undermine his general impressions about life and how to live. *World Gone Water* roves the deep terrain of our want for emotional connection and is a devastating narrative about love, sex, and friendship.

Garden Lakes (2016) finds Charlie employed as an Arizona newspaper columnist who has built his career on a deception he committed that inadvertently stirred up anti-immigrant sentiment, casting a pall over the state. But Charlie's story is really one of serial deception, a life of prevarications he traces back to a summer fellowship program he attended while a junior at an all-boys prep school. The chosen fellows were tasked with undertaking supervised construction of a house in a half-built development donated to the school by the bankrupt developer. The fellows lived and worked together and were tested when a ~~~~~ girl wandered ~~~~ e development after the disappearanc ~~~~~~~~~~~~~~~~~~~~~~~~ nes. What happened at *Garden Lakes* re\ ~~~~~~~~~~~~~~~~~~~~~~~~~~ it especially Charlie's, which is forever

D1166243

Author photo by John Laprade

Jaime Clarke is a graduate of the University of Arizona and holds an MFA from Bennington College. He is the author of the novels *We're So Famous, Vernon Downs,* and *World Gone Water,* editor of the anthologies *Don't You Forget About Me: Contemporary Writers on the Films of John Hughes, Conversations with Jonathan Lethem,* and *Talk Show: On the Couch with Contemporary Writers,* and co-editor of the anthologies *No Near Exit: Writers Select Their Favorite Work from Post Road Magazine* (with Mary Cotton) and *Boston Noir 2: The Classics* (with Dennis Lehane and Mary Cotton). He is a founding editor of the literary magazine *Post Road,* now published at Boston College, and co-owner, with his wife, of Newtonville Books, an independent bookstore in Boston.

www.jaimeclarke.com

www.postroadmag.com

www.baumsbazaar.com

www.newtonvillebooks.com

VERNON DOWNS

WORLD GONE WATER

Garden Lakes

JAIME CLARKE

THE COMPLETE **CHARLIE MARTENS** *TRILOGY*

Roundabout Press   2021

For Robert —

w/ admiration + Thanks

Published by
Roundabout Press
PO Box 370310
West Hartford, CT 06137

by arrangement with
Bloomsbury Publishing Plc.
50 Bedford Sq, London.

Copyright © 2014, 2015, 2016 by Jaime Clarke
All rights reserved

ISBN: 978-1-948072-06-9

This is a work of fiction. Names, characters, places, and incidents either are the
products of the authors' imagination or are used fictitiously. Any resemblance
to actual events, locales, or persons, living or dead, is entirely coincidental.

Cover design Pete Hausler
Book design by Josephine Bergin

First printing: April 2021

To read about the last days of Charlie Martens, send a
blank email to frank@baumsbazaar.com to receive autoreply.

VERNON
DOWNS

Praise for VERNON DOWNS

"*Vernon Downs* is a gripping, hypnotically written and unnerving look at the dark side of literary adulation. Jaime Clarke's tautly suspenseful novel is a cautionary tale for writers and readers alike—after finishing it, you may start to think that J.D. Salinger had the right idea after all."

—TOM PERROTTA, author of *Election*, *Little Children*, and *The Leftovers*

"Moving and edgy in just the right way. Love (or lack of) and Family (or lack of) is at the heart of this wonderfully obsessive novel."

—GARY SHTEYNGART, author of *Super Sad True Love Story*

"All strong literature stems from obsession. *Vernon Downs* belongs to a tradition that includes Nicholson Baker's *U and I*, Geoff Dyer's *Out of Sheer Rage*, and—for that matter—*Pale Fire*. What makes Clarke's excellent novel stand out isn't just its rueful intelligence, or its playful semi-veiling of certain notorious literary figures, but its startling sadness. *Vernon Downs* is first rate."

—MATTHEW SPECKTOR, author of *American Dream Machine*

"An engrossing novel about longing and impersonation, which is to say, a story about the distance between persons, distances within ourselves. Clarke's prose is infused with music and intelligence and deep feeling."

—CHARLES YU, author of *Sorry Please Thank You*

"*Vernon Downs* is a fascinating and sly tribute to a certain fascinating and sly writer, but this novel also perfectly captures the lonely distortions of a true obsession."

—DANA SPIOTTA, author of *Stone Arabia*

I

CHARLIE HAD TRAVELED a long, indirect route to Summit Terrace. He could hardly recall a time he hadn't known the name Vernon Downs, though in truth the discovery was in the not-too-distant past.

"He's Olivia's favorite writer, dummy," Shelleyan had said that day in the Milky Way Café at Glendale Community College, where Charlie and Olivia were creative writing majors. It was his second stint at GCC; he knew from his first stab, after graduating from high school, that even though he was pushing thirty, he wasn't the oldest student on campus. That Olivia was twenty-two separated her—and him—from the student body full of teenagers who mostly behaved like they were still in high school, and the retirees taking classes as a hobby. Only Shelleyan could make him self-conscious of his advanced age. He ignored her, long used to Olivia's roommate as the price of Olivia's companionship. He'd met Olivia, an international student from London, the previous semester in Intro to Creative Writing. Over the prior summer, Charlie had read an interview with a writer who had a background similar to his—the writer was an army brat and had lived all over the world—and how that sense of impermanence informed his writing. Whether or not the writer was being self-deprecating, Charlie couldn't tell, but the piece spooked him a little, as the writer seemed to intimate that there was no place in the workaday world for those with such an upbringing. And so he enrolled in the creative writing class with more hope than ambition.

Discovering Olivia across the conference table seemed to confirm the impression Charlie had taken away from the interview. Olivia's nationality gave her an air of otherness, and Charlie perceived a kinship in the way she was both present but from somewhere else entirely. Olivia hadn't told her parents that she'd dropped out of Arizona State University the first week of the fall semester so she could pocket the difference in tuition between ASU and GCC. If anyone could fully comprehend the narrative of his past and, more importantly, overlook its irregularities, it was Olivia, who confessed that she liked the attention, which was all the encouragement Charlie needed. What began as a crush on a pretty girl with a sexy accent quickly evolved.

"What did he write?" Charlie asked Shelleyan, the name Vernon Downs vaguely familiar. He glanced at Olivia as she combed through that day's goulash with her fork.

"*Minus Numbers*," Shelleyan answered automatically, scooping a forkful into her mouth.

He looked at Olivia for help, but she was apparently absorbed in thoughts of Vernon Downs and *Minus Numbers*. More troubling than the notion of Olivia's secret admiration was the apparent truth that Shelleyan had been privy to the information but not him.

"You should really read it," Olivia said.

"You never finished it, liar," Shelleyan accused.

Olivia shrugged her off. "Of course I did."

"You just think he's cute," Shelleyan said. She turned to Charlie and he flinched. "He's in the movie for a second. He only has, like, one line."

Olivia giggled, embarrassed. "So what?" she asked. "He wrote the book it's based on, didn't he?"

"The book is nothing like the movie," Shelleyan snorted. "But I guess you wouldn't know that, huh?"

"So what?" Olivia said again. She had never found Shelleyan as intimidating as Charlie did.

He wondered how long it would be until she missed him. Really missed him, the way he knew he'd miss her once she was gone, a visa issue stripping her of her international student status after the spring semester. He dreaded the first time he would miss the candy aroma of her perfume, her smiling, freckled face drawing near, the harrowing moment when he would understand her loss in terms of his happy future thieved, stolen away back into the wilds of England.

Olivia had never mentioned Vernon Downs or *Minus Numbers* as far as he could recall, and he thought for a minute that they were putting him on. He awaited the punch line, the gentle ribbing that signified that he was still an intimate and not an ignorant outsider. He wasn't sure which he preferred: Olivia's having a simple infatuation with Downs or her actually admiring his writing, which, though he hadn't read anything by Downs, he was satisfied was facile and gimmicky. Hadn't he seen Downs in *GQ*? Serious writers didn't appear in the pages of *GQ*.

He was overcome with sadness at Olivia's leaving. Charlie knew intimately what it was to have something ripped out of your life, enervating your will, and senselessly: his parents, sure; but also the Kepharts, his maternal grandparents, in Denver, who helped him secure his Batman costume so he could burst into his third-grade homeroom, his new best friend, Jesse Mason, trailing in the Robin outfit, Mrs. Holstein looking on calmly as they scrambled after George McLean, the only Asian at Elrod Elementary, whom Charlie had talked into dressing as the Joker. The Kepharts had helped him crumple tiny pieces of aluminum foil, filling the bag of fake diamonds George clutched in his hand. Charlie's classmates squealed as the pursuit led them across the room, the chase continuing into the adjoining homeroom, as per his design. He explained to the principal that the drama would be more believable if the entire school was captivated by the play, a syllogism the principal accepted, much to Charlie's amazement. What Charlie didn't confess to the principal was that the production was simply a stunt to impress Suzy Young, whom he'd been caught kissing after the bell.

And the McCallahans, his aunt and uncle in Santa Fe, where he'd gone to live after the Kepharts admitted they were too old to raise a child. The McCallahans couldn't look at him with the same eyes they laid on their son, Ian, with whom Charlie had built a fort in the backyard out of empty boxes from Mr. McCallahan's job at Southwest Peterbilt. Only afterwards did he realize that Ian was technically his cousin, a fact that never arose while he was staying with the McCallahans.

And the Alexander-Degners of Rapid City, a cousin of his father's who was married to his high school sweetheart. Their childless neighbors had a dog that often found its way into the Alexander-Degners' yard. Charlie would play with the dog, chasing it up the grassy berm in their backyard that led to the freeway. The new neighbors were rarely seen, so that when a short, bearded man knocked on the Alexander-Degners' door to discuss erecting a fence between their yards to keep the dog from roaming free, Mr. Alexander assumed the man was the husband of the woman next door. Charlie learned only by eavesdropping that the man was a boyfriend, and that the couple had rented the house to get away from the woman's husband, a fact that the neighborhood discovered the morning after the boyfriend loaded his shotgun into his station wagon and drove to the local bar to call the husband outside and fire a slug into his chest, ending the alleged harassment the boyfriend and the woman next door had suffered at the husband's hands. The murder shocked their street, more so as no one knew the boyfriend or the woman, who had endeavored to live anonymously among their neighbors. Charlie retraced the neighbor's short drive to the bar in his mind, hearing him call the husband out onto the street, away from the innocent patrons, raising the shotgun to chest level. He imagined the husband, drunk, not begging for his life but daring the boyfriend to pull the trigger. Charlie heard the pop, smelled the smoke, saw the bewildered look on the husband's face. What were his taunts? How had he harassed them? Charlie tried to imagine the satisfaction the boyfriend must've felt when the threats evaporated. He wondered what it felt like to erase the past just like that.

He missed the Wallaces of San Diego too, another aunt and uncle, with whom he'd lived on base. Mr. Wallace treated him to trips to the flight simulator on Saturdays, until the Wallaces were dispatched to an air force base in Florida, a place Charlie, for some reason, couldn't go.

And of course he'd miss the Chandlers, his Arizona family, who'd enrolled him with every good intention at Randolph College Preparatory, an all-boys Jesuit high school of which Mr. Chandler was an alum. The Chandlers lived next door to his first cousin, twice removed, who agreed to take him in when the Wallaces left for Florida. The first cousin was a salesman for something called Simco and went missing for long stretches of time, leaving Charlie in the care of a succession of older women the first cousin called "friends." Charlie noticed the surfeit of kids living in the brown and white ranch next door and quickly found himself welcomed by the Chandlers, who were foster parents to six kids, including Talie, whom Charlie followed around like a puppy dog. With the first cousin's permission, the Chandlers helped Charlie file the paperwork to emancipate at seventeen, the family court judge scowling at him as if he were making the mistake of a lifetime, the glare lasting an uncomfortably long time, ruining the pizza party at Pistol Pete's that the Chandlers had thrown to help him celebrate his entree into adulthood.

Charlie had admitted his fractured past to Olivia and was relieved when she didn't consider him the alien in landscape he mostly felt in his day-to-day life. He anticipated the moment in any social scenario—especially potentially romantic ones—when his past would arise, which always required endless qualifications. He'd omitted the gaping hole in his life that was Jenny, the Mormon girl he'd met in high school. Jenny's sudden marriage just after she graduated was a wound that wouldn't heal, and Charlie was too embarrassed to admit to Olivia the hold his memories of Jenny held over him. Or his secret hope that Olivia would be the one that would make him forget about Jenny forever.

"Did you see he's coming to Phoenix?" Shelleyan asked. She pulled her reddish brown hair back and adjusted her scrunchie, revealing the dabs of sparkle she'd applied high on her cheeks. She didn't know it, but the joke among those students who knew her was whether or not they could get sparkled by Shelleyan. A few had, and still others dreamed of it.

Olivia's eyes grew wide. "You're lying."

"It was in the paper, dummy. He's got a new book coming out," Shelleyan said, gathering up her napkin and utensils. "No picture, though. He hates having his picture taken. Don't you read the paper?" Charlie hated the way all of Shelleyan's questions intimated that everyone else was in the know, and he suspected her questions were really aimed at him specifically, to dunce him in front of Olivia. "I gotta jet," she said, keeping one eye on Miles Buchanan, a hotel restaurant management major—and current focus of Shelleyan's affections—as he sauntered past the table and gave her a not-too-subtle wink, then drifted toward the door. Charlie guessed they were headed out to the parking lot, to make out in the backseat of Miles's silver Ford Bronco; Miles had told Shelleyan he'd tinted the windows with just those aspirations.

Lunch ended with Olivia promising to meet Charlie after classes, as usual, but he couldn't concentrate in his British literature class, distracted by the revelation about Vernon Downs. His need to be the center of Olivia's life flushed him with jealousy as he stared at the copy of *Pride and Prejudice* open on his desk, Professor Rudrud's words droning on. He hadn't been able to read the novel beyond the first few chapters, as the phrase "It is better to know as little as possible of the defects of the person with whom you are to pass your life" upset him so much that he couldn't continue, and he knew he would recall Austen's words verbatim every time he heard the book's title.

The plan to write Vernon Downs and arrange a private meeting while he was in Phoenix, lunch maybe, formed before the end of class. Charlie felt sure that Downs would agree to lunch, maybe dinner, with a couple of fans. He dogged it to the library, rounding the deserted stacks of the fiction section. He browsed the multicolored spines—Danticat, Dickens, Didion—halting when he saw the prize in the hunt, and reached for those by Vernon Downs. He arranged the books in a neat row in one of the study carrels, studying the covers, taking them in all at once, then focusing on the name Vernon David Downs as if trying to decode its mystery. He flipped the books over to reveal the author photo on each and was taken aback at how young the Vernon Downs who wrote *Minus Numbers* was. *He looks like a kid*, Charlie thought as he studied the cool pout, the tousled hair, the black and white suit. He marked his own passing resemblance to Vernon Downs and wondered if Olivia had a type. The author photo on the back cover of *Scavengers*,

Downs's second book, was hardly recognizable—the hair a little less abundant, the lines under the eyes, a cardiganed Downs hunched over on the steps of a nondescript brownstone. The studio shot on the back of *The Vegetable King* featured Downs in profile, his chin tipped up like an actor on a movie poster. "The powerful new novel by the controversial author of *Minus Numbers* and *Scavengers*" ran above the photo in bold lettering. He wondered if Downs's reticence to be otherwise photographed was simple vanity, and was surprised at how much pleasure the thought afforded. Was he jealous of Vernon Downs? The real question superseded this: What did Olivia see in Vernon Downs? He would've given anything to know how Olivia had first discovered Vernon Downs. What had drawn her in? The primary-color book jackets, the author photo, what? The novels were seemingly about the rich and affected, a class of people he'd never known Olivia to be particularly enticed by. Olivia's stories in workshop were mostly realist and were gently criticized for occasionally lapsing into sentimentality. Charlie read into Olivia's work and gleaned from her fiction that she was someone who prized kindness and life's small coincidences over the themes of apathy and perversion that Downs seemed obsessed with.

He toted the books to the bank of gray metal microfiche projectors and ordered a spate of reels from the portly, skeptical student working the front desk, a worn copy of *Zen and the Art of Motorcycle Maintenance* splayed on the counter. Charlie wheeled through article after article about Vernon Downs, gathering and absorbing the biographical ephemera.

He began to unravel the mystery, the slow calculus computing. Vernon Downs wasn't a writer in the sense that other writers referenced in workshop were writers. Vernon Downs was as famous as the company he kept at nightclubs in New York, and restaurants in L.A. named

Spago and Pastis and Bossa Nova. That he was a writer was incidental to his incredible celebrity.

Charlie couldn't calculate what excited him more: the prospect of arranging the lunch for Olivia, or announcing it in front of Shelleyan. In retrospect, he wished he hadn't been so confident in Vernon Downs's response, a confidence that tricked him into writing a short, breezy letter wherein he briefly described Olivia's admiration and their willingness to come to his hotel if that was more convenient. He cringed when he remembered his casual salutation—"Hey, Vernon"—that opened the letter, as if they were old friends. And he regretted not lying about his own admiration for Vernon Downs's books—he'd planned to catch the movie version of *Minus Numbers* so he could converse intelligently about the novel. Each minute after Charlie dropped the letter addressed to Vernon Downs in care of his publisher in the mailbox ticked by with a torpidity that bordered on cruelty.

He might've maintained his silence about the surprise, but circumstances conspired against him. First, the announced date for Downs's reading at Arizona State University was Valentine's Day, which lent his plan urgency. Then he opened the Sunday Arts section of the *Arizona Republic* to find the same studio shot of Vernon Downs from the back of *The Vegetable King*. The recognition felt personal, like seeing a picture of someone he knew. Just as startling as the photograph was the attendant article about the furor caused by the publication of *The Vegetable King*. The elements of said furor seemed outrageous: sections of the book being leaked to *Time* magazine by staffers at Downs's publisher who were horrified by the content; a boycott instituted by the National Organization for Women because of the graphic torture and murder committed by the main character, Nick Banks; the pulping of the book by its original publisher, who allegedly bent to the will of its parent company, Gulf and Western, the book subsequently being snapped up, along with a short story collection called *The Book of Hurts*, by another publisher, which resulted in Downs being paid twice for the same book, Downs retaining the original six-figure advance. Charlie gulped back the information as quickly as he could, reading and rereading the article, converting the details into talking points whose vitality dimmed as the days expired without word from Vernon Downs. He knew the article would come up, and he even guessed correctly that Shelleyan would be the one to reference it. He had to wait only as long as Monday's lunch.

"That picture was hot," Shelleyan said. "He could be a model if he wanted."

"I can't wait to meet him." Olivia sipped her 7UP. "I don't care how long the line is." Abundant enthusiasm was just one of Olivia's attributes that enchanted him.

"Are you going to ask him to sign your book 'love'?" Shelleyan joked.

Olivia smirked at Shelleyan. "Very funny."

The words tumbled out before he could stop them. He hadn't heard so much as a word from Vernon Downs, but he felt his position in Olivia's life continually slipping as the date of her return home approached, and drastic action was the only recourse available to him.

"I was going to wait to tell you," he said, his temples pulsing, "but we're going to have lunch with him when he's in town. It's all arranged. I wrote to him and told him what a huge fan you are, and he's staying at the Phoenician—you know, the hotel on Camelback Mountain, really fancy, Madonna stays there when she's in town, so it must be . . ."—his breathing was so shallow he thought he might pass out, but he pressed on—"you know, pretty cool."

The look of astonishment on Olivia's face was worth every ounce of the lie, which didn't feel so much like a fabrication when Olivia jumped up and wrapped her arms around him, kissing him lightly on the cheek, a promise, he hoped, of more gratitude later. Charlie glanced at Shelleyan, whose quiet smile he purposely interpreted as jealousy and not the pure, undistilled doubt that she made no effort to conceal.

"You can get him to sign your book at lunch and avoid the lines," Shelleyan said drily.

As the weeks counted down to Vernon Downs's Phoenix appearance, Charlie nervously checked the mail with a frequency bordering on schizophrenic. He falsely accused his roommate, a stoner from Illinois who had dropped out of GCC the previous semester, of losing mail, making him promise not to visit the mailbox at all, for any reason. Worse, Shelleyan began alluding to the impending lunch with Vernon Downs with open hostility.

"What are you going to wear?" she asked Olivia at lunch one day in the cafeteria.

Another time: "Do you think he's a vegetarian? What if he orders, like, a salad?"

A week before the alleged lunch: "Ask him who designed the cover for the book. Tell him from me that it's pretty gross."

Charlie decided to take action. He called information for the phone number for Downs's publisher. He carried the number in his pocket for a day or two, allowing the mail one last chance to deliver salvation. Finally he called. The line rang just once before a sweet-sounding operator answered. Charlie mistook the person as an ally and confided his eagerness to treat his girlfriend to lunch with Vernon Downs (her favorite writer!) when he visited Phoenix next week. He may even have offered to pay for the lunch, in case the financial end of the thing was what was holding up a decision.

"Hello?" Charlie said after a short silence.

"You need to contact the author's agent," the operator said, all the succor drained from her voice. He timidly asked for that number, and after a lull where the real possibility that the operator had hung up loomed, she gave him the number for Downs's agent, Daar Baumann, and hung up. He held the phone long after the operator had clicked off, the name Daar Baumann resonating; it was listed in the acknowledgments of most of the important books published over the last decade or so.

"Can I say what this is regarding?" a mellifluous voice asked after he dialed the number he'd been given.

"Vernon Downs," he answered, trying to imitate a reporter, or some other persona that Downs's agent was comfortable dealing with. He yearned to better understand the foreign land he was touristing.

"One moment." The voice was suddenly replete with a dull apprehension.

Charlie self-consciously crossed his fingers during the silence, uncrossing them when the voice returned, flatter than before.

"She's in a meeting, can I take a message?"

He left a message, knowing it wouldn't be returned.

"Do you really think it would be okay to bring my book and get it signed?" Olivia asked as the phantom lunch date neared. "Or should I wait until the reading?" He nodded, searching for an equitable moment for confession. "Is it rude to bring more than one copy, do you think?" Her childlike worship might've infused a lesser man with jealousy, but Charlie only felt helplessness and defeat.

"I think it would be okay," he said.

He skipped classes the day before Vernon Downs's reading, trolling hotel switchboards, hoping to reach out to Downs personally. An hour or so spent calling the Phoenician and other luxury hotels in the metro Phoenix area, asking to leave a message for Vernon Downs, proved a fantastic waste of time, as none had a reservation under that name. He devised and then scuttled an elaborate plan whereby he'd take Olivia to an expensive restaurant and then claim Vernon had stood them up.

He would have to confess, simple as that. There was every chance that Olivia might be so angry with him that she would refuse his company thereafter. A night of fitful sleep left him agitated and hostile. He transferred his irritation at not being able to track down Vernon Downs to Shelleyan, brushing by her when she said, "Bummer, eh?"

"Fuck off," he grunted, prizing the shock on her face.

She called out after him, but a gaggle of administrators passed, drowning her out. He loitered in the parking lot to dodge the usual congregation in the cement amphitheater that functioned as the campus nerve center where he and Olivia and Shelleyan and others would meet before and after classes. He could successfully dodge Olivia until lunch, but lunch would bring its own set of problems, namely Shelleyan, and so he was skipping ahead after sociology when he spotted Olivia.

"Hey," she said. Her smile undid him and he feared abrupt tears, not only hers, but his. She opened her backpack and he spied her copies of *Minus Numbers* and *The Vegetable King*. She threw herself at him, her face buried in his chest. "It's so disappointing," she said, his secondhand Polo shirt muffling her cries.

The full import of what he'd done registered only then. "I know," he said. "I'm sorry." He'd hoped the simple confession would suffice, but he intuited that his future would be brimming with more contrition.

Olivia wiped a tear from her eye. "Stupid, right? I mean, think of Vernon. He's got it worse, right?"

The campus began to thin as he and Olivia moved dangerously toward tardiness. He tried not to betray that he didn't know how Vernon Downs had it worse. She passed him the carefully folded article from the *Phoenix Gazette* titled "Vernon Downs Cancels Tour." Charlie read with wonder as the article recounted what he already knew—the grim circumstances surrounding the publication of *The Vegetable King*—and what he didn't: the death threats, the organized protests, the stalker that showed up in city after city until rented bodyguards became a daily reality for the author. He held the article gently, as if it were an archive document, or a religious parchment that held the divination pilgrims had been seeking their whole life. He handed it back to Olivia and grabbed her up in his arms, both to comfort her and to cloak his elation at having been so gloriously bailed out.

They consoled each other with repeated viewings of *Minus Numbers* at his apartment, exploiting Charlie's roommate's absence owing to a funeral in Michigan. They collaborated on a rebuttal to a scathing review in *Entertainment Weekly* of Downs's story collection, *The Book of Hurts*, published quickly to capitalize on the notoriety of *The Vegetable King*, and were elated when the magazine printed it in a subsequent issue:

> Once again a reviewer has overlooked the technical and literary genius of one of the brightest authors of our time, Vernon David Downs, whose work *does* represent the state of hip fiction today. We'll wager everyone who works at *EW* thinks Douglas Coupland is hip.
>
> —*Charlie Martens & Olivia Simmons, Phoenix*

The dig at Coupland, a popular writer, was especially satisfying to Charlie. His early investigation of Downs and his work had prompted him to class Downs and Coupland as the same kind of writer, but Olivia had begun preaching the virtues of Downs's work, the clinical satire, the wicked humor, the moral empathy at the heart of his seemingly immoral characters, and Charlie had been persuaded of Downs's talents.

A profile of Downs in *Vanity Fair* filled in the blanks about his canceled tour and gave an update about his whereabouts: He was ensconced in an unnamed town in Virginia with a friend, attempting to begin a new novel. The article described Downs as "bulky," a detail in direct opposition to his author photo, but didn't include any photographs, instead employing a full-page caricature emphasizing Downs's cherubic features. The odd detail of Downs picking up a bath towel and sniffing it to see if it was clean stayed with Charlie longer than it should've.

"Let's write him a letter," Olivia said. "A real fan letter. I've never written a true fan letter."

Charlie convinced her the better idea was to write a letter to the editor of *Vanity Fair*. "He might see it," Charlie reasoned.

Olivia crafted a note she hoped Downs would read, rejoiced when it appeared:

> Finally a quasi-revealing profile (as much as we'll ever know, I'll bet) of one of the most talented writers of our time. As a creative-writing student at Glendale Community College, I can say that Mr. Downs is among the most revered authors of my generation, admired for the fluidity of his prose style and his eye for context and detail, which, on the surface, appear ordinary enough but are really, under Mr. Downs's microscope, threatening and truly unnerving. I quiver with anticipation for the arrival of his latest masterpiece.
>
> —*Olivia Simmons, London*

The sexual innuendo of the last sentence bothered Charlie like an itch he couldn't reach, but he was more troubled by Olivia's identifying herself as a Londoner, a reminder that she was but a provisional visitor who would return to her homeland in a matter of months. He suppressed those emotions and they spent the next few days driving around the metro Phoenix area, buying up copies of *Vanity Fair.*

....

The idling cab, pulled to the curb at Summit Terrace, was a cocoon: Once Charlie stepped from it, the final act of his plan to win back Olivia would begin. Camden had been a trial run—everyone in the summer writing program would forever associate him with Vernon Downs and vice versa. The stage was bigger now. How to replicate the effect, he wasn't exactly sure. Olivia's words—"We can't see each other anymore"—still rattled him, though increasingly he thought of them as a challenge. He'd said he'd come the first chance he could, which meant financially, which was easily solved by an afternoon spent filling out preapproved credit card applications offered along with free T-shirts at various tables around campus. As the cards began to appear in the mail, he planned his trip to London and was devastated and confused when his weekly phone call didn't find Olivia at home. When he finally reached her, he wouldn't hang up without an explanation, and Olivia gave him an unbelievable one she had clearly contrived under duress. Perhaps her parents had learned about how she'd switched enrollment from Arizona State to Glendale Community College and were punishing her.

A desperate scenario in which he'd locate Vernon Downs in New York emerged. What would happen after that was anyone's guess, but he let himself be guided by impulse. He charged a one-way trip to New York City and studiously pored over a map on the flight, wondering where along the colored grid he'd find Vernon Downs. He traced the route from LaGuardia into the city so he wouldn't be taken advantage of by the unscrupulous taxi drivers of popular imagination. He laughed now as he remembered the look of surprise on the cabbie's face when Charlie instructed him to take the Triborough Bridge. He hadn't known that the Triborough was a toll bridge and that the Midtown Tunnel was the faster, free alternative. Other surprises lay in store, like the hotel in Times Square that was really a hostel, necessitating a pair of flip-flops from the corner CVS in order to use the communal shower; and how everything in New York cost at least two dollars more than it did in Phoenix. But the biggest surprise was the absolute lack of any trace of Vernon Downs anywhere in Manhattan. All the articles he'd read had Downs starring in nightly debaucheries, but as Charlie haunted the entrances of bars like Nell's and Balthazar and clubs like Tunnel and Limelight, he understood that everyone who entered those venues did so seeking debauchery.He stood squinting up at the office of Downs's literary agent, Daar Baumann, but knew nothing but disappointment awaited inside. Recognizing dead ends was a useful skill he'd developed early on.

The stench of defeat dogged him until a new plan spontaneously emerged, based on a flyer for a summer writing conference at Camden College, Downs's alma mater, that was stuck on a bulletin board at the New School, where Charlie had taken refuge from an early blast of summer heat. Camden had figured prominently in a number of Downs's books, and the conference featuring lectures and writing workshops would at the very least bring Charlie closer to the world of Vernon Downs. It seemed like the logical next step in his quest to win back Olivia.

....

Charlie cursed himself for scrimping, the late arrival time the result of a cheaper red-eye ticket that imprisoned him at the Albany bus station until six a.m., the first available pickup time that could be arranged by the car service, the only means of travel available to the remote college campus. This rookie mistake was obvious in retrospect as he trudged in circles through the tiny terminal, willing the sun to appear. He contemplated a hotel room, but the balance on one of his MasterCards had crept perilously toward the limit, and he vowed to eschew unnecessary purchases. He'd wait it out. He clutched the postcard of the Empire State Building he'd purchased at the Port Authority, debating about sending it. Olivia would see the beseeching lines he'd scrawled and know his longing for reconciliation. He slid the postcard into a mail slot and immediately began to worry that Olivia's parents would find the missive in the mail and trash it instead of delivering it to its intended reader.

He curled up on an uncomfortable half bench, the strap of his duffel bag looped around his arm to prevent robbery; the suede pouch within, given to him by the Kepharts, secreted keepsakes from his travels and was the sole possession he valued. He longed for the comfort of his bed back in Phoenix, though he knew his ex-roommate had found someone to rent his room after Charlie announced his plans to go east. Sleep came fitfully and then was banished forever by the whir of an industrial vacuum cleaner as the terminal underwent an early-morning cleaning. Six o'clock was forever in arriving, and despite his excitement at escaping the bus terminal, he dozed off in the back of the hired Lincoln Town Car, waking to marvel at the Vermont countryside. The sun glinted off the green fields and he took in the rural landscape.

The car sailed through a red-planked covered bridge eroded by time, the verdant landscape filtering in through the latticework, the car's interior spotted with sunlight. The Town Car shot out the yawning mouth of the bridge, delivering them into the town of Camden, a picturesque New England hamlet populated with wide lawns running back toward quiet houses nestled far from the road.

The driver nosed the car through the gates of Camden College, itself set deep in the woods. An admixture of anxiety and excitement coursed through Charlie as the car crept along College Drive, finally slowing to a stop at the Barn, the two-story structure that functioned as the administration building. The driver let him off, and he signed for the service and the tip, which was more than he'd anticipated. He watched the black car drive away until it turned the corner, a curtain of morning sunlight falling over the still campus. The buildings appeared deserted: the Commons ahead and Crossett Library to his left, the manicured Commons lawn a quiet runway extending toward the End of the World, the abrupt terminus from which endless miles of Vermont woods and sky were visible.

He wondered what Olivia would say.

He wished he could know.

The single thought that he was finally within the inviting bosom of Vernon David Downs's alma mater was surreal. His sole preoccupation on the bus ride from New York had been how to breach the campus successfully—he'd run several scenarios involving multiple deceptions to finesse any security—and once the awe at how easily he'd been able to infiltrate Camden had subsided, he realized he knew very little about Downs's existence on campus. Which of the green and white clapboard dorms had he lived in? McCullough? Booth? He set his bag down on one of the picnic tables outside of the Commons, distressed by extreme weather and extreme temperaments, searching the campus for any sign of life. *Vernon Downs probably sat at this picnic table*, he thought. He tried the door to Stokes, surprised when the handle gave easily, and roamed through the vacant dorm, choosing an empty room down an empty hall farthest from the entrance as his own. *He probably stared out this window*, Charlie thought. The distant mountaintops retained their snowy caps, even in the summer. *He may even have lived in this very room*, he thought as he drifted off to sleep, exhaustion washing over him as he spread out fully clothed on the soft bed.

Faint laughter woke him some time later. He squinted at the bluing light as he tried to gauge where he was. The gauzy curtains blew in the evening breeze, the air suffused with a floral sweetness. Out his window, dark figures moved against the gray landscape, some struggling with overpacked bags, others darting furtively in and out of their dorm, unpacking idling cars double-parked on the single-lane road that wound past the student housing.

His fellow Camdenites had finally arrived.

Charlie hurriedly showered and dressed, then sauntered toward the Commons, which cast rectangles of light across the darkening lawn, the destination of the flow of people appearing in doorways or emerging in tributaries from points unseen. He kept his head low, hoping to blend with those who were actually enrolled in the summer program. Experience had taught him that he could persuade people he was invisible, which invariably emboldened him in any new social situation, so he was bewildered by how nervous he felt. He followed a woman in her eighties wrapped in an oversized yellow Windbreaker, as if expecting a storm, into a dimly lit room crowded with amiable and eager faces, all congregated at a long wooden bar stocked with self-serve beer and wine, which was being grabbed up by nervous hands. Charlie tried to mix into the crowd, cradling a sweaty bottle of Budweiser, listening in on conversations that cut violently from how hard it was to find time to write, to a short list of favorite books, to which of the teachers huddled near the dormant stone fireplace was the recent National Book Award winner.

Camden's recent history was very much on everyone's minds too. Charlie gathered the bits and pieces of conversation to sew the narrative together: Just a year before, the college had taken the extraordinary step of abolishing tenure, firing a third of the

professors who taught at Camden, invoking the ire and censure of
the academic community. The air was polluted with uncertainty
about Camden's future, which provided the perfect cover for
Charlie's impersonation of a Camden student. He quickly fell into
the proscribed banter, asking people where they were from, if they
wrote fiction or poetry or what. He readily provided answers when
the same was asked of him, sometimes recycling answers he'd been
given moments before during a similar inquiry. There was something
intoxicating about rotating in a crowd of aspirants. Anything was
possible. Even getting Olivia back.

That night, he dreamed what he would do.

Early the next morning, he strolled into the Barn and located
the alumni office.

"I'm a student here and would like the address for an alum,"
he said to the straw-thin girl with wispy blond hair behind the
counter. "Vernon Downs." A rising nervousness pulsed through
him. He regretted betraying his earlier instinct to employ a believable ruse. He'd considered several on the walk to the alumni
office: that he was with the local newspaper and wanted to interview Downs; that he worked in the library and needed to forward a package someone had sent Downs; or that someone at the
campus bookstore wanted to ship a carton of *The Vegetable King* to
Downs for autographing. But none of the deceptions appealed to
him, and it was better to go in straight than to proffer a lie he wasn't
completely invested in.

"I'm just watching the desk for my friend," the girl said. "I actually work in admissions."

"Oh," Charlie said. He leaned on the counter in what he hoped
was an unassuming pose. "Which is better?"

The girl made a face. "Both are boring," she answered. "But it
beats working in the cafeteria with the rest of the losers."

Charlie laughed. "I suppose it does." The girl glanced absently at the clock on the wall, the red second hand gliding slowly across its face. "I like the food here," he said. "I mean, I like that someone else takes care of it."

The girl smiled. "I'm a vegan, so I only really eat at the salad bar."

Charlie worried that his request would come under scrutiny if the girl's friend reappeared, and he debated leaving. But something in the way the girl behind the counter nervously began to scratch her elbow betrayed that she and her friend were likely up to something, or she was worried that she'd be found out for spelling her friend, who was off doing who knew what, and Charlie reversed course.

"I'm sort of in a hurry," he said, affecting impatience.

"God, where is she?" the girl asked. "She's been gone for, like, ten minutes."

"Is there someone else who can help me?" Charlie asked, searching the obviously empty office.

"I'll just do it," she said. The girl tapped something on the computer. She handed him a yellow Post-it note, a phone number scrawled in her slanted handwriting. "It says the request for an updated address is pending, sorry." Charlie thanked her and memorized the phone number in case something disastrous happened to the Post-it, which he folded into his wallet, with the intention of transferring it to the safety of the suede pouch. He absented the alumni office quickly, as if he might be called back to account, the creaky floorboards singing underfoot. An errant left brought him face-to-face with the director of the summer program, a large bearded Irishman with tortoiseshell glasses whom he recognized from the writing program flyer.

"Hello," the director boomed.

Charlie gave a short wave, an understatement he hoped the director would let stand.

"Good man," the director said, slapping him heartily on the back, which propelled him in an unplanned direction, around the nearest corner and away from the director, who bounded out the door and into the brightening sky. Charlie strolled down the hall strewn with cluttered corkboards and stacks of unstained wooden chairs, hunting for an exit that would circumvent the director and thus avert an embarrassing conversation he was sure neither of them wanted to have.

A murmuring wafted through the breezy hallway, and Charlie slowed at the open door bearing an engraved plastic plaque advertising the summer writing program office. He feigned interest in the flyers pushpinned to the bulletin board outside the door while straining to hear.

"We should make them pay when we accept them," a voice tinged with anger said. "That would keep them from dropping out without notice."

"They'd just want a refund," a smaller voice said. "There's no way to guarantee they'll show up."

"But canceling at the last minute," the first voice countered. "If he would've had to pay in full, that would've forced him to attend."

Charlie lifted an outdated flyer about summer studies abroad and focused on an announcement about a film series at the local cinema featuring movies inspired by books. Some days the fantasy that Olivia could see him was all he had to motivate him, and her phantom presence had become so ingrained that he often acted as if he were on a stage, with the audience just off in the wings.

"The workshops are all screwed up now," the first voice said, exasperation replacing anger.

"Can't we draft the closest wait lister?" the small voice said.

"Not at this late date," was the reply.

Charlie stared dumbly at the bulletin board. He had what he'd come for, and extending his stay on campus could only increase the chance of exposure. But there was an allure about all he didn't know about Vernon Downs and his time at Camden. He reasoned that an education in All Things Vernon could only aid in his overall goal to ingratiate himself with the author. Plus, it was more economically feasible to spend ten days in Vermont than ten days in New York City. He crept away from the open door, the floor creaking underfoot, threatening to expose him as he formulated what exactly he'd say. He didn't consider it lying, exactly, but an expedience that benefited all parties involved—a cousin to a white lie, or at best, an act of charity whose currency was simple, harmless untruths.

He circled the Barn, gathering courage before striding into the writing program office. The air-conditioning had been turned low and Charlie shivered as he approached the counter.

"Can I help you?" The small voice he'd heard earlier belonged to a round, dour woman behind a wooden desk weighted down with stacks of shuffled papers and a computer monitor three technologies old.

"I need to pay my tuition," he said confidently, smiling sheepishly, as if the joke was on him in some way.

"What's the name?" the woman asked as she pulled a pair of reading glasses from her worn sweater.

He gave her his name and she typed it slowly into the computer. A dark figure moved behind a pane of frosted glass in the door guarding an inner office. The dour woman frowned. "I don't have you in my computer," she said.

Charlie smiled casually, knowing this was the critical performance. "Maybe I'm still on the wait list," he suggested. "I was wait-listed at first." He rubbed his hands together and then dropped them to his sides, shrugging in a mimic of a small child waiting instruction from a parent.

The woman clacked the keys of her computer again, a look of consternation on her face. "Hmm," she said, and Charlie could see

the conceit he'd planted in her mind take bloom. "Wait one moment, please." She swept out of the room, easing behind the door
to the inner office, which was consumed with urgent whispering.
The door opened and closed again, and the woman rounded her
desk, a curiously thin file folder in her hand. "Found it," she said,
sighing dramatically. "Computers can't beat a good old-fashioned
filing system."

Charlie chortled dutifully. "They never will," he agreed, nodding at the prop file. He was amazed but not surprised that the trick
had worked.

"How would you like to pay?" the woman asked.

Charlie placed his MasterCard on the counter, and the woman
fished a carbon from the top drawer. He smiled as she copied down
his credit card number, confident that the summer writing conference would be over before the transaction was processed, at which
point he would call MasterCard and refute the charges, feigning
ignorance about what or where Camden was.

Charlie moved into the cramped room assigned him in
Booth, no longer having to squat in Stokes on the fringe of the
summer program, though his official admittance left him feeling
exposed. He nodded politely to the girl who lived at the end of the
hall, alarmed that she'd try to trap him in a conversation about
books or writing. A low-level fear accompanied him as he
rotated on the outside of groups of students that formed and broke
apart with the speed of supernovas. His artistic resume—two
semesters of creative writing at Glendale Community College—
represented the least distinguished credentials among those
in attendance, who all seemed either to be enrolled at Iowa or
Columbia or Williams, or to have decades of life experience,
which lent an air of authority to their theories about writing and
what constituted art.

Workshop was another matter entirely. He spent evenings in his room conscientiously reading the stories passed out that afternoon. The quality of the stories was markedly better than those he'd seen at GCC—several read as smoothly as published stories—and he couldn't find anything substantive to say, so that by the third meeting, he was the lone participant who hadn't spoken, forcing Jane Martin, the workshop leader and author of a famous book set in an eponymous small town, to call on him. He fumbled through a string of exhortations about the quality of the writing and plotting, aping speech he'd heard in the hallways and dining room, finally making an original point about the likability of the narrator, a widowed herpetologist who falls in love with a woman half his age. The con held, though he wasn't sure that all his workshop mates were convinced he belonged there, a suspicion he feared would be confirmed as the deadline for him to hand in his story approached. His small cache of original work was archived on a blue diskette he kept in the suede pouch, and he reread everything he'd written on a computer in Crossett Library, but none of it exhibited the quality of the work they'd been considering at Camden. One of the first stories he'd written, "My Last Jenny," was too upsetting to finish reading. Another, about people all over the country mistakenly spotting Lee Harvey Oswald in the moments after the Kennedy assassination, rose in his estimation, but the story was too personal, written during a sensitive time—he hadn't even shared it with Olivia—and he wasn't eager to hear it dissected in workshop.

The situation plagued him all through the field trip arranged by Jane Martin for the purpose of an elaborate writing exercise designed around the tragic disappearance of Paula Jean Welden, the Camden sophomore who walked out into the campus woods in the mid-1940s and vanished.

Charlie tramped along the worn trail, the campus receding behind the group of students lacquered with astringent bug spray. They listened as Jane Martin described Paula Jean's disappearance, how she'd marched out the front gates in the December cold without a jacket or scarf, how a garage owner closing for the night was the last to see her alive, if you discounted the bus driver who claimed Paula Jean had grabbed the last bus to New York City, or the waitress at the Modern Café who swore she'd served Paula Jean a plate of scrambled eggs and sausage with a side of pancakes.

"The rumor that she was underdressed led searchers to believe that Paula Jean was rendezvousing with someone who had a car or a cabin," Jane Martin said. She gathered the group under a stand of birch trees, the sunlight spotting the faces of the would-be scribes, anxious to please. "So take out your notebooks," Jane Martin said, "and sketch out a few paragraphs about what you think happened to Paula Jean."

Notebooks and pens were wrestled free of bags and backpacks. Charlie took out a pocket-size Camden notebook he'd shoplifted in the campus bookstore. He held his pen to paper like a reporter but drew a blank. The other workshoppers scribbled furiously, constructing whole lies out of the scraps of a girl's unsolved disappearance. Charlie found it exhausting to speculate about Paula Jean, a little disconcerted that the others found it so easy. Weren't they worried that adopting a tendency to fabricate would leak over into their real lives? The girl standing opposite him swatted at a red spot on her tanned leg with her notebook.

Jane Martin called time and all but a few pens stopped scratching out make-believe. "Who wants to go first?" she asked.

Predictably, the eager, bird-faced brunette from Wisconsin, whose workshop story was roundly criticized for flowery language and corny sentiment, shot her hand in the air.

"Go ahead, Charisse," Jane Martin said without a hint of reluctance. Charlie wondered how a professional and published writer like Jane Martin could summon the patience for wannabes like Charisse and the others in the group. The only legitimate answer was the amount of the paycheck, he surmised.

Charisse proceeded with a spiel about Paula Jean and a mystery lover, taking the obvious cue and running. In Charisse's version, the mystery lover was a disfigured local boy whom Paula Jean had befriended. Longing to shrug off their shackles—in Charisse's take, Paula Jean was sick of being rich and bored—they plunged deep into the woods to live simply and shirk the value system imposed on them by a superficial society. "I didn't get to finish," Charisse lamented. "I think they had children, too, who they raised accordingly."

Charlie suffered through an outpouring of implausible plotlines involving UFOs, Bigfoot, kidnappers, and sinkholes. Jane Martin tried to convey that the *how* was less interesting than the *why*, compelled to hold up Charisse's ridiculous response as an example of interior versus exterior. He understood perfectly what she was trying to impart. He thought about Paula Jean leaving all that she was behind, trusting in the unknown. How fearful she must've been that she'd be caught, dragged back to the present she was trying to outrun, consigned to the life she wanted to give back.

Paula Jean's struggle was mighty compared with his own life, Charlie realized. How easily had he slipped from place to place, a new set of friends, a new school, everything new, new, new? Pride surged within him as he realized how much Paula Jean would've envied his life. The fresh slant on his own history enthralled him until the gross similarities between Paula Jean's disappearance into the Vermont woods and his exodus from Denver, and Santa Fe, and Rapid City, and San Diego, struck him. The bothersome thought that he could simply walk away from Phoenix, and from Olivia and the memories they shared, couldn't be dislodged from his mind, no matter how distasteful the idea. He refused to surrender to the hypothesis, afraid of the power of admission. It was like using a relative's death as a fake excuse for missing school—once proffered, the evitable would follow. To forget Olivia would be to forsake the one person who could provide his one real chance to quit the dizzying carousel of towns and fleeting friendships that had accrued over the years. He lamented surrendering his apartment, his only real tether to Phoenix, even though he'd had to financially. He'd never doubled back before and had discounted its comfort as a fallback. An afternoon wind rustled the leaves, and he clung to his memories of Olivia, battered by the awareness foisted upon him by the stupid writing exercise. An outer dark loomed beyond the group of workshoppers, the bleak future that awaited Charlie if he succumbed to cataloging Olivia as just another person in another town that he'd known.

He heard his name called, Jane Martin bringing him back from the precipice. The group eyed him, waiting, but he shrugged. "I couldn't think of anything," he said, closing his notebook.

....

Charlie strode across the short, thick grass of the Commons lawn, glancing up in time to avert being hit by a stray shuttlecock from a scratch badminton game being played by other Camdenites, all of whom were swatting at the birdie with their free hand, the other hand minding their full plastic cup of wine or beer. The campus was in its postdinner lull, the sun still high in the sky, the faculty readings still hours away. An esprit de corps had enveloped the campus, and those with cars motored into Camden to haunt the shops for trinkets for their children or significant others, or to stock up on the basic necessities at the newly constructed Wal-Mart. Charlie had skipped dinner to stroll around the fetid pond and through the tall, ragged grass of Jennings Meadow, which led to Jennings Hall, the granite mansion that housed the music facilities. The summer writing program was mostly contained at the other end of campus, and the foot traffic on the trail to Jennings thinned noticeably as he broached the imposing house. He'd overheard vague tales about how Jennings was haunted, how music students practicing in the converted studios would hear strange, unmusical noises that would chase them back to their dorms and trouble their dreams, but he didn't believe in the supernatural and dismissed the rumors as campus mythology.

A rush of wind blew across the naked meadow and he turned his back to it, his T-shirt and shorts billowing in the gale. The warm air cooled as it subsided, swaying the maple saplings that ringed the mansion. He listened for music—a prim group who ate at a table in the windowless corner of the dining hall were rumored to be music students stranded at Camden for the summer—but Jennings was quiet. The front door caught when he tried it. He read about the Jennings family on the historical marker bolted to the stone facade, about how Mr. Jennings had been a powerful lawyer in New York City who died in his midsixties, widowing his wife, who ultimately donated the house for the creation of Camden College, a Depression-era college for women. The engraved words EST. 1880 appeared in smaller type at the bottom of the plaque, and Charlie ran his hand over them, his fingers lingering over the numbers, the one and the eights and the zero. *More than a hundred years old*, he mused. *Older than the state of Arizona.* He thought of the hastily abandoned Mrs. Jennings and shuddered. Without warning, the parade of friends he'd left behind filed through his mind. He'd made widows of them all as he bounced here and there. He was curious to know if he'd left a trail of heartbreak. He'd never before considered that his previous experiences and relationships were anything more than finite—their separateness had given him pleasure, the compilation of memories a zoetrope always spinning in his mind. That he'd been a bit player in an array of people's lives, against a myriad of backgrounds, seemed impossible. Yet he acknowledged the probability that he hadn't widowed anyone, but simply passed through their lives with an inconsequential nod and a polite smile.

....

The end of Charlie's time at Camden was marked with turmoil. As he stood in Tishman, the subterranean lecture hall, barely looking up from the lectern, he was unable to measure the audience's enthusiasm for his selection for the recreational after-dinner readings. Most read selections from authors that had made them want to become writers, and Charlie was enamored of the idea of lineage. He became obsessed with publicly sharing what had led him to Camden, associating himself with Downs in the minds of others.

Vernon Downs was by far one of the most successful writers in Camden's history, but his name was whispered in the halls with a mix of shame and admiration. By comparison, students talked loudly about Bernard Malamud, who had taught at Camden for decades; or Robert Frost, who had lived in a house on campus and was buried nearby; or Jamaica Kincaid, who lived in a beautiful wood house behind the campus. But no one ever spoke openly about Downs. Charlie silently dedicated the reading to Olivia, then began, immediately recognizing that he'd started reading the wrong page. He'd intended to read a comic scene involving business cards but had inexplicably opened the book to a scene that included one of the most violent passages in *The Vegetable King*. As he neared the conclusion of the reading, he gazed out awkwardly and smiled at the applause. He was aware that some had walked in late—the lecture hall doors had swung open and shut loudly during the reading.

Mike Conway, who occupied the suite opposite his and with whom he'd exchanged pleasantries, approached. "Did you hear those people walking out?" he asked.

"What do you mean?" Charlie asked.

"When you started reading the part about the rat, a bunch of women got up and walked out."

Mike approached him again at breakfast the next morning. "There's something on the bulletin board in Commons you might want to read," he said solemnly. Previously, the bulletin board had served as a collage of cartoons cut from the pages of the *New Yorker* or anonymous diatribes about laundry room etiquette, so the sober note Mike struck was troubling.

Charlie followed him to Commons, and they waited for the group of students clustered around the bulletin board to disperse before stepping up. Charlie scanned the letter tacked in the center of the board.

I am deeply offended by Charlie Martens's public reading of Vernon Downs's work. Downs has the right to write what he chooses, Martens has the right (in the privacy of his own mind) to read what he chooses. I also have the right not to fill my mind with graphic depictions of sexualized violence against women. To be subjected to such images out of the blue (images I may never be able to erase from my thoughts) is a violation.

As writers, we are all concerned with freedom of speech, but Martens crossed the line—his action was disrespectful and unacceptable. I, for one, take issue with what he did—I protest.

The note had been annotated by others, the addendums written in different-colored inks:

> I agree (and I had previously read the passage out of <u>choice</u>).
>
> It would have been nice to have had the option to leave the room (or go read the passage myself if I wanted) before this gratuitous reading. It was nothing less than mental rape.
>
> I agree. What was the point?

Mike told Charlie not to worry about it. Mike's dismissive attitude comforted him, though for the rest of the day Charlie felt like others were staring at him. He assuaged his discomfort by telling himself the letter was a stunt that would die by lunch, an idea he believed until a follow-up letter was posted:

> 1. Charlie Martens could have offered a handout of the VDD passage, then any consequent debate would have been, as it should have been, about <u>it</u>, not about his method of presentation.
> 2. This debate isn't about censorship, but about courtesy, specifically about ways of demonstrating respect for others' sensibilities.
> 3. Providing those of "tender sensibilities" an opportunity to leave would not have been a good solution. The image of women rising + leaving raises attendant images of women withdrawing from men after dinner—to the (with)drawing room. A solution that literally separated us would be no solution at all. Isn't common ground a precondition of community?

Followed by another:

> The material of Vernon David Downs is strong, unpleasant, and

to my mind, not very important, which is why I chose not to attend. But should what is presented here be shaped to the most vulnerable among us? With all respect for the sensitivities of those who find the material offensive, as a woman I find it ironic that we seem on the verge of returning to the time when someone else decided, "The material is a bit rough. Perhaps the ladies would like to step outside," or even worse, to a time when in the back rooms others would say, "This material is something that might be important to hear, but in deference to the ladies, we can't even consider it."

I didn't come here to be protected, thank you.

Charlie's reading and the bulletin board postings were the rage in the dorms and on campus. His paranoia about being gawked at was validated as his peers averted their eyes whenever he attempted to make eye contact in lecture. He began skipping lectures in favor of camping out in his room. The cafeteria became an arena of liability too when an older woman he'd never seen before accosted him, leaning in so that her face nearly grazed his. "I think you're disgusting," she said. She waited for a reaction of some kind, but he just shrugged, knowing he could not convince her otherwise.

Charlie considered vanishing, but he had begun scratching out notes for a story based on his relationship with Olivia and wondered if workshopping the story might bring some clarity about his situation. So for the rest of the conference, Charlie attached himself to various groups revolving through campus, trickling into pools of conversation, mostly unnoticed, though he affected an agreeable tone when included in whatever was being discussed. It seemed that while everyone had heard about the public outcry over his reading of Downs's work, very few people actually knew Charlie by sight. Right when the controversy

threatened to wane, the soap-operatic narrative folding in on itself—
where people stood on the issue boiled down to whether or not they
were fans of Downs's work—Mike knocked on his door.

"There's something you should see," he said.

Charlie read over the shoulders of the group gathered around the
bulletin board:

Dear Charlie,

It may please you to know that Vernon David Downs went down
fighting. As I fed the first page of The Vegetable King into the fire, a
cluster of flames leaped out from beneath the paper and scalded my
thumb. He went down like the condemned man before the firing squad,
spitting in the soldiers' faces. What else can they do to him? Vernon did
not beg or bribe or whimper. He took his punishment like a man.

But we burned him like women. Gently. Not like Nazis burned
books, with the false and grandiose notion that we can actually eradi-
cate the text, the idea, the memory. No, we burned him the way a
woman burns the letters of an ex-lover. The way a woman burns the
letters of an ex-lover when she has lost him to violence—his. She
burns them gently, grieving for her lost innocence. She knows now
that loving can be dangerous. Just as listening can be dangerous.
Trusting the words of your soft mouth not to harden like a hand that
once caressed hardens into a fist.

We cannot unbruise our ears from this or any other unwanted
intrusion. Vernon David Downs has carved his initials into us like
the trunks of trees. But we burned the pages and called the names of
women. Strangers, women we know, women we love, women in our
families, who have been raped or beaten or brutalized. Real women,
not the inexhaustible legions of women in fiction who offer themselves up willingly. Real women.

I am lucky. I have a voice that tells me everything important. Shortly after your reading began, it told me to leave. Now, I was comfortable, and it was humid out. But one of my favorite gospel songs says, "I'm gonna do what the Spirit say do." Spirit said leave, so I did. I didn't hear the passages you read, but I saw them in the distressed faces of the women who are my friends and colleagues.

Is that why the flames chose my hand as we sacrificed Vernon into the fire? Was it because I had been unscathed by the words? Maybe it was a reminder that although we are right, the element of fire does not prefer Vernon's flesh over mine. Perhaps it was to remind me that burning Vernon wasn't without danger.

After we finished, one of my friends gave me a clear plastic cup of ice water. As I rewound the tape in my cassette player, I stuck my thumb into the cup to soothe the burn. Then we played Queen Latifah's "U.N.I.T.Y." and danced.

We won this little battle, but not because we burned The Vegetable King. We won because despite the infinite number of tortures real women experience every day, we are also real women, and we were with each other, and we were making ritual, and we were dancing.

It didn't take long for news of the ritualistic burning to sweep across campus. Conversations were held in muted tones. There were those among the population who were appalled by the act and expressed their opinion vocally; others were equally appalled by Charlie's presence, and their silent glaring communicated their disgust. The entire student body was enveloped in a foul stink. The reactions were too extreme for Charlie to register them as anything other than self-aggrandizing, though he secretly relished the episode as the twinning of his narrative with Vernon's.
. . . .

Charlie thought to review his questions in the cab, but he'd memorized them—even their order—and didn't want to sully the reporter's notebook he'd charged at the stationery store in Union Square as a backup to the mini recorder he intended to return with the receipt to the electronics store near Grand Central Station. As the hands on his watch moved toward ten, he was seized with worry: Were his loafers too weathered? Was his haircut cool enough? Did he look like a poor student on financial aid, or could he somehow pass as the sort of hipster Downs wrote about and probably socialized exclusively with? *Don't come off as too eager*, he admonished himself, knowing a misstep could halt the forward progress he'd made since leaving Phoenix. He ducked under the green and white awning of Summit Terrace, the doorman nodding as he pushed through the etched glass door.

"Yes?" the doorman asked, balancing a copy of the *Village Voice* on his lap.

"I'm here to see Vernon Downs," Charlie said carefully.

"Name?" the doorman asked.

"Vernon Downs," Charlie repeated.

"No," the doorman said sourly. "*Your* name."

He gave his name and the doorman announced his arrival in the receiver of the white phone on the desk. "Okay," the doorman said into the mouthpiece. "Okay." He hung up. "He's not ready for you yet. Be five minutes."

Charlie paced the octagonal brick and glass lobby, the strong urge to urinate visiting him. "Do you have a bathroom?" he asked.

"Basement," the doorman said. "Door by the elevator."

He followed the passageway to the maintenance room but was so paranoid that Vernon would descend and find the lobby empty that the emergency abandoned him and he retreated. "You can go up," the doorman said without looking at him.

The ride to the fourth floor was short, and Charlie nearly fainted as he raised a tremulous fist to knock on Vernon's door. The journey from Phoenix to New York to Camden to Summit Terrace had been longer than he had expected, riddled with setbacks he could never have anticipated on the bus from Vermont. His previous foray into Manhattan had in no way prepared him for life on the East Coast. He didn't possess the skills to procure the kind of job necessitated by astronomical rent and utility payments, a riddle that vexed him as he ambled the city streets, down skyscraper-lined Fifth Avenue, to the South Street Seaport, over to Wall Street, and back up the West Side, cutting over to Central Park and looping through the Great Lawn. He avoided the subway, certain that it was a death sentence based on the wild rumors he'd heard growing up in the West about murder after murder being committed on the tracks, until he counted up the colossal sums he was spending on cab fare and forced himself to take public transportation. The roar of the hot subway was more exhilarating than expected, and once he effected his first successful transfer at Times Square, he felt he was mastering the art of life in New York.

His living situation had finally stabilized too. A brief stay at the Holiday Inn in Midtown maxed out one of his MasterCards and he checked out, leaving the cut-up plastic remains in the waste-basket. Charlie traipsed around Manhattan, realizing quickly that if he wanted a place to live, he'd be relegated to one of the less fashionable boroughs, either Queens or the Bronx, maybe Staten Island. He rode the N train to Astoria, a heavily Greek neighborhood in Queens, and spent an afternoon climbing the stairs in prewar apartment buildings to look at all there was for rent. Astoria's proximity to Manhattan had corrupted rent prices, so that renters were being shuttled deeper into Long Island City, or to New Jersey. Dismayed, Charlie boarded the N train back into the city, hatching a fallback plan wherein he'd ride the subway all night with the other homeless if it should come to that.

A stopgap solution revealed itself in the form of the night front desk position at the Yale Club, but he was fired after two days when the day manager caught him sleeping in one of the well-appointed guest rooms, a sleep mask and white-noise machine Charlie had purloined from Guest Services obscuring the day manager's footfalls. A suite of embarrassments followed: the older woman he'd met at a bar in Greenwich Village forcibly asking him to leave her apartment when she returned early from a trip to Paris, angry that he'd let himself back in, after they'd said their good-byes, by tricking her aging doorman; being rousted by the Pakistani teenager whose bed he'd stolen at the Big Apple Hostel in Times Square; the waitress threatening to call the police if he didn't pay up and leave; the security guard discovering him camped out in the accidentally unlocked first-editions room of the New York Public Library.

The miracle that stabilized his living situation first appeared to him a mirage. A heat-induced chimera in Shelleyan's likeness sauntered down Minetta Lane one particularly airless afternoon, checking her hair in the reflection of the Black Rabbit, a wood-paneled bar on the corner.

Charlie peered at her, overtaken by serendipity. Surely her presence was an omen that he was treading the right path, that the hazy journey from Arizona to Vermont to New York would bring him back to Olivia. He straightened his back, shifting his dirty duffel bag to obscure his meager possessions. Perhaps Shelleyan would even act as the conduit.

"It is you!" Shelleyan cried. "I thought it was. How are you?" She looked exactly the same, as if the Arizona Shelleyan had a twin living in New York City, save for the stylish haircut that gave her the air of working in an office.

"Fine," he answered, "I'm fine." She lunged at him for a quick hug. "I've been in Vermont."

"What have you been doing in Vermont?" she asked.

"Studying writing at Camden," he said, baiting her. Would she remember Camden as the school Downs had made famous? He regretted it instantly, the scene where Shelleyan taunted him about his ignorance of Olivia's penchant for the works of Vernon Downs was still fresh. If she asked him what he was working on, or what he'd written, he knew he'd blank, incapable of even devising a fake title to offer as proof of his new phantom identity.

Shelleyan nodded. The clue eluded her, which convinced him that what she had professed to know about Vernon Downs she'd aped from Olivia's interest only to harangue him, and he hated her for it anew.

"What are you doing here?" he asked.

"I live here," she answered.

"Where?" he asked. Had she seen him living on the streets, working up the courage to approach him, maybe at Olivia's insistence, from whatever safe roof housed her?

"Williamsburg," she told him. "Or East Manhattan, as we say in Billyburg."

Charlie was baffled by what she was talking about, but nodded nonetheless.

"I transferred to Parsons," she continued. "Where are you staying?"

"East Village," he lied. It was the only neighborhood he could convincingly speak of.

"Very cool," Shelleyan said.

A cab lurched down the lane and they both watched as it rolled to a stop at the entrance to the shuttered Minetta Lane Theatre. An athletic cabbie with shoulder-length hair braided against the heat shook the locked theater doors and then drove off.

"Have you heard from Olivia?" she asked, as if intuiting the thought that had dried on his lips.

His nerves jangled at the sound of her name. He felt the sudden

need to confide his ploy to impress Olivia with his connection to
Vernon Downs, but all there was to disclose was his objective and its
unsuccessful execution. "You guys stay in touch?" He winced as the
question landed. The answer would tell him how much she knew
about what had been said between them during that last phone call.

"She doesn't have my new address," Shelleyan admitted. "I need
to write her."

Charlie clenched his bag. "Sounds like a plan," he said, baffled at
why Shelleyan had engaged him in such friendly conversation, if not
at Olivia's bidding. The concept that he and Shelleyan would be
friends so far from home seemed improbable. Their roles had been
cast back in Phoenix, their relationship previously defined. "Hey,
I've got to run. I'm meeting someone. . . ." He motioned in the
direction of the Black Rabbit.

"Is this your regular?" she asked, appraising the bar.

"It's just a bar," he said. "Great to see you."

"Okay," Shelleyan said, and he rushed past her, touching her on
the shoulder to evade the good-bye hug he sensed was imminent.
"Wait!"

He turned around, his dirty duffel swinging violently.

"Let me get your number." She rummaged in her bag. "Be fun
to have old home week, huh?"

The open door to the Black Rabbit was less than fifty feet away.
"You can always reach me here," he said, jamming his thumb at the
gold-stenciled window. He laughed to indicate it might be a joke and
it might not, waving and disappearing into the dark, cool bar. He spied
Shelleyan copying the phone number into her address book. The sight
of her provoked a set of fragile emotions: On the one hand, a sense
of welcome familiarity gripped him, as if he and Shelleyan and
Olivia had lunched together in the Milky Way yesterday rather
than forever ago; but all that had happened to him since reminded

him that Olivia, too, was off somewhere living her life while he was absent from her life. He longed to staunch the accumulation of time spent apart, and Shelleyan's presence was a further insult to his situation.

Charlie watched from the safety of a dim corner until Shelleyan was lost in a sea of NYU kids migrating toward Sixth Avenue. The empty bar had the clean smell of freshly polished wood. The elderly bartender nattily attired in a pressed white cotton shirt and vintage gold vest busied himself with aligning the bottles of liquor behind the bar, rotating the labels face out, putting his eyes in the mirror only when Charlie turned to leave.

"Drink?" the bartender asked. A streak of late-afternoon light lit a dust mote that floated aflame across the vacant bar.

Charlie hesitated. He knew that wood-paneled bars like the Black Rabbit were generally more expensive than the sinkholes on the Lower East Side—he'd wandered into the Oak Room at the Plaza Hotel after an afternoon idle in Central Park and was dismayed at the fifty-dollar check for two vodka tonics and a watercress sandwich. He hadn't even known what watercress was, and while he enjoyed the sandwich, he would forever associate it with that afternoon's extortion.

"Maybe a glass of water," Charlie answered, "if you can spare it."

The bartender smiled. "You look like you need something a little stronger than water."

Charlie pulled out a barstool, convinced that this old man was going to sucker him by selling him a drink he needed but couldn't afford. His insides were still electrified from Shelleyan's unforeseen appearance, and the fortitude he needed to endure the harsh conditions on the streets of New York had momentarily been flushed from his system.

The bartender poured a tall, frosty glass of amber ale and set it in front of him. "On the house," he said without fanfare.

A store of self-pity welled up and it was all he could do to refrain from leaping over the bar to hug the bartender, or to curb the tears tickling the corners of his eyes. He lifted the glass in the bartender's direction. "Cheers," he said, the first taste of the cold beer going down a little too easily.

The bartender gave his name, and Charlie listened as Frank related how he'd once been a Broadway producer, "back when New York was New York," telling about the theater he had called home and all the wonderful friends who were long gone. "Some of them are on the wall," he said, indicating the framed pen and pencil caricatures that lined the establishment. Frank poured Charlie another beer, then one for himself. "What do you do?" he asked.

"I'm a writer," Charlie said, sipping the fresh beer.

"What have you written?" Frank asked.

Charlie babbled an unintelligible monologue about a novel that too closely resembled the mashed-up plots of two of Vernon Downs's novels, and he hoped that Frank wasn't a rabid Downs fan. "So far unpublished," he added quickly.

"Just takes luck," Frank said. "So many people in the theater had the most amazing stories about finding fortune. Some owed their whole career to standing in the right spot at the right time." He raised his glass. "To luck."

Charlie lifted his half-full glass. "To luck," he repeated.

Frank drained his glass and quickly washed it in the bar sink, replacing the sparkling pint on the pyramid of glasses behind the bar. "My friend owns a small publishing house in Brooklyn," Frank said. "You should send him your book."

Frank's mounting kindness toward him washed away all of Charlie's anxieties, and he deeply wished the imaginary manuscript existed, if only to repay the charity that Charlie knew he didn't deserve. He pocketed the address Frank scrawled on a cocktail napkin bearing a foil silhouette of a small black rabbit.

It was a number of days before Charlie learned that Obelisk Press was in the Williamsburg neighborhood in Brooklyn, the same neighborhood where Shelleyan lived, and the notion of paying a visit—he was slowly learning that every connection in New York deserved tribute—gave him the heebie-jeebies. Accident brought him to the crumbling concrete steps of the gray building in the Puerto Rican section of Williamsburg one Wednesday afternoon: He was enjoying an afternoon getaway from the city courtesy of a flyer he'd found in the subway advertising a kickball tournament in McCarren Park, in Greenpoint, the neighborhood abutting Williamsburg. As the sun set on the kickballers, Charlie trudged back toward the subway, his stomach full from the free hot dogs and watery beer served to spectators and players alike by the Turkey's Nest, a dive bar that was also the tournament's sole sponsor. An adventurous jaunt down a quiet side street designed to prolong the redemptive afternoon led him instead to the discreet plaque advertising the publishing company Frank had steered him and his imaginary manuscript toward.

He knocked on the door, unsure what he'd say. No one answered. He knocked again, spying the buzzer at knee height. He bent down, his back aching from leaning or lying on the grass all day, and pressed the buzzer. The front door was jimmied open by an enormous man in his sixties dressed in an impeccable three-piece suit, a neatly trimmed white beard the only hair on his pink head. Charlie introduced himself as a friend of Frank's. He didn't know Frank's last name, and Frank had only suggested mailing his imaginary manuscript, not showing up at the address in Brooklyn, but Charlie's instinct was stronger than reason and always prevailed. The man was searching Charlie's face, trying to fathom what it was he was saying, when Charlie remembered the folded napkin in his wallet. He offered the napkin with Frank's scrawl and the man's eyes lit up. He hoped Frank wouldn't learn of this misapplication of his kindness, though he was fairly sure he would never see Frank again, or could avoid him if it became an issue, so he dispatched the worry as quickly as it arose.

"Ah, yes," he said. "Come in."

The man introduced himself as Derwin MacDonald, though his affiliation with Frank from the Black Rabbit was to be forever unknown. Obelisk Press occupied the entire first floor of the building, the second being Derwin's living quarters. Charlie accepted Derwin's offer of a strong cup of coffee and, grateful for a comfortable chair, settled into the low-lit living room as Derwin recounted his days as a hanger-on in London, on the fringes of the third incarnation of the Bloomsbury Group, which Derwin explained was a group of intellectuals, writers, and painters. He glossed over the group's demise owing to vanity and fervent self-publication, Obelisk rising from the ashes of the immolation to publish the writers and thinkers he admired most.

"Do you write?" Derwin asked.

"I'd like to be a writer," Charlie admitted.

"Ah," Derwin said. "That's not the same thing."

Charlie shrugged and peppered him with questions about London, what it was like to live there, how expensive it was compared with New York, what single people did for fun, etc., keeping silent on the nature of his inquiry. He was dismayed at the glorious portrait Derwin painted, worried that Olivia might realize that she was already living in one of the most desirable world capitals and lose any interest in returning to America, for any reason.

By the end of the evening, he felt as integrated as he had since he'd left Phoenix, and by the end of the week he was squatting in the tiny studio apartment on the third floor, above Obelisk Press, with

Derwin's permission. A foldout couch sat unevenly on the hardwood
floor next to a table with spindly legs piled high with copies of Obelisk titles. A small counter installed under the far eave supported a
toaster and a defunct coffeemaker. What he mistook for a closet was
actually a half bathroom. The room suited him fine. He'd long ago
given up trying to personalize any of the spaces he inhabited.

His apprehension at bumping into Shelleyan on the streets of
Williamsburg faded as he acclimated to his new lodgings, and when
Derwin offered him a part-time job as his right-hand man, he felt
landed enough to call Vernon Downs, whose number he still knew
by heart.

....

As he knocked on Downs's door, Charlie was revisited by an old
humiliation from his first week in New York. Fearing that he'd be
chased from the city and never have the chance, he had managed
a call to Downs. Their staccato conversation—mostly Charlie giving a nervous recitation about what had transpired after his public
reading of Downs's work—was cut short with a proffered invitation,
a book party at the National Arts Club in Gramercy Park. Charlie
thanked him profusely, and Vernon said he was looking forward to
meeting then, which provoked a crippling anxiety that lasted until
the party. It was some small relief, then, when the doorman at the
National Arts Club forbade him entrance for lack of a jacket.

"Gentlemen wear jackets," the doorman snobbishly suggested.
The snub ignited Charlie's inclination toward flight, which he'd felt
when he first arrived at the Kepharts', and the McCallahans', and
the Alexander-Degners'—on down the line. Over the years, he'd
noticed a tickle when inaugurated into a new situation, one that
implored him to turn back, or to press on quickly. He fought against
the feeling but bailed from the foyer as the doorman hunted up a

club jacket for him to wear. An aggregate of humiliation could only lead to certain ruin. But would Vernon remember Charlie standing him up? Or worse, had he somehow witnessed his humiliation as the doorman shook his head sternly, like the nannies did their charges in Gramercy Park on the sunny days since that Charlie had spent canvassing the scene of the crime, the interior of the National Arts Club a mystery still? He had considered calling Vernon the next day and leaving a cheery message saying he'd see him later that night, pretending to be mistaken about the date, ultimately glad that he hadn't. One of the dilemmas about an uncertain present was an indecipherable future.

He'd had to invent a pretext for a second call, especially after his unexplained National Arts Club absence, and he manufactured an assignment he hadn't been given: He asked Vernon if he could interview him for *Oneironaut*, an online pop culture magazine whose founder he'd befriended in line at Starbucks.

"Sure," Vernon had said. "Be happy to."

The door opened slowly, a pair of cautious eyes peering from behind it. The door opened further and Vernon Downs stood before him, a tall, bulky man in his midthirties, a half smile on his cherubic face, the living embodiment of the description from the *Vanity Fair* profile he and Olivia had read repeatedly. A slight embarrassment passed between them.

"Come in," he said, his baritone voice filling the cavernous loft as Charlie entered.

II

"FOR OLIVIA?" Vernon asked.

Charlie nodded as he fished the tattered copy of *The Vegetable King* Olivia had left behind from his bag.

"This looks pretty beat up," Vernon said, fanning through the curled pages. "I think I can do better." He slid back the doors on the white and maple sideboard table packed with books and, not finding what he was searching for, reached under the unmade bed for a plastic bin crammed with copies of his work. He selected a pristine copy of *The Vegetable King* and signed it to Olivia. He signed the worn copy too, splaying the book out on the black granite kitchen counter, the only shadow anywhere in the gleaming white loft. "You can sell this one for a couple of bucks at the Strand." Charlie nodded, remembering the mammoth bookstore on Twelfth Street from when he'd cased Vernon's block upon learning Vernon's address.

The light outside the oversized windows was fading, a dusky glow painting the white walls gold. The stainless steel fan Vernon had switched on during the interview rotated, its blades flashing, the breeze rippling the cloth folding screen in the opposite corner that sequestered a table and computer. Vernon flicked on the track lighting and the loft, which had previously felt like a theater stage, took on the warmth of a habitable apartment. Charlie's anxiety at meeting Vernon had dissipated over the course of the interview, and he had become captivated by Vernon's answers, querying him exhaustively with the ambition of knowing every nuance about the author and his life. In the span of an afternoon, he'd become the world's expert on all things Vernon Downs, and for a brief moment he wished to time-travel back to the Milky Way Café at Glendale Community College so that instead of uttering "Why do I know that name?" he could proclaim "Of course, Vernon Downs."

"I'll ride down with you," Vernon said as he stabbed his cigarette into the pewter ashtray engraved with WORLD'S GREATEST DAD, which had slowly filled during the interview. Vernon cradled the ashtray and moved them into the elevator with a jauntiness that belied what must've been the incredible stress of the last couple of months. His smooth face was unblemished and he projected a vigor Charlie associated with health spas and resort living and not virtual exile in a small loft in New York City. "Be sure to show me the interview before you send it," he said. "Just to make sure I didn't say anything, you know, ridiculous."

Charlie promised he would. The elevator opened on the second floor just as Vernon said, "I'm having a little party," and Charlie was too exhilarated at the invitation to Vernon's famous annual Christmas in July party to really register Vernon's scattering the remnants from his ashtray in the hall, the heaviest concentration of butts littering the doorway of apartment 2D. Vernon stepped back into the elevator and it completed its descent to the lobby. "You should definitely stop by."

Charlie suppressed his elation. "I will," he said, "thanks a lot," regretting the "a lot" as soon as it left his mouth. The division between those on the inside and those on the outside was just circumstance and chance, he thought.

"And I'd love to see some of your work." Vernon slipped the ashtray into the back pocket of his black jeans.

"Oh," Charlie said, more in surprise than in response to the enormous gratitude the gesture inspired. He shifted into the rote supplication he could conjure at will while he considered what work he could show. He had his Oswald story, but he'd also managed to finish the story loosely based on him and Olivia for his Camden workshop. He'd feigned illness rather than attend workshop the day his story was to be discussed—he hadn't changed Olivia's name and understood too late that he wouldn't be able to weather others speaking about her in any way, even as a fictional character, so much so that he left the copies with his workshop mates' edits unread in a trash can in Booth before lighting out for New York. He was curious what Vernon would make of the story, though, and was also thrilled that he would soon be introduced to Olivia, albeit only on the page.

The genuineness of Vernon's invitation to the party and his offer to read some of Charlie's work caught Charlie off guard, and he exited the lobby before he could utter something foolish that might persuade Vernon otherwise, but Vernon was engrossed in conversation with the doorman, complaining of someone smoking in the halls. The doorman promised to investigate, and Charlie wondered what the gag was.

. . . .

In honor of the invitation to Vernon's party, Charlie bought a new shirt. He'd spent the afternoon at Century 21, the discount clothing store near Wall Street. Previously, his fashion sense had been limited to the rudimentary understanding most men held about colors that clashed. He had enlisted the help of the salesgirl, who smelled like vanilla, and he gave a start when the elevator to Vernon's loft opened on the second floor and a woman wearing the exact same scent emerged from apartment 2D. Charlie glanced guiltily at the carpeted hall, which had been recently vacuumed. He smiled at the woman, who was wearing a cornflower blue silk pleated dress that matched the color of her eyes.

He held the door for the woman and she disappeared into Vernon's party like quicksilver. Charlie maneuvered through the crowded loft with the manila envelope containing a copy of the story he'd written at Camden. Trajectory after trajectory was aborted, guests crashing into him as he sought out his host, who was sequestered in the corner with the rented sound system that rendered conversation in the loft impossible. As he cut through the crowd, he found himself next to an actress he recognized from one of Olivia's favorite movies. The actress was drunk, relying on the nearest blank wall to keep her upright. He surveyed the loft and realized the party was peopled with celebrities. The lead singer of a band he had worshipped one summer in high school was chatting up Vernon, and Charlie stalled his approach.

Vernon waved him over.

"Thanks again for inviting me," Charlie said, awkwardly sticking out his hand, as if they hadn't previously met. In one unbroken gesture, Vernon shook his hand and introduced him to the lead singer, whose name he couldn't hear over the blaring music but knew nonetheless. "I brought a story," Charlie said, offering up the envelope, intuiting just then that it was completely the wrong venue and occasion to pass work to Vernon. Vernon responded by gracefully nodding and taking the envelope, slipping it behind one of the speakers. The hardwood floor was littered with silver and gold confetti, and a bodybuilder in a Santa suit hoisting a tray of hors d'oeuvres slipped and fell, scattering his payload, though hardly anyone noticed.

Charlie felt like a child who had strayed into a parental gathering, past his bedtime, and excused himself on the pretense of getting a drink. "Can I get you anything?" he asked Vernon, regretting this sycophancy, but Vernon didn't hear—or pretended not to—and Charlie slunk away, inching through the mob toward the make-shift bar. He felt a hand squeeze his arm and turned to find himself latched to a woman with enormous red lips.

"Vernon!" the lips shouted, and then just as quickly, "Oh, I'm sorry."

"I'm Charlie," he said, but the woman was skimmed away by a tide of revelers.

The movie poster for *Minus Numbers* loomed over the bar, the actor who had played the lead pointing at the poster, his face be-traying the years since the film's release, as he strove to convince a skeptical blond woman that he was the actor on the poster.

"It's really me," the actor argued, a drunken grin spreading across his face.

The blond woman rolled her eyes and departed the bar with her drink, nearly charging into Charlie, whom she looked past as she scrutinized the faces in the loft.

The bartender, a tall, tanned woman in a gauzy dress, cupped her ear as he shouted his drink order, nodding as she poured out the last swallow of a bottle of tonic. Jeremy Cyanin materialized at Charlie's side. In all but a handful of the gossip column accounts of Vernon's alleged antics in bars and nightclubs from the Lower East Side to the Hamptons, Cyanin had been implicated as Vernon's ac-complice, the two often referenced in the same breath. Cyanin's first novel, *Fiesta!* was published to critical and popular success simulta-neous to Vernon's *Minus Numbers*, and as both novels explored dis-affected youth, the press rendered the two writers interchangeable and began confusing them in print regularly. Their author photos from the decade previous had been reprinted thousands of times, so that the casual reader couldn't tell them apart, or recognize them now. Cyanin's reputation had been enhanced by a short stint as an ambulance driver during the first Gulf War—though a leg injury had deposited him safely stateside, where he continued his job as a fact-checker for the *New Yorker*—and from his surviving a small-plane crash during an African safari he'd taken with his first wife. (Cyanin had been married multiple times, each marriage beginning on the heels of the last.) The couple had been rescued by a passing sightseeing bus, only to have their second plane crash. Cyanin had suffered a ruptured spleen, a sprained arm, smashed vertebrae, a burned scalp, and a transitory loss of all feeling in his hands. To his eternal amusement, he had been declared dead and read his own obituary in a café in Venice, a fact he often mentioned in interviews.

"Another," he said to the bartender.

"One sec," the bartender said, holding up a finger as she turned to rummage through the cardboard boxes of unopened bottles of gin, tequila, vodka, whiskey, and rum.

Charlie grasped for something to say to Cyanin, but his thoughts were hijacked by the memory of Vernon referring to Cyanin as obsequious when Charlie tried to initiate small talk while waiting for the elevator. "He's still an obsequious presence at nightclubs." Vernon had meant "ubiquitous." The malapropism had plagued him, a catch in his throat that surfaced as he stood side by side with Cyanin. To his relief, Cyanin paid him no attention, staring straight ahead until a murderous shriek broke his trance. A woman grabbed Cyanin and kissed him on the lips. Cyanin pulled back, pretending offense.

"Is that a promise or a reprimand?" he asked, oozing a phony charm.

The woman hiccupped loudly and then proceeded not to be embarrassed when it was discovered that she'd mistaken Cyanin for her ex-husband, a bond trader for Salomon Brothers. "You actually don't look a thing like him," she said.

"He's a very lucky man," Cyanin said, swiping his fresh drink from the bar without breaking conversation. Charlie grabbed his vodka tonic as well, pointedly thanking the bartender, and turned away from Cyanin to face a platoon of thirsty partygoers impatiently questing for another drink.

"I loved your book," a bespectacled man said.

"Excuse me?" Charlie said. The vodka began massaging his brain.

"I said I loved your book," the man repeated, the scent of whiskey on his breath. Charlie noticed the man teetering slightly in his tasseled loafers. "I thought the characterizations were . . . real and the story . . . believable," the man said.

Charlie smiled, nodding as the man continued to praise whatever book he was referring to.

"Is it hard to write a book like that?" the man asked.

"Yes," Charlie said. "Very hard. Harder than you'd think."

"I'm Peter Kline," the man said. "I'm with the *Times*."

Charlie suspected Kline wouldn't remember the conversation and indulged him, grateful for someone to talk to.

"What I really liked was the way you couldn't tell if the main character—what was his name again?" Kline exhaled a stream of sour breath as he fumbled.

"I'm sorry," Charlie said. "I'm deaf in one ear. What did you say?"

"The main character in *The Vegetable King*," Kline said. "His name is escaping me."

"Nick Banks," Charlie said.

"I liked the way you couldn't tell if Nick Banks was really doing those murders, or if they were all just his imagination," Kline said.

Charlie sipped his drink, annoyed. "You couldn't tell? Thought it was obvious."

Kline didn't register the barb. "This is some party," he said. "Lots of celebs. Saw you with Jeremy Cyanin over there by the bar. Your partner in crime, eh?" Kline winked conspiratorially. "He says you don't like your picture taken."

Charlie smiled sheepishly. "Just doesn't seem like a good idea," he said. The cadence of Vernon's speech had been indelibly recorded in Charlie's brain, and he contorted his mouth to imitate the smirk he'd seen Vernon employ when he'd asked him the same question.

Kline winked again, making a gun with his fingers. "Gotcha. Lots of nut jobs out there." The commotion around a handstand by an attractive woman whose dress gathered down around her shoulders obscured Kline's good-bye as he joined the tributary of people moving slowly toward the balcony. Charlie swayed with the crowd until Kline was gone and then made his way for the door. He'd stayed long enough to recount the party to Olivia and glanced toward Vernon, hoping to give a salute across the noisy room, but Vernon was still in the corner, the woman with the cornflower blue dress whispering into his ear. He laughed and she leaned her body into his.

A boisterous foursome burst into the lobby, late arrivals for the party raging upstairs. Charlie lingered, eavesdropping on their excited chatter about meeting Vernon Downs, before catapulting out into the night, his senses ablaze with a privileged glimpse of the world Olivia must've dreamed of a thousand times over.

. . . .

Charlie announced himself to the doorman, who registered a faint look of recognition. The doorman hung up the phone. "He's coming down." Charlie had almost missed the message Vernon had left the day before at Obelisk, asking him to join him for lunch. He had spent most of the previous day uptown with Derwin, who had arranged a launch party for Jacqueline Turner, one of his oldest authors, at Bemelmans in the Carlyle Hotel. Derwin had advanced him his paycheck so he could buy a suit for the occasion, again with the assistance of the vanilla-laced salesgirl at Century

21, who remembered him, or pretended to. New York's reputation as a cold, heartless metropolis was unearned, in his judgment. Eastern Star, the former speakeasy on the same block as Obelisk, had become Charlie's local, and he was amazed at the disparate population he'd encountered at the Star's lacquered and pockmarked bar: faces from Florida and Texas and Oregon, or Canada and Europe and Asia—each as friendly as the last, always inquiring what had brought Charlie to New York. He always demurred and instead luxuriated in their answers to the same question, drinking in the various biographies and ambitions. The Vietnamese girl who was studying fashion at Pratt; the Australian couple who hoped to open an apiary somewhere in Brooklyn; the kid from Detroit who had dreams of becoming a hatter. Their ambitions were endless and Charlie lamented only that he'd never know if any or all of them would come to fruition.

Charlie's stomach gurgled, reproof that he hadn't eaten since the Southern-themed launch party at Bemelmans the day before. The plate of leftover pecan-encrusted sliced chicken breast drizzled in honey and red-skinned mashed potatoes he'd wolfed down was a distant culinary event, and he hoped Vernon's plans for lunch were more than liquid. Jacqueline Turner had abstained from the delicious fare at her launch party, which Charlie ascribed to nerves. Leading up to the party, Derwin had been distracted with the details. What was left unsaid was that with Jacqueline being eighty, this would surely be her last novel, and even Derwin knew that it would not be remembered or read in the future. Charlie wondered if the same was true for her first novel, *Esque*. A framed enlargement of the cover hung over Derwin's desk, the author photo a stunning portrait of Jacqueline in her youth, her even features lending her an aura of grace. The knowing eyes bored out from the frame as Charlie considered the art deco design on the cover. The novel had won several of the major fiction prizes the year it was published, and Jacqueline had written two more in short order that sold well enough to her new audience, which thinned with each subsequent title, until she stopped publishing altogether at the young age of forty. Charlie bristled at the notion that it was possible to go from gracing the cover of *Time* magazine to obscurity within the same lifetime. Vernon Downs would be famous his entire life, probably posthumously, too. Jacqueline's death would merit an obituary in the *New York Times*, and Derwin would keep her work in print as long as he was alive, but it would probably suffer the miserable fate of being stacked in warehouses waiting for readers whose attention had turned elsewhere. The launch party for Jacqueline's new novel—sparsely attended by friends of Derwin's as well as a smattering of Jacqueline's contemporaries, and none of the press outlets Derwin had Charlie fax his carefully worded press release to—telegraphed just such ignominy. Charlie had helped himself to seconds after the small gathering had cleared, the caterer's assistant eyeing the same prize. Charlie knew the hunger with which free food was devoured, and he imagined the assistant would be lunching on pecan-encrusted chicken sandwiches for weeks.

"Sorry, sorry," Vernon said as he hustled into the lobby. "I have to go uptown."

A black sedan Charlie hadn't previously noticed idled out in front of Summit Terrace. His hunger rose up against his inclination toward genuflection but was defeated. "No problem, really."

"Ride with me," Vernon said. "I read your story."

The driver opened the door for Vernon and grimaced as Charlie skirted around to the other side, never having had a car door opened on his behalf. The leather interior was remarkably hard, and Charlie bounced in his seat as the car turned uptown, sailing up Park Avenue South. The landscape transformed dramatically as they sluiced through the tunnels at Grand Central, awash in the gilded moraine of centuries of wealth accumulation. Across Park Avenue, across the wide boulevard of landscaped tulips, a silver Jaguar gleamed heroically in a showroom window.

The interim between Charlie's handing over his story to now had been teeming with grand designs of becoming Vernon's protégé, fêted up and down Manhattan as the Next Big Thing, perhaps replacing the dull, aging Cyanin as Vernon's literary yin. If simply knowing Vernon was currency in Olivia's eyes, his becoming a protégé would make him richer by ten. The fantasies about celebrity-studded book parties and lucrative film offers were brought low now that he was cocooned in the sedan with Vernon. Charlie hadn't done more than transcribe his and Olivia's story, the pages likely rotten with florid language as a result of the seismic ache in his heart. That Vernon Downs would be remotely intrigued by the story suddenly seemed a severe miscalculation.

"I read it twice," Vernon said, tapping his slender fingers on the armrest between them. "You're onto something, but it's not happening on the page yet. Nothing happens, for one. Characters need backstory, but Alice is down the rabbit hole on page one, if you get me. And action is borne from motivation. So for instance, the girlfriend doesn't just move back home. They're engaged and she breaks up with him to marry someone else. But even that is too boring. She marries the other guy because the other guy has money, which is important because the girlfriend's family fortunes are dwindling. Maybe the result of scandal. Etcetera."

Charlie swallowed the revulsion he felt at the idea of Olivia marrying someone else, or marrying someone else for money. The offense was too grievous to consider, even fictionally. Vernon's advice called to mind those critics who had wondered where the emotional heft was in his work, complaining that his novels were too often peopled with ciphers meant to channel the author's ennui. One particular critic had called Vernon's work "everythingless."

Charlie mentally argued against Vernon's critique but was distracted by Vernon adding, casually, "I think I know an editor who would consider it if you revise." The hard truth that he needed Vernon's approval, craved the apprenticeship, stifled all his argumentative impulses.

"I'll definitely have another go at it," he said. "Thanks. Really, thanks."

"Pull over here," Vernon told the driver. The car found the nearest curb and Vernon turned in his seat. "Here's how you can return the favor." The directness of his tone spooked Charlie and he was taken aback by the cold fear he felt. He hadn't previously considered Vernon to be dangerous, but even the driver averted his eyes. "Write me five hundred words on why kids are ruining America."

"You mean like an essay?" Charlie asked, laughing.

Vernon smiled, clenching and unclenching his fists as if the reps were part of a daily exercise routine. "It's for *George* magazine. I told them I'd do it, but that was only because I wanted to meet JFK Jr. I'm just not into it now." He searched Charlie's face for complicity. "Do this for me and I'll show your story to my friend the editor."

Charlie nodded, knowing the hunger for ingratiation. "Sure. When do you need it?"

"Yesterday." Vernon grimaced. "Why don't you bring it with you to KGB tomorrow night. There's a book party. Seven p.m."

"Okay," Charlie agreed. It was easy to agree without considering what he was agreeing to.

"This is you," Vernon said. It took Charlie a moment to realize what Vernon was saying.

"Watch traffic," the driver warned from the front seat.

"Sorry about lunch," Vernon said.

Charlie waved good-bye and walked up Sixty-eighth Street, ir-
resolute about the direction he was headed until Central Park came
into view, orienting him. He was lost as a tourist uptown—his second trip in as many days—and almost collapsed in frustration until
the doorman at the Plaza indicated with a nod the direction of the
subway entrance under the hotel.

....

Charlie mounted the steep stairs to KGB, emerging at the tiny
second-floor bar whose walls were lined with Soviet memorabilia,
framed posters of Stalin and Lenin and other unnamed politburo
chiefs menacing the crowd of oblivious hipsters from above. He
spotted Vernon under a poster of Yuri Andropov. As he knifed
through the throng, he spied Jeremy Cyanin behind a near-life-size
black-and-white head shot of the author whose books were stacked
on the corner of the bar.

Charlie crept forward. He'd been confused by the lack of real
instructions for delivering the *George* magazine piece—he surmised
that Vernon hadn't asked him to e-mail it to avoid an electronic paper
trail—and felt foolish for bringing it to the book party, even if those
were Vernon's instructions. He'd nearly abandoned the assignment, unable to come up with a slant that seemed worthy of a slick magazine,
until he'd solicited Derwin for his assessment of youth culture. Derwin
had given him a soulful look. "Murderers, rapists, gamblers," he'd said.
"You never heard of these things when I was young." Charlie had no
independent knowledge about whether the comparison was true or not,
but once he embraced Derwin's point of view, the piece flowed quickly:

Teens are running roughshod over this country—murdering,
raping, gambling away the nation's future—and we have bills
for counseling and prison to prove it. Sure, not all kids are bad—

but collectively, they're getting worse. Why should we blame ourselves? Things have changed drastically in the last twenty years, to the point where one can really only chuckle in grim disbelief. Cheating on exams? Smoking cigarettes? Shoplifting? You wish. Murder, rape, robbery, vandalism: The overwhelming majority of these crimes are committed by people under twenty-five, and the rate is escalating rapidly.

He'd gone to sleep feeling mentally fatigued, spent from rearranging sentences and auditioning words and phrases, searching for artistic expression of his borrowed idea, but also from the charge of aping Vernon's cool attitude.

Vernon nodded in his direction, calling him over.

"You made it," Vernon said.

Charlie made a nervous joke about having gotten lost, even though he hadn't.

"This is Jeremy Cyanin," Vernon said, pointing.

"Hey," Cyanin said coolly, scanning the room. "I suppose you're mad at Vernon too."

Charlie smiled dumbly, unsure what the gibe meant, forcing Vernon to explain that he'd been spending time with some models as research for his next novel and had even participated in a photo shoot, but changed his mind about signing the release form. Apparently, everyone was angry about it, much to Cyanin's amusement. Charlie processed the information in the uncomfortable silence, which was broken by a woman dripping in gold lamé who squealed when she saw Vernon and Cyanin. "It *is* you," the woman said, raising her arms to allow the writers to hug her. Cyanin obliged, while Vernon lifted his glass in the woman's direction. "Hello, Vernon," she said. "I haven't seen you since your Christmas party. You never did say where you hired those elves from."

"The elves were two years ago," Cyanin said, laughing. He rocked back on his heels, unaware of the swaying.

The woman's expression changed. "Yes, I'm on some sort of blacklist, apparently." Vernon shrugged and rattled the ice in his glass. A cloud settled over the woman, whose gold lamé dress appeared rusty in the red-lit room.

Cyanin leaned into the bar, and Charlie passed the folded pages to Vernon, who slipped them into his suit jacket pocket with a half smile.

"Looks like a rip-off of *Minus Numbers*," Charlie said, indicating the blowup of the cover.

"You could say that," Vernon laughed.

The writer being celebrated appeared, a jaunty kid wearing a very authorial jacket, complete with elbow patches, and shook hands with Vernon as Cyanin emerged from the bar. Charlie exploited the seam created by Cyanin and reached out for the lip of the bar to pulley himself to the front of the crowd.

"That's a slick move," the man standing next to him said.

"Thanks," Charlie replied.

"If you can get the bartender's attention, you'll really have done it." He stuck out his hand. "Warren Thomas."

Charlie shook hands. "Your name sounds familiar," he said, having recently realized this was the correct thing to say in writerly circles.

"I write for *Esquire*," he said. "With Josh." He indicated the author whose book had brought them all together.

"Right," Charlie said, reaching into the recesses of his mind to seize the elusive strand that incorporated what he knew about Warren Thomas. The information bobbed up like a sunken piece of driftwood finally freed. "You wrote 'The Case for Vernon David Downs,'" right?"

Warren nodded. "Good recall."

Charlie gushed about how Warren's piece about the *Vegetable King* controversy had clearly been written by someone with a cool head, not someone caught up in the rhetoric and the heated moment. "He's here," Charlie said.

"Yeah, I saw him." Warren attempted to flag down the bartender, without success. "I heard he's finally crawling out of his cave. Good for him. A shitty way to have to live. I'd stand in the corner too, though. You never know who's out there."

"Do you think *The Vegetable King* is his best book? Or just the most famous?"

Warren finally reeled in the bartender, who didn't look up when Warren gave his order, then pointed at Charlie.

"Same," Charlie said.

Warren turned to him. "Truthfully, I think he's a sensationalist hack with a gift for self-promotion. That piece was assigned to me and I wrote it. But it was mental torture. I didn't come up with the headline and never felt like I was making the case for anything, frankly. Just doing my job. I could make a case for him being a talentless douche bag. Easily."

The bartender splashed the vodka tonics down on the bar. Charlie tipped a buck, like he'd seen others do, but the bartender didn't notice, and when Warren didn't follow, Charlie slipped the dollar back into his pocket.

Warren hoisted his glass and said, "Sorry to disappoint," before being swallowed up by the crowd, which had grown exponentially. Charlie cut a half-moon through the bodies to reach Vernon and Cyanin, who were in the corner, their backs to the crowd. A cumulus of cigarette smoke hung thickly overhead. The spiced fragrance of a clove cigarette filled his nose.

"Have some," Vernon said, palming a small chrome bullet into Charlie's hand. The tiny cylinder felt hot to his touch, and he instinctively set his drink on the nearest table and unscrewed the top. Charlie had never favored anything more than drink, but reading Vernon's work had been, among other things, a study in the usage of drug paraphernalia. He scooped a tiny pyramid of cocaine with the miniature spoon inside and held it under his right nostril, inhaling quickly. A searing sandstorm blasted across the back of his throat, and his tongue involuntarily clamped to the roof of his mouth. Heart palpitations drowned the whirring in his brain as he resumed possession of his vodka tonic.

Vernon skulked in the corner, his arms crossed, striking the same pose he had at the Christmas party. Cyanin never strayed from his side, his animation contrasting violently with Vernon's passivity. Charlie felt his spine straighten as the cocaine massaged his doubts and fears about winning Olivia back into confirmation that all would be well. Something within him vindicated all designs of his thinking, vanquishing the interior monologue that constantly reminded him that he knew nothing definitively and that his life was essentially a streak of guesses.

Josh, the celebrated author, ducked into the bathroom in the hall. An acrid odor assaulted Charlie as he followed. His field of vision narrowed. Josh was at the sink, dabbing his wet fingers through his black hair. The phoniness of the assortment of bracelets on his right wrist struck Charlie as pathetic. Josh peered at Charlie in the mirror and Charlie tipped his chin. "Great party," he said.

"Cool," Josh said. The bracelets jangled as his hands dropped to his sides.

"I liked your book," Charlie said.

Josh turned and edged against the sink to let Charlie pass. "Thanks, man."

Charlie's heart raced and he stifled a cackle. "I mean, I liked it when it was called *Minus Numbers*."

The author grimaced, squinting.

"Seems like a pretty poor imitation," Charlie continued. "Actually, truth be told, it looks like garbage. I'm surprised there isn't a stack in here to wipe your ass with." The words issued from his mouth like gunfire.

"You're entitled to your opinion," Josh said. He pivoted, but Charlie barred his exit.

"Oh, it's more than an opinion," Charlie sneered. "It's an established fact."

"Can I pass?"

"Fact," Charlie repeated.

"May I pass?" Josh asked again.

"Sure." Charlie acquiesced, stepping aside. "You can do anything you want," he said. "Except come up with your own ideas, apparently."

"Fuck you," Josh blurted out as he lurched out the door.

Charlie lunged at the sink, his pulse quickening until his vision was permeated with bright constellations. He pressed his forehead against the mirror and watched his eyeballs shimmy in their sockets. He drank ravenously from the rusted tap, splashing the cool water on his face. Back in the bar, Vernon and Cyanin were sitting at a table, drinking and smoking. Charlie took the steps two at a time until he reached the street, the humidity lashing his forehead with sweat. He made his way toward Union Square, traffic blurring around him. As he plummeted into the swampy subway station, an immense exhaustion overtook him and he clutched the rail. A young girl with a blond beehive hairdo asked him if he was okay, and he moved on without answering, thinking about the question.

....

Charlie realized that a pain he had mistakenly diagnosed as a sore throat was actually a bad tooth. He disregarded the throbbing until it prevented him from sleeping, finally giving in to the unbelievable fire in his jaw, seeking treatment at the New York University dental school on the advice of Derwin, who'd had a successful cleaning there at a fraction of the cost. "Not to fret," Derwin said. "The students are supervised by faculty."

The days leading up to Charlie's appointment, mostly spent in agony in his cramped and stuffy studio apartment above Obelisk typing up his interview with Vernon, passed slowly. When he finally breached the doors of the dental clinic, it was with a sense of hope. He waited patiently to be called onto the floor, a cavernous space as big as a gymnasium outfitted with dental chairs and dental equipment, shiny and new enough to assuage Charlie's fears that the school was nothing more than a chop shop. He was introduced to the student who would be attending to his dental needs, a Russian whose name he didn't catch. A bit of pantomiming couldn't elicit his name again, and Charlie finally surrendered to the Russian's entreaty for him to open wide.

After a few moments of prodding, the Russian brought him upright and motioned for Charlie to follow him. He draped the heavy apron over Charlie and pointed for him to take a seat in a metal booth. The Russian pressed a cardboard splint loaded with film into Charlie's gums until they bled, finally finding the position he wanted. The Russian aimed the arm of the X-ray machine at his cheek and scampered away. As Charlie anticipated the high-pitched squeal of the X-ray machine, he noted a smear of dried blood on the booth that almost made him faint.

The Russian managed the words "root canal" and Charlie nodded, glad to have the problem out in the open. The Russian bade Charlie to follow him back to a dental chair, and he was quickly surrounded by three other heads that began speaking rapid-fire Japanese into his open mouth. Charlie had somehow assented to a root canal, and the foursome was going to extract the root in his ailing tooth right then and there. He wanted to protest, but the pain radiating from his mouth persuaded him to give it a shot.

The Novocain injection put the operation on the right footing. *These guys really know what they're doing,* Charlie thought. He relaxed as best he could as the Russian drilled open his bad tooth. He knew from previous root canals that the next step would be to remove the infected pulp tissue, which would alleviate the agony. The drilling was endless, though, exciting the Japanese students, whose instructions in Japanese the Russian didn't seem to understand. Charlie could sense the Russian becoming flustered, until he raised his arms in surrender. The five of them sat in silence, catching their breath, while Charlie stared at yet another dried bloodstain, this one on the overhead lamp. After a moment, the Russian wanted a second chance, which turned into a third and a fourth try. An hour passed while he tried to get at the infected tissue, and finally a balding man in a lab coat, who Charlie later learned was the instructor assigned to walk the floor, banished the foursome to another torture assignment and quickly finished extracting the tissue. He cleaned out the root canal and sealed it with a temporary filling.

"You'll have to come back on another visit to continue the procedure," the instructor said gruffly. "Make an appointment on your way out."

Charlie stood at the checkout desk, shaken, while a student wearing headphones looked into a computer monitor, booking him for an appointment he knew he wouldn't keep.

"Something in your teeth?" Vernon asked over drinks at the Gramercy Park Hotel bar. The drink was in celebration of Vernon's victory in a legal matter involving a studio and a director who had stolen the premise of one of Vernon's early published short stories, and Charlie had shown up on time, hoping to disappear before the arrival of Cyanin and the rest of Vernon's cadre of friends.

"Had a root canal this morning," Charlie said without elaboration. He knew not to burden Vernon with his personal problems.

"I hope that means painkillers," Vernon said.

"Tylenol Three," Charlie replied.

"Sucker," Vernon said, flashing him a half smile.

Charlie expected Vernon to comment on his piece for *George* magazine, but Vernon gave no indication that he'd even read it. Maybe he'd read and tossed it, instructing his agent to cancel the contract. Entirely possible. His heavily revised short story could meet the same fate. After agonizing over the sacrilege, he accepted Vernon's challenge and portrayed the character based on Olivia in the unsympathetic light Vernon had suggested. The story was now the tale of an idealistic young romantic whose heart was maliciously broken. When the young romantic chases the object of his affections to Europe, she tells him she had an abortion and that she can never see him again. Back home, the young romantic runs into a mutual friend, who tells him that the abortion was just a story to get rid of him. The ending leaves ambiguous what the young romantic does next.

"I took your advice," Charlie said. "About my story, I mean."

Vernon drained his vodka. "Cool," he said, crunching a piece of ice. "E-mail it and I'll have a look."

As Vernon dictated his e-mail address, Charlie was astounded at the simplicity of the combination of letters and symbols. He'd idly speculated that Vernon's e-mail address would incorporate something from one of his books, a character's name or a character's favorite restaurant or bar. The realization that the address was an AOL account simply prefaced with Vernon's initials was stupefying. The relief for those panic-stricken weeks back in Phoenix when he was frantic to arrange lunch with Olivia and Vernon could've been puzzled out if he weren't always trying to be clever. Sometimes the answer was simple, not a code to be broken. "He's Olivia's favorite writer, dummy," Shelleyan had said. He wished his answer could've been, "I'll drop him an e-mail and see if he's up for lunch."

"Excuse me, Mr. Downs?" The impeccably groomed waiter with the shiny black ponytail approached. "This is against hotel policy, but I wondered if you might sign a book for me." He presented a copy of *The Vegetable King* from the waistband of his black apron. "I hope it's okay to ask."

Charlie said, "Possible to get another drink?" before Vernon cut him off with a smirk. "It's no problem." He commandeered Charlie's pen and signed the book while the waiter glared at Charlie.

"I truly appreciate it," the waiter said. "I'm a tremendous fan, going back to *Minus Numbers.*"

"Thanks," Vernon said quietly, rolling the pen back to Charlie. "You're not going to sell it at the Strand, right?"

"No, never," the waiter said.

"Possible to get a couple more?" Charlie asked brusquely.

"Same?" the waiter asked Vernon pointedly.

Vernon nodded, turning to Charlie as the waiter sauntered away. "Quit abusing my fans," he laughed.

"Just thought it was uncool," Charlie said reflexively.

Vernon regarded him with an air of amusement. The chandelier overhead dimmed and the red velvet lounge shaded, casting his features in relief. Charlie knew he'd overstepped, and waited for a rebuke. Instead Vernon said, "Would you be up for some apartment sitting?"

. . . .

A sharp pain flashed through Charlie's brain and he slumped against the pillow, rubbing his dry eyes. Yesterday's *Post* lay on the floor, open to the piece that had brought on the frenzy he hadn't fully been able to subdue:

Vernon Downs Evades History

Vernon Downs has always had a knack for getting press, but young writers looking to hitch their wagons to his publicity mule should look elsewhere. *The Vegetable King* author tells us he is refusing to cooperate with an oral biography of his life and work being written by Jonathan Erdahl. According to anonymous sources, Erdahl intends to interview such literary folk as David Gomez, Jeff Lawrence, and Jeremy Cyanin. So why won't Downs touch the project with a ten-foot pen? A friend of his tells us, "He just isn't in the mood." Well, we're sure Erdahl will dig up something.

Charlie had no idea who in the fuck Jonathan Erdahl was, but the crest of jealousy that crashed over him as he reread the article was disorienting. That Vernon had never mentioned him assured Charlie that this Erdahl was just one more wannabe, someone Vernon had vanquished by leaking a quote that was certainly devastating to the project. Erdahl was finished. He wouldn't be digging up anything of any interest to anyone anytime soon.

The faded blue iguana stamped onto his left hand brought the previous night into focus, the no-name club where he ended up with Stacey, the woman he'd met at Bull & Bear, the restaurant at the Waldorf Astoria, who claimed to work for some sort of design company. He'd gone to Bull & Bear to remind himself that he could act like a gentleman, quietly sipping a Ketel One martini at the elegant bar while the youngish pianist played indistinct classical music. The cigar smoker in the suit might've assumed he was an investment banker, someone who lived uptown or off Central Park, or one of those computer gazillionaires who might be in from California to broker a deal. For the first time since he'd moved to New York, Charlie felt the pliant personality that had allowed him to move from town to town, home to home, school to school, emerge, and when Stacey sat down beside him and ordered a vodka sour, he decided to enlist his old powers. He could do that. Slough off the heavy baggage he'd ferried from Phoenix, always concentrating on the high-wire act he was trying to orchestrate. He said hello and remembered what it was like to pretend. He had Stacey calling him James, he had her riding in a cab going downtown, he had her drinking bourbon straight up at the International on First Avenue.

Then she had him dancing in a club full of people in Soho. Everything was green, the walls, the lights, the liquor they drank out of plastic cups. "This isn't crème de menthe, is it?" Charlie asked, but Stacey didn't hear him and then she was gone, swept up in a wash of green. He slipped into the bathroom and vomited until the toilet bowl matched the rest of the decor, and then he glided out the front door.

Charlie rubbed his eyes again. He had the feeling that he was forgetting something, leaving something out, but he could not summon a picture of what had happened next. He looked at the inch-high red digits on his alarm clock. He had guessed it was around noon and was dismayed to read that it was nearing five o'clock. He snatched up a half-eaten bag of lime-flavored tortilla chips and sat on the end of his bed, crunching loudly, the tinge of salt and lime filling his mouth and throat, wondering the extent of the hit his credit card took during the previous evening's escapades. When he learned later that his Visa was maxed out, he bent it in half and then in half again and flushed the pieces down the toilet.

A survey of his closet revealed that Charlie hadn't done laundry in a while. Why couldn't he remember these crucial chores?

Derwin had invited him to use the washer and dryer in the basement anytime he wished. Charlie slipped on a pair of jeans not too dirty to wear and pulled on his favorite black T-shirt. He took the stairs gingerly and meandered to what was quickly becoming his favorite neighborhood bar, Iona. The bartender, Ailish, was the incarnation of Talie, the girl in foster care at the Chandlers' in Phoenix that he'd been close to, and it amused him to watch the place fill with men—some from Manhattan—waiting for their chance to flirt with her.

"How are you, Charlie?" Ailish said from behind the narrow bar, the playground for so many late-night conversations and flirtations. The track lighting overhead cast shadows around her as she emptied the pint glasses out of the dishwasher.

"I'm okay," he said. "What's new?"

"Remember that song you were trying to think of the other night?" Ailish had been playing all '80s music, and a lyric he couldn't identify had popped into Charlie's head. Charlie had argued it was a band called Camouflage, but Ailish said for sure it wasn't, though she couldn't remember exactly who it was.

"It was Camouflage," Charlie said, smiling.

Ailish slapped the bar towel at him. "I told you it wasn't fucking Camouflage," she said. "It's Real Life." She put her arms up over her head in victory.

"Yeah," Charlie said. "Real Life covering Camouflage."

"Oh, give it up," she said.

"I think you owe me a drink, then."

"How is it you got the answer wrong and I owe *you* a drink?" She acted incredulous, and it was one of the things Charlie loved about her, how any small thing could become a good time.

"How about if I buy me one and then you buy me one?" he offered.

"That's a *much* better deal," she laughed, and poured him a pint of Bass, which was how it always started.

By eleven o'clock, Charlie had lost sight of Ailish, not knowing it would be the last time he ever saw her, that a death in her family would call her back to Dublin. He looked at the apartment building across the street. All the windows were dark. Everyone was out somewhere, having a good time, or having a shitty time, he thought. Living their lives, regardless. Derwin had gone out of town for the weekend to visit his brother in Baltimore. Charlie didn't want to be the only soul in the building, which was how he ended up in a cab with two girls who were afraid to take the subway from Brooklyn late at night. He asked them their names twice as the cab sped over the Williamsburg Bridge, and then the girls ignored him, sorry they'd offered him a ride (he had just stepped out for some air, but the way he looked at the cab made them think he wanted to share it). Charlie got out at Houston and Broadway and handed the girls a five-dollar bill. "Nice to meet you, Becky and Julie," he said. "Thanks for the ride."

"Sandy and Emily," one of them said as Charlie slammed the cab door.

Charlie parted the black curtain under a neon sign on the Lower East Side, and his eyes dilated in the dark bar. Two girls dressed in identical pink plastic dresses looked up from the sofa by the door, their faces obscured in darkness. Charlie waved as if he knew them, and they looked back at each other and continued their conversation.

An uneasy feeling came over him as he battled for space at the bar. Finally he planted himself on the long couch in the back room. He would trade every good thing in his future if only Olivia would appear, kiss him on the cheek, rest her head on his shoulder. His heart contracted and he gasped for breath, sure that he was about to die. Two short breaths and he exhaled deeply, the weight he'd felt lifting right as the waitress poked her head in.

"Vodka tonic, please," Charlie said. "Stoli."

A song that had been popular when Charlie lived in Santa Fe played loudly overhead, and by the time it was finished, two empty glasses were keeping each other company on the table near the couch as he recounted for Lynette—a girl who had come in looking for her friends, for a birthday party—the different meanings the song had held for him at different points in his life. Charlie was making a very moving point about his childhood when Lynette interrupted him to ask the difference between a Sea Breeze and a Bay Breeze. Charlie couldn't guess and said so. He put his head on Lynette's bare shoulder and she didn't seem to mind. He felt her body vibrate when she told the waitress, "Sea Breeze, please," and he started humming the song that had just ended. By the time he was in the cab with Lynette, headed to an Albanian nightclub Lynette knew about somewhere in the Bronx, Charlie was humming the tune for the cabdriver, asking if the cabbie knew the name of the song, or who sang it.

"I have to get up early," Lynette said to no one in particular. A mole on her neck would be unsightly once Lynette was older—she'd likely have it removed—but Charlie thought it was so sexy he wanted to lean in and kiss it.

"Where do you work?" Charlie asked, but he didn't listen to the answer.

The cab flew up Madison Avenue, the streets desolate except for the occasional couple strolling in front of backlit windows, peering in at chicly dressed mannequins wearing frozen expressions.

"Take us to Fifty-fifth and Fifth," Lynette yelled, leaning through the plastic divider. Charlie glimpsed a second beauty mark on her breast that mirrored the one on her neck, and he yearned to trace an arc between the two.

"Is that where you live?" Charlie asked.

"There's a cool bar," Lynette said, her thoughts drifting. "I went there once with my father."

The cab stopped on Fifth Avenue and Charlie paid the driver, then tipped the doorman at the Peninsula Hotel. Lynette pressed the button for the elevator, and Charlie slipped into the men's room, vomiting in a stall, bracing himself against the cold steel walls. He fixed his hair in the mirror, and the elevator rang as the men's room door closed behind him.

The bar on the roof of the Peninsula was unoccupied, and Charlie looked at his watch: 3:30. A light breeze swooped down and made him shiver.

"What are you drinking?" Lynette asked.

Charlie ordered a vodka and cranberry from the tuxedo-clad bartender. "We're closed after this," the bartender said, and brushed his crew cut.

"So are we," Charlie said, but no one laughed.

The cranberry juice tasted like food to Charlie as he slowly tilted his head back. He opened his eyes and spied the moon peeking through a jumble of clouds. He thought he could feel the light coming off the moon, not heat but a soothing coolness, like the water in the pool Lynette spotted on their way to the elevator, her dress already poolside by the time Charlie splashed down. Floating on his back, he was unsure if they'd paid for their drinks. He closed his tired eyes and put his hands at his sides and began to sink toward the bottom.

....

The doorman nodded at Charlie as he whisked through the lobby of Summit Terrace. He reflected on the progression of faces the doorman must log during the course of the day and felt pleasure at being recognized. Several of the faces passing through Summit

Terrace were likely famous, too, a fact that astonished him when he thought of how amiable Vernon was with the famous and unheralded alike. To believe the papers was to believe Vernon was a celebrity hound, but Charlie never heard him mention other celebrities and was simultaneously impressed and jealous at how easily commoners like himself were integrated into Vernon's life.

The woman who answered Vernon's door startled him.

"I'm Jessica," she said. "You must be Charlie." Her quick smile indicated that she'd grown used to people like Charlie in Vernon's life. A tattoo of one of the Powerpuff Girls—he didn't know which—peeked over the waist of her jeans as she sprinted for the whistling teakettle. "Would you like some?" Her brunette bob flounced as she reached for a box of tea.

Charlie declined as Vernon burst through the front door, led by a panting white pug on a leash. Vernon dropped the leash and the pug snuffled against Charlie's leg. "I see you've met," he said, indicating Jessica, who was ladling sugar into her teacup. "Oscar, stop."

"We're old lovers, actually," Jessica said.

Charlie demurred, picking up on the vibe between Jessica and Vernon. Instead, he laughed and handed Vernon the envelope with the typed interview. "A first draft," he said.

"Great, thanks," Vernon said. "I'll take it with me." He dropped the envelope on the kitchen counter. "Did you make an extra key for Charlie?" he asked Jessica.

She replaced the teakettle and scowled. "I thought that's what you were doing."

"I was walking the damn dog," Vernon said, exasperated. He unhooked the leash and Oscar bolted for the metal bowl in the kitchen.

"Why didn't you walk him to the locksmith's?" Jessica asked evenly.

Vernon exhaled. "Because I thought you'd already done it."

"I got the mail," Jessica said, her counterpunch landing squarely with Vernon, who dropped the issue of the extra key and took up his mail.

"I'll have to get the key to you another time," Vernon said to Charlie as he opened an envelope from Camden College. For a moment, Charlie worried that the letter was about him. A warning perhaps. The irrational thought passed when Vernon said, "Camden wants my archives." He laughed and flung the letter onto the counter.

"That's an honor, right?" Charlie asked, affecting a false naïveté in case there was something unstated about giving your archives to your alma mater that he didn't apprehend.

Vernon shrugged. "I guess."

"You could get a lot of that junk out of the apartment," Jessica chimed in.

Oscar's bowl skated across the hardwood floor as he dug his face into it, crashing into Jessica's foot. She nonchalantly guided it back to the corner.

"You have to organize it all," Vernon snapped. "You can't just send them a truck full of stuff."

More out of instinct to interrupt the fight than anything else, Charlie said casually, "I can organize stuff if you want."

"An apartment sitter, dog walker, *and* archivist," Jessica said. "Very handy." She smiled playfully at him.

"Oscar is staying with you," Vernon said. "We discussed that."

"We discussed it," Jessica said, "but I didn't agree. I don't want him slobbering all over my place. Plus, my roommate hates dogs."

Vernon sighed.

"It's no problem," Charlie said. His purpose in this scene was apparently to agree to everything. The ease with which he adopted the guise of a sycophant was disturbing to him, but he was powerless to stifle the instinct.

"Do or don't," Vernon said.

"You'll get used to 'do or don't,'" Jessica laughed.

Charlie took the phrase to mean he was fully initiated into Vernon's inner circle, regardless of Jessica's sarcasm.

A buzzer sounded and Vernon picked up the receiver mounted on the wall. "Send him up," he said. "Sorry," he said to Charlie, "can you come by tomorrow and we'll go over everything?"

"I'll bet it's no problem," Jessica mocked, half smiling.

Charlie couldn't discern if the retort was targeted at him or Vernon, and he shrugged it off as Vernon walked him to the door. "Come by early, before I leave," he said. He opened the door and to Charlie's surprise John F. Kennedy Jr. stood in the entranceway, dressed in cargo shorts and a loose green T-shirt, poised to knock. His nearness to JFK Jr. was breathtaking, and an involuntary hitch in his step almost caused him to stumble. He lingered, with a burning desire for acknowledgment and the expectation that Vernon would introduce him. He knew Vernon wouldn't reveal him as the true author of the *George* magazine piece, but a handshake with the famous son of a president would be a treasured memento. He settled for a startled "hello" from JFK Jr.

"See you Friday, then," Vernon said, and waved JFK Jr. into his loft.

Charlie could hear JFK Jr. greet Jessica before the door clicked shut on Oscar's barking. In the perpetual retelling of the encounter, Charlie and JFK Jr. shook hands. Possibly exchanged words. In future tellings, the story would likely be that JFK Jr. complimented him on the ghostwritten piece, and Charlie would come to believe it. With so few witnesses, veracity would be lost in the fog of time.

He punched the button for the lobby and the elevator descended, opening on the second floor. Charlie half expected the woman who smelled so strongly of vanilla to appear, a replication of his previous experience, so it was startling to see the words SMELLY VAGINA spray-painted across the woman's door in blood red. A maintenance guy and an albino in a suit one size too big entered the elevator and spoke in hushed tones.

"How did he get into the building, is my question," the maintenance guy said.

"It's the doorman's responsibility, ultimately," the albino said. "Union will bitch, but this is cause for dismissal."

As the elevator closed, Charlie observed the distinctive V, the same flatness at the fulcrum as in Vernon's signature, which he'd practiced over and over since first seeing it in the inscription Vernon wrote to Olivia.

Jogging down Broadway—he was late for an event that had been on his calendar for at least a month, a reading at the Astor Place Barnes & Noble by Robert Holanda, his creative writing teacher at Glendale Community College—he doubted Vernon had graffitied the door. His brain was still swirling from his late-night escapades, and his synapses clearly weren't firing correctly. Vernon Downs, a famous author, vandalizing his own building. It was too fantastic.

The tiny theater of metal chairs assembled at the top of the escalator on the second floor were mostly unoccupied save for half a dozen people or so. Charlie marveled at the giant poster of the cover of Holanda's new novel, imagining a poster of his own first novel, his name as large as the title. A stench permeated his surroundings and he sourced it to a homeless woman clinging to her tattered plastic bags full of who knew what. He guiltily moved a few rows forward, closer to the podium. From his new vantage point, he could make out the details of the cover image, a blurred Ferris wheel exploding with yellow and red and blue fireworks.

An overweight woman wearing Barnes & Noble green and a lanyard with a badge strolled up to the microphone with a brave face. The loudspeaker annoyed a man in a suit sitting near the front, and he took the book he was flipping through to a quieter corner. As the woman introduced Holanda, mispronouncing his surname, a group of young women paraded in and took seats in the front row, whispering, the distraction compelling the B&N employee to repeat a sentence from her carefully crafted introduction. Charlie recollected two of the women as talentless classmates from Glendale Community College. Their presence in the Astor Place Barnes & Noble was unnerving, and for a breathless moment Charlie wondered if Olivia would be in the crowd, possibly with Shelleyan in tow. The ludicrous was sometimes made possible, as Charlie knew. At the first appearance of Olivia's long, flaxen hair, or the silhouette of her small features, he would retreat into the rows of magazines. He could still hear the transformation in her otherwise sweet voice as she breathed matter-of-factly into the phone, "I just wanted to have a fling with an American," as if answering a question from a stranger. Always able to see all the avenues, he estimated that she had been coerced by her parents. She'd been planning to leave her parents and her homeland behind for good, and somewhere in the house her parents were lurking, listening. He'd nodded solemnly at the click that ended the transatlantic call, adrift in the mystery of what exactly could activate the pulley that would bring her, hand over hand, back to him.

Vernon Downs immediately came to mind. All memories of Olivia not involving her love of Vernon Downs fell away so that when he thought of her, he thought of Vernon Downs, and vice versa.

Holanda appeared from behind a door next to the podium sporting a blue plaid beret, a hat Charlie didn't recollect Holanda wearing at GCC, and smiled at his former students lined up like bowling pins in the front row. Charlie scowled condescendingly at the backs of their heads, their attendance a painful reminder of recent, happier times. Holanda boomed into the microphone as if speaking to a packed hall. Charlie couldn't follow the story, lost in thoughts of how Olivia had been one of Holanda's favorite students, Holanda encouraging her before the rest of the class, which caused some hard feelings among the other aspiring writers, including those currently ensconced up front. It was hard to know if any of them had any real talent—Charlie included—so encouragement had become the foundation of the reward system they all lived by.

After the reading and the short Q&A—and after his classmates had exited the space, tittering about the plans for the rest of their vacation in New York—Charlie approached Holanda, who was signing stock at a table near the podium.

"Charles," Holanda said, standing. "Were you lurking, as usual?"

Charlie smiled and they embraced. "Congratulations on your book. It sounds terrific."

"Can I sign one to you?" Holanda asked.

Charlie knew the hardcover purchase would dent his dwindling credit, but he'd walked into the trap unawares and agreed enthusiastically. The Barnes & Noble employee waited patiently while Holanda scribbled a note on the title page and handed it to Charlie.

"And how is our Olivia?" he asked, returning to the job of signing stock.

Charlie wondered if his desire to attend the reading was actually about this moment. He must've known Holanda would inquire about Olivia, though he'd failed to prepare the pat answer that would rescue him. He hardly suspected himself of a masochistic streak, but as Holanda's question hung between them, he stood mute, his flesh searing. He couldn't answer.

"Oh," Holanda said. "Well, that happens." He continued signing the mountain of books B&N had ordered for the reading, the B&N employee expertly handing over the books open to the title page. "What are you doing in New York?"

Charlie regained his faculties in the face of the question he'd anticipated. "I'm spending a lot of time with Vernon Downs," he said. "He's become somewhat of a mentor to me."

Holanda arched an eyebrow. The B&N employee fixed on him with sudden interest. "I didn't realize you were a fan of his work."

"I came to it late," Charlie said truthfully.

"I find his stuff to be a little . . . light," Holanda said.

"He's the nicest person in the world," Charlie said. He hadn't anticipated defending Downs to his former teacher. The opposite, really: He had expected Holanda would be impressed, perhaps asking Charlie to introduce him while he was in town.

"I'm glad to hear it," Holanda said. He finished signing and stood up, stretching. The B&N employee thanked him and carted off the signed books, deserting them in the empty arena. "I didn't want to say this in front of her," Holanda said, nodding toward the retreating bookseller, "but Downs is really a terrible writer. I'm speaking not as a teacher, but as a reader. His books are just gimmicky diatribes contrived to draw attention to himself."

"Have you read his new collection, *The Book of Hurts*?" Charlie asked. He speculated Holanda had only read *The Vegetable King* because of all the press attention—*Minus Numbers* didn't seem like the sort of book readers of Holanda's generation would read—and he'd probably been put out, perhaps even jealous, at all the ink spent excoriating or defending the book.

Holanda shook his head in a manner that indicated he would never, under any circumstances, read *The Book of Hurts*, the answer Charlie had hoped for. "It's some of his more mature stuff," he said definitely.

"I'm glad to hear it," Holanda repeated, and another piece of Charlie's past broke free from his inventory of memories.

Outside, in the dusky triangle of Astor Place, he flipped open the cover of Holanda's book and read the inscription: "To Charlie, who always believed in the possibilities of fiction." He closed the book and carefully placed it on a stack of *Village Voice*s inside a plastic kiosk, leaving Holanda's words behind as he trudged toward the subway.

....

Charlie delivered the Obelisk manuscript to the copy editor in Chelsea, as he promised Derwin he would, and decided to walk across town to meet Vernon for the key. The west side of Manhattan had remained a mystery to him, and he gawked like a tourist at the men holding hands in Chelsea, pausing to window-shop for wine he could never afford, loitering out in front of the Hotel Chelsea. He fell into a stream of people flowing down Seventh Avenue, marking Madison Square Garden, people rolling off the escalator under the JumboTron announcing the upcoming Aerosmith concert like products on a conveyer belt. An ambulance roared by and Charlie fantasized about the feeling of rescue afforded the rescued: Someone else in charge of the big decisions, and there's every anticipation that everything is going to turn out okay.

He cut down Thirty-second Street and through the jungle of vendors hawking knockoff designer wear, watches, scarves, and prints of famous landmarks in New York and abroad. Koreatown was a long block of signs in both English and Korean, pictures of deliciously glazed food plastered in restaurant windows. He bobbed down Fifth Avenue, guided by the space oddity of the Flatiron Building. He was perplexed by which direction he should take and guessed incorrectly that either side of the Flatiron would lead him to the East Village. He had to cut across Twentieth Street when Fifth Avenue led him astray, then took Broadway to Union Square, where a farmers' market was in full bloom.

He was still a little early to meet Vernon, so he browsed the stalls, splurging on a hunk of dark chocolate cleaved from a slab the breadth of a manhole cover by a cute girl wearing a yellow bandana. He nibbled the chocolate as he scanned the tables at the Barnes & Noble that loomed over Union Square. Robert Holanda had signed the copies of his book on the front table, and Charlie felt a degree of condescension toward his former teacher. The image of Holanda slinking around town hunting for his own book in bookstores and signing the copies he found, possibly moving them himself to the front table, lowered his opinion of Holanda. He turned Holanda's book over in his hand, smirking at the author photo, reading the blurbs with irony. The writers who had given Holanda blurbs were hardly famous, and he even recognized some as writers who taught at the state universities in Arizona. Holanda could say what he wanted about Vernon Downs, but he'd probably have killed for a blurb from him.

The doorman at Summit Terrace smiled when Charlie approached. "He's not in, but he left this for you." He handed Charlie an envelope with the key, though when Charlie reached the loft, he found the door unlocked. He knocked and then entered. The loft was vacant. All the windows had been thrown open, negating the efforts of the struggling air conditioner. A large television stationed in the middle of the floor played a pornographic movie on mute. "Here boy, here boy," he called out, not remembering the dog's name. No answer. Vernon must've left early and taken the dog to his girlfriend's place against her wishes. He conjectured Vernon triumphed more often than he didn't. He snapped off the television and pushed it back into the corner, closing the windows against the day's heat.

The pull of his unfettered access to Vernon's loft was seductive. He previewed the cupboards, the dearth of any food products or surplus cans of fruit cocktail not a shock, considering how often Vernon dined out. An impressive cache of rum and vodka and whiskey was an unexpected bonus. The kitchen junk drawer was a repository of expired lottery tickets. He slid open the door to the sideboard table and was in awe of the collection of signed books. The books were for the most part unread, but judging by the inscriptions, the authors were either friends or admirers of Vernon's. Charlie hauled out the bins underneath the bed and investigated the trove of work by Vernon, including the prepublication galleys printed by Vernon's publisher in advance of the actual book. Holanda had imparted that galleys were notoriously brimming with mistakes and misspellings, and Charlie casually hunted through the galley of *Scavengers* for typos.

The phone rang, giving him a start. He shoved the bins back under the bed. The answering machine picked up and Vernon's recorded voice boomed sonically. After the beep came "Yo, Vernon, I think I left one of my shoes at your place. Alligator loafer? If not there, then in the cab ride home, dude, so let me know." Charlie rewound the answering machine tape without rummaging for the loafer. He relieved himself in the bathroom, squinting against the white light. As he washed up, he noticed a tube of Aim in the medicine cabinet. He regarded the toothpaste as an archaeological find. *Vernon Downs uses Aim*, he noted. The loft was as intriguing as the lost city of Atlantis, every household article or utensil or effluvium found floating in junk drawers holding an unintended significance. It seemed inconceivable that he once spent an ignorant afternoon hearing about Vernon Downs and *Minus Numbers* from Olivia and Shelleyan, and all these months later he had free reign over Vernon's loft.

The phone rang again, but this time the machine didn't answer. The ringing continued until Charlie realized the source was not the phone, but the intercom system with the doorman.

"Yes?" Charlie breathed into the receiver.

"Someone from *George* magazine is here," the doorman reported. Charlie wondered if it was JFK Jr. but guessed JFK Jr. would've given his name, or that the doorman would've recognized him.

"Send them up," Charlie commanded, adding, "please."

A few moments later, the elevator arrived and Charlie cracked the door to the loft, as Vernon had done for him the day they met. At the sound of a faint knock, he swung the door open to reveal a young man in his early twenties, his shaved head gleaming in the light. Tiny silver hoop earrings shimmered in both ears.

"I'm here to deliver the proofs for your piece," he said, nervously patting his leather messenger bag.

"Come in," Charlie said, affecting Vernon's cool tone.

"Wow," the messenger said. "Great place."

"Thanks," Charlie said.

The messenger produced a white envelope stamped with the words GEORGE MAGAZINE and CONFIDENTIAL. Charlie spied a copy of *The Vegetable King* in the bag as well.

"Just need you to sign for them," the messenger said meekly. Charlie took the receipt over to the kitchen counter, the nearest writing surface. He began to draw a C on the receipt, when the messenger said, "I was hoping you could sign this, too," and stood apologetically with his copy of *The Vegetable King*. "I'm probably not supposed to ask, so if you don't want to, no problem."

Charlie signed the receipt with Vernon's practiced signature, a perfect counterfeit the result of hours spent tracing the letters in the book Vernon had signed to Olivia. "Be happy to," he said, taking the book. "Who should I sign it to?"

Charlie scrawled the messenger's name onto the title page, his mind humming, the thrill from the deceit producing a kind of mental levitation. He scribbled "Hope you enjoy this" on the title page and repeated Vernon's signature.

"Here you go," Charlie said. "Just don't sell it to the Strand."

"No way, never," the messenger said, bowing slightly. "Thank you." He tucked the novel back into his bag without inspection and did the same with the receipt for the proofs. He thanked Charlie again and drank in the loft. Charlie imagined the stories the messenger would tell his friends back in Brooklyn about his visit to Vernon's.

"I know I missed your Christmas in July party," the messenger said nervously. "But is there any way it would be cool if I came next year? My girlfriend would just die."

"Of course," Charlie said. Granting the messenger's wishes mollified his sense of right and wrong.

"Too cool of you," the messenger responded. He continued to thank Charlie as he called for the elevator, one last thank-you slipping out as Charlie closed the door. He moved in the glow of charity as he opened the envelope to find the proofs of the piece he'd written for *George* magazine. The initial irritation at seeing Vernon's name in the byline subsided as Charlie gaped at his words emblazoned on the page. Vernon hadn't changed so much as a comma. A fantasy quickly developed whereby Olivia would pick up a future copy of *George* magazine based solely on a piece by Vernon Downs in the table of contents, running home to read it, lying across her bed while frantically flipping the pages, his words filling her eyes. He would need to make a photocopy of the proofs as evidence for when he confessed the ruse to her later. The fantasy rewound and replayed through a celebratory tumbler of Vernon's whiskey, continuing through the meal of Chinese takeout he spilled across Vernon's countertop. The scenario, along with the whiskey and Chinese food, lulled him asleep in the early evening.

A clattering woke him near daybreak. He started awake, a blurring figure hovering near the door. The bleary visage of Vernon

Downs bore down on him. "Why the fuck are you here?" he asked, his hair tousled as if he'd ridden an all-night roller coaster at Coney Island. Charlie had forgotten to turn off the air-conditioning and the loft was frigid.

"I thought . . . ," Charlie said. "The doorman gave me the . . ."

Vernon jittered through the loft, grabbing up random objects: a fistful of CDs, something from a drawer in the kitchen, the opened bottle of whiskey. "You weren't supposed to come until . . . ," Vernon said. "I mean this is not a good . . . Whatever." His eyes were small and red, and Charlie wondered if he was high. "Everything is totally fucked. My fucking dog is missing and I have to leave for Vermont and . . ." Vernon recounted in profane outbursts how Jessica had taken Oscar for a walk and the dog had bolted from his leash. Vernon had canvassed the area around Jessica's Murray Hill apartment before retreating to a Kinkos to produce a flyer he'd spent the early hours affixing to any flat surface he could.

"I'm sorry," Charlie said. "I didn't know."

"You have to be vigilant," Vernon said, a globule of spit landing near Charlie. "If anyone calls about Oscar, you have to go meet them. Here." He dug into his black jeans for his wallet and swiped all the cash, handing it to Charlie. "Just do whatever you have to."

"I will," Charlie promised.

"And call me immediately when you find him," Vernon said.

Charlie nodded and Vernon disappeared into the bathroom among a clattering of toiletries. Charlie quickly counted the money, which amounted to over four hundred dollars. Vernon emerged with a duffel bag and a suitcase on wheels. He'd smoothed water through his hair, and the adrenaline that had fueled his all-night vigil had recessed, leaving him limp, barely able to scrape the luggage across the floor. "I meant to tell you," he said. "The editor at *Shout!* magazine likes your story. He said he'd publish it in the fall fiction issue."

Charlie guiltily longed for Vernon to leave so he could bask in his great fortune. "I can't thank you enough," he said. Vernon waved him off, distractedly checking his answering machine for news of Oscar, deleting the message about the lost loafer before it finished. He trundled into the hall, a rumpled, near lifeless figure, and left without saying good-bye.

ON HIS WAY out for coffee, Charlie didn't recognize the new doorman, who was leaner and had a militant air about him. He was also appreciably older than the doorman Charlie'd felt friendly toward. "Where's the other guy?" he asked, but the new doorman just shrugged and returned to sorting some cards on his desk. He reckoned the doorman had taken a sick day, or maybe even a personal day to play hooky. Good for him. Outside, a hulking moving truck idled at the curb. Charlie casually wondered if the woman on the second floor had found another apartment somewhere far away from Summit Terrace.

Waiting at the corner bodega for his coffee and egg sandwich, he flipped through the *Post*, landing on a small item about Vernon offering to name a character after the person who found Oscar. He was amazed at the press's preoccupation with every facet of Vernon's life. Back at Summit Terrace, he exited the elevator to find a woman with a brunette ponytail fidgeting with the lock on her door. "Hold the elevator," she called out, but he had already let the elevator go.

"Sorry," he said as he slid the key into Vernon's door.

"You must be Vernon Downs," the woman said, apparently forgiving the faux pas. "I'm subletting while my sister is in Paris," the woman said, the dimples on her cheeks and the tiny cleft in her chin forming a flawless frame for her soft smile. There was a tomboy element buried deep within, Charlie sensed, a toughness

masquerading as delicacy. "I'm a huge fan." She held out a manicured hand. "I'm Christianna."

He returned the smile and shook Christianna's hand. "Nice to
meet you," he said. He felt no guiltier about giving this misimpression than he did earlier in the week when someone had mistaken
him for someone else, calling and waving from across the street.
He'd waved back as a courtesy and the woman moved on. There was
little harm in fulfilling expectations, he thought. Besides, he could
always plead ignorance with Christianna if the truth emerged, convincing her the miscalculation was her own.

"How long have you lived in the building?" she asked. Uncertain
of how long Vernon had been in residence, Charlie was about to cover
with "Not long," but Christianna didn't wait for his reply and said, "I
just have to say"—she put her hand on his arm—"that the party scene
in *Scavengers*, you know, the End of the World party? That's exactly
how it was at my college. The tiki torches, everything. God, I'm sorry
I missed your Christmas party."

"Oh, really? Where did you go to college?"

"That was at Hampshire. I'm at New Haven now," she said,
eager for a reaction. "Drama school. I want to move to New York
to be an actress." She called for the elevator and it opened, having
never descended to the lobby. "Well, see you around, Vernon," she
said, and was gone just like that, the swirl of lilac perfume dying in
her wake.

He avoided Christianna over the next week or so, pretending to be
in a rush if she waylaid him in the lobby, or in the elevator, or on their
adjacent balconies looking down on Thirteenth Street. Christianna's
alarming intimacy, as well as her penchant for reciting her favorite
scenes from Vernon's works, had become disquieting.

The first time she caught him in the elevator, on his way to meet
someone who mistakenly thought he'd located Oscar: "You know

what I loved about *The Vegetable King*? The stuff about Huey Lewis
and Phil Collins and Whitney Houston. I laughed my ass off when
I read it."

The first time she cornered him at the mailboxes in the lobby:
"You probably hear this all the time, but that story in *Book of Hurts*,
the one set in Hawaii, is one of my favorites."

The time she caught him people-watching on the balcony had
spooked him the most. Christianna appeared on her balcony, swaddled
in a royal blue cotton bathrobe, and addressed him as one of the characters from *Scavengers*. It was a moment before he realized she, too, was in
character. He mimicked deafness and shouted something vague about a
phone call he had to make, before scurrying back into the loft, easing
the sliding glass door shut.

Two days later, exhausted from following a bogus tip about
a dog matching Oscar's description wandering off leash near the
World Trade Center, Charlie watched as a silver envelope was
thrust under the door, followed by the echo of Christianna's door
closing. He opened the elaborately calligraphed invitation to a New
Year's in August dinner party and knew he would not be able to
devise an excuse grand enough to evade the gathering. The homage
to Vernon's party was slightly troubling, a fact that menaced him as
he grudgingly dry-cleaned the one suit he owned after discovering
that the suits in Vernon's closet wouldn't fit.

In the days before her dinner party, Christianna was noticeably
absent from the building, and Charlie happily resumed the task of
separating and sequencing Vernon's papers. He rarely left the loft,
save for a farewell lunch with Derwin, who was decamping Brooklyn for Fire Island for the rest of August. Derwin was keen for details about the archive project, but in delineating his duties, Charlie
admitted that the endeavor was a free-form exercise with little direction, and had been undertaken with more passion on Charlie's

part than Vernon's. "My only real responsibilities are to check the mail and to report any important phone messages or e-mail," Charlie confessed. He was too embarrassed to reveal his primary responsibility, finding Vernon's lost dog.

"Your Obelisk training is paying off," Derwin laughed as he picked up the tab for the boozy lunch, the afternoon faded by the time they parted, with plans to reunite back in Brooklyn upon Derwin's return after Labor Day.

Charlie didn't encounter Christianna once, and he began to root for the possibility that the dinner party had been canceled, a hope that was dashed when a catering van appeared on the afternoon of the appointed date. He reluctantly dressed, fishing through the leftover liquor for a full bottle of anything, finding an unopened pinot noir. He paced the loft until half an hour past the designated time, in order to skip the predinner cocktails, and then grabbed the bottle and presented himself at Christianna's door.

"Well!" Christianna said dramatically. "This is very exciting!" She was overdressed in a pale blue gown more suited for a ball, or a fairy tale. "Welcome," she said by way of introduction to the expectant faces populating the loft, which had the same floor plan as Vernon's. "You traveled a long way to be here with us tonight," Christianna added, but the other guests didn't understand her joke, and he worked the room, shaking hands with the segment producer at MTV, the budding fashion designer who lived with her parents in Ronkonkoma, the manager of several rap acts who kept saying he had to "leave soon," and an actress who turned out to be Christianna's roommate at Yale. The oldest guest by far was familiar, and as the bespectacled man offered his hand, Charlie recollected him as the *Times* reporter from Vernon's Christmas party.

"Peter Kline," the man said. "We met at your party."

"Peter's a reporter for the *Post*," Christianna said helpfully.

Charlie waited for Kline to correct her, but Kline nodded and smiled. "For my sins," was all he said. Charlie smirked at Kline's having elevated his journalistic pedigree. *Typical*, he thought as the group gathered around the hand-carved mahogany table boasting a pewter candelabra in which cinnamon-scented candles were burning.

The catered meal was served by Christianna, who made no mention of the food having been prepared by caterers, absorbing compliments like "This is delicious" and "This is so yummy" as if she'd cooked the food herself, a personality quirk that Charlie found oddly endearing. She exuded sureness, and he admired how easily she assumed the pose.

Dinner conversation ranged from the vagaries of trying to start a fashion design business to the latest MTV gossip to how hard it was to audition for female directors. Charlie politely solicited information about the rap world from the lone dinner guest who seemed content to sit back and listen, but his questions were answered with a short yes or no and, not really being interested in the subject, he gave up.

Christianna's Yale roommate—she'd been introduced as Diane or Diana, he couldn't remember which, though she'd haughtily corrected the rap manager when he called her by the wrong name—raved about an off-Broadway play she'd just seen having something to do with the Wright brothers and their illegitimate sister.

"I tried out for the part of the sister for the Williamstown festival," Christianna said mournfully.

"You would've slaughtered whoever they have in the lead now," Diane or Diana said.

Christianna smiled appreciatively. "So many parts, so many parts," she said.

"I could never do that," the MTV producer said. "Put myself out there like that. To be judged. I couldn't stand to."

"How do you keep doing it?" Charlie asked, genuinely interested.

"If you keep wanting it, you'll get it," Christianna said simply. "Nobody can take that from you." Christianna and Diane—he'd decided it was Diane—hooked their pinkies in a secret handshake.

"Tell us what you're working on now," Christianna said to Charlie.

"Are you a painter?" the fashion designer asked, forking a piece of sweet potato casserole into her mouth.

"You're kidding, right?" Christianna said. "This is one of our greatest living authors. Haven't you read his work?"

"I have," Kline said, raising his hand pointlessly.

The actress turned to Christianna. "Remember that year we watched *Minus Numbers*, like, everyday?"

Christianna nodded.

"Have you seen *Minus Numbers*?" the actress asked, the table turning on the fashion designer.

"Umm, maybe," the fashion designer said.

"That the one with what's-his-name?" the MTV producer asked.

"Oh," Christianna said. "I love him."

Charlie watched this conversation develop with some amusement.

"Julian really needs you right now," Christianna said to the actress, who in turn uttered the next line, the two playing out one of the pivotal scenes in *Minus Numbers* for the benefit of the dinner party. The table erupted in applause and Charlie felt himself bowing in his chair.

Candlelight slowly became the only light, obscuring the guests' faces. Successive bottles of wine were opened, the wine a precursor to cocktails that activated a buzz in his brain. At some point, Christianna left the table to put on some music, the notes of a classical piece fluttering around them like small birds. Between rounds, the fashion designer and the MTV producer and the rap manager begged off. The actress excused herself to go to the bathroom, grabbing the table for support as she rose, and never returned. Christianna would later find her passed out on her bed. Charlie was planning his own exit strategy, the warmth of the food and liquor in his stomach hindering his good-bye, when Kline asked him a question that sobered him.

"How about letting me do a profile," he said.

Charlie pretended not to hear, an absurdity considering the room was empty except for the three of them.

"Who, me?" he asked, hoping to brush off the request.

"You didn't think he meant me, did you?" Christianna asked. She laughed at her own joke, but no one else did.

"What about it?" Kline asked.

"Maybe when the new book comes out," Charlie said.

"When's it coming out?" Kline asked, slipping into his reportorial persona.

"Who knows?" Charlie said. The conversation began to hang heavy around his neck. The candles burned dangerously low, flames skating on pools of wax. He stood abruptly. "Best dinner party ever," he said grandly, bringing Christianna to her feet. "Peter," he said, holding out his hand. "Always a pleasure."

Christianna escorted him to the front door and kissed him on both cheeks only after he promised they'd do it again soon. He made the short walk to Vernon's loft with considerable effort, fumbling the key in the lock. Inside, he threw off his clothes and hopped into the shower to cleanse his mind of the entire evening. He checked Vernon's e-mail, the messages falling into the inbox like snow. He clicked on an incoherent e-mail from Jeremy Cyanin involving a party he'd attended at the Soho Grand. Charlie deduced that Cyanin was speaking in some sort of code he and Vernon shared, which provoked an irrational tizzy about his trying to undermine Charlie's budding friendship with Vernon, and Charlie deleted the e-mail, cleaning out the trash folder as well to erase all traces of it.

An e-mail from a famous writer whose new book was being adapted for film by Tom Cruise asked if he and Vernon were still on for drinks at Lucy's, and Charlie took the opening to inform the famous writer that Vernon had left New York for the foreseeable future, signing his full name, adding "Asst. to Vernon Downs" after reading the e-mail four times for typos. When the famous writer replied that he, too, was in Vermont, as was Lucy's, Charlie switched off the computer to stanch his severe embarrassment; a clutch of days passed before he could bring himself to fire it up again, finding a lone e-mail from a woman named Shannon Hamilton with the subject line "From a fan." He rolled his eyes and clicked on the e-mail.

Dear Mr. Downs,

Where to start? I'm guessing you get a lot of letters like this one, and I'm not sure how much you read before you stop reading, so I'll dispense with the usual chatter about how big a fan I am of your work and go right to the heart of it: Like you, I'm a graduate of Camden College, but unlike you, I'm a writer that no one has heard of. I did my Camden thesis about you and am wondering if you had any advice as I start out into the real world. A lame question, perhaps, but the answer is very important to me, so if you can see your way through to write back, I'd appreciate it.

Sincerely,
Shannon Hamilton

Charlie deleted the message, instinctively discerning that Vernon would not waste his time responding to Shannon Hamilton, but something compelled him to retrieve it. He read the e-mail a second time. Before he realized it, he'd clicked reply and had written, "Dear Shannon." He contended that Vernon wouldn't want to slight a fan over an unanswered e-mail. Better to dispatch with the e-mail, he thought, regarding the chore as one of his clerical duties. He'd mention it to Vernon and they'd both chuckle and then forget about Shannon. Convinced, he touched his fingertips to the keyboard.

Very many thanks for your e-mail. As you might imagine, I get numerous queries such as yours, both through my agent and in my personal mail, but I'm always happy to hear from a fellow Camdenite. (Flattered about your thesis, by the way.) I guess I'd say the best advice is not to let anyone dissuade you from what you want to do. If you want to write, write. Don't take no for an answer. Good luck.

Charlie proofread the e-mail and then typed Vernon's name. A thrill ran through him as he clicked send. He deleted both Shannon's e-mail and his response.

....

Where to start? Charlie thought as he lorded over the boxed archives. A binder dated around the time of the publication of *Minus Numbers* revealed Vernon's previous attempt to chronicle his early years, despite the impression he'd given Jessica when announcing Camden's desire for his papers. He scoured the index to see what had come before, a little surprised by the sentimental entries:

1972.01	Sunshine-gram from Mrs. Ormiston (2nd grade teacher) for excellent penmanship
1973.01	Photo from *Los Angeles Times* dated April 19, 1973, re: Vernon in Cub Scout parade at Rose Bowl

1975.01	Article from Los Angeles newsmagazine dated October 14, 1975, re: Mrs. Cotton's 5th grade class trip to courthouse; incl. photo of VDD
1977.01	Manuscript—"The Mystery of Dead Man's Grave." Original.
1977.02	Pocket Books' declining letter for "The Mystery of Dead Man's Grave," dated April 8, 1977.
1978.01	*No-Name News*—broadside for Fowler Elementary
1981.01	Receipt for private phone line for bedroom
1982.01	Manuscript—"The Last Lemonade Stand on the Block." First draft.
1983.01	Beverly Hills High yearbook—1983

Thoughts of Vernon as a Cub Scout amused Charlie as he read through the index, matching his personal chronology to Vernon's, remembering his own unhappy days against Vernon's popularity at Beverly Hills High, the catalog of manuscripts and love notes faithfully labeled as correspondence; the notebooks and tests for each class carefully maintained, the instructor's name appearing in the binder entry; the letters of recommendation to Camden, Vernon's Camden application, and his acceptance letter the last entries in the archive. Charlie realized that he'd be responsible for cataloging the bulk of Vernon's public life. He eagerly dived into the material. He opened an unmarked box and reached for a black folder containing a sheaf of email from the Bank of America in Sherman Oaks, all sent at the same date and time, the body of the email left blank. He fanned through the printed e-mails, looking for some indication of what they represented—were they documents or correspondence?—and quickly became frustrated by the lack of identifying detail. He was disheartened, too, to find the sealed envelope with the typed interview buried on Vernon's desk, though he had decided to try to publish the interview with a more established outlet than *Oneironaut*, so there was no hurry for Vernon to proof it.

He cracked open a window and let the street noise permeate the loft. The first order of business would be to create piles by year. He marked out a space on the floor for 1982 and then paced off a spot for 1983, and so on. He doubled the volume of the space for *The Vegetable King*, assuming that a preponderance of documents would be dedicated to the controversy the novel had inspired. Next he unpacked the boxes and scattered their contents into their respective spots. In all, it took him two days to separate the material, a feat Charlie celebrated with a tall glass of a leftover cabernet. With the sorting stage complete, he assessed the loft, a paper landscape of letters and reviews and drafts of manuscripts.

After a quick lunch at the Blimpie on the corner, and against the blazing *Minus Numbers* soundtrack, Charlie began picking through the piles. An item he'd previously resisted—a folder marked CAMDEN – ADV. CREATIVE WRITING—called out to him, and he leafed through drafts of early chapters from *Minus Numbers*, line-edited by Vernon's mentor, Harrison McInnis. Charlie hungrily devoured the early work but put the folder away short of the conclusion he was hurtling toward: The early drafts of the novel weren't very good. He agreed with the comments McInnis had written in the margins: "Melodramatic" or "Too dark" or "Is this supposed to be funny?"

A folder from the 1981 pile labeled PHANTASM caught his eye. The folder contained hand-drawn flyers for what apparently was a high school band in which Vernon was the keyboardist. Charlie studied a heavily xeroxed photo of the band posing with the Beverly Hills High auditorium in the background. A packet of lyrics buried behind the flyers fell to the floor and Charlie scooped them up, saying the words out loud.

Touch Me   *Words and music by Vernon David Downs*

The touch of your hand

Can tame any man

You're an obsession

No one can have

You walk across the room

And I shiver and shake

My heart's beating faster

I just can't wait . . .

Please!

(Touch me!)

With your tender touch

(Touch me!)

You can't love me too much

(Touch me!)

Touch me all over and you'll see

All I want

Is you to touch me

I don't know what you've got

But I know I want it

I don't know what you've got

But I know it's hot

It's so hard to ignore

Just reach out and touch me

Don't let up

Keep givin' me more

Please!

(Touch me!)
With your tender touch
(Touch me!)
No, no, you can't love me too much
(Touch me!)
T-t-t-touch me
So true
Touch me
I want it all from you
(ad-lib, repeat & fade)

He caught himself singing the lyrics as he pecked his way through the archives, selecting an envelope marked THE ANGEL'S TRIP – CHRISTMAS 1971 that contained a handwritten story about an angel atop a Christmas tree who falls on Christmas Eve and follows the tinsel trail back to the top, encountering villainous ornaments who orchestrated the angel's fall and who prevent her ascent before Christmas morning. Charlie noted the genesis of Vernon's adult handwriting in the child's hand, the disconnected letters, the violent Rs, the pointed Ds. He couldn't imagine the discipline and patience required to stick with a passion from childhood through adulthood. How had Vernon not been diverted by wanting to be a center fielder, or an astronaut, or a lawyer, like practically everyone did? Vernon's tunnel vision gave Charlie hope for his reunion with Olivia. The fact that Vernon had committed to what he loved, and had found success in his fidelity, seemed to bode well for the future, he thought.

The song Charlie liked best on the *Minus Numbers* soundtrack filtered through the speakers, and as he moved to turn up the volume, he skidded on a folder peeking out of the stack for *The Veg-etable King*, crashing hard to the floor, causing the CD to skip. He massaged his left knee and could feel the bruise forming under his skin. He kicked at the file folder, trying to shove it back where it belonged. He lifted the stack and pulled the folder free, a swatch of manila sticking to the hardwood floor.

The unmarked folder held a letter from Vernon to someone named Burton LaFarge, dated the previous May.

Hey, Burt,

Your letter shook me up some, especially since I stood up for you when they first talked about kicking you out of Camden. I even went before the administration for you, do you remember that? Hope you do. Hope you remember it as I try to deal with what you're saying re: *The Vegetable King* and the manuscript I helped you with sophomore year. A lot of people sent me stuff that year and I looked at it all, so I find what you're suggesting to be an incredible coincidence. It's been a dark year for me, people coming at me from all directions. Can't use any more bad publicity. Just can't use it. Remember that, Burt? That was your line whenever someone handed you drugs after you were already out of your mind. Just can't use it. I ask you to remember those days as we work through this. Is there any chance you'll come down from the figure you mentioned in your letter? It's a lot of money, as you know. I mean, if that's the figure, then that's the figure. But if there's a different figure, will you let me know?

V-E-R-N-O-N

A business card for a detective agency in Jersey City was paper-clipped to the letter. Charlie replaced the letter and slipped the folder back where he found it, as if he hadn't seen it. He started the *Minus Numbers* soundtrack over from the beginning and poured himself a vodka tonic, which stayed the onslaught of questions raised by the letter.

....

Charlie sensed an impending drink invitation from Christianna long before it arrived in the form of spontaneity in the elevator—"I'm meeting some friends at Aviator, would you like to join us?"—and he knew, too, that he would accept, not least because he was addicted to her fawning over him, the Famous Writer. He'd just returned from the Upper East Side, someone having claimed to have found Vernon's dog, but who in reality only wanted to meet Vernon Downs and get him to sign a book, which Charlie obliged. He'd found cataloging Vernon's archives a lonely endeavor, his days taken up with boxes of memorabilia celebrating Vernon Downs's success and with little else, leaving him restless and utterly alone once he stopped shuffling papers for the day. So much so that Charlie began to participate actively in the archives: An envelope containing correspondence with an author Charlie had vaguely heard of sandwiched between drafts of *Minus Numbers* provided the details of a small literary feud involving an article Vernon had written for *USA Today*. Charlie judged the feud to be too trivial to ruin a friendship and penned a short note of apology to the author in Vernon's handwriting.

And so he said yes to drinks at Aviator, though he claimed he needed to meet her there. "Prior obligation," he lied. Christianna was oblivious—did she notice that he hardly left the apartment?—but delighted that he would join her and her friends. In truth, the cash Vernon had left in aid of the fruitless search for Oscar had dwindled, spent mostly on takeout and cabs. Charlie convinced himself that the sustenance and transportation were precisely what Vernon had intended the money for. He further convinced himself that the idea to sell off some of the signed books in Vernon's collection to the Strand to keep liquid—and thereby primed and ready to answer any alleged Oscar sighting—was sound. The first doubts were quashed by Charlie's supposition that authors were always sending Vernon signed books—he'd found three in the mail from debut writers since he began apartment sitting—and so he cherry-picked a dozen or so books and waltzed them over to the Strand, pocketing an easy hundred dollars from the curmudgeonly buyer behind the counter, who raised an eyebrow at the inscriptions but remained silent on the matter. Charlie caught the buyer regarding him, and he signed Vernon's name to the receipt acknowledging the transaction. The buyer gave him a half smile and nodded as he swept the signed books aside and called for the next person in line.

The crowd at Aviator was unusually small, which Charlie ascribed to the hour, just past six. He was two vodka tonics in before Christianna finished her story about an exploitive audition she'd had that morning. "It was a student film," she said. "Guess I shouldn't have been surprised."

"You should turn him in," Charlie said, pulverizing the lime at the bottom of his glass with a red plastic straw.

"I was thinking the exact same thing," Christianna said, sipping her White Russian. "Funny thing was he resembled my friend James. Made me feel a little sorry for him, I guess. He died when he was nineteen."

"Jesus, sorry," he said.

"It's okay," Christianna said, finishing her drink and handing the empty glass to the waiter, who replaced it with a fresh drink. The waiter also set down a plate of mozzarella marinara that Charlie didn't remember anyone ordering.

"How did it happen?"

"He was trying to light a cigarette—well, I'm pretty sure it was a joint, but what does it matter, right?—and his BMW flew off the freeway. I was following him. It was Labor Day weekend and we were going to stay at his parents' place."

"Awful," Charlie said, eyeing the dish between them. He poked at it with a fork, opting to partake in the free food. He presumed that since Christianna had extended the invitation, she would treat.

"He always ordered this," Christianna said with a sigh.

"What," he asked, "White Russians?"

"The mozzarella marinara," she said, sighing again.

He put down his fork, forcing himself to swallow the gooey cheese, trying not to envision it as a chunk of flesh. "Was this when you were at Yale?" he asked.

Christianna bobbed her head, but he couldn't tell if she was indicating yes or no. The story felt familiar and he couldn't figure out why. (Later he would come across a letter in the archives from one of Vernon's friends describing how the story Vernon had written for *The Book of Hurts* about the death of their friend outside Palm Springs—in the exact manner that Christianna had described her friend dying—had helped the friend cope with the loss.) "Speaking of death," Christianna said, launching into a tale about her college roommate OD'ing, which Charlie recognized as being right out of Vernon's novel *Scavengers*.

"So I come back after a night of drinking at the Pub and find her on the floor and it looks like she's not breathing. I look around and see a half-empty bottle of whiskey"—Dewar's in the book— "and think, *Oh my God, she's going to die*. So I grab a freshman in the hall and we drive my roommate to the emergency room"— Charlie remembered a funny exchange from *Scavengers* about one of the characters thinking the closest hospital was in Keene, New Hampshire, but he stifled his smile at this bit of comic relief absent from Christianna's version—"and the doctor can't find a pulse." Ditto the book. "The doctor says, 'Your friend is dead,' and I'm standing there thinking, *This can't be, this can't be,*" Christianna continued, "and then my roommate opens her eyes and says, 'Am I really dead?' And the doctor says, 'Yes, you are. I can't find a pulse.' Can you believe that?"

He said he could not.

"So I say to the doctor, 'How can she be dead? She's talking!'" Christianna said, shaking her head at the absurdity. "But the doctor insisted. He kept saying, 'Your friend is dead. Your friend is dead.'"

"That is something," Charlie agreed, signaling for another drink. Christianna grew quiet, and he wondered if she'd recounted these plagiarized stories from Vernon's work to test him or to impress him. A game was afoot, but he couldn't grasp the rules. Christianna's left thigh brushed his and he moved away reflexively, wishing he hadn't. A general sexual frustration that had been accruing for weeks begged for an outlet, though he felt sure that sleeping with Christianna would be a monumental mistake. The perceived rebuff chilled the pleasantness the table had enjoyed; if he didn't manufacture an excuse to leave, the two would share a constrained stroll back to Summit Terrace or, worse, he would be made to pick up the check.

"Hey, look," Christianna said, brightening.

Jeremy Cyanin strolled into Aviator in a charcoal suit, leading a dark, petite woman to a table near the bar. "Oh no," Charlie said, slumping down in the booth.

"What?" Christianna asked.

"Great," he said.

"*What?*" Christianna asked again, this time intrigued by his playacting.

He improvised an escape. "Cyanin's been harassing me about some coke he left at my place," he said.

"So?"

"I did it, like, two weeks ago," Charlie said, affecting lament.

"And I'm fresh out." He detected a spark in Christianna's eyes at the prospect of participating in the melodrama. "I'm going to try to sneak past him," Charlie said, adding, "the bastard."

"I'll cover you," Christianna said conspiratorially. "I'll go up and talk to him. Distract him."

"No, no," he said. "At all cost, you must not engage him or he'll talk you into drinks, and when he finds out you're my neighbor, he'll weasel his way back to the building and we'll never be rid of him."

Christianna nodded. "Oh, I know the type." She squinted at Cyanin, wrinkling her nose in mock disgust.

"Got an idea," he said, motioning for the waitress, a young girl who didn't look old enough to drink, much less serve. "I want to play a prank on my friend," he said, whispering for no reason. "I want to send a Sex on the Beach to that table"—he pointed to Cyanin's table—"but I want you to say it's from that table." He pointed to a booth in the far corner where two comely lesbians were sitting side by side. "Okay, I'm out of here," he said. He reached for his wallet, but Christianna shook her head.

"I've got this, you've got next time," she said, and before he could process the ramifications of "next time," he had kissed her on the cheek and was slithering along the bar, Cyanin with his back to him, the waitress bending to set the cocktail on his table, motioning toward the oblivious lesbians as Cyanin swiveled in his seat. He could hear Cyanin's explanation to his date: "They're fans, what can you do?" Charlie forged through the crowd, spinning away from a woman at the bar who turned precipitously with a martini in each hand. He grasped for a stool, his balance deserting him entirely, and he could only manage to spring forward, falling helplessly into the crowd pushing its way into Aviator. He collided with Peter Kline, the two of them falling against the hostess station.

"Leaving so soon?" Kline asked.

"I . . . have . . . to . . ." He gestured toward Fourth Avenue.

"I thought we were having drinks with Christianna," Kline said, confused.

He engineered an answer along the lines that Christianna was indeed still inside, but that he was feeling ill and had to cancel. "I'm sorry," he said, and took a step toward Summit Terrace.

"Wait," Kline said. The crowd at the door plunged forward and Charlie found himself alone on the sidewalk with Kline. "I was wondering if you'd like to have lunch," he said.

Charlie nodded, not really concentrating on what Kline was saying.

"Thursday?" Kline asked, hopeful.

"Sure," he answered. He would've agreed to anything short of homicide to abort the conversation.

"Thursday at noon," Kline said. "At Jackson's. The paper is buying."

Charlie nodded idiotically, wanting to object. Someone or something tapped him on the back, but when he spun around, he was bewildered to find no one there, surprised further by the rush of vomit he spewed on the sidewalk, chunks of undigested mozzarella falling like wet clouds tumbling from the sky.

"Hey, you okay?" Kline asked, but he held up his hand and began walking backward, away from Kline and the orange and white stain he'd left in front of Aviator. "See you Thursday," Kline shouted, and Charlie waved his arms wildly, both as confirmation and in protest, but the looming threat of lunch with Kline was less urgent than his roiling stomach, and he felt his way down Thirteenth Street, back to Summit Terrace, spending the night in the tub for its comforting proximity to the toilet.

. . . .

Cyanin's flat voice came at him like an assault. He shrank against the porcelain tub, shivering. Who had let Cyanin into the

loft? A thought he hadn't considered spooked him: *Cyanin has a key.*
He hoisted himself out of the tub, carefully navigating a splotch of
dried vomit that had missed its mark. The loft was quiet again and
he peered out the bathroom door, ready to be cornered. But the loft
was empty. A cold breeze swirled through the kitchen. A small cy-
clone of paper danced across the promontory of the highest stack of
archives, floating and finally settling at his feet. He quickly shut the
window he didn't recollect opening, realizing he was alone.

After a long, revitalizing shower, the blanket shrouding his brain
lifted. The flashing light on the answering machine called out to
him as he pulled on his jacket, and he pressed the button.

"Hello?" It was Cyanin. "Hello?"

He froze, as if Cyanin were at the door.

"Hello, hello, hello." A pause. "Are you back? You're back. I
guess the question is, why? A better question is, what was that shit
at Aviator? The best question is, why did I have to read about your
return in the *Post*? Call me back." Another pause. "P.S. I slept
with those two lesbians."

Charlie erased the message, but it was burned in his memory. He
opened the *Post* to Page Six, the notorious gossip column, spotting
Vernon's name in bold in the "Sightings" column:

Bad-boy novelist Vernon Downs was seen stumbling out of Aviator
on Fourth Avenue, laughing maniacally at a prank he'd just pulled on
his fellow bad-boy novelist Jeremy Cyanin.

He skimmed the column—the notice of the actress arrested for
shoplifting (again), this time at an antique shop in the Bowery; the
underage pop star caught drinking at a club in Noho; the socialite
who fled her suite at the Four Seasons without paying—but he
invariably drifted back to the mention of Vernon, dumbstruck

at how the *Post* had ascertained this bit of false information. It took half a bottle of Gatorade before he put together that Kline was most likely the author of the gossip. Infuriated, he pounded on Christianna's door, the brass knocker vibrating under his fist. He heard Vernon's answering machine through the open loft door: "Vernon, it's Daar. Are you back? Why are you back? Call me." He erased the message, wondering if the *Post* article would reach Vernon. He remembered Vernon's description of his self-imposed exile in Vermont—"submarine down" were his exact words—and hoped that there weren't copies of the *Post* onboard that submarine. He couldn't imagine Vernon caring about the gossip item upon his return at summer's end and found solace in this rationale, which he also applied to the e-mail response from Shannon Hamilton:

Dear Mr. Downs,

Thanks for replying. I appreciate your taking the time. And I'll take your advice to heart. Really. So thanks. I meant to ask in my last e-mail: What was it like when your first novel was published when you were so young?

Your fan,
Shannon

Charlie smiled. He was still grinning as he grabbed a six-pack of Corona from the reach-in cooler at the deli on the corner with one hand and a couple of limes from a plastic basket on the counter with the other, opting for a little hair of the dog over the bagel sandwich he'd set out for. Back in the loft, he opened a Corona and shoved a wedge of lime down its neck, taking a long pull as the computer warmed up again. He unearthed the typed interview, spreading the pages out before him. He opened Shannon's e-mail and clicked reply.

Dear Shannon,

Seems strange to me to be thinking about that book again after all these years. The last time I reread it, I remember thinking I was too young to write a book like that. I also remember thinking that I shouldn't have taken a lot of the editorial advice I received. The first draft of *Minus Numbers* was very, very long and a lot of melodramatic things happened. But what I was going after was to have all these melodramatic things drifting in and out of the characters' lives and to have the power of these melodramatic things completely diminished because of all the fluff that's surrounding their lives. So there could be murders and rapes, but all this other garbage floating around the characters mutes the power of these horrifying things happening to people. This idea probably interested me the most when I was working on *Minus Numbers*.

When the book was edited down—and it was pared down a lot—by the editing process, a thirty-or-so-page sequence near the end of the book was left intact and stands out as way too melodramatic. I think the book holds up until then, but then I just find it to be a little embarrassing. Everything pretty much reads as I wrote it, but since a lot of stuff was edited out of the middle, these last pages really bother me, or did bother me when I last reread it. I also think the editing toward this kind of ending probably helped make *Minus Numbers* a more popular book too, and it helped make it a more successful book than it perhaps would've been if I'd had my way.

Yours,

V-E-R-N-O-N

Dear Mr. Downs,

Wow, thanks for that insider's look into the publication of *Minus Numbers*. Sounds like publishers really have the ultimate say, huh? Sucks. Curious about your writing habits. And about your favorite

books. But if you don't have time to write me back, don't worry. I've
taken up too much of your time already!

sh

The seduction of the lowercase signature was a whisper that
hovered, filling the room with promises and praise: *Shh, this is
between us. Shh, I'm your biggest fan. Shh, trust me with all your secrets.*
He shuffled the pages of the interview and stroked the keyboard:

Dear Shannon,

I don't write every day. I think about writing every day, but I don't
write every day. There are days where I write a lot, and there are days
where I can't do it. Some days I have either notes or parts of things
that I put into my computer, reorganize, or edit. It really depends on
what's going on in my life, it really depends what kind of mood I'm
in. Sometimes the material overrides the mood and makes you push
forward and say, "I really want to do this, I have the impulse to do
this right now, I'm gonna do it." And there are other days where you
feel like crap and you can't do it. You can't will a good paragraph, you
can't wish it to work out. You've really got to be in a mood, and there
are a lot of times where I just sort of wander around the apartment,
wait for the mail, open up the refrigerator, wait for the mail some
more, open up the refrigerator, turn on MTV, hope I get some good
magazines in the mail, walk around the corner, go to a movie, things
like that.

As for books, my advice is to read whatever you can get your hands on.

V-E-R-N-O-N

Charlie crawled into bed. He couldn't shake the fantasy about
how he'd respond if a fan note from Olivia appeared in Vernon's
inbox. The idea electrified him no end.

....

Charlie flipped back and forth through the weathered copy of *Zagat* he found in Vernon's top desk drawer, but Jackson's was not listed. Knowing that restaurants in New York sometimes had their official name and their popular name, he searched the index for the name of the restaurant Kline had suggested. Charlie was running late anyway—a burst of energy had propelled him through a midnight session with the archives; he was through 1993 now—but he'd use his inability to locate Jackson's in *Zagat* as his excuse, rubbing it in Kline's face as a salve for what little irritation remained from the Kline-inspired *Post* article. He finally called information, the operator informing him that Jackson's was on West Fifty-fourth Street, and the cabdriver circled the block before finding the unmarked place with blackened windows. Charlie stuck his head through the front door, his eyes adjusting to the dim light made dimmer by the crushed-velvet walls and ceiling. He spotted Kline waving wildly from a table next to the kitchen.

"You made it," Kline said benignly.

"Place is hard to find," Charlie said, his rising annoyance competing with the kitchen clatter. *Vernon wouldn't sit by the kitchen*, Charlie thought.

"This is an old newsman's hangout," Kline said proudly, as if he'd invited Charlie to his private club.

"It's a little dingy," Charlie said. He hoped Kline wouldn't recognize that he was wearing the same suit he'd worn at Christianna's dinner party, then realized he didn't really care. The criticism about the restaurant stung Kline, and Charlie let go of any residual anger about the *Post* gossip piece.

"The food's good," Kline offered.

Charlie had readied himself in case Christianna had told Kline about how he'd taken her to the apartment of the famous actor who lived on Central Park West, an invitation extended by e-mail from Vernon's film agent, someone named Bill Block. "He really wants to meet you," Block had written. Charlie was a fan of the actor, as was Christianna, and they'd spent an animated evening in the actor's company, drinking expensive bourbon from cut crystal glasses while overlooking Central Park. Charlie signed some first editions of *Minus Numbers* and *The Vegetable King* before they left, the actor calling him "mate" as they waited for the private elevator. But Kline seemed oblivious of this latest escapade, and Charlie endured his soliloquy about how he had become a reporter, how he'd come to work for the *Post*, how he coveted a job covering the Yankees. Charlie focused instead on his steak tartare, zoning out on Kline, trying to remember when he'd last eaten steak tartare, if ever. He intended to soak Kline for the best lunch possible.

"So, that was something about what happened when *The Vegetable King* came out, eh?" Kline asked, slipping the question in at the end of a long dissertation about power hitters in the American League. "Seems like it came out of nowhere."

Charlie nodded. "It *was* sudden," he said. "But if I look back over it, there were a lot of warning signs. The publisher not publishing the book was the most sudden thing, though. All that stuff about the cover designer and the in-house personnel complaining about the content of *The Vegetable King* was really just background noise until the publisher dropped the book."

Kline held his water glass in midair. "Who told you the book was cancelled?"

Charlie relished the attention and paused dramatically before answering. "My agent called and said, 'Listen, we're going to have to move this book because they're not going to publish it,'" Charlie said. "I was *floored*. It really, really shocked me. And when the editor called to say that this was in fact the case, I was numb. I guess I thought they would publish it, and people would be upset by it, but I would've never guessed with a million guesses that they wouldn't publish it. It was genuinely shocking."

"Dessert, gentlemen?"

Kline waved off the waiter before Charlie could pad the bill with a custard he'd spied on the menu.

"Where did you get the idea for *The Vegetable King*?" Kline asked. "If that isn't too banal a question."

Charlie sighed. "If I had a dollar."

Kline feigned an apologetic look but waited for the answer.

"Let's see," Charlie said, staring into the space of the near-empty restaurant. He tried to recall Vernon's words, thrilled with Kline's rapt attention. "I knew I wanted to write a book about New York—I find the city inspiring—and when I moved here after Camden, I found myself in the midst of all these guys who worked on Wall Street—brothers and friends of my friends from Camden—and I thought, *Perfect, this is perfect.* These guys were making a tremendous amount of money—hollow money, really—for doing next to nothing, which was a metaphor I liked."

"So you were hanging out with them?" Kline asked.

Charlie shot him a look. "Yeah, that's what I said."

Kline waited for the rest and Charlie made him wait for it. He waved to the waiter. "I'll have the custard," he said. "You want anything?" he asked Kline.

"Coffee," Kline said.

Charlie waited for the waiter to bring the custard and the coffee before restarting his story, as a penalty. He was having great fun and he appreciated why Christianna engaged in such role-playing.

"You were saying," Kline said, stirring cream into his coffee.

"Yeah, so I was hanging out with these yuppies," Charlie continued, "after they'd get off work. We'd meet at Harry's, usually, and I'd just sit and listen while they raved about their summer place in the Hamptons, or their new model girlfriend, or some great car they were thinking about buying. It was wild. And so I knew that was the tipping point to start writing the novel. Also"—Charlie stopped for a bite of custard—"the book is informed by a severe black period I was experiencing then, which is why I often refer to it as the most autobiographical of my books."

"It's really an incredible book," Kline said. "Do you ever wonder how it would've fared if it hadn't had all the prepublication hoopla?"

Charlie shrugged. "Guess we'll never know." This wasn't the answer Kline was looking for, which pleased Charlie. "Hey, this custard is first-rate. Think I'll have another." He registered his order with the waiter, who brought another bowl.

"It must've been pretty traumatic," Kline sympathized.

"In some ways it damaged my reputation, probably," Charlie said through a mouthful of custard, "but in other ways it completely enhanced it. See?" Kline nodded as if he understood. "I guess it made me wary of the publishing business—editors always covering their asses, et cetera, but I don't really see the experience as anything but positive. In the end I got to publish the book I wanted to publish, and people got to read it, end of story. I doubt the experience left any sort of imprint on my life, though."

"You're a stronger man than I am," Kline laughed. "I would've held a grudge against all those who tried to ruin the book. At the very least, I would've been angry at the boycott organized by NOW."

"I was angry at the time," Charlie said. "But their puppet show was revealed when they called for a boycott of not just the book, but the products and services mentioned in the book. American Express must've been laughing their ass off about that."

Kline emptied his coffee cup. Two men wearing harried expressions entered, and one saluted Kline, who saluted back.

"Colleagues," he explained, though Charlie hadn't asked.

"Last question," Kline said. "What do you think people get wrong about you?"

Charlie laughed and reclined in his chair. "I think everything that's been said about me is pretty much dead on. Or I should say, I don't think there's been anything said about me that I strenuously disagree with," he said. "Sometimes I read profiles of myself written by newspapermen I don't know"—Charlie paused for effect—"and I don't recognize the person they're describing. It's usually just a convenient version of me, but it isn't who I really am. What might not be true is that people assume I wrote *The Vegetable King* for reasons other than the simple fact that this was a book that I needed to write. That would be untrue. But other than that . . . people just write what they want to write." An urgent need broke Charlie's concentration. "Where's the head in this joint?"

Kline indicated the men's room and Charlie slid out of his chair. "If the waiter comes, order me a coffee." He strolled down the hallway to the bathroom, passing a waiter whose face he could barely see in the darkness. He laughed at how Kline had fallen for the charade and slipped out the back, silently bidding Kline adieu.

The new doorman at Summit Terrace, whose name Charlie still hadn't learned, regarded him as he blew through the lobby, hurrying to sign some of the copies of Vernon's work in order to catch the book buyer at the Strand before he left for the day.

. . . .

Unlike the calls from Staten Island, Harlem, and even Westchester County, the sighting of Oscar on the Lower East Side seemed plausible. But the twins in the Grand Street loft were another imposture. They beseeched Charlie to take their manuscript, a novel involving talking cats, and he grabbed the pages and deposited them into the first wire trash bin he encountered. Responding to phantom dog sightings was his most important responsibility, he knew, but he grew to dread them. Charlie no longer cared about the dog's fate. Oscar likely had a new owner and was being fed and petted by the next set of hands, which was just the way it turned out sometimes.

He was startled to find Jessica in the loft.

"I didn't mean to frighten you," she said calmly as she crouched, a green agate pendant swinging on the end of a necklace made of tiny purple beads, sorting through the selection of DVDs stored under the television. Dark circles ringed her eyes. Charlie hadn't noticed the storage space, and the discovery piqued his curiosity about what else might be hidden in the loft. "I see you've made yourself at home." She nodded toward the assemblage of takeout containers and empty beer bottles forming a small cityscape on the kitchen counter. Mountains of paper littered the loft. Charlie hadn't even had the chance to utter "Hello," and he guessed that Jessica was adept at controlling conversations. "I suddenly *had* to see this movie," she said. She plunged her hands deep beneath the television, mining an assortment of foreign films and pornography that didn't seem to embarrass her. "You haven't seen it, right?"

"Which?"

"The one where the guy is trying to get back to his apartment and he's out of money and can't. His money floats out the cab window. He tries to take the subway, but they've raised the fare and he doesn't have enough."

The movie sounded familiar, though he couldn't name it. "Something with mannequins," he offered.

Jessica snapped her fingers. "Yes, exactly. You know it."

"I don't *know* it," he answered. "I may have seen it."

"What's it called?" she asked hopefully.

The phone shrieked and they both froze, waiting for the answering machine. Vernon's voice floated through the loft, swarming around them in deep tones, and Jessica hugged herself absently. Charlie peered into middle space in an effort to coax the title of the film, counting the seconds left in the answering machine message he now knew by heart. The caller hung up without leaving a message and Charlie shrugged.

"I thought you were supposed to be useful," Jessica teased as she returned the DVDs to their rightful place. Charlie admired the seam of Jessica's blouse, tracing it along the curves as it rose and dived this way and that. She stood and Charlie looked absently out the window, causing her to glance over her shoulder.

"I'm told I'm very useful," he said. In his mind, the retort was flat and uninflected, a cold piece of steel brandished as a weapon against any misunderstanding that might arise between them, her being Vernon's girlfriend. Later, after Jessica had left empty-handed, he blamed the disconnect between his intention and his playful tone for the exchange that followed.

"I'll bet." She smiled, closing the distance between them. He smelled a lemony soap, her freckled skin close enough to touch. "What did Vernon tell you about me?"

Her expectant gaze knifed him with guilt. Vernon hadn't so much as uttered a word about her. Charlie didn't even know her last name. He became flushed with the same rank embarrassment he'd felt earlier, at a Starbucks upon his return from the false lead on the Lower East Side. Two overweight girls, both with hair dyed unnatural colors, obviously in high school—and obviously in glee club by the way their conversation was punctuated with outbursts of song—earnestly promised to marry each other if they weren't married by their late twenties. "Do you promise you'll marry me?" the one asked. "Absolutely," the other agreed, "except for the physical stuff, obviously."

Jessica read his reaction accurately. "Not surprised," she said. A shadow crossed her face as she bit her lip. "It's hard, Charlie. Very hard to be with someone who doesn't see you exclusively."

Charlie inadvertently raised his eyebrows.

"He didn't even tell me where he was going," she said, her voice infused with a soft whine.

"You mean where in Vermont?" he asked.

She looked at him askance. "He didn't even say he was going to Vermont," she said bitterly. "Let me guess, Richard is with him, right?"

"Who is Richard?" Charlie was desperate to exit this line of inquiry and hoped to devise a change of topic while Jessica ranted about Richard.

"He's a protégé, like you," she spit out. "A fucking waiter at the Gramercy Park Hotel. Classic. Just classic. The never-ending train of wannabes is tiring. 'Do or don't' extends to his sex life, too, and it's mostly 'Do.'"

The shocking reality of Vernon's bisexuality—Charlie was terrible at guessing people's ages, so naming their sexuality was outside his abilities if asked—was overshadowed by the realization that Vernon and Richard the waiter from the Gramercy Park Hotel had absconded to Vermont, leaving Charlie to dicker with dog sightings and jealous girlfriends. An aberrant hurt at Vernon's not coming on to him passed. Perhaps it meant Vernon took him seriously as a writer. Once the shock receded, he resisted the bitter feeling that even though he was orbiting Vernon's world, he was a faraway, unnamed planet.

"I guess I need to find my own protégé, eh?" Jessica asked.

Possession overtook him as he regarded Jessica. Had she really come over to look for a DVD? The scheme seemed impossibly juvenile. If you encounter an embittered girlfriend crouched in your space, if only temporarily your space, what are the gears in the machinery that brought her to you? And if you're both feeling betrayed and looking for consolation, what is allowed and what is forbidden? He could reach out. He could touch her on the arm, signaling his submission to whatever purpose she'd arrived at, riven with the idea that she could deliver him from his subordination. Every apprentice was one part assassin.

"I could ask around," Charlie offered, floating it as a joke to gauge Jessica's reaction. The suggestion caught and she narrowed her eyes. She crossed her arms and her smooth biceps flexed involuntarily. He wanted to break the long gaze between them but knew that to do so would be to lose the powerful cord they were momentarily tethered to.

"I'd need someone discreet," she continued. She moved toward the stereo. An old copy of *Details* magazine featuring a profile Vernon had written about the actor Val Kilmer caught her attention and she turned the pages absentmindedly.

"I thought you weren't exclusive," Charlie said, leaning against the kitchen counter.

"I'd like to be," she admitted, the confession squandering a measure of the playful tension that had been building. "I'm normally a one-man kind of girl." She tossed the magazine back toward the pile of media he'd carefully gleaned from the rest of the archives, fluttering the mountains of correspondence, fan letters, and manuscript drafts.

The moment for conquest—if it really existed—slipped away with Jessica's acknowledgment of her true desires. The erotic haze that had briefly hung over them cleared, leaving him stifled and slightly sick to his stomach.

"But if, when you're out serving your master, calling 'Here boy, here boy' around the neighborhood, you run into a suitable candidate, give me a shout," she said, swinging her pocketbook over her silky shoulder. "Don't look too hard, though," she added. "For the dog, I mean." She glided for the door.

"Why not?" he asked, turning but not following.

"Sucks to have something you love withheld," she said.

Charlie took a step toward her. "You took the dog?" he asked.

"He only cares about the dog because it's new," she said. "I was new once too. So were you. Remember that."

"Will you bring him back?" Charlie asked. "We'll say that he just came home on his own. Vernon will never have to know."

Jessica opened the door and grimaced. "What makes you think I still have it?" she asked, and then was gone.

....

"Hurry the hell up," Christianna called from the other side of the screen. She hunted through a Depeche Mode CD, sampling the first beats of each song before skipping ahead.

Charlie reread Shannon's e-mail:

Did you write a draft of the screenplay for *Minus Numbers*? Were you involved with that process? If you had to rank your books according to how successfully you completed what you started out to do, how would that list go?

The titillation of writing Shannon while Christianna waited in the loft was palpable.

S,

I was still in college when I found out they were going to turn it into a movie. I was sent a script by someone, I saw a couple of more scripts, but I was not involved in the process. I didn't want to be involved. When I was first asked if I wanted to be involved, I realistically didn't think I could do it because I was finishing up school, and then I did go back a week later to my agent and said, "Well, maybe

I do want to do this." She said, "It's too late, I already told them you don't, and you should finish school anyway." But you know what? I would've done the first draft and it would've been very close to the book and there's no way they would've made it. This was a movie that should never have been made by a big studio, and it should never have been a big, glossy Hollywood movie filled with a lot of stars, directed by a very slick video director. It just shouldn't have been done. It probably would have been much more successful if it had stayed true to the book and was made on a very low budget. There was no way that a big Hollywood studio run by the parents of the children in the book were going to make an honest movie out of that book. So it was hopeless anyway. I could've written a draft, but it wouldn't have mattered.

As for ranking, wow. You have an idea for a book and you're really lucky if you get fifty or sixty percent of that idea down. In your head, you have this grandiose idea of a great, awesome book where you're going to write about this, or this, or this, and when you start writing, reality sets in and you kind of get to the point where you think, *Okay, if I can just get through this, if I can just move it on to here, I'll have done some work and it will have worked out.* Sometimes writing a novel can be so overwhelming and so exhausting emotionally that you're really lucky if you can get fifty or sixty percent of what you really wanted to initially down on paper. I think, for example, *The Book of Hurts* is probably sentence for sentence the best writing I've done by far. I don't know if it's the best book, but I do think that the writing is, let's just say, very unembarrassing to me. I still think *Scavengers* is the one book that I really got down everything that I wanted to do. I wrote a book that really threatened to annoy a great many people. At the same time, I just really have a soft spot in my heart for *Scavengers*. That might be because *Minus Numbers* and *The Vegetable King* were these big bullies that could take care of themselves. *Scavengers* was so slammed because it was about these really annoying, atrocious kids nattering on and on about their lives at college and "Oh, he doesn't love me" or "She doesn't love me" or whatever. It got a tremendous amount of flak that I thought really wasn't due the book. So I sort of have a soft spot for it.

I really can't reread the books, it doesn't really interest me that much. They define a certain time of my life and what was going on during that time of my life, and I don't know, to me they're not that interesting to reread again. They were interesting to write, but to reread them . . . I don't know if I'd get that much pleasure out of that. Or if it would be particularly instructive.

Charlie proofed the e-mail against the typed interview and sent it. He checked Vernon's inbox for anything that seemed urgent. A request from his paperback publisher was difficult to decipher and he decided it could wait. Practically everything could wait, he guessed. At first, he expected daily phone calls demanding updates on Oscar; but the silence from Vermont portended that nothing that was going on in New York was of any importance to Vernon. He heard Christianna open the refrigerator and exhale a long "ew."

"It's nine-*thirty*," she whined. "I thought we were having drinks at Aviator."

Didn't we do that already? he thought. He moved to switch the computer off just as a reply from Shannon drifted into the inbox. His intuition that an unhappy Christianna was a dangerous Christianna warned him that he should save the e-mail for later, but Shannon on the other end of the connection, hoping to catch him in real time, was irresistible.

It seems like it would be easier to write "nice books." It seems you risk so much with technique, with the things you do. At a certain point don't you think, is it worth it?

So much risk, so much risk. He flipped through the typed interview to find Vernon's answer to a similar question Charlie had asked previously, dispirited by the apparent unoriginality of his interview questions. How many times had Vernon had to answer the same question, or some version of it?

It's very strange to me that you say this because in the end it's really not a choice. It's really just a reflection of the writer, whether the subject is vampires, Japanese businessman taking over Los Angeles, evil corrupt law firms, or whatever. It's just a reflection of who you are. I don't think you can force yourself, at least not to the end of an honest book, to write in a way that you don't really want to write. You write how you write. Some people will like it, some people will not like it. But it's not really about pleasing people or making people understand things. Writing is really a very selfish thing. You're writing a book because *you* want to write a book and *you're* interested in these characters and *you're* interested in this story and *you're* interested in this style and *you're* basically masturbating at your desk with all these papers and these pens, and if it goes out there, hits a nerve, fine; if it doesn't, well, fine too. It's really about expressing yourself in a lot of ways, *to* yourself and not to anyone else. You're pleasing yourself when you're writing, you're not pleasing a bunch of other people. You're not constructing a little candy house, or a little gingerbread house that everyone can take a piece of and feel sweet and nice and that makes themselves feel good about themselves or about reading a book. Writing a book is actually a very selfish and very aggressive thing. You're writing this book and putting it out there and it says, *Read me! Read me! Read me!*

He sent the e-mail. His stomach rumbled just as Christianna's patience reached its limit. "Let's go," she demanded.

They negotiated the crowd at Aviator, his brow sweaty from the short walk through the humid August streets, as Christianna steered them toward the same table, creating a sense of déjà vu.

"You should never keep a lady waiting," Christianna chided him. "Tsk, tsk."

"A lady never complains," he joked.

"Oh, you are such a beasty," she said.

"How's that?" he asked.

"You are such a total beasty."

Charlie remembered this bit of dialogue from a Christmas party scene in *Minus Numbers*—it was possibly the only line from the book to appear in the movie—and he scoured his memory for the next line. He concentrated through four swallows of his vodka tonic before Christianna uttered, "You're such a Grinch," a line from a Christmas party scene in *The Vegetable King*, confusing him, though he knew the next line from that scene.

"Bah humbug," he said.

Christianna delivered the response without missing a beat. "What does Mr. Grinch want for Christmas? Has he been a good boy?"

The scene between Nick Banks and his girlfriend, Evelyn, came back to him with clarity—it had been one of Olivia's favorite scenes—and he fell into his role effortlessly, trying to remember his lines. "I want a Gucci wallet, I want a silver sherbet scoop from Lotus, I want a car stereo—"

"But you don't *even* have a car," she said, as if on cue.

"But I *need* a car stereo," he said.

"We'll see what we can do," she said.

Eventually Christianna would respond only to "Evelyn," and Charlie asked twice if she wanted to leave once Aviator was overrun with the preclub crowd. Christianna didn't answer, but Evelyn finally said, "Let's go to the Soho Grand," and he instructed the cabdriver to the corner of Canal and West Broadway. After a couple of rounds of fifteen-dollar margaritas, paid for with the last of his Strand money and served to them while they lounged on oversized armchairs in the hotel air-conditioning, Christianna-as-Evelyn wanted to get a room, a fact she communicated by sitting on his lap and whispering it in his ear, and even though he didn't remember this particular scene from the book, he obliged, the girl at the front desk saying "Welcome back" when he charged the room to his American Express card. The confluence of alcohol and the possibility of sex was amplified when he spied Jessica at the bank of elevators dressed in a black miniskirt and halter top, hanging on Jeremy Cyanin's arm. Her gaze penetrated the dim lobby and she smiled as the elevator claimed them.

When he woke back in the loft, an empty bottle of vodka resting on its side next to the bed, Christianna in her loft, blaring the soundtrack from *Flashdance*, Charlie replayed his memories of the previous night, substituting Jessica for Christianna until the reverie seemed authentic.

Charlie drained a glass of orange juice, toeing the unmarked folder containing Burton LaFarge's letter as he shuffled to the kitchen for a refill. A faint knock gave him a start. He knew who it was and refilled his glass quietly, gliding noiselessly back to the computer.

An e-mail from Shannon erased any further thoughts about Christianna.

What did you want to be before you wanted to be a writer?

The lone question bespoke a familiarity that was both alarming and alluring. Gone were the days of "Dear Vernon," and Charlie lamented the disappearance of Shannon's lovely electronic signature, the tiny *s* and *h* importing its own message. He hoped to revive the tradition by not falling victim to the new parlance, instead addressing Shannon as always.

Dear Shannon,

Before I was a writer I wanted to be a musician. In fact, I still have fantasies of being a musician, and that's one thing I definitely was going to embark on before Camden. I was in a band in high school— Phantasm, which was not the name I thought of, but one the guitarist did. It was the summer before going to college. I had been accepted to Camden, and it was that summer where the decision was either to stay with the band and see what would happen, or go to Camden and major in creative writing, read everything, and start to concentrate on that. Being the really kind of wimpy, safe adolescent I was, I choose to go to college, and the band broke up.

V-E-R-N-O-N

The orange juice was impotent against the hunger seizing him. He dressed haphazardly and listened at the door before exiting by the back stairs. Breakfast at Baxter's, the diner on First Avenue, was the remedy. The diner had started to feel more like a sanctuary than the loft on Thirteenth Street, so he was dismayed to look up from his omelet to find a college-aged kid with dirty-blond dreadlocks standing beside his table.

"Mr. Downs?"

"Yes?"

"I'm Shannon," the young man said, flipping his sunglasses up on his head. A day-old beard camouflaged a ridge of adolescent acne scars on Shannon's wide chin.

"Oh," he said. "Hello."

Charlie bit down on the inside of his cheeks to squelch both his supreme disappointment and the anxiety of having been watched. Though he never imagined meeting the recipient of his late-night e-mail correspondence, he'd nonetheless begun to fantasize about what Shannon might look like, mostly a compilation of the best features of girls he'd known. Olivia had been curiously excluded from the anthology, which he attributed to the illicit thrill of cheating on his own feelings whenever he answered one of Shannon's e-mails. All that mental expenditure was gone, but the need to delicately extricate himself overtook his anger at what was clearly an inappropriate situation.

Shannon towered nervously over the table, fingering the strap on a new messenger bag. Charlie masked his annoyance by asking Shannon to sit.

"Thanks," Shannon said.

"How did you know who I was?" Charlie asked. "I mean, how did you recognize me?"

"I saw you come out of the building," Shannon answered, momentarily embarrassed.

"How did you know where I lived?" Charlie asked.

"Oh, um, hope it's okay," Shannon said. "The alumni office at Camden gave me your address when I asked for your e-mail."

"Oh," Charlie said. The pain of recognition was unbearable. "So. You're a . . . man."

He'd hoped for levity as a stall tactic, but Shannon blushed. "Um, yeah. Did you think—"

Charlie cut him off before the embarrassing realization could land. "Just an observation," he said.

"I wanted to, um, thank you for, you know, taking the time to write to me," Shannon said, the mangled sentence barely making its way from his lips. "I'm, uh, sure that you have better things to do."

"No problem," Charlie said, regaining his composure. He was the famous writer, after all. "Happy to help."

"It's really nice of you," Shannon said.

Charlie sipped his coffee. "You live in the East Village?" he asked.

"Hoboken," Shannon said.

The two sat in silence and Shannon's nerves gave first. "I, uh, was hoping you would read my book," he said, hoisting a manuscript from his bag. "And, you know, you wouldn't have to line-edit it or anything. Unless you wanted to."

Charlie sipped his coffee again, stalling.

"Fine," he said.

Shannon stood, gazing at his watch. "Anyway, I hope it's not a bother and thanks again. Take your time. I gotta run. Nice to meet you."

"Likewise," Charlie said. He ordered another cup of coffee, relieved, his dull headache receding with every slurp. He fanned the pages of Shannon's manuscript, embarrassed at the revelation that Shannon was not a sexy female fan, but was instead just another male writer who wished he were Vernon Downs.

. . . .

Shannon dropped an e-mail a week later crafted to seem innocuous—"Have you had a chance to read my manuscript yet?"— and Charlie answered quickly that he had, and that he liked it. He hoped this was all the encouragement Shannon sought, but Shannon persisted to know what exactly he had liked, and he generalized about the originality of the main character's plight as well as the role chance played in the lives of all the characters. Shannon assailed him with direct questions about the manuscript, but his deft circumlocution kept Shannon at bay until, weary, Shannon asked him point-blank if he would recommend him to his agent. The query came after a long day of e-mailing wherein Charlie tried to make up for his brutal evasiveness by actually reading the first chapter of Shannon's manuscript—he discovered he'd been spelling the main character's name wrong, which likely as not had aroused Shannon's suspicions—and so he answered, "Yes, I will." Shannon replied with a smiley face drawn with a colon and a closing parenthesis.

Another e-mail the next day was devoid of any pretense of endearment. Shannon asked again if Charlie would recommend him to Daar Baumann and again Charlie promised that he would. Shannon thanked him, adding, "I was thinking it might be helpful to have a blurb from you. Possible? Thanks. Your fan, Shannon."

"Hey, Shannon"—Charlie hoped the casual salutation would temper Shannon's aggressiveness—

You should send the whole manuscript. She'll want to read it front to back, guaranteed. Give her this quote from me:

"With this novel, Shannon Hamilton pulls off a magic act of sustained imagination. Hamilton's prose sings, his characters intrigue, and I have no doubt the publication of this book will bring favorable comparisons to some of our most revered authors, not least among them Salinger. This book is an updated *Catcher in the Rye*."

Charlie appended the note with Daar Baumann's e-mail address and signed off with "Good luck—you won't need it!" He expected that would be the last he'd hear of Shannon Hamilton. The potent feeling of control over the small mess he'd gotten himself into with Shannon was fleeting, supplanted by a worry and anxiety he hadn't known since leaving Arizona, since Olivia had packed her bags and flown out of his life.

He'd been unsettled by a chance encounter with Shelleyan, who had shrieked his name from across Union Square Park the day before. She'd dyed her hair a shiny chestnut color and had cut it at a severe angle. He hardly recognized her. "So there you are," she said. "I've been leaving messages for you." Charlie shrugged and moved down the sidewalk. Shelleyan kept stride. "Olivia is coming to New York," she announced theatrically. "I'm picking her up at the airport on Tuesday. She's going to stay with me. And I thought maybe we could all get together."

He mumbled an apology about being very busy.

"I've been temping at *Shout!*" she said. "Congrats on your story. You've come a long way in a short time."

The calculus whereby Shelleyan sneaked a copy of Charlie's story to Olivia, who had probably read it in disgust, was easy math. He was convinced that Olivia's sole motivation in coming to New York was to confront him about his fraudulent portrayal of their time together. As the crowds hustled around them, a thrumming in his head spread to the rest of his body. His nerves frenzied, as if Olivia might turn the corner and find him, exposed, caught on the verge of escape. He hadn't considered until that moment how much his scheming nourished him, and that her complete silence sustained the whole of his ambition to get her back. But Shelleyan's invitation threatened proximity, and proximity would only mean exposing his rapidly withering dreams. None of what he'd undertaken would mean anything to Olivia. Worse, he was clueless what her reaction would be upon learning of his last few months. He couldn't summon a response plausible enough to be Olivia's, one that could be ascribed solely to her and not to any one of the faceless strangers passing by. It was like they'd never met; she was a featureless ghost, and he searched his mind for any tangible proof that he'd ever known her. Even Shelleyan appeared unrecognizable; she bore a vague resemblance to the girl from a lost time who berated him for not knowing who Vernon Downs was, or that he was Olivia's favorite writer—insinuating there was a reservoir of things he didn't know and could never understand—but she was far removed from the tiny community college cafeteria thousands of miles away in Arizona where they'd once crossed paths, and it seemed preposterous to be standing on a sidewalk in New York, listening to her prattle on about reunion. A fleeting thought grew manifest within him: That his connection to the past was just his own fanciful imagination. The Kepharts, and the McCallahans, and the Alexander-Degners, the Wallaces, the Chandlers, and now Olivia. What he thought he knew about her—about any of them—was just pure invention.

. . . .

"You have to call me *now*," Vernon's agent said after the beep. No "Hello," no "Hi, how are ya?" "I don't know why you're not answering the Vermont number you gave me, but the *Post* has something and we need to talk about it. Call me, Vernon. I'm serious."

Before Daar Baumann finished her message, Charlie was out the door, struggling with the buttons on his shirt as he called for the elevator. Christianna's door opened and she emerged dressed for an evening out. She sized him up, but before he could spit out Kline's name, she withdrew into her loft. The elevator sounded and he suffered the interminable ride to the lobby, rushing out of Summit Terrace for a cab that was about to pull away, his breath a hot smoke against the windows.

The *Post* offices were grungier than he'd expected. A gruff security guard he tried to finesse wouldn't let him pass, instead calling up to Kline to announce his arrival.

"This *is* a pleasure," Kline said, greeting him as the elevator opened on the sixth floor. The glass cubicles in the bull pen were occupied with interns and secretaries, none of whom paid any interest as Kline ushered them into his office, a cramped space cluttered with papers and Yankees memorabilia. "My favorite player," Kline said when he caught Charlie admiring a baseball signed by Mickey Mantle. "Kid had two bad legs and kept hitting. Amazing, no?"

He didn't answer, didn't know what Kline was referring to, didn't want to know.

"Have a seat," Kline said, indicating a ratty leather chair opposite his messy desk. "To what do I owe this visit?" he asked.

Kline's coyness riled him and Charlie struggled with his lines. He had choked back tears earlier in the cab when he imagined Vernon's irate reaction to Kline publishing whatever article he proposed to publish.

"How did you find out?" Charlie asked.

Kline put his hand on his heart. "Find out what?"

"C'mon." Charlie leaned forward in his chair, measuring his breath. "How'd you figure it out?" On the cab ride over, he had considered forsaking Vernon Downs entirely and bolting from New York, later presenting the episode as an anecdote that would maybe amaze Olivia. But he was curious about the publication of his story in *Shout!* and wasn't ready to submarine what might be a burgeoning literary career. Could he manage both? It all depended on Kline, to his supreme amazement.

"That you're not Vernon Downs?" Kline waved at someone passing outside the office. "I bumped into Vernon when I visited Christianna after the party. I was just playing my cards close."

Charlie exhaled. He'd underestimated Kline by disregarding him, and the penalty phase was about to commence. "What's the pot?" he asked.

Kline pitched forward. "You ever had a nemesis?" he asked.

A crowded field of faces from the past came to mind. "So?"

"Mine is another reporter—he prefers 'journalist,' excuse me. He was accepted at the more prestigious *J* school, works for a more prestigious paper, gets the plum assignments, on down the line." Kline's phone rang and he glanced at it. "I first heard about his writing an unauthorized biography of Downs from a mutual ex-girlfriend." He held up his hands. "I can't even verbalize that situation, but anyway, she told me and so I just showed up at his Christmas party. Did you know anyone can go? You don't have to be invited. If you know about it, you just go. Pretty remarkable for someone so mysterious. I knew the address from Christianna's sister, and it didn't take much investigation to uncover the when."

"Does Christianna know?" Charlie asked. The thought hadn't occurred to him until just that moment.

Kline shook his head. "I don't care about what you're up to with her," he said. "She'll never say anything to her sister, if that's your concern."

Charlie was unsure of his primary concern. "I still don't know what this is all about," he said, shifting.

Kline shoved a piece of paper across the desk. Charlie recognized it at once, the letter that had turned up innocently in Vernon's archives, a letter he guessed Vernon hadn't meant to keep.

"It's a copy," Kline said, warning in his voice.

Charlie reread the letter from Burton LaFarge, the accusation of plagiarism infinitely more menacing as he sat in Kline's office than it had been when he'd first discovered it in the safety of the loft. "Did you write this?" he asked, tossing the letter back across the desk. Stall, stall, stall.

"You know I didn't."

He thought of another tack: "How did you get it?" He guessed breaking and entering wasn't a talent Kline possessed.

"I told Christianna I could get her a couple of auditions," Kline said without a trace of chagrin. "She should take some acting lessons from you, though. That day at lunch? An amazing performance."

The emotional swing brought on by Christianna's betrayal was sickening. He'd never be able to explain to Olivia about why and how he'd come to New York and ended up embarrassing himself by pretending to be Vernon Downs. He wouldn't be able to use as an excuse how expert he'd become at pretending. It was all over if Kline printed what he knew. He began the cost-benefit analysis he'd employed in previous situations created out of his eagerness to fit in, or his yearning to be liked, measuring what had been forfeit against what could be revised in his favor, and he realized that the option to simply move on to the next thing, whatever it was, was his to exercise. Whatever mistakes or missteps he'd made in Denver, and Santa Fe, and Rapid City, San Diego, and Phoenix, had always accrued mercilessly until he'd wish for another move if only to wipe the slate clean.

But maybe it could all be salvaged, he thought. Perhaps Kline would barter the LaFarge letter for a raunchy tale about Jeremy Cyanin involving hookers and a substantial quantity of cocaine, insinuating that Cyanin was a bagman for a local crime family and that he might have participated in a hit. Or a believable story about Cyanin's sexual depravity, something involving ropes and turpentine, but that lie paled in comparison to Charlie's impersonating Vernon Downs, and the mental narrative he began to spin about Cyanin and the mob spiraled out of control and out of the realm of believability. He surrendered to his compromised position.

"What is it you want?" he asked.

The passing crowd barely registered as he exited the *Post* building, nearly tripping over a homeless woman squatting out on a flattened refrigerator box, Kline's outrageous request for access to Vernon's archives to write the better biography as the price of

Kline's silence, both in the pages of the *Post* and with Christianna, ringing in his ears. Kline had pushed for Charlie's help in securing authorized status for the biography, but even Kline knew this was overreaching. Charlie assented to the request simply to win his freedom. Late-August humidity swarmed the city, the stink of garbage piled high on the sidewalk nauseating. Sweat trickled down his back as he waved in vain for a cab during rush hour.

. . . .

The lock to Derwin's brownstone resisted Charlie's key. He leaned against the diamond-shaped window scarred by weather and vandalism and peered in, but the entryway was deserted.

"He died." Mrs. Cooper, the ancient Puerto Rican neighbor who could pass entire days loitering on her stoop, told about Derwin's fall, the ambulance that whisked him away, demolishing his summer plans for Fire Island and forever after. She couldn't answer Charlie's question about who changed the locks, but uttered something incomprehensible about Derwin's brother in Baltimore.

Charlie glanced up at his former residence, the tiny studio apartment sealed like a tomb. He felt the first tremors of hysteria as he grieved for what was lost, mostly the suede pouch from the Kepharts that held his valuables:

The aluminum diamonds from the long-ago Batman and Robin performance had traveled with him for so long they'd turned yellow. The skit had ended triumphantly, good finally trumping evil as Charlie skated across his homeroom floor, undercutting the Joker's legs so that the bag of foil diamonds soared, spraying the tiny silver jewels under the desks of their classmates, a choreographed move they'd practiced in the hall. George proudly wore the remnants of the white makeup used to paint him as the Joker that wouldn't wash off, the three of them accepting the wows of their peers, who they believed considered them superheroes. The Joker's capture and the players' ovation weren't the close of the drama for Charlie, however. The conclusion of the play would be asking Suzy Young to be his girlfriend. He'd chosen breakfast in the gymnasium as the venue for his proposal, but he waited a couple of days, allowing for the legend of the Batman and Robin skit to propagate, he imagined, before approaching Suzy. He'd purposely stayed clear of her to avoid losing his new sheen of celebrity, which was why he was oblivious about her father's abrupt transfer to Idaho, the reason Suzy was absent from breakfast on the day he'd hoped would be their happiest. Charlie frantically searched the gymnasium, asking her friends if they knew where she was. Suzy's desk remained empty during the morning classes, and he finally asked Mrs. Holstein about Suzy as the others filed out for recess, collapsing in tears when Mrs. Holstein told him the awful truth.

Gone too was the wedding ring Michelle Benson had given him in the fourth grade. Michelle's friends had been the inspiration to take the relationship to the next level. "Why don't you just ask her to marry you?" they chimed, a dare Charlie converted into proposal, asking Michelle if she would marry him in a note before lunch. Michelle gamely accepted, less flattered than amused, he thought— she was always more amused by him than anything else—though he was the last to know of her decision, since it was Wednesday, which meant boarding the bus that pulled up outside Mrs. Selby's class and honked in the middle of the day, Charlie the lone student from Lewis and Clark in the Gifted and Talented Program hosted by Webster Elementary. He bemoaned his showy cleverness at the annual spelling bee—he discovered an ability to spell words whose definitions eluded him—an exhibition that landed him in the gifted program. He dreaded Wednesdays, not because he sensed his classmates staring at him and his cumbersome backpack as he climbed onto the near-empty bus, or because he had to walk home alone from Webster through an unfamiliar neighborhood, but because of the menacing he and his fellow gifted students suffered on the Webster playground.

His enrollment in the gifted program was a source of tension in the McCallahan household, too: The McCallahans never asked him about it, and Wednesdays came and went like the other days of the week, so that it felt like Charlie's secret, a quiet he associated with the school nurse's diagnosis that Ian was dyslexic, though when Charlie overheard Mrs. McCallahan telling Mr. McCallahan, she said the word in a way that betrayed her disbelief in the nurse's medical qualifications. For his part, Ian never let on that the gifted program bothered him, though Ian barely came out of his room when Charlie knocked to say good-bye before being shipped out to Rapid City without a chance to properly divorce Michelle.

Charlie's wedding day was attended by most of the girls in his class. The event was booked for the early recess, near the monkey bars. One of Michelle's friends made a crown for her to wear, and Charlie fashioned two rings out of twist ties. The ceremony was quick and consisted of Michelle and Charlie holding hands while they were pronounced man and wife by Michelle's best friend. "You may now kiss the bride," someone yelled, and he angled forward, Michelle taking the kiss on her cheek.

Lost was the letter from Ms. Slater, his first-grade teacher, her acknowledgment of the carefully wrapped package containing a necklace and a ring from the machine at the grocery store that spit out plastic bubbles full of wonderful prizes that he'd left on her chair the last day of class. Charlie would stare moon-eyed at Ms. Slater from his seat near the back of the room, listening but not listening to whatever subject they were studying. He didn't endeavor to impress her with his academic work; that route was too pedestrian. His own burgeoning affinity for the dramatic was born out of the anonymity that had claimed him since his parents died. Instead he chose "My Bonnie Lies over the Ocean" from the songbook his piano teacher had given him and practiced it incessantly, working for perfection, willing himself to tears on the refrain "Bring back my Bonnie to me." He dreamed of performing the ditty to a packed concert hall, smiling in Ms. Slater's direction after the touching performance, the only variation on the dream being the hairstyle Ms. Slater wore. The recital dream was so real he could summon its emotional aftershocks at will, reveling in it over and over so that the moment felt like a shared secret, an illicit romance his classmates were oblivious to. Worried that she'd forget him—and slightly paranoid that she'd vanish before the start of the next school year—he hoped the jewelry would serve as a reminder of his affection and that she'd look forward to seeing him as eagerly as he looked forward to seeing her in the fall. A tizzy threatened his summer until he found a letter addressed in Ms. Slater's hand:

Dear Charlie,

I was so surprised to find a present on my desk after school. Thank you so much for the lovely necklace and ring.

I have been having a nice summer. Mostly I've just been lazy—doing a lot of reading and sunbathing. I have a new car and will probably be going on a trip later this summer. I plan to visit my sister in Spokane and my parents in Portland, and go to Seattle for the King Tut exhibit.

I hope your summer is a lot of fun.

Love,
Ms. Slater

He'd never again hold the Mormon dance card he'd acquired so that he could attend dances with Jenny, his high school girlfriend. His theory that Mormonism was the sole obstacle to a secure future with Jenny had been wrong. He guessed that swaying Jenny from Mormonism would be a nearly impossible task, but everything hinged on it, so when he read about a documentary proving conclusively that Mormonism was substantially make-believe, he perceived it as his last last chance. Jenny's letters from college had ceased leading up to Christmas, and he hoped her silence was simply reticence to engage his harangue that religion was just a form of governance, rather than a repudiation of him entirely.

Jenny's expression when she opened the door, the aroma of her family's dinner wafting in his direction, revealed how far he'd fallen. "This isn't a good time," she said, as if he were a salesman conniving for just one cup of coffee. Her expression contracted when she spotted the documentary he was cradling, tears streaming down his face. She'd already disowned him, he could see that, but the glint in her eye communicated how much his materializing with the anti-Mormon video violated the last sacrament between them—the remembrance of how much they'd once loved each other—rendering the memory impotent. Jenny's look hardened and Charlie divined the shattering news that he had been unaware of: She had moved on. A downdraft whipped through the yard and Jenny stepped away from the screen door. The sonorous vibration of laughter burst from the house, and Jenny glanced reflexively toward the dining room, the same dining room where he'd supped on numerous occasions, encircled in prayer around the polished table with Jenny and her family, giving thanks, Charlie finally drawn completely into the comfort of home. He stammered a valediction about his embarrassment at having interrupted dinner, but Jenny cut him off again with "This isn't a good time," and the expression he must've worn his first day in Denver, and Santa Fe, and Rapid City, and San Diego, and Phoenix—the look of someone who was starting over—spread across the constellation of freckles he used to spend afternoons counting with clandestine kisses. And although he'd worn the expression in countless circumstances, he'd never had to suffer it—he'd always been the one moving on, leaving friends and familiarity in his wake—and the effect was devastating. As Jenny closed the door, her silhouette rejoining the festivities, he stood in darkness, drowning in Jenny's disdain, his losses mounting, his eyes wet with regret.

Charlie turned his back on the brownstone and Mrs. Cooper, who had struck up a conversation with the girl from the corner Laundromat, out circling the block on her afternoon smoke break, and walked away. The initial exhilaration that visited him when a new chapter began predictably shaded into depression. Unlimited freedom didn't guarantee happiness, he knew firsthand, though it always promised it and he thirsted for that promise.

Charlie migrated unencumbered toward the subway, disguised in the crowd as somebody racing toward something. A swell of warm, recycled air escaped from somewhere deep underground as he paced the L platform, the launching point for whatever was next. He refused to acknowledge the emotional attrition invested in every next adventure, every new face, every new terrain.

"Who are you?" Kline had asked as Charlie stormed out of the *Post* offices, but Charlie had no answer.

IV

CHARLIE GRIPPED THE leather wheel of the black BMW, raindrops from the brief rainstorm as they crossed the border into Pennsylvania sparkling on the hood. The instrument panel cast an orange glow over Vernon's features as he slept coiled in the passenger seat. The lush green landscape darkened as the car raced west along the ribbon of wet highway. He'd had to force his way into the driver's seat in a showdown with Vernon in front of Summit Terrace. The days between Charlie's meeting with Kline and Vernon's frightening appearance had been filled with uncertainty about what exactly was next. He'd camped out at Vernon's, indiscriminately shoving the archives back into boxes, having unplugged the answering machine. Christianna's presence just beyond the lofts' common wall was felt but not seen, her betrayal enmeshed with that cancerous Kline, the hallway eerily quiet each time Charlie had food delivered. A low-level dread about Jessica appearing unannounced corrupted his sleep, so that a fogginess plagued him through the daylight hours as he tried to dream up a new scheme that would propel him to the next new world, wherever that was.

As the date of Olivia's arrival drew near, a series of bargaining positions hampered his ability to plan. He was convinced he was hanging around Vernon's loft, delaying, because he was going to keep the date with Olivia and Shelleyan, until he was doubly convinced that he would not, which made urgent an errand he'd been avoiding.

He'd been carrying the name Harold E. Turnbull around forever, since he noted the signature scrawled on the police report from
that awful day. The police report judged his parents' death accidental,
caused by a gas leak in the basement. Charlie knew the basement
had filled with gas, and was made to understand it was the pilot light
that had sent the house into orbit. When he subsequently secured a
copy of the report by mail, he searched for clues that it could've been
otherwise. Couldn't it have been some other type of accident?
Couldn't there have been a defect in the hot-water heater? Wasn't
there someone else who could share the blame? Would he have to
wake with the same heavy sadness that put him to sleep night after
night? As he grew older, he would toss in his tiny bed under the eaves
of his aunt and uncle's soundless house, convinced that he'd seen a
shadowy figure lurking that fateful day, though by morning he was
always devastated by the awareness that it simply wasn't true.

Harold E. Turnbull lived on Mott Street in Chinatown; the
computer in the New York Public Library had imparted this bit of
information as easily as it churned out queries by subject, author, or
title. Previously, he'd uncovered a rat's nest of Turnbulls in Minnesota, and he'd called every one, hoping for a relative. It wasn't until
he found respite from the oppressive summer heat at the New York
Public Library that he even thought to try New York, or anywhere
east of the Mississippi, for that matter. And there he was, residing
on Mott Street the whole time, waiting for him. Harold E. Turnbull. Of Mott Street. New York, New York. He wondered what sort
of person Harold E. Turnbull was: Did he have a family? Was he
from California? Had he ever before seen a house reduced to sticks
and scraps of metal, the occupants of the house gone, gone, gone—
gone into the atmosphere?

Mott Street wasn't any wider than an alley, and the cab cruised
slowly, the cabbie scanning for the address. The car halted and

Charlie paid the fare and stood alone in front of a dark building appointed with a gray door. His hand shook as he pressed the button under the name H. E. TURNBULL. A husky voice answered: "Yes?"

He didn't know this part of it. He barely knew what he would say when he got into Harold Turnbull's apartment, much less how to gain entrance. "You don't know me, Mr. Turnbull," he said, "but I've come to speak to you. It's about my parents."

"Hello?" the husky voice asked again.

Charlie cleared his throat and started again. "I've come to—"

"Hello? Who is it? Hello?" the voice barked, and then clicked off. Charlie's heart sank, and he searched the shadowed street for a pay phone—he'd copied Harold Turnbull's phone number, too, and would try to call and explain—but he managed only two steps before the door buzzed, and he pushed it, slamming it against the wall. The door caught and closed slowly as a trapezoid of plaster plummeted to the floor.

Charlie used the handrail to navigate the unlit stairway to the fourth floor. The door to Harold Turnbull's apartment strained against the gold chain, and a set of owl eyes blinked out from behind a pair of enormous spectacles.

"Hello? What do you want?"

Charlie stood back, not wanting to distress his prey. "I think you knew my parents," he said, choosing an expediency rooted in truth. "In Modesto. It was a long time ago. You were the city inspector there, right?" He flinched when the door swung open. The smell of ripe bananas escaped the apartment.

"It's nice to have a visitor," Turnbull said. Charlie figured him to be about seventy-five, but it was impossible to tell because his loose flesh and bald head gave him the appearance of having been dead for a long time, resurrected only by Charlie's visit.

The tiny apartment was cluttered with unread newspapers, some still in their plastic sheaths. Empty orange juice cartons were stashed behind the recliner positioned directly in front of the televi-sion. A dozen or so chocolate bars were spilled across the tiny black-and-gray-flecked Formica kitchen table. A familiar scene from an old sitcom squawked from the television and they both stood and stared at it.

"I'll clear this away," Turnbull said. A foul odor emanated as he swept a rack's worth of bundled magazines off a ragged couch.

Charlie lost his nerve. What if Turnbull looked at him and said, "Yes, it was your fault"? What if he said, "If you and your friend hadn't been fucking around in the basement, your parents would still be alive today"? It hadn't occurred to him that the only reason he'd sought out Harold Turnbull was that he wanted absolution, to have him testify it was an accident, that it might've been something else, anything—a meteor falling out of the sky, a bomb planted by terrorists, a rocket mistakenly fired from the local army base.

Turnbull plunked into the recliner and elevated his feet. "Circu-lation," he said, wincing. "Now, what is this all about?"

Charlie fingered an imaginary spot on his pants. He felt Turn-bull staring over his socked toes at him, and he summoned the Olympic courage he sometimes willed to power him through situ-ations that he'd misjudged as easy but that proved surprisingly dif-ficult. He told Turnbull about that day when he was seven, about him and his sixteen-year-old sitter, the neighbor girl, Kyra, roller-skating in the basement—it was safer than the street, where a car could roar around the corner and kill you dead just like that. It was his mother who had suggested it, actually. "Why don't you go down in the basement if you want to skate," she'd said. Charlie wouldn't have come up with that idea in a million years, as appealing as it was. He told Turnbull about coming home later from the store, Kyra in tow, and discovering a gap of sunlight where his house had stood. He confessed how he sometimes saw the house in his dreams.

Not the same exact house; sometimes it was red or green or blue, sometimes a single-story ranch, but no matter what color or shape, he always recognized it as his childhood home, the house disintegrating into colored confetti when he turned the brass knob.

"Very interesting," Turnbull said.

"And so," Charlie said, weary from the effort it took to expel the story he'd secreted away for most of his life, "I just need to know if you think what happened that day might have been an accident."

Turnbull removed his glasses and pinched the bridge of his nose. "It was a lifetime ago," he said.

"I brought this," Charlie said, handing him the yellowed copy of the police report.

Turnbull held his glasses aloft, inspecting the document. "That's my signature, all right," he said. Charlie inched forward on the couch. He'd grown accustomed to the stench in the apartment. "The thing is . . . it was a lifetime ago."

"Are you saying you don't remember?" Charlie asked. "How many houses have you seen blown to pieces?"

"Just hold on," Turnbull said. He kicked himself out of the chair and handed back the report. "Let me just—would you like a drink? I find a drink sometimes helps."

Charlie demurred. His heart was pounding. Turnbull poured himself two fingers of bourbon and flushed it down. He poured another glassful and returned to the recliner. Outside, a siren wailed and Turnbull's apartment was briefly flooded with emergency.

"Were your neighbors affected?" he asked.

The question staggered him. His memories of that terrible day and since had never accounted for the neighbors, and he strained to conjure any details about them. The one across the street had maybe been a dentist, and he definitely remembered a patch of sunflowers in the yard adjacent to his, the sunflowers coming into

view when he and Kyra kicked higher and higher on the plastic
swing set his father had staked to the ground with metal chains the
previous Christmas. But he couldn't be certain. His neighbors in
Denver had had sunflowers, and it was conceivable the dentist had
actually lived opposite him in Santa Fe. A flush of embarrassment
overcame him, dubious about whether Turnbull was chastising
him for his self-absorption, or whether a detail or two about those
who lived on his childhood street in California would really help
spur his memory. The conceit that his neighbors, whoever they
were, had carried on with their lives after his house had immolated
seemed incredible—the street had assumed the form of a tableau in
Charlie's mind, untroubled by the present or future—and triggered
the discomforting thought that someone had more than likely built
a house on the ruins of his parents' house, a sacrilege that he'd never
considered. Did Kyra still live in the neighborhood? Why hadn't he
wondered that before? Maybe Kyra was keeping his memory alive
on that tiny street. Maybe she wondered what had become of him,
and he was startled at how powerful the feeling was.

"What do you want me to say?" Turnbull asked. "Do you want
me to say it wasn't an accident? How could it be anything else?" He
took another swig of bourbon. "Do you want me to exonerate you,
assure you that you were not the cause of the accident?"

Charlie didn't respond.

"Well," Turnbull said, "maybe. Maybe the leak was caused
by something else. Maybe it wasn't a leak at all—hell, back in
those days if a house blew up, we *assumed* it was a gas leak. We
couldn't do what they can do now." He finished the second
glass of bourbon. "I will tell you this," he said. "Accidents happen
and sometimes they change your life, but they're still accidents.
You shouldn't try to look for meaning in them. An accident is
an accident."

Turnbull sat back in the recliner. Charlie tucked away the photocopy of the police report. He thanked Turnbull for his time, but Turnbull started to snore loudly, so he let himself out. Something had just happened—he felt it—but what? Had anything Turnbull said made any difference, or was he saying that nothing anyone could say would make a difference, and by extension, that the past was the past and had no bearing on the present or the future? It was a homily he had trouble believing. The sun was starting to set on Mott Street, and Charlie fruitlessly hailed a cab, somehow sorry that he'd finally found Harold E. Turnbull, the years of hope and comfort he'd derived from the name whisked away on a hot afternoon wind of regret.

The visit to Turnbull had been so taxing and left him so rent he failed to make it to the lobby to collect the mail, the annoyed doorman delivering it one afternoon wrapped with a thick rubber band. Among the mail was the unopened apology he'd mailed to the famous author Vernon had quarreled with, marked UNDELIVER- ABLE. He opened the letter and was reading the heartfelt apology when a disheveled Vernon Downs appeared, his hair matted to his head as if it were raining, his normally smooth face unshaven, a barbaric spark in his eyes. Charlie had girded against rebuke, but Vernon muttered something about California, his words slurring as he grabbed random articles from the loft and deposited them into paper shopping bags, Charlie revolving around him silently, the two pirouetting through the unkempt loft until Vernon hefted the two bags by their handles and stalked toward the door. The rush of excuses that had flooded Charlie's brain when Vernon appeared evaporated, and without being asked, he followed Vernon down the emergency stairs to the street where the BMW languished amid the cacophony of honking cabs and animated, competitive sidewalk conversations. Vernon dropped the shopping bags in the backseat on top of his luggage from Vermont. After a confused moment where Vernon begged to drive to calm himself, Charlie slipped behind the wheel and listened to Vernon's harangue against his editor, who had driven him to the fringes of madness over the latest revision of the new novel, punctuated by directions on how to flee the city by car.

"'Make it more Vernon Downs–y,'" Vernon repeated incredulously, his eyes bulging, his breath stale from cigarettes. "What does he know about it?" he asked angrily. "Take the George Washington Bridge." Charlie followed Vernon's directions, Manhattan slowly receding, the skyline shrinking into miniature. "What does anyone know about it?" Vernon asked softly.

"What did the editor mean?" Charlie asked.

Vernon cracked the window and lit a cigarette. "It's a tired impression at this point, is all," was the answer. "You take what they give you and you burnish it, indulging it even," he said, "and then you realize you're in a prison of your own construction. I mean, I let it happen. This unrecognizable person in the papers was infinitely more interesting than I was. I'd read what they wrote about me and aspire to their interpretation. That was my mistake. I didn't understand how important it was to control your own narrative.

"I remember when I first learned *Minus Numbers* was going to be published, I was elated that something I'd dreamed up was going to find its way into print. That was it"—he exhaled through the open window—"but everything after that got . . . easier. I struggled and worried and fussed with *Minus Numbers*, and after it was published, I swear I could've published an annotated grocery list and it would've gotten the same reception as the books I did publish. You want to know why? Because the machinery was already in place to dictate the outcome. You're young, you write a book, you become famous, maybe make some money, which unleashes praise and jealousy in equal measure. So from then on out, a certain number of people worship you and a certain number of people loathe you. It's a mirror of everyone's life, just played out in the press." Vernon stubbed the cigarette out in the ashtray, where it smoldered among a salad of empty candy wrappers. "You once asked me what the most untrue thing anyone ever said about me was. 'Controversial and reclusive East Coast literary novelist.' The person who first coined it should've trademarked it. If words were money, that person would be rich beyond rich. Ask anyone, there's nothing controversial about me personally. You see something, you translate it into words and create *fictional* characters to generate meaning, and then you're liable for these things that you simply witnessed and recorded. And they call you reclusive if you don't want to answer questions asked by someone who either hasn't read the work or wants to confuse your characters with you. And worse: You take the bait and start equivocating on earlier denials that your work is any kind of reflection on your life. You have some fun blurring the edges, fanning the embers of the secret desires people who hardly know you harbor. Disappearance is the only remedy. What other answer is there? I'm forced to disappear if I want to wake up and live the way I was before *Minus Numbers* and everything else. I can't go back to New York. There's no peace in New York."

Vernon had leaned against the window as he rambled on about the ways his self-impersonation had gone astray, how he had allowed what was said about him to inform his perception of himself, how he had acted his way through life accordingly. He fell silent and Charlie assumed he'd finally dozed off. "Against all my better instincts, I went to the tenth anniversary of Nell's," Vernon said, barely audible, his voice shot through with sadness. "I went there very early with a friend of mine; we thought we'd have a glass of champagne and it would be like the Haunted Mansion at Disneyland. I hadn't been there in five years, and we realized it would be really scary but we had to do it. We had spent so much time hanging out there with so many. It was really at one point the nexus of publishing. It was the hub of where everyone who was involved with publishing in New York would hang out. So we walk in and we sit in the same booth we always sat in whenever we were there, and then we noticed that a couple of us were drinking Diet Cokes, people were smoking light cigarettes, no one was doing blow on the table, everyone was checking their watch. Basically we all felt really old. Everyone was controlled by how manic the times were, which sort of demanded that you rush out to every restaurant you possibly could, party with every famous person you possibly could, buy everything you read about in magazines, act this way, look this way, do this."

Vernon's monologue saturated Charlie's mind as he struggled against the monotony of the road. He resisted Vernon's interpretation, ascribing it to fatigue and a toxic moroseness induced by whatever had happened in Vermont. He guessed Jacqueline Turner and the other authors gathered at Bemelmans on that not-so-long-ago afternoon would've traded some privacy for an ounce of Vernon's exposure. Everything had a price, he knew well, and it was either paid voluntarily or forcefully extracted. Still, Vernon's madness was real. They were on their way to California, to his mother's house in Los Angeles. That was real. He wondered at Vernon's game plan for a second act in L.A. Perhaps it was just to be closer to friends and family. But his money would run out eventually. Vernon's celebrity would hamper his ability to interview for the variety of jobs people held to pay their bills, much like Charlie's own resume, which was largely a chronology of absence.

"You never said where you were from," Vernon said, yawning. "With most people . . . it comes up." Vernon yawned again. "Just stay on the I-80 West."

Charlie struggled with the question, rescued by a suite of sighs that preceded a light, melodious snoring. A calm settled over him as the extent of his liberation unfolded. Kline's demands, the drama with Christianna, the threat of reunion with Olivia with Shelleyan as witness—all erased. Like in Denver, when he'd forsaken Jesse Mason's friendship after the Batman and Robin skit to throw his lot in with a group of popular kids, a transition Jesse's mother and Mrs. Kephart ignored as Jesse's birthday party loomed, the awkwardness aborted when Charlie landed with the McCallahans, who were ignorant of the drama involving Michelle Benson. Not his pretend nuptials, but that after a brief acrimony toward the boyfriend she'd broken up with to be with him, he and the ex-boyfriend became friends, to Michelle's chagrin. Charlie eventually spent more time with the ex-boyfriend than he did with Michelle, and soon they were distributing He-Man Michelle Haters Club cards they'd printed on the ex-boyfriend's home computer. He recoiled when he thought about how easily he adopted the manners and interests of others as a coping mechanism for always being the new kid in the new school. He still didn't drink orange soda because Michelle hated it; he adopted Jesse Mason's opinion that the moon landing had been faked, something Jesse's parents had told him. He became a Vernon Downs fan because of Olivia. He could think of endless examples. Vernon had liberated him from the mess back in New York like his move from San Diego to Phoenix had freed him from academic embarrassment, his short tenure as Miss Wade's student aide. His chemistry teacher's initial attentiveness was flattering, and he held the position with a pridefulness that other students must've found distasteful. But when he began to hear whispers that Miss Wade was a motorcycle-riding lesbian—rumors that were never confirmed—his attitude underwent a transformation, and it wasn't long before he was leaking the answers to Miss Wade's exams to anyone who asked,

which was briefly a fountain of popularity. Miss Wade quickly
discovered the hustle when the exact sequence of correct multiple
choice answers were applied to an alternate test she'd utilized so that
students couldn't pass answers from class to class. Charlie's demotion
to study hall wasn't as perilous as the ire of the student body, and
he was mulling begging the Wallaces to allow him to transfer high
schools when he was shipped out again, to Phoenix, the immediate
threat ameliorated just like that. Same for the trouble he'd gotten into
with some classmates the summer of his junior year at Randolph Prep;
the emancipation the Chandlers helped him engineer bailed him out
of having to testify to the administration about how the fellowship at
Garden Lakes, a sort of summer camp, had gone awry.

He slowed as the night sky colored red and orange, the taillights
of the cars ahead of them flaring. The nose of the BMW almost kissed
the bumper sticker on a yellow VW that read, IF YOU WERE AN AIRLINE
PILOT, WE'D ALL BE DEAD. Charlie obsessed over all its meanings as
the line of cars snaked forward in the dark. Vernon shifted in the
passenger seat, his sleep cycle unbroken. The car at rest, and without the lullaby of the tires on the road, Charlie was wide awake. A
police cruiser with its lights flashing passed silently on the shoulder,
followed by an ambulance. He wondered idly if the driver of the yellow VW was embarrassed about the bumper sticker in this instance,
when it could be that someone did actually die, and possibly due to
poor decision making. Or did the driver even remember that the
bumper sticker was there? Charlie could envision a scenario where
the driver slapped it on, as either a statement or a joke, and then
quickly forgot about it, maybe only remembering it when he noticed it, or if someone asked him about it, where they could get one
too. The bumper sticker morphed into a provocation as Charlie was
compelled to stare at it when traffic came to a standstill. The deep
woods on either side of the interstate bred a claustrophobia he at-

tempted to abate by turning on the air conditioner. The slight breeze simulated enough movement to quell the aggravating implication that Charlie was as disconnected from his various experiences as the driver was from the bumper sticker on his car. It had meant something to him once, but he barely considered it now. To his relief, the yellow VW put on its flashers and pulled over to the side of the road. As he passed, Charlie smiled at the driver, a bearded man in his fifties who jumped out and popped his trunk.

....

By sunrise, they were well into Ohio. Charlie had stopped to relieve himself and fill the tank, waving the Speedpass on Vernon's key chain at the Exxon station off I-80 as Vernon slept in the passenger seat. When he finally awoke, just past Springfield, he said, "Take I-75 South," and they veered off the exit, headed for Cincinnati. Without inquiry, Vernon gave a thumbnail account of the reason for their detour: that his ex-wife, Jayne, and nine-year-old son, Robby, lived in Blue Ash, a suburb just outside Cincinnati. Charlie absorbed the facts, that Vernon had met Jayne when she was a model in New York, right after he'd published *Scavengers*, that they had had a long, protracted battle involving private detectives over Vernon's paternity—"We kept calling each other John and Jane Doe after it was finally resolved," Vernon said—followed by a quick marriage that lasted a mere three months. After a quiet divorce, Jayne had moved to Blue Ash and made Vernon swear not to utter a word about them as he went on with his life. "Not for their own privacy," he said, "but because I'm an embarrassment as a father and ex-husband." The story staggered Charlie, as did Vernon's ability to keep it out of his official biography.

The modest white and blue ranch house on Laurel Avenue was shrouded behind clouds of hydrangeas. A red Jeep Cherokee sat in the driveway, the back passenger door inexplicably left open. Vernon stared uneasily at the open car door, perhaps sensing the visit was a mistake, the signs of apology troubling his brow. He fortified himself with the last of the cigarettes that had substituted for his breakfast. A golden retriever bounded across the lawn toward the Cherokee. "Victor," Vernon said. "That dog hates me." Charlie braced for Vernon to make the connection between the golden retriever and Oscar— Vernon had amnesia about the missing dog—but Oscar had apparently been consigned to the past, just as Jessica predicted.

A slender woman in blue jeans and a yellow sheer chiffon button-front blouse appeared in the driveway, shading her eyes. Her long black hair fluttered in the morning breeze. Vernon stepped out of the BMW and waved. The woman lowered her hands and retreated inside. Vernon leaned into the car. "Come back tomorrow," he said, shutting the door and sauntering across the thick grass. The golden retriever ran aimlessly toward him and then pulled up, changing direction and jogging ahead of Vernon toward the front door.

The separation caused Charlie a moment of panic, which quickly converted to anger at being abandoned. Regardless of his intellectual preparedness, it was always a wonderment, that first prick of panic and then the wall of anger that rendered him powerless until he could hack through his emotions to take inventory of his new circumstances, which would reveal what would be required of him to survive. In the case of Vernon's precipitous exit, the primary concern was that he'd be obliged to sleep in the BMW, his funds mostly depleted from his summer in Manhattan. As he cruised the quiet suburban streets, idly guessing at what it would be like to grow up in the bucolic heaven that was Blue Ash, he scouted for camouflage, which would only need to hold until tomorrow morning, when he could legitimately go for breakfast, or find a bookstore to satisfy his curiosity about whether the good citizens of Middle America read Vernon Downs. But after unsuccessfully trolling the local radio station for a soundtrack to his latest dilemma, Charlie fished for a CD in the leather armrest and discovered a stash of twenties he hoped Vernon wouldn't remember. A quick alibi—that he'd used the money to gas up in Pennsylvania—would be believable until Vernon received the bill for his Speedpass, at which point Charlie guessed it wouldn't be an issue. His cover story thus salted away, he rented an antiseptic room at a Motel 6 and fell on the blue and green checkered comforter in his clothes, staring at the television to dull his mind of all that had transpired.

He awoke after midnight, restless. The Motel 6 complex was a hulking ghost ship in a sea of suburban sprawl. The warm August night draped the landscape in a purple bloom, specks of headlights roving in the distance. The vending machine in the concrete courtyard swallowed Charlie's quarters without reciprocation. He pummeled the glass, but the Hostess cupcakes slumbered behind their wire guard. He unsuccessfully rummaged the BMW for more change, though his hunger ebbed when he discovered a cardboard box stashed under Vernon's luggage containing typewritten pages, the new novel. Charlie turned the pages carefully, sprawled out on the sheets back in his room. The novel was without a title page but involved several characters from Vernon's second novel, *Scavengers*, many of whom had gone on to become models. The narrator shared the same name as the golden retriever, and he chuckled at the connection. As he read, the narrative became a hybrid of satire and thriller, involving models as terrorists, the overt thesis intimating the tyranny of beauty.

Charlie set the pages aside. The myth of Vernon Downs—even after it had been punctured by the madness that had them scampering across the country—was so ingrained in his mind, so saturated in association to bygone days with Olivia in Phoenix, that he was incapable of judging if the book was any good. Were reviewers right about Vernon? Was he a hack, a sensationalist, a writer more famous for being famous than for being a writer? He recalled a scurrilous accusation he'd read somewhere—that if not for the controversy surrounding *The Vegetable King*, Vernon would still be published by his original publisher, whose reputation as a purveyor of celebrity biographies and gimmicky books had been cemented in recent years. Regardless, however the new novel turned out, it would be published, a record of Vernon's particular interests and thoughts at a certain time in his life. The book would be a written record, a permanence in an otherwise transitory existence, and Charlie traced his attraction to writing back through his want for a little attention to this lust for immortality. If only he could bead his experiences on a chain, not just to memorialize them in print for posterity, but to search them for threads of meaning or instructive themes.

The sun ascended in the milky sky, the beginning of another humid summer day. Charlie checked out, too early to arrive at Vernon's ex-wife's place. His restlessness from the night before had ripened into a full-blown anxiety, a wariness that Vernon's visit with his ex would have them reversing course, back to New York. He slowly drove the streets of Blue Ash while its residents awoke. Without any concrete evidence to support his theory, he surmised that Blue Ash closely paralleled the neighborhood in Modesto where he'd lived with his parents, who had, over the years, become little more than a fact. He'd had parents, like everyone. But because both his mother and father had been substantially younger than their siblings, and had never been close with the kin who tended him, Charlie had left his biological family without any memento or recollection of them. His features were too ordinary and symmetrical to provide a sketch of familial resemblance, and without that mental purchase, he was helpless to speculate about what kind of people they were, if they subscribed to the tenets of religion and politics that most employed to define themselves, if they were college educated, if they were employed, if they were liked by their neighbors, if they saw people socially, if they were involved in neighborhood concerns, if they ate regularly at local restaurants, liked spicy food or unusual pizza toppings, if others recognized and regarded them when they walked down the street, if they were more likely to dispense wisdom or seek advice, if they paid their bills on time or pleaded for extensions, if they happily agreed with taxes for community improvement or resented the governmental intrusion on their personal finances, if they were progressive or given to bouts of racism and sexism, if they were inclined to help someone in need or pass by quickly, pretending not to see, if they liked pop music, if they went to the movies regularly, followed sports, if they had the newspaper delivered to the house or bought it occasionally, if they read books, listened to talk radio, if they drove a new car or a used one, if they rented or owned their home, if they had planned to save money for his college education, if they showered him with kisses or treated him like they would an adult, if they assiduously researched the quality of the local school system or not, if they harbored secret crushes on neighbors or coworkers, if they drank coffee or tea, if they were vegetarians, if they smoked, if they were afraid to fly, if they had a history of cancer, if they feared technology, or nuclear war, if they would've been the kind of parents he was proud or ashamed of, if he would've forsaken them for adventure or stayed close as he grew older, if he would've been closer to his mother or father, if he would've begged them for a sibling or basked in the attention of being an only child, if he would have made them proud or been the cause of disappointment, if they would've boasted about him to friends and neighbors or been bound to shake their head with chagrin, if they would've been a close-knit family that took vacations together, celebrated all the important holidays, and been devastated when one of them was grievously injured or gravely ill, rendered inconsolable by death.

He wished he could know.

....

Vernon appeared rejuvenated by his overnight visit. His clothes had been laundered, and a shower had all but resurrected his previously beleaguered form. But Charlie noted that neither his ex nor the boy accompanied him to the car. Vernon motioned that he wanted to drive, so Charlie dutifully crawled into the passenger seat. They slipped back onto the freeway in silence, Vernon making lane changes without utilizing any mirrors or looking over his shoulder. He wasn't concerned about where Charlie had spent the night, or how he'd occupied himself during the gulf of time he'd been abandoned, and so Charlie stared out the window until he nodded off.

Vernon insisted on driving the rest of the way, darting off the freeway somewhere in Illinois, telling Charlie to stay in the car as they pulled up to a white clapboard house perched on a hill. The name carved in relief on the wooden sign in the shape of a tractor posted in the small garden out front—McInnis—was that of Vernon's onetime mentor at Camden. Vernon shook hands with the tall, gray-haired Harrison McInnis, who invited him in. Charlie reclined the seat, the BMW's air-conditioning vanquishing the first signs of heat. The cool, quiet chamber was broken moments later as Vernon climbed in, sweat on his forehead, his hair tousled and a sunburst-patterned red mark on his right cheek.

"We're off," he said, making a U-turn for the freeway.

"What happened?" Charlie asked.

"Just saying hello to an old friend," he answered.

Somewhere between the two Kansas Cities, Vernon fished a pill bottle out of his luggage and intermittently chewed small white tablets as they screamed across the Kansas plain, the darkness as pure as any Charlie had ever witnessed. The lone incandescent lights from gas stations and forlorn strip malls flashed by at metronomic intervals and Charlie fought sleep. Vernon cracked his window and increased the volume on the Stone Roses CD they'd listened to three times through. Conversation had been sparse, constrained to where to stop for fast food and gas, Vernon preoccupied with a point somewhere far along the horizon. Along a particularly endless expanse of pavement, the trance was snapped and the BMW eased to the shoulder.

"Christ," Vernon exhaled. He leaned his forehead on the steering wheel, completely deflated.

"I can get us to Denver," Charlie volunteered, and they wordlessly switched places, a tractor trailer blowing a torrid exhaust giving them a wide berth.

Charlie was so consumed by an intricate design whereby he might ditch Vernon at the hotel in Denver to surprise the Kepharts, the grandparents he hadn't seen or heard from in years, that he couldn't fathom the maze of one-way streets that would bring them to the towering chain hotel Vernon had pointed to, demanding sleep. The hotel mocked him as it drew near and then receded, none of the streets seemingly the answer to the riddle. "I thought you said you used to live here," Vernon said. Just when frustration threatened to flow like lava between them, the hotel's portico appeared. Vernon heaved his bag and disappeared through the electronic sliding doors while Charlie parked. Vernon's mental state made it impossible to predict how he'd react to the idea of borrowing money for a hotel room, so Charlie used the pay phone in the hotel lobby to call American Express to ask for a limit increase. He'd prepared a spurious anecdote about how he was starting a new job soon that would significantly boost his previously insubstantial income.

The joyless voice denied the request, so Charlie climbed into the backseat of the BMW and rested his weary body on the leather seat. His head buzzed with thoughts of the Kepharts, replaced with a worry that they'd be disappointed to see him now, to know anything about what had happened to him since he left. He preferred they remember him as the little boy they'd briefly known so long ago.

....

Vernon appeared to believe the staged drama in the lobby about how Charlie had already checked out and was impatient to light out, and so the road trip recommenced, Vernon behind the wheel and Charlie the passenger. Charlie tongued the hole in his back tooth where the temporary filling had been. He must've swallowed it in his sleep. The tooth would likely weaken from infection before he could manage a way to fix it, he thought.

The blue snowcapped mountains disappeared as they crossed into Utah, plunging into valleys of red rock, the arid landscape reminding Charlie of his proximity to Arizona, a place he was sure he'd left for good. The overnight stop in Denver and the sojourn through the desert southwest confirmed that the geographical backdrops of his personal history continued to exist into the future, even though for Charlie they were frozen in amber, the glass bottles glinting in the sunshine of his mind. A secondary thought, about the historical supposition about heading west in search of a better life, or to make something of yourself, appeared as false as anything.

As they skirted Las Vegas, Vernon regaled Charlie with the amusing anecdote about how when he was in high school, his parents discovered drugs in his room—"My sisters ratted me out!"—and they sent him to work in his uncle's casino outside Vegas, forgetting that he'd mentioned it previously in the interview, their first encounter, which seemed to Charlie like several lifetimes ago.

A calmness descended on Vernon as they merged off the I-15 and onto the I-10, passing signs for Pomona, West Covina, El Monte, and Monterey Park, the locales sounding to Charlie as exotic as foreign countries. A bronze minivan and a blue Camaro, both with Michigan plates, tried not to lose each other in traffic. A silver pickup truck changed lanes, momentarily separating the two vehicles. Charlie watched with interest as the minivan slowed to force the pickup truck to pass, reuniting the van with the Camaro. He thought about the drivers planning for just such a problem, devising the stratagem to protect each other all the way from Michigan.

"I was born in Modesto," Charlie said between songs on the radio.

"Northern California is a whole different thing," Vernon said. "It's Oregon, basically." His mood brightened as they broached the Los Angeles city limits. "I haven't been back in forever," he admitted. "Everyone out here calls me Dave. Harrison McInnis made me put my full name on the manuscript of *Minus Numbers* before he sent it to his agent. But I'm known to my real friends and family as Dave. I guess that punctures any remaining fiction about Vernon David Downs," he laughed. He stopped for a red light. "The myth is useful for a whole bunch of things, but it's a bummer when people buy into it too heavily. Like you did." He turned and looked at Charlie, who was processing the revelation, counting up the myths he'd adhered to for so long, a life with Olivia as rescue from his life of spirals overshadowing the rest of the list. "Hopefully you'll find something that means more to you than my literary facade." The light changed to green and the BMW rolled forward. "Unfortunately for me, I'm addicted to the fictional me," he added. Charlie took the admission to be Vernon's way of saying that he would ultimately return to New York and resume the life he'd fled a few days earlier. Charlie envied him the easy cover his image provided, in spite of its hazards and occasional nuisances.

They exited the freeway near Century City and headed toward Beverly Hills. "My father had an office in Century City," Vernon said. He spun a narrative about his previous life in Los Angeles, growing up in a pink stucco house on Valley Vista in Sherman Oaks, hanging out in Westwood at a Fatburger, the restaurant on Melrose where he used to have drinks with his mother, mobbing the twenty-four-hour Du-par's in Studio City, or Pages in Encino if Du-par's was packed. Vernon made a sequence of turns and noted how he used to wait patiently at the bar at La Scala Boutique, eating chopped salad and bribing the waitress to bring him red wine while his sisters shopped with their father's platinum AmEx card. "You used to go to La Scala Boutique to dodge the people who went to La Scala," he laughed, "which is impossible now, I'm sure." They passed a restaurant called Chasen's and Vernon said, "Christmas with the family there every year." Charlie admired the recitation, the parsing of Vernon's personal narrative, indifferent to the landmarks, which meant nothing to him. Only the Hollywood sign was familiar, but they motored under it without comment. "There used to be a yellow train on Sunset," Vernon lamented. In the middle of a story told with incredulity about how his parents had taken him to a place called Sambo's in Westwood when he was a kid, he broke off to ask, "Is today Sunday?"

Charlie wasn't sure, and said so, but Vernon became convinced and they drifted through the streets. The sky had been darkening all afternoon, the sun fighting through at intervals, the momentary brightness fouled by the thunderclouds approaching from the west. The Santa Monica Pier came into view, lit green and yellow and red against the black sky.

"We used to come down here on Sundays," Vernon said excitedly. "The last time I visited, I was shocked that people from my high school were keeping the tradition alive."

An exodus for cover was taking place as they pulled into a parking spot. Lightning streaked the sky, a sonorous crackle following. The ocean frothed, expelling the last swimmers. Vernon stood atop a pylon and shielded his eyes. "They're here somewhere," he said.

Charlie hoisted his duffel from the car as Vernon jogged down the dark beach. The car alarm engaged as he shut the door, and he was filled with wistfulness for the safe interior of the BMW, like driving by the home you were born in, knowing you would never live there again. He shouldered the bag and watched as Vernon receded into blackness, a web of lightning illuminating his outline, the lone figure marching toward the ocean while others ran for cover.

As Charlie moved inland, a light rain began to fall, the menace of a downpour in the air. He made for the taillights of a city bus as it pulled away from its stop, waving for the driver to stop, but the bus roared away. He'd hardly stepped into the shelter of the bus stop when the sky unburdened itself, unleashing a torrent that bathed the streets, rain bouncing off the hardened ground. He wondered if Vernon was looking for him, or if he'd turned to introduce him to his friends and shrugged when he found Charlie had disappeared. Neither really mattered. Either Vernon did or he didn't, and the consequences were the same to Charlie. Vernon wouldn't be surprised either way. He was right: Charlie had invested too much in Vernon's myth—they both had. Charlie often thought of his lack of a belief system—in anything—as a handicap, but wasn't life just a series of beliefs that mostly turned out not to be true? Or as true as you needed them to be? Wasn't the need to believe more interesting than the belief itself? In a sense, each new beginning in his life had been a rebirth, another chance. So many rebirths annihilated any thought of death, allowing recklessness to become his guiding principle.

"No more buses," someone shouted over the din of the hard rain, a vagrant taking refuge.

"No more buses?" Charlie repeated.

"Tomorrow is Labor Day," the vagrant said.

Charlie remembered the time he'd tried to take Olivia out to dinner for her birthday only to find all the restaurants closed on account of Thanksgiving, a fact they discovered after driving from restaurant to restaurant, playfully bargaining about the types of food they were willing to eat as they encountered each closed establishment, until they darted around Phoenix trying to locate a fast-food drive-through that was open.

"How could you not know it was Thanksgiving?" Olivia had asked. "Isn't it one of your biggest holidays?" He failed to explain that Thanksgiving was mostly a gathering of family and served no purpose for those who had grown up in a procession of tribal communities.

He smiled at the memory as the rivulets of rain collected in small tributaries. He wasn't devastated by Olivia or any of it, his ability to tie things off a skill he assumed most people would admire as they became bogged down by the minutiae of their lives. Back in New York, Christianna's sister was likely returning from Paris, ending Christianna's summer sublet. And Olivia and Shelleyan were probably strolling around Manhattan, Shelleyan relating what she knew about Charlie and his time in New York, which wouldn't amount to anything. The week before Vernon reappeared had been fraught with anxiety, and a small part of him was disappointed that he wasn't going to be called to account. Olivia meant more to him than he did to her, he had known that from the beginning. But he would never doubt that in time he would've won her completely over, like he would've Suzy Young and Michelle Benson, and like he did Jenny, before he lost her.

A chill gripped him as the wind gusted, but he was cheered when he recalled the copy of his short story—the Camden version, before Vernon's edits—buried deep in Vernon's archives. He hoped someone far into the future would stumble upon it and marvel at reading the thoughts and true feelings of someone who had lived a long time ago.

A black Cadillac splashed through the flooded street and Charlie was suddenly troubled by the thought that maybe his wasn't a skill anyone would admire at all. The mechanism he had so heavily relied on throughout his life—his innate ability to box his experiences—occurred to him as an impediment against making connections that might allow for personal growth. Even acknowledging the fact, he understood it academically but not emotionally, which was a worry and a lament. However his recent experience had turned out, any vulnerability had passed and he would always remember it as a time when there was a writer named Vernon Downs, and a girl named Olivia, a summer spent in Vermont and then New York, a road trip across the country. When the astounded future listener asked, he would say that the plan all along was for him and Olivia to move to New York, once Olivia had flown back to London to settle her affairs, tell her family and friends. His misguided adventure would be reduced to a few anecdotes about how he spent his time in New York while he was awaiting Olivia's return.

Over time, the entire episode would even occasion nostalgia.

Praise for WORLD GONE WATER

"Charlie Martens will make you laugh. More, he'll offend and shock you while making you laugh. Even trickier: he'll somehow make you like him, root for him, despite yourself and despite him. This novel travels into the dark heart of male/female relations and yet there is tenderness, humanity, hope. Jaime Clarke rides what is a terribly fine line between hero and antihero. Read and be astounded."

—AMY GRACE LOYD, author of *The Affairs of Others*

"Funny and surprising, *World Gone Water* is terrific fun to read and, as a spectacle of bad behavior, pretty terrifying to contemplate."

—ADRIENNE MILLER, author of *The Coast of Akron*

"Jaime Clarke's *World Gone Water* is so fresh and daring, a necessary book, a barbaric yawp that revels in its taboo: the sexual and emotional desires of today's hetero young man. Clarke is a sure and sensitive writer, his lines are clean and carry us right to the tender heart of his lovelorn hero, Charlie Martens. This is the book Hemingway and Kerouac would want to read. It's the sort of honesty in this climate that many of us aren't brave enough to write."

—TONY D'SOUZA, author of *The Konkans*

"Charlie Martens is my favorite kind of narrator, an obsessive yearner whose commitment to his worldview is so overwhelming that the distance between his words and the reader's usual thinking gets clouded fast. *World Gone Water* will draw you in, make you complicit, and finally leave you both discomfited and thrilled."

—MATT BELL, author of *In the House upon the Dirt between the Lake and the Woods*

Why I'm Here
Charlie Martens

I am not a good person. I don't need anyone to tell me that I am not a model citizen. People can always improve and I want to be a better person. I want what better people have. In my own defense, though, I do have moments when I reach up and brush my fingers on the brass ring of kindness, charity, and compassion.

In further defense of myself, I have to say that I am principally proud of who I am, proud that I have navigated so well with what some have called a faulty compass. Before anyone in here judges me, or starts an intense investigation into who I am, first you have to come to grips with the following ten ideas:

1. I am not a son of privilege, yet I am not an orphan of poverty.
2. I do not hold degrees from institutions of higher learning.
3. I am not handsome enough to operate on looks alone.
4. I have no family traditions.
5. I have the same dreams everyone else has, dreams whose origins are in the common myths of our time.

6. I am easygoing but will sometimes tend toward violence, if
   provoked.
7. I believe in equality.
8. I am a protector of those things in life that are smaller and
   weaker than I am.
9. I can't stand ignorance, idiocy, or intolerant behavior.
10. People talk about me in terms of sweetness and charm.

I don't pretend that these ten ideas define me, but they help you get a better view from where you are, looking down on me. The view from here is not one of looking up, I assure you, but merely looking out.

An eleventh idea is that I do not judge people.

If you want to know how far I've come, you have to understand what I've overcome. I don't just see things, I *feel* them. You can blame a fascination with appearance and how things seem on any modern thing you like. I did. But I didn't find any answers in blame, and maybe the only truth I know is this: You have to feel something to understand it.

You ask me why I'm here, and I'll tell you that I'm here to feel my way further into the world. I haven't been remanded to your custody. I simply took Detective Rodriguez's advice. Your only job is not to judge me based on what you see.

Exit Interview Report

I, Jane Ramsey, in my capacity as a clinical psychologist employed by Sonoran Rehabilitation Center, located in Maricopa County, Arizona, do hereby swear that this exit interview report contains my personal evaluation of Charlie Martens. This exit interview is being conducted after the completion of Mr. Martens's voluntary nine-month stay.

STATEMENT OF FACTS: Mr. Martens was a person of interest in a sexual assault investigation in the state of Florida, though he was never charged due to the unreliability and ultimate disappearance of the accuser. On the recommendation of Detective Florio Rodriguez of the Boca Raton Police Department, Mr. Martens enrolled in SRC. Upon his successful treatment, Jay Stanton Buckley has guaranteed Mr. Martens's position as a functioning member of society, gainfully employed by Buckley Cosmetics in a public relations capacity.

TREATMENT: Mr. Martens participated in every aspect of SRC's program. His monthly journal entries and essay assignments are appended herewith. At Mr. Martens's request, his creative writing exercises have not been admitted to the record.

OBSERVATIONS: Mr. Martens's rehabilitation at SRC has been a concentrated effort to even out his mind about the opposite sex and relations with women. An unexplained, alternating inborn hostility and passivity toward women has, in my opinion, been leveled, and a truer, more mature personality has been erected in its place. During his stay at SRC, Mr. Martens has displayed mannerly and cordial behavior toward the women here, both on staff and inpatient alike. Personally I find Mr. Martens a pleasant and charming individual. His presence in group and on the campus here shall be missed.

The following is a complete record and true account of Mr. Martens's rehabilitation.

Signed and dated this day——

If you ask me about Jane, I'll tell you that she is a fine woman. It is true that in the catalog of women in my life, Jane would come under *P* for "plain," but she is tender and we go together pretty good. Besides, I prefer not to make aesthetic judgments.

The thing I like most about Jane is that she looks best without makeup. On one of our first dates, right after I left SRC, Jane had put on bright red lipstick, and the whole night I tried not to stare at it, because it looked like she was smiling even when she wasn't, and by the end of the night I was self-conscious about it. I think she sensed I didn't like it, or maybe she was uncomfortable with it too. Jane has never worn lipstick again.

We keep each other at arm's length most of the time and that is really for the best. (She knows it too.) I guess one could say our relationship is not complicated by love. We are, however, into each other totally. Our relationship is utopian. Utopian relationships last longer than marriages because emotions like jealousy and envy are removed. I never think about anyone but Jane, and Jane always tells me I'm the one for her. It wouldn't be fair if it weren't that way, and it is the only real promise we've made.

It wasn't always like that, though. At first, Jane thought I was dangerous. She didn't say much , but she warmed up when I showed her what a nice guy I can be. Jane said she'd come off a relationship with a fellow who had probably once been in prison. You have to take the good from your last relationship and put it in future ones, I told her.

And that's what we did, creating our present utopian relationship, which provides her with whatever it is she wants. This is the sort of relationship a woman like Jane deserves. It is the sort of relationship I like to initiate.

If I could change one thing about Jane, though, I wouldn't make her such a big Christian. I don't have a problem with religion per se, but sometimes Jane can really confuse the issue. Besides, like I've told her over and over again, there is no religion in Utopia.

But then, Jane thinks I am the Antichrist. "You're the devil," she is always telling me. If she says it too often, I start to get a pinched feeling in my head and I have to yell at her to stop. I won't yell at her in public, though, and I never take it out on her in bed.

Jane is moving to California, but I want her to stay. I make a point to say "California is *not* Utopia" at least once a day, just slipping it into a conversation casually. Jane raises her eyebrows and shrugs in a way that lets me know she is on the fence. I'm convinced I can get her to stay.

"What's in California?" I ask her.

"You could come with me," she answers. She knows from my sessions with Dr. Hatch that because my parents were killed when we lived in California, it's a blank spot on my mental map. Even my short stay with my aunt and uncle in San Diego feels like it took place out of time, and out of country. Of my own will, I will never return to California, a fact Jane knows well.

"But I don't want to move to California."

"Charlie, you could easily come."

"But I don't want to," I repeat, and this signals Jane that I don't want to discuss it.

So I'm in the mood for a good time, and Jane and I are getting ready at her apartment to go out for the usual—dinner and whatever. She sees that I am on the verge of what could almost pass as euphoria, and I see that look on her face that lets me know it won't be smooth sailing.

And sure enough on the way to dinner Jane gets me uptight by demanding to know the name of the restaurant. When I don't tell her—when I say that I want it to be a surprise—she pursues the question about what kind of food this restaurant serves with an irrationality that becomes so frightening I finally do tell her, and though I'm disappointed about the deletion of the only mystery the evening holds, I'm glad this has happened, that the glitch is out of the system, that I can now breathe easy through dinner.

Sometimes I think I would like to marry Jane, but I know that our relationship couldn't survive the rules and constraints of a formal institution like marriage. Still, she carries herself in such a way that someone across the room looking at her would think, *Hey, that girl crossing the room could make a pretty good wife.* Someday someone should marry Jane and I'm pretty sure someday someone will.

Depending on Jane's mood after dinner, we will either go to the Sugar Bowl for ice cream or go straight back to her place. I always hope we will go for ice cream because I like to watch Jane coo like a little girl between licks of mint chocolate chip. Not only is it an amazing transformation, but it always signals the start of at least an hour of foreplay that lasts all the way from the Sugar Bowl to her bed.

Tonight dinner clearly makes Jane pensive, and I can sense that she won't want mint chocolate chip and indeed the whole rest of the night may be in jeopardy. I dread the thought of going back to my room at the Hotel San Carlos, my temporary encampment courtesy of Buckley Cosmetics, alone. The historic boutique hotel is situated in a part of downtown I hardly know at all, and when I return to my room, I have to pretend that I'm just a tourist to stave off the depression brought on by my small pink room. Regardless of Jane's mood, her apartment is always preferable to another night in the hotel.

"I'm going to California," she says, as if trying to cheer herself up.

"I'll go with you," I say, and wait for her reaction. The skin under her eyes tightens, confirming my suspicion that she doesn't really want me to.

"I thought you wanted to stay here." She tries to act like she hasn't been caught off guard.

"I could stay or I could go," I tell her, shrugging.

"Well, *I'm* going," she says, realizing I am toying with her. My coyness cheers her up and again I am sure I can convince her to stay.

As the result of a bet I lost concerning how long I could pleasure Jane in bed (although I was just seven minutes shy of the promised thirty minutes, which, Jane assured me, was only average), I have to go to church with her every Sunday this month.

"If you can prove you're omnipotent, you don't have to go," she teased. But, of course, I am not.

Jane being the Catholic she is, we sit in one of the back pews, like I used to at mandatory Mass at Randolph Prep, in the Gallery of Heathens. When Mr. Chandler, my guardian's neighbor, used his pull as an alum to help me transfer to Randolph, he didn't mention that it was an all-boys Catholic school, though it hardly mattered. I was all but finished at the public school where his foster daughter Talie went.

The priests march in an impressive parade, dressed in black and red garb, holding long staffs with banners that could have been made during the Crusades, and the head priest—the Pontifex Maximus, the one leading the way—bows prayerfully from side to side.

The entourage halts in front of the congregation, and the priests assemble in an indeterminate order behind a long counter on a stage.

I look over at Jane, who knows I am about to say something snide and ignores me.

The magic act begins with a bowl on the table belching white powder, and I crane my neck to get a better glimpse. One of the elderly priests on the left of the Pontifex Maximus, dangling a charm on the end of a gold chain, begins swinging the chain back and forth, the audience mesmerized. Some sort of liquid is poured into the bowl and now suddenly all of the priests are busy with their hands, and in my mind I superimpose the title *Cooking with Catholics* over the whole scene. I lean over to share this with Jane, but she leans away from me.

After an inordinate amount of standing and sitting, singing and muttering, standing and sitting, I feel the end is near. Anxiety washes over me as I anticipate the benediction, like the anxiety a smoker in a business meeting feels when he senses he will finally get to step outside for a cigarette. There is an unquiet silence and those in the very front pew stand . I groan to myself and fold my hands on the pew in front of me and rest my head in the empty triangle they form. The shuffle of feet and the murmuring of the Eucharist become a drone in my ears as I close my eyes, wondering what I would pray about if I prayed.

I imagine Jane on her knees, at the foot of her bed. Is she praying that we'll get married? Or is she praying for things only for herself—her family's wellness, or for the right decision about California?

Without warning, an image of Jane and her next boyfriend praying together, heads down, hands together, appears in my mind. The suddenness of seeing them quickens my pulse and a bitter irritability creeps through me. The image is static and overpowering, like a giant poster plastered on the wall of my brain, and the thought occurs to me that Jane probably *will* pray for me, given her good, religious nature. Privately she asks the Lord to watch over me and protect me from evil. This thought stays with me until we are out in the parking lot, and as we climb into Jane's car, I say, "Fuck church."

"You're the devil," Jane says.

Essay #1: A Proper Introduction

Before I was anything, I was an Elrod Bullet.

Ms. Saltonstall, my second-grade teacher at Elrod, told me I was her favorite. I was her helper because I held the spoon full of sugar while she held the flame under it during science, because I read longer passages than anyone else during English, because in math I didn't have to go to the board, since Ms. Saltonstall knew I hated it. The girls in my class noticed this and began to believe that I was special too. Whatever I didn't know then, I felt some sort of special force working in my favor—to the exclusion of all the other boys in my class, and it made me a king.

My main group of friends—Wendy, Ronda, Cheryl, and Sally Ann—and I were always together. We would hang off the monkey bars and squeal, or see who could swing higher on the swing set. These girls liked to match whatever I did. If I jumped out of the swing, they'd try to jump farther.

Sometimes Wendy and Ronda went to Cheryl's house, or Cheryl and Wendy would go to Ronda's house, or Cheryl and Ronda went to Wendy's house, or they would all go to Sally Ann's, but I never went to any of their houses. They would invite me, but my grandmother wouldn't let me go. I invited them over once, but when my grandmother found the five of us in my room playing a game of Sorry! in our bathing suits, she called their mothers, who said they'd assumed my mother was home when they granted permission for the girls to join me for afternoon snacks. I taught the girls a new phrase, "Never assume. It makes an ass out of you and me," and we laughed about that until Wendy and Ronda and Cheryl and Sally Ann said they didn't want to play with me anymore.

On the last day of school there was a field trip to the Denver Observatory. Even though it was daytime, we were staring at stars through a giant telescope. "How can there be stars?" Wendy asked. None of us understood it, or heard an answer.

If I ever see Wendy or Ronda or Cheryl or Sally Ann—which seems doubtful now; they appear not real but as ghosts in my mind—I'll tell them what I know: that if you really look, you can see what others can't.

Most Likely To

My then-best-friend-now-ex-best-friend Jason handles it real cool. He was our high school's master thespian.

"How much each?" he negotiates with the one in the faded Michael Jackson *Thriller* T-shirt.

"Are you cops?" she asks, reaching inside the passenger window. She gives my soft crotch a squeeze.

"We're not cops," I say. I was against this at first, on principle, but Thriller's touch is warm and I can feel the wheels in motion. Suddenly I'm gung ho.

"I get thirty dollars," she says. That leaves me with the pregnant one, who turns out to be more expensive, fifty bucks.

Thriller tells us to circle the block, and we take out all our money, counting out what we need, putting the rest in the glove box. When we get them in our headlights again, the pregnant one is pointing toward the alley.

"Just stay relaxed," the master thespian says. "But keep your eyes open."

Jason's car reeks of his girlfriend's perfume, even though it's been more than an hour since we dropped Sara off, right after we dropped off Jane. Jason and I have sought out common ground with these hookers; it's where we left off, what we used to do when we were both transfer students at Randolph Prep, outsiders in an exclusive club. Bumping into Jason in the cereal aisle at an Albertsons, it was like yesterday we threw that cup of warm piss on that guy riding his bike home late, or the time we climbed in the fountain at City Hall, stripping and shitting until we had good-size pieces we could pitch. "Hey, batter, batter. He can't hit, he can't hit, he can't hit, *swing* batter."

Sure, I felt the old stuff, too. Our jealous rivalry, kept alive in high school more by him than by me, a rivalry that faded the summer of our junior year, when I was selected for a prestigious summer fellowship and he wasn't. The way he produced Sara as evidence that he had the perfect relationship. I introduced him to Jane too, and I could see in his eyes that he was anxious to size me up, see who's who.

Thriller and Preggers wave for us to pull in, dancing impatiently in the headlights.

"What should we do?" I ask.

Jason is watching the two hookers, studying them. In situations like these, his mind is a steel trap. "I'm going to give them a scare."

He flips the headlights out. Thriller and Preggers disappear into the dark and Jason rolls down his window, yelling "Fucking whores" as he pushes the accelerator to the floor, plunging toward the streetlight at the end of the alley.

Jason knows about what happened to me, and I appreciate the way he treats me like it was just yesterday we were two transfer students at Randolph, him from New York and me from nowhere. It's a good friend who will overlook what other people think about you.

Aztecka

Jason's bar, Aztecka, is packed, the strobes lighting the massive movement of people on the dance floor. I cross Camelback Road and walk up to the door. An ultra-yuppie couple appears, their noses turned up at the industrialites crowding the dance floor, desecrating their mahogany and green plush carpet. "All I wanted was a kiwi margarita," the woman says.

It isn't really Jason's bar. He's the manager, and since I've been back, I've been helping him out on the busy nights.

I've always thought the best part of working in a bar, obviously enough, would be meeting women.

The worst part is seeing what people do to each other. A bar is the perfect environment to do real harm to someone you don't really know.

Miles, the relief bartender, hands me an apron and we face the throng at the bar, two deep. It still takes me a minute to orient myself, but once I do, I feel like I never left La Onda, the bar I tended in Boca Raton, where I went to escape memories of Jenny and ended up finding Karine.

I'm making four or five drinks at once while having two or three more orders shouted at me, and suddenly I hear a *whack* and then it seems like everyone freezes and I see this guy and this girl and the girl is holding the side of her face and she's begging him not to leave her there and that's when I notice another girl waiting off to the side, impatiently, and the first girl is in tears, blubbering. I hear the guy say, "If *you* won't do it, *she* will." I look over at the girl to see if she really will, and our gazes lock and I can't make myself look away. The first girl's pleading becomes pathetic and she starts convulsing; her voice crescendoes and everyone is listening but the guy doesn't realize it and he smacks her across the face again. I start in the direction of the guy and he faces me, scowling. The showdown. I reach under the bar, go for an invisible bat, and he sees this and grabs the girl-in-waiting and cuts through the crowd to the door.

There's a hum and then the bar is at 140 decibels, the noise swallowing the girlfriend who is left standing in the corner, holding her face. People are screaming for their drinks, but I ignore them and call out to the girl. I wave a drunk guy off his stool and motion for her to sit.

"Are you okay?" I ask.

Clearly embarrassed, she just nods.

"What was that all about?" I ask.

"Can I have a drink?" she asks.

"Sure. What do you want?"

"Just water."

I hand her a glass of water and she takes a sip and sets it back down on the bar.

"Want to talk about it?" I ask, feeling like I can really help her, but she just shakes her head and asks me to call her a cab.

When the cab arrives, I search the bar for her, and just as I'm about to shrug at the cabdriver waiting in the doorway, the girl emerges from the bathroom. I wave, trying to get her attention, but she isn't looking at me. Instead she turns away and heads to the pool room in back. I signal the cabdriver to stay where he is, and go after her.

I find the girl leaning against one of the pool tables, and when I walk up to her, she gets a strange look on her face like she wonders who I am. Her boyfriend is back and he comes up to me. "What do you want?" he asks, sneering.

"Your cab is here," I say to the girl.

"I don't need it," she says, turning away.

"The driver's waiting out front," I tell her, trying to persuade her to go home, where she'll be safe.

"Look, I already said I didn't want it. Are you deaf?" She scowls at me, and now her boyfriend moves in closer and I consider throwing him out, but I begin to feel a shift in loyalties on the girl's part and I turn and start to walk away. A hand grabs my arm and I whirl around, ready to deck the asshole, but it's the girl and she asks me: "Do you know where we can score some smack?"

I'm still hearing the girl's question when I'm back behind the bar, not so much the words, but how she asked it. Sometimes you can mistake unhappiness for despair.

Jane gets me into helping people and it turns out I'm a natural.
The first deal didn't turn out so well: I guess I'm not great with
children.

I had been volunteering with Jane at the crisis nursery for
only about a week when I hurt someone (it was an accident). I was
playing along fine with the kids, running around and screaming, in
and out of the miniature wood house, an old set piece from some
play, donated by a local theater company. I had chased some kids
into the house, ducking into the tiny front room, where the kids
were pressed one on top of the other in the corner. I pretended like
I was going to really get them, and this little Mexican kid started
kicking me in the leg. I yelled at him to stop, which made the kids
laugh, and this little Mexican kid kept doing it until I put my hand
on his head and pushed him back against the wall.

Of course there was a big stink about who did what. The little
Mexican kid accused me of hitting him. I said the little Mexican
kid fell. I said I was sorry about it. I said I felt bad. I think they
believed me, but I didn't get to help out at the nursery anymore.

I told Jane this story (minus what I did to the Mexican kid), and
she suggested I volunteer for the March of Dimes Bowl-A-Rama,
which turned out to be a right-on suggestion.

"Thanks for coming," Katherine said.

"Glad to help out," I said grandly.

"We've got several volunteers for today," Katherine said. "If you like it, maybe you'll think about staying on."

"Sure," I said. "We'll see."

I was assigned to a girl named Janice. Janice couldn't talk very well and walked like she might pitch forward or backward, depending on how you looked at her. And she couldn't stop smiling.

Janice seemed to like me right away, and I helped her with her bowling. The March of Dimes had these special ramps set up in front of the lanes that looked like slides at the water park.

"Like this," I said, showing Janice how to put her fingers in the holes and lift the ball up onto the ramp. Janice watched the ball roll down, picking up speed, until it thumped in the lane and slowly rolled toward the pins.

Janice clapped wildly as the ball veered into the gutter, grounding past the upright pins.

"You try it," I suggested, and she said something unintelligible.

She lifted the ball with both hands and loaded it onto the ramp. "Like this," she said.

"Good job, Janice," I said. Her ball guttered, and we both stood wondering what to do next.

"Watch," I said, pushing the ramp to the side. I took up a ball and let it fly down the lane.

"Wheeeeee!" Janice screamed. Everyone looked over, and I thought for a minute I might get into trouble, but the sound of the pins crashing into one another brought cheers and applause from the others, and I just smiled blankly at everyone.

"Are you my brother?" Janice asked.

"What's that?" I asked.

"You're my brother," she said.

I didn't know what to do, and Janice started pawing at me in a surprisingly lewd manner. I stepped back and Katherine rushed up.

"Sorry," Katherine said. "She thinks all men are her brother."

"Oh," I said.

Janice ignored us and picked up another bowling ball, peering into it as if it were a mirror.

"Where is her brother?" I asked hesitantly.

"He's in jail," Katherine said.

"Really?"

"He molested her."

I nodded my head like I understood, because I didn't really know what else to do. The information didn't mean anything to me—I had just met Janice and I didn't know her brother and I was pretty sure her brother's molesting her hadn't made Janice handicapped. Mostly I felt like I couldn't really do anything for Janice even though I knew this about her.

I was sulking about what a crappy person I probably was when Katherine said, "She thinks all men are her brother, so she thinks it's okay for all men to do to her what her brother did."

Janice began dropping balls right onto the lane, one after another, clapping madly at their dull thumps.

Katherine lunged to stop her.

I thought about men taking advantage of Janice.

I wondered if *I* would.

I wondered if I knew anyone who would.

I could picture several.

Essay #2: I Touch Clouds

All the boys in high school thought my neighbor Talie was pretty, and they all tried to get dates with her. She wasn't as pretty as some of the cheerleaders, but those girls only had what you saw. With Talie, boys knew she felt things most girls didn't, and they wanted to feel them too.

Talie had natural grace. When I wanted to learn how to dance for the Christmas formal, Talie volunteered to help. We would practice in her foster parents' living room, the coffee table standing awkwardly on its end, pushed in the corner to make more space. We pretended we were at a grand ball, hooking up arm in arm in the kitchen doorway, entering the room stride for stride and turning to each other. I bowed and she curtsied.

"Not too fast," Mrs. Chandler, her foster mother, would say, marking the time by slapping her hand against her leg.

Talie moved majestically and I tried to follow, becoming lost in the way she looked directly into my eyes before she dipped me. My head went right for the floor until I thought I would bring us both down, but her arm would catch, saving me, bringing me back up, making me look graceful too. Talie would spin me out, away from her, and I would rotate like a satellite, pulled back in by her gravity.

**

"Not too fast," Talie said. "You're hurting me."

I eased up.

"Don't stop," she said. "Just don't go so fast."

I remember the pain and fear I would feel when I would come while masturbating, but with Talie, things felt different. Her breath was warm and touching her was like running your fingers along clouds.

"Doesn't it feel good?" she would ask.

"I'm going to come," I said, warning her.

"Shit," she said, stopping suddenly. "I don't want to get pregnant."

Talie climbed off and lay on her side, facing me. I felt her fingers on me, moving back and forth, and I did the same for her. We came out of sync, me first, then her. She cupped her hand to keep me from making a mess on the sheets. I watched her lean over the sink in the bathroom as she scrubbed her hands.

Most of the time she would just come over and ask me to. We wouldn't kiss on the mouth or anything corny like that. She would just say she wanted to, and I don't think there was ever a time when I didn't want to. I'd just ask if the coast was clear, and she would nod and lock the door.

"You're learning," Mrs. Chandler said.

It didn't matter that no one at the formal would dance.

I was glad.

I didn't want to show anyone what Talie had shown me.

From the Deep End

Jason wants to come in and say hi, but I tell him it's better if he drops me at the front gate. "I haven't seen JSB in forever," he says.

"Maybe next time," I say, and he gets it.

I wait until Jason is out of sight to punch in my gate code. I'm surprised that it still works and the heavy metal gate rolls back on its track, retracting behind the concrete walls of Arrowhead Ranch.

The red Land Cruiser that JSB is going to loan me is parked in the far corner of the driveway. If I could jump into the Land Cruiser and drive away, I would.

Heading up the back walkway, I kick through an overgrown row of birds of paradise, their orangish flowers drooping and rotting. The upright arm of the giant saguaro outside the back kitchen window has rotted too, and it rests elbow-out at the top of the walkway. Weeds sprout up through the graveled cactus beds underneath the picture windows.

I knock on the back door. Through the kitchen window I see a pizza box next to an empty plastic pitcher of iced tea on the cutting block in the middle of the kitchen. I consider going around to the front, to where the bell is, but knock again, harder, until JSB shuffles into the kitchen, sees me, and smiles.

He opens the door with considerable effort, and a stiff foulness rises to my nose when he opens his arms, a smile somewhere deep within him barely visible on his face.

"When?" he asks.

"While you were in Canada," I say apologetically.

JSB nods. "Was there any trouble there?" he asks.

I shake my head no. "They were fine," I say.

"I told them to call me if there was—"

"There wasn't," I say.

We sit at the rattan kitchen table, and JSB reaches for an invisible glass, looks back toward the refrigerator and then at me, leaning comfortably in his chair.

"Did Talie tell you?" he asks.

"That you fired your landscapers?" I ask, smiling.

JSB glances out the window and snorts. "Buckley Cosmetics is going to file for bankruptcy," he tells me.

I lean back in my chair, stunned. I know so little about the world that I didn't know it was possible for a company to file for bankruptcy twice in its corporate life. The trauma of the previous bankruptcy, when I first came to work for JSB and Buckley, was easily summoned.

"We're so far in the red we need the protection," he says matter-of-factly. "We were hoping the new line of cosmetics would save us, but the development has been delayed by at least six months and the banks won't cooperate anymore."

"Can't you take a personal loan?" I ask. I can't remember when I'd last offered advice to anyone. For the first time in a long time I feel like I am really helping someone.

"My credit lines are overextended," he says, shrugging.

I'm turning it over, trying to come up with the solution, when there's laughter on the walkway. I look out the window, but JSB sits still in his chair, not turning when the door opens and a woman—a girl, really—who looks like Victoria, JSB's girlfriend when I left for Boca Raton, blond and honey-kissed, but who is not Victoria, saunters in with an embarrassed dark-haired kid no more than eighteen in tow. "Hi," she says, kissing JSB lightly on his graying hair.

JSB smiles and fingers the pepper shaker on the table.

"We want to use the pool," the girl says. "Is that all right?"

"Sure," JSB says. "Help yourself."

The two disappear as quickly as they arrived, and JSB gets up, motioning for me to follow.

"Thanks for loaning me the vehicle," I say.

We're in front of the smoked-glass picture window overlooking the pool. JSB drags over a couple of chairs and we sit.

"What's her name?" I ask.

"Erin," JSB answers.

"How long have you been seeing her?"

"Six months," he says, sighing.

If a woman in JSB's life lasts six months, it's like ten years in a regular relationship. The six-month anniversary at Arrowhead Ranch usually calls for a locksmith and a reprogramming of the front gate.

"Where is Talie?" I ask, looking toward the end of the house, in the direction of her bedroom.

"I haven't seen her," JSB says, not taking his eyes off the pool, where Erin and Erin's friend are pushing a volleyball back and forth across the water's surface. "I've been thinking of making Erin . . . permanent."

"Really?" I'm as surprised as I was when JSB called from Atlanta when I was seventeen, freshly emancipated, working for JSB as a corporate runner for Buckley Cosmetics—a job Talie helped me get—and told me he was engaged to his high school sweetheart, whom he'd met up with again. By the time his plane landed in Phoenix a week later, there was no mention of the high school sweetheart, and the whole episode remains an aberrant dream among the very real personalities of the women he's been with before and since.

"The secret is to let them think they're going to get a piece of everything," JSB used to tell me. "By the time they figure it out, you're ready for the next one." This advice resurfaced in my mind now and again because it was an unusually calculated thing to say, especially coming from a man who so passionately believed in romance. This advice was repeated with a frequency that suggested it was a joke, something he'd picked up from someone who'd said it, or half said it, or was making a joke too.

Erin and her friend are sitting on the steps in the shallow end, leaning back on their elbows. They collapse in laughter and Erin puts her head on the boy's chest. The boy buries his nose in Erin's wet hair and JSB puts his hand up to the glass window.

"I should probably go," I say, wondering where Talie is.

JSB awakens from his trance. "The keys are on the counter," he says. He pats my knee and smiles.

I nod and he turns his gaze back toward the pool, not able to look away from what shines in front of him.

Essay #3: An Ideal Day Sometime in the Near Future

This is an ideal day sometime in the near future:

I meet someone who can appreciate me for what I can offer and we spend a lot of time together. But we don't get trapped by love. We just like being together and we realize that it isn't forever, that eventually we'll move on, but that we'll always remember what we had with each other.

And after that relationship is over, I meet someone else who can appreciate me for what I can offer, etc.

Tuesdays, Jane volunteers at the crisis nursery, and Tuesdays put Jane in a good mood. We both always look forward to Tuesday nights, and this Tuesday night seems especially good because afterward, our backs against the crumpled sheets, we solidify the Utopian Love Code:

"If a man makes promises to a woman and does not keep his promises, another man shall fulfill the obligation," I start. "If a man has stolen another man's woman, and if that woman was unhappy, that woman shall remain with the man; however, if the woman is said to have been happy, she shall be returned to the man from whom she was stolen."

This makes Jane giggle and she adds: "If a man has put a spell upon a woman, and has not justified himself, the man shall plunge into the holy river, and if the holy river overcomes him, his intentions are bad; but if the holy river bears him out and shows him innocent, his intentions are good and he may proceed with his sorcery."

"If a fire breaks out in a woman's heart and a man extinguishes the fire, he shall be set fire himself."

"If a man has married a wife and has not made her feelings and her property part of a whole, she is no wife."

"If a woman's reputation is besmirched by another male without just cause, he shall throw himself into the holy river for the sake of the purity of Utopia."

Jane props herself up on her elbow and adds: "A woman's feelings cannot be hurt, taken for granted, abused, or ridiculed."

I frown at this and tell her that the rule about besmirched reputations covers this, and she just stares at me and then rolls away, and I guess we've pretty much covered the basic tenets, but I review them silently for oversights.

Their days always appear to me this way:

Jenny saunters through the house, opening the curtains, everything in full view. As always, she boils water in the microwave for her morning oatmeal—maple and brown sugar. Gray light pours in as she sits at the table in a white terry-cloth robe, a purple satin nightgown peeking out. After she tilts the bowl and scrapes it twice with her spoon, Jenny rinses it in the sink and walks back to her bedroom, which is on the far side of the house. When Jenny reappears, she is dressed for her job teaching first grade at the elementary school in town.

And when school lets out, Jenny drives home, stopping by the market, browsing through the aisles, wandering back and forth across the store, then, realizing the time, she hurriedly fills a basket.

Ben pulls up as Jenny is unloading the groceries, and he kisses her on the cheek before lifting a paper bag from the station wagon, slipping on the shoveled driveway, catching himself as the bag hits the ground. He picks it up again, pretending nothing has happened.

My stomach turns when I think of Ben—weak, not a challenger, not a contender, kept in only by her will—who is unable to understand Jenny the way I did.

She loves me. She loves me not. She loves me. She loves me not. She loves me but doesn't know that I still love her, more than anyone in the world, and I see the light in the living room go out, the house dark for a moment, Jenny sitting on the edge of the bed, Jenny smiling when Ben walks in and closes their bedroom door and kisses her on the forehead before he draws the blinds.

I imagine me at their wedding (even though I wasn't invited): The redbrick church appears to be receding into the pale summer sky, purely an optical illusion brought on by the sun and the whiskey sours I drank earlier, and I wonder if anyone in the church can see me, down the street, hidden behind the drooping oleanders.

I unbutton the vest of my suit and check my hair in the mirror on the visor. The last invited guest arrived ten minutes ago, and I am debating how I will make my entrance: before or after the ceremony? I can imagine the look on Jenny's face, everyone staring at me, bewildered. I fondle the dozen red roses I've been keeping cool in my refrigerator. The street is empty and I stare hard at a lone palm tree swaying back and forth, obscuring part of the church steeple, fanning the heat back toward the shimmering yellow sun.

The doors of the church swing wide and Jenny's uncle appears, walking hurriedly to his van, not fifty feet from where I am. The van door groans deeply, echoing in my head, and he lifts out his camera bag. I slide down in my seat, and as Jenny's uncle slams the van door, he recognizes my car. A sweat breaks out on my forehead while he stares, trying to see past the window tint, and he takes a step toward me. I reach down for the gear shift, my hand quivering, and slowly press in the clutch. He sets his camera bag on the neatly manicured lawn, looks both ways, and crosses the street toward me, shaking his head. I feel my body convulse as I pop the car in gear, lurching forward, spilling the roses around my feet, barreling down the street, crying.

**

Junior year, when my focus should've been on my new classmates at Randolph Prep, I met and fell in love with Jenny, a freshman saxophone player at a public school on the west side of Phoenix. Mr. Chandler had given me a saxophone abandoned by one of his foster kids, suggesting that I join band at Randolph as a means of making friends quickly. I knew firsthand that transfer students were easily made pariahs and followed his advice; Jason knew too, which is why he signed up for theater the first day of classes.

The randomness of Jenny and me sitting together on the bus ferrying selected students to the statewide marching competition was not random at all: The months of Saturday practices on the empty fields of Scottsdale Community College had provided hours of close infantry training. The trip to Northern Arizona University in Flagstaff, the competition venue, was merely the culmination. Jenny and I sat together on the two-hour trip, flirting. As we neared Flagstaff, I nervously popped my saxophone reed into my mouth, claiming to have to moisten it before the competition. "Try to bite it," I said playfully, sticking the small reed out like a tiny wooden tongue. I pulled back as Jenny shyly inched forward and snapped at the reed like a guppy. "Try again," I said. This time I didn't pull back, watching as she zoomed toward me, her green eyes sparkling. She bit the reed and held it, finally releasing it. "Again," I said softly, this time dropping the reed in my lap as she leaned in, kissing her, the spark of our long-suffering flirting a danger to the pine trees that whisked past us as the bus entered the Flagstaff city limits.

"She's a Mormon, dude," someone said when I confirmed my interest.

I shrugged, unsure of what that meant.

From that time forward, Jenny and I were inseparable. I quickly assimilated into her circle of friends, who were exclusively Mormon.

The Mormon kids at her school were not a small population and were generally good students and well liked, and I found their approval and acceptance easier than that of the rich kids at Randolph. Jenny's family was a first-generation conversion (someone her father worked with had convinced them to convert), and when, upon meeting me, her mother asked her in front of me if I was LDS, I had no idea what that meant. Jenny answered that I wasn't and I let the matter drop, my happiness at being with Jenny blocking out the white noise around me. Her parents wouldn't allow us to officially date until Jenny turned sixteen, so our courtship took place entirely at her house after school. The matter of where I lived never arose, and it was some time before it surfaced that my birth parents were dead and that I'd been shunted from distant relative to distant relative before landing in Phoenix at the home of my first cousin twice removed. That I attended an all-boys Catholic school didn't seem to register with them, and I hid from them the fact that I'd recently been legally emancipated.

Still, the ease and speed with which our relationship grew serious might've been alarming to Jenny's parents, but their recent separation consumed them, and Jenny and I were essentially left alone, free to wander her family's property, an unworked farm outside of Phoenix, a parcel among parcels in what was primarily farmland. We rode the family three-wheeler back and forth to visit her cousin, who lived on an adjoining parcel; sometimes we took her horse, who spooked me. Usually we watched television or listened to music while we shot pool in her living room, her pool skills far superior to mine. I was always aware that her mother was lurking around the house, though, maybe looking out a window, or listening for the quiet that portends making out. Her home was a sanctuary that offered us a place out of time in which to get to know each other. That she had never seen my house (her mother forbade her) or that we didn't hang out with my friends (a small population, but still) was not a concern. We did manage outside dates of a sort: Every so often a couple of Mormon stakes (each church or ward was part of a stake; Jenny belonged to the Tolsun ward, which in turn belonged to the West Maricopa stake) got together and hosted a dance.

Anyone could participate in the dances, regardless of religion; however, before attending your first dance, you had to acquire a dance card from the local bishop. I made the requisite appointment. The bishop, an older man with prematurely skeletal features, welcomed me and asked me into his spartan office. We exchanged a few pleasantries—I told him about how Jenny was my girlfriend and ran down the roster of my friends who attended the Tolsun ward—and then settled into business. The bishop handed me a small yellow piece of paper, the dance card I'd come for, invalid without the bishop's signature, which he was happy to sign after I read and consented to the rules on the back of the card:

1. Ages 14–18
2. Valid dance card must be presented at the door for admission. (We will accept valid dance cards from other stakes.) Replacement charge for lost card is $5.00.
3. The Word of Wisdom to be observed: No tobacco, alcohol, or drugs are permitted inside the building or on the premises.
4. BOYS shall wear dress pants (no Levi's, jeans, denims, or imitations of any color, or other non–dress pants). Shirts must have collars. No sandals are allowed. (Nice tennis shoes are OK.) Socks must be worn with shoes. No hats, earrings, or gloves.
5. GIRLS shall not wear tight-fitting dresses or skirts or have bare shoulders (blouses and dresses must have sleeves). Hemlines of dresses are to be of modest length (to the knee). No dresses or skirts with slits or cuts above the knee.

6. After admittance to the dance, you are to remain inside the building.

7. No loitering or sitting in cars on church grounds.

8. Automobiles shall be driven in a quiet and courteous manner, so as not to disturb the residents in the area.

9. No acrobatics, bear-hugging, bumping, rolling on floor, or exhibitions.

10. Personal conduct and behavior shall be that expected from exemplary young ladies and gentlemen.

"Can you agree to these rules?" the bishop asked.

I said that I could.

"Very good," he said, taking the slip of paper from me and laboriously signing his name to it. "Have you considered joining our church?" he asked as he handed my dance card back.

I hadn't. "I might," I said, knowing that was the answer he wanted to hear. He regarded me cautiously.

"You might attend with Jenny and her family," the bishop said. I wondered if he knew about Jenny's parents' marital status, guessing that he didn't. The topic was never broached in Jenny's house, or in her cousin's house, everyone pretending like the fact that Jenny's mother and father were still married but not living in the same house was as natural as their counterparts living together.

The next question caught me off guard. "Have you and Jenny been intimate?"

I couldn't tell if the bishop was joking or not, so I laughed, suppressing a sickening feeling that was building in my stomach. I answered no automatically, not just because it was the truth but because I hoped the answer would stifle the look of surprise on my face.

"Have you been tempted?" he asked.

I fumbled through a series of "ums" and "wells," stuttering until I gave up and smiled.

"It's okay," the bishop said. "We're all tempted. Moral character is defined by how we react to temptation. I hope you'll continue to consider your moral character in the face of temptation. And Jenny's, too."

I assured him I would, and we both stood, shaking hands. I excused myself and wandered through the empty church halls, treading on the brown carpet past the chapel, stocked with plain wooden pews. I couldn't imagine then that the room would be the venue for one of my most dramatic and regrettable performances.

Wednesday

I know Jane can't leave me. She knows I'm irreplaceable, and I'm glad because frankly I don't want to replace her. We have got a good thing and not everyone can keep a perfect balance like we do.

"Are you coming with me or not?" Jane demands.

"Why does it matter where you live?" I ask. "I don't want to live in California."

"Well, I do," she says.

"Why can't we just keep doing what we're doing here?"

"I'm tired of being here."

Then I say: "Look, I want you to stay."

Jane starts to melt and I feel a little guilty for employing such tactics, but the truth is I *do* want her to stay. But I also know it's only because I want to sustain what we have and that someday our relationship will inevitably ebb and float away.

"I can't imagine staying here." Her voice softens.

"What you imagine happening somewhere else is exactly what will happen here," I say.

"What does that mean?"

"It means that if you're going to run, make sure you're running *to*, and not *away*."

"I'm not running *away* from anything," she shoots back.

"What are you running *to*, then?" I ask.

"I'm not running, *period.*" Her voice grows louder. "I'm simply just *tired* of here." The emphasis on "tired" insinuates that she is tired of me, too, but I pretend that I'm oblivious and I just sit there and smirk.

"Why do you have to be so confrontational all the time?" I ask, knowing what this will do to her.

"Me? You're the one that's confrontational."

"And defensive, too. You're always defensive about something." I am pouring gas over the fire.

"You are probably the most impossibly"—she angrily spits the words out at me—"most fucking impossibly . . . *stupid* fuck—"

"Stupid? Is that the best you can do?"

Jane lunges for me, at first in anger, but soon we are both on the floor of my living room, laughing so hard we have to hold ourselves.

"You really are stupid," Jane says, still laughing. "You know that, right?"

"Yeah, I know. So are you." I kiss Jane on the forehead. We lie there silent for a minute, and then I tell her, "I hope you stay." It comes out sounding like an apology, and in a lot of ways, it is.

Journal #2

When I was first shipped to Phoenix, we took a car trip to a cabin my first cousin twice removed owned up on the northern rim of the Grand Canyon. As we ascended out of the valley, I remember worshipping the beautiful red rock formations and the cacti and the vast sky that opened up in front of me. But I also remember feeling afraid. I stared at a cactus in the distance and thought, *I could get hurt out there.* I stared at an endless brown field, every acre a carbon copy of the rest, and thought, *Everything here is dead.*

We stopped in Sedona for lunch. I went into the gift store of the restaurant to look around while my first cousin twice removed finished eating.

"Don't dawdle," my guardian warned. I was careful not to linger looking at any one thing for too long. I wanted a magazine for the ride back. The gift shop didn't seem to have any. I really wasn't surprised when I returned to our table and my guardian was gone.

Without panicking, I walked out to the parking lot to confirm that I'd been left behind. I headed back toward Phoenix on foot, looking over my shoulder now and then to see if any of the approaching cars were being driven by my first cousin twice removed. None were.

Less than a mile out of Sedona a white pickup truck pulled over.

"Where you going?" the guy—a rancher—asked, vaguely concerned.

"Phoenix."

"This is your lucky day," he told me.

I hopped in the truck, which smelled of dust and sweat and dogs, and we raced down the highway. The rancher asked me typical hitchhiker questions, and I made up a story about how I was seeing America via my thumb. The rancher liked this story, as much as he didn't believe it, and launched into one of his own about how the youth of America weren't as patriotic as they were in his day and how more people should get a feel for the land, to cultivate an appreciation for what nourishes and sustains them, and I nodded my head all the way back to Phoenix, thinking, *Christ, what a bummer.*

Essay #4: Amends

Dr. Hatch wanted me to call all the people I'd hurt and ask them for forgiveness. It was part of the program, Hatch said, like the essays and the journal and the writing exercises. Child molesters called their sons and daughters, adulterous husbands called their wives and said sorry. Didn't I want to call Karine? I couldn't make Hatch understand: I didn't hurt anyone.

Here's what happened: I met Karine one night at La Onda, the bar where I worked in Boca Raton, my attempt to put Jenny behind me for good. Karine hung around the bar most of that night, talking to me while I poured drinks. At first I thought she was merely friendly, or lonely. As the night wore on, I could tell that Karine was hanging around waiting for me.

"My shift's about over," I said to her. "You want to get out of here?"

"What do you have in mind?" she asked.

I cleaned empty glasses and wiped the bar in front of her.

"Nothing in particular," I answered. I told Karine she could come upstairs to the apartment that came with the job and wait while I changed. She said sure, she could do that.

After showering, I came out into the front room and Karine was sitting on my couch, looking around.

"I hate to wait," was all Karine said, but it was the way she said it that let me know she didn't actually want to go anywhere, that what Karine really wanted was for me to give her one good time in the vacuum of the dreariness of her life.

A surge of power came over me and I sat next to Karine on the couch. She seemed even sadder when I got up close to her, but instead of feeling sorry for her, I reached out and stroked her arm. She flinched but didn't make a move to resist, so I leaned over and kissed her hard on the lips. I could taste alcohol on her tongue, but I didn't gag, and she put her hand on the back of my neck and forced her vodka-soaked tongue all the way into my mouth.

We sat like that for a while, until I moved to untuck her shirt. Karine helped me by wriggling a little and I lifted it off over her head. Soon we were both naked and on the floor. I crawled on top and started kissing her madly, really getting into it, until she pushed me away.

"Do you want to stop?" I asked.

She just looked at me.

"We'll stop if you want to," I told her, but she didn't say a word and I put my hand back down between her legs and she started moaning again.

Just when we started to get back to where we were, I could feel Karine hesitate once more. As much as I wanted to give her what she needed, I couldn't spend a lifetime doing it, so I quickly moved inside her. Her whole body tensed up. I was gentle. She tried to fight it, but I felt she wanted me to take control, to convince her of what she wanted. When we were through, she was in a hurry to leave and I didn't get a chance to hold her. I guessed she didn't need that part of it.

We Finish Nice Guys

The first thing Dale wants to know is what it's like in rehab.

"Is it like in the movies?"

"Worse."

Dale and I are waiting for the bartender to notice us at the crowded bar. The restaurant side is pretty empty, and we could easily get a table and have our drinks delivered, but the thought of being chained to a table for an entire meal with Dale is too intimidating, especially without Talie as point man for topics of discussion and interesting interjections.

Dale is satisfied with my answer and doesn't need to hear any details, which surprises me. Talie's letters to me at SRC were full of details about this "great guy" she met through a friend of hers, and since most of the guys I knew at that time weren't "great" in *any* sense of the word, I secretly began to look up to Dale, or at least the ongoing composite of him drawn from Talie's letters.

It surprised me how much something so little could mean. Somehow it pleased me to know Dale drove a blue Volvo, that Dale had his clothes dry-cleaned, that Dale took Talie out faithfully every Saturday night. Dale is in real estate in a way that's too complicated for me or Talie or anyone we know to really understand. I imagine

Dale in dark oak rooms with dim light, convincing people to buy, or sell, or to buy more, to lend him their lives.

I didn't expect Dale to be a pretty boy when I finally did meet him, when the two of them picked me up from SRC. Obviously, Talie had told Dale about me; he seemed "ready" to meet me. I could tell he was putting the nice on a little when he shook my hand. That would have been okay—I almost expected it—but I recognized Dale right away as one of those ironic guys, dangerous because they could draw you out with sympathy and mock interest, and then leave you flapping your arms uselessly in the air.

"What are the tricks to getting attention?" Dale asks.

"Wave money," I suggest.

Dale pup-tents a twenty and waves it at the bartender, who registers us with a side glance.

"Look at that," Dale says as we sit. He nods at a guy approaching two women at the bar. We watch like kids in front of a TV, waiting for the shuttle to lift off, anticipating the noise and smoke and breaking apart of intentions, of ideas. "God, I'm glad I don't have to work for it anymore," Dale says.

"Yeah," I agree, trying to figure out if that means Dale's glad he found Talie, or if it means something more sinister.

"I could never really get into it," Dale goes on, still staring. "I mean, I always felt like women knew what I was doing when I was on the make. How could they not?"

This question pretty much says it all.

"Did you say you have to go back?" I ask. It seems like a lame thing to ask, but I'm having real difficulty coming up with things to say.

"Uh, yeah," Dale says, sips his beer. We're both confused about this, him not remembering if he told me he had to go back to work or not, me not sure either, whatever.

There's a pause, followed by a critical comment of someone's appearance, followed by another drink, followed by a pause, and so on.

"Where did you say you had to go earlier?" I ask, remembering something he said on the phone.

"Oh," he says tiredly. "I had to meet this old cocksucker friend of mine from school at Propheteers. He's an investment banker from New York and was meeting a client there for dinner."

I quit lobbing questions altogether as Dale leans back in his chair, liquefying.

"I'm really in love with Talie," Dale says, nodding grandly, his head tomahawking through the fog of cigarette smoke.

"Yeah?"

Dale, swear to God, puts on his puppy dog face right there at the bar. "I can't believe I found someone like her," he says.

I'm thinking, *Please, Christ, don't start crying.*

"Well," I say.

"You've got to convince her to marry me," Dale says, reaching out and grabbing my arm. His vise grip causes an involuntary recoil and he lets go.

"Yeah, sure," I say. I look away from Dale and into the gaze of two women at the bar checking us out.

"You see those hooks looking at us?" Dale asks without moving.

"Yeah," I say. "I see them."

"I shouldn't call them hookers," Dale says, apologetic. "They're not as dignified as whores."

I notice: *Hey! Dale is drunk!*

"See, hookers were great." Dale leans in. "They knew what you wanted and you knew that they knew."

I wonder if Talie knows about this. "Didn't you worry about diseases?" I ask.

"I did get something, once," he says. "I gave it to my bitch girlfriend, too."

I was hoping I wasn't ever going to hear the man who was thinking about marrying Talie use that word.

"I mean, I didn't have *that* many," he says, guessing what I was thinking. "It just worked out."

He sits up and smirks, satisfied.

The women are no longer looking at us.

"I know a lot of women who aren't vultures," I say, making what I think is my point.

"Some women aren't," he agrees. "And not all men are assholes, either."

"True," I say.

"I mean, look at us: We're nice guys. We're the exception."

Here Dale realizes he's talking like a drunk and shakes himself, draining the alcohol from his mind.

"They're looking again," Dale says.

I smile, a little amused, both by the women and by Dale's delusion that he is a nice guy. The more I think about it, the funnier it gets.

Journal #3

That's me at the conference table with two FBI agents, the seat still warm from Teddy, who had finished his interview a few moments earlier, his last question to the agents, "Should I get a lawyer?" jangling my nerves.

The summer after my emancipation proved a watershed time. I'd enrolled in summer classes at Glendale Community College to gain a head start on those who had the advantages I never would, a plan that evaporated the moment I encountered Talie having lunch in the atrium of Scottsdale Fashion Square with an older man. My immediate thought was that Talie had found her birth grandfather, but Talie had never mentioned any sort of search for her birth family. Instead, Talie introduced her lunch companion as Jay Stanton Buckley, founder of Buckley Cosmetics.

I'd heard of Jay Stanton Buckley before his name became a regular fixture in the papers, though. Randolph College Prep boasted a Buckley Hall, the honor bestowed after Buckley donated a nice sum toward the construction of Randolph's library. JSB also regularly placed in the top ten of the Phoenix 40, an annual compilation of the forty wealthiest and most influential businessmen (whose sons invariably attended Randolph). Certain titillating rumors about JSB reached the populace via profiles in newspapers and local magazines: that he hopped between real estate holdings by helicopter; that he kept a private plane in a hangar at Sky Harbor International; that he hired only young, staggeringly beautiful secretaries, who were collectively known as Buckley's Angels.

I had all of this in mind when I arrived at Buckley Cosmetics for the interview Talie had arranged when I mentioned that I would never be truly emancipated without my own money.

Buckley's offices on Camelback Road consisted of two buildings—a two-story building that housed administration (top floor) and legal (bottom floor), and a single-story building that housed accounting. An impressively clean driveway separated the buildings, the asphalt tributary running around back to the employee parking lot, each space carefully stenciled with the initials of the space's owner. At the far end of the parking lot, a basketball hoop mingled with the fronds from a neighboring palm tree, which was undergoing pruning by the team of Tongan landscapers imported from the archipelago of South Pacific islands by JSB himself, all outfitted in turquoise polo shirts bearing the Buckley logo.

The receptionist invited me to wait in a nearby conference room, showing me to a couch in a room towering with boxes. Through the floor-to-ceiling drapes I could see men in suits sauntering through the hallways. The electronic buzz of the switchboard was nearly constant.

The conference room door clicked opened and a man in his early seventies appeared, closing the door behind him. "Hello," he said, introducing himself as Dr. Theodore F. Weber. "You can call me Teddy." Teddy asked me a few questions about myself, genuinely interested in the answers. Eager to talk about the job, I mentioned that Mr. Buckley had made a generous donation to my high school. "That's the kind of man he is," Teddy said enthusiastically. "If you come to work for us, you'll see that for yourself. The thing is this: We all work for Mr. Buckley. He's the captain of the team, and everything belongs to him: the bats, the balls, the playing field, everything. And we're his team." That was the closest we'd get to discussing the job. Instead, we diverged into the fact that Teddy had come to work for Mr. Buckley through his son-in-law, who worked at Buckley, after running a successful medical practice in Chicago. He'd moved with his wife to Scottsdale to be closer to his daughter and had magically been tapped by Mr. Buckley to head up the department of runners, the foot soldiers that were the backbone of Buckley Cosmetics.

"So when can you start?" Teddy asked.

I told him I could begin immediately.

We stood and shook hands, and like that I was Buckley Cosmetics' newest runner, a position I learned had an amorphous set of responsibilities. There were certain absolutes: The three supply rooms, one on each floor of both buildings, were to be inventoried and restocked daily; the out-of-state lawyers fighting JSB's various legal wars were to be shuttled to the airport on Friday afternoons and picked up again on Monday mornings; a catered lunch was to be provided daily on each floor, each entrée from a different restaurant (JSB's theory about this was that if he catered lunch, the lawyers were less likely to disappear for hours in the afternoon); the buildings were to be opened at 7 a.m. and closed at 7 p.m. I came to understand that the largest responsibility, by far, was to be ready to be called into action should the need arise: a last-minute run to FedEx; spinning one of the family's Mercedes through the local car wash; beating the clock at the courthouse clerk's office with a legal filing, etc.

My first day on the job, I was certain I'd made a serious error in judgment.

"We could lose our jobs any day," my fellow runner Trish said on my inaugural courthouse run. "We're all just waiting to get fired. A lot of people have already quit."

Trish's grim prediction spooked me. I'd hoped that I'd quickly rise through the ranks to more hours and more money. More importantly, to be identified with Buckley, a brand everyone knew, would go a long way toward obliterating my anonymous past. The possibility that the opposite would happen was a disaster, and I began to wonder what I'd do if it came to pass.

I envisioned myself a foot soldier under JSB's command.

And no job was too small.

When JSB needed someone to fetch a tie from his gleaming mansion, I volunteered, punching in the gate code, letting myself into the empty house. My worn loafers clicked against the Italian marble floor as I took in the spectacular view of Phoenix from the kitchen bay windows. I opened the refrigerator to peek at the groceries of the rich and famous, expecting the labels to be fancier, the foods richer, surprised by the inventory of everyday brands you could find in *anyone's* refrigerator. I traipsed through the tastefully decorated living room (furnished with the same style and color of furniture as the Buckley offices) into the master bedroom, a room as large as the front room. I stood before the bathroom mirror and ran my fingers through my hair, marveling at my infiltration of such a nice house. I thought about how my ghostly footprints would never be known by JSB or any of the fabulous people who most certainly came through JSB's front door, how once I stepped back out into the driveway, it would be like I'd never been here.

I finally saw Jay Stanton Buckley again the second time I paid a visit to his house, some two months after I started working at Buckley. JSB sometimes liked to walk the few miles between the office and home for exercise (shrugging off the concerns for his safety from the investors who wanted his blood, according to the papers), and so one of the runners would drive his Mercedes to his house at lunch, with a runner in a company vehicle following. As the last hire, I was never offered the lead position in this two-car caravan; but one day JSB walked home without notifying anyone, calling for his car after all of the other runners had gone home, save me and Trish. Trish had no interest in driving JSB's Mercedes (she was afraid she'd wreck it), and so I confidently took the keys from Teddy, barely hearing his warning to be careful.

I had, to that moment, driven every car in the Buckley fleet except JSB's Mercedes. Once every week or so, two runners would spend an entire day driving the company cars through the car wash that was a mile or so away, including the company's twin tan Cadillac limousines, which sat like sleeping tigers in the back of the employee parking lot. But I'd never been closer to JSB's Mercedes than walking by it on my way into the building (it was the lead position in the row of employee parking, closest to the door, and directly in sight of JSB's office window, so I rarely stopped to admire it). It was like no Mercedes I'd ever seen, and there was a rumor that it had been imported from Europe. The dark blue interior matched the custom paint job, and I had to adjust the driver's seat to account for the difference between JSB's 6'2" frame and my 5'11" reach. I carefully started the immaculate car, the dashboard and stereo lighting up as I surveyed the gauges and JSB's preset radio stations. After adjusting the rearview mirror (but not the side mirrors; I couldn't figure out how), I backed the car out of its spot and pulled into traffic, Trish behind me in the company van.

The drive up Camelback Road to JSB's house was a short one, but I savored every mile, the Mercedes floating along the streets, banking softly with the slightest turn of the steering wheel, as if the machine were reading my mind. I eased the car into JSB's driveway, punched in the gate code, and touched the accelerator to climb the sharp incline. My instructions were to leave the keys in the car, but I recognized my chance and strolled through the marble portico and knocked on the solid wood of the front door. Trish threw her hands in the air and shrugged, and I smiled back.

The heavy door swung open and JSB stood towering over me, beaming, his jacket and tie replaced with a polo shirt bearing the Buckley logo.

"I . . . I brought your car," I said, stammering, caught without anything to say.

"Great!" JSB said. "Do you want something to drink?" He stepped back to let me in.

"Who is it?" a voice asked. A smallish, impeccably groomed woman appeared from the kitchen. "Oh, hello."

"This is Charlie," JSB said. "He's a good guy." JSB slapped me on the back with a force that propelled me forward. That JSB knew my name was an unaccountable thrill.

"Very nice to meet you," the woman said.

"Here are the keys," I said dumbly.

The woman disappeared into the kitchen and JSB followed her, reappearing with two cans of soda. "For the road," he said. I took the cans, wanting instead to be invited for dinner, to eat from expensive china and hear conversations littered with references to JSB's friends: Ivan Boesky, the Wall Streeter who was eventually busted for insider trading; Michael Milken, the genius junk bond financier at Drexel Burnham whom the government charged with securities violations (my economics teacher at Randolph, a former broker at Drexel, first introduced me to the idea of junk bonds, and to the name Michael Milken; he began every class by pulling a bottle of Pepto-Bismol from his leather briefcase and chugging a healthy swig); or Sir James Goldsmith, the billionaire merchant banker.

I relished the idea of annotating this fantasy dinner conversation with what little I knew about anything, indicating gently that I was willing to learn, wanted to be an apprentice.

My new ranking among the runners was quickly apparent when Teddy approached me about a mission JSB wanted carried out. The noose was tightening around Buckley Cosmetics, it seemed, and JSB was making plans for life post-Buckley, having rented office space up the road for a real estate consulting firm. Few knew that JSB had handpicked a group of executives to move with him to this new business, and he wanted to furnish the new offices with furniture from the Buckley offices. So as not to alarm those employees who were not in the know, the furniture would be moved before and after working hours, JSB and others placing a small orange sticker on items that were to be moved up to the new offices.

Secrecy was an essential element of the transition, and Teddy deputized me and Lance, another runner, for this very important responsibility. At first, Lance and I moved effortlessly, making a run in the morning and one in the afternoon; the offices up the road filled quickly with expensive furniture. We moved silent as cat burglars until a marble credenza we could barely lift wouldn't fit in the elevator.

"Should we even be doing this?" Lance asked me, exasperated. Lance had, from the outset, agreed to the mission simply because he wanted the overtime.

"I'm sure it's fine," I replied, unsure if it was or not.

"Then why do we have to sneak around like this?"

I smelled revolt and did my best to quell it. "Teddy wouldn't involve us in anything underhanded," I said, a truth Lance couldn't deny.

Lance waited with the credenza, which we parked in the atrium of the small office building, the other occupants glancing at it curiously as they filed in for another day at the office, while I called

Teddy to apprise him of the situation. The twenty or so tenants seemed to know that Jay Stanton Buckley was moving into their building, and they watched from their windowed offices as Lance and I brought expensive piece after expensive piece through the front door, up the elevator, and down the hall to the newly rented corner offices.

Teddy's instructions about the credenza did not make Lance happy.

"This is ridiculous," Lance said as I relayed Teddy's directive to take the credenza to the unused stables on JSB's property.

The code for the back gate was the same as the code for the front, and we committed the combination to memory as we punched it in time and time again, the gates opening slowly as we ferried the overflow of furniture to the stables. Three or four runs in, Lance asked to be relieved of his overtime duties, and Teddy took his place without comment, gabbing with the Tongans who landscaped JSB's property while we unloaded our take in the crisp fall morning air. I hoped JSB would remember my stamina when he made the move from Buckley to his new offices.

My interest was more than simple employment: If I could catch JSB on his next upswing, a new life could be made, I guessed.

The government had caught wind of JSB's intention to flee, and upon my early arrival one morning I was met with the unhappy news that the FBI wanted to talk to me and Lance and Teddy. In fact, Teddy was already being interviewed in the conference room in legal. I sprinted across the compound to find out what was going on, a wild look in my eyes, bumping into William, a Southern lawyer who worked for JSB.

"What is it?" he asked.

I explained to him what was happening and he called me into his office and shut the door.

"What's the truth about the furniture?" he asked, sitting behind his desk.

I told him the whole story, about Buckley's new offices, about the moving expeditions before and after work, about the stash of furniture in JSB's stables. A horrified look clouded William's face. In the short time that I'd known him, I'd come to know that he was an aboveboard guy who did not tolerate dishonesty.

"My advice is to tell them the whole thing," he said. "It's a felony to remove property from a bankruptcy estate." It was the first time I understood that Buckley Cosmetics had filed for bankruptcy, rather than having the impression that it was an option. William's words were not the legal comfort I was searching for. I wanted him to jump out from behind his desk, outraged, ready to defend me against the crush of a maniacal government run amok.

It occurred to me that I might be in real trouble and I cursed JSB for putting me in a vulnerable position.

The conference room door swung open and a red-faced Teddy charged out, asking over his shoulder, "Should I get a lawyer?" The two young, fresh-faced FBI agents answered that that was up to him. Teddy spotted me coming out of William's office. "The boys had nothing to do with it," Teddy added.

"Thank you for your time," one of the agents said, motioning for me to take a seat at the conference table.

The legal conference room was a naturally dark room, its eastern exposure partially blocked by the accounting building across the compound. The FBI agents did not turn on the lights, but took their seats across the table from me. The credenza populated with tiny crystal tombstones commemorating Buckley's various product launches caught what light was available, twinkling like a constellation behind them.

"We already know from Teddy about your recent activities," the one agent said. "We just want to hear it from you."

The agent's use of Teddy's nickname frightened me.

"Are you aware that what you've done is a crime?" the other agent said. "One felony count for each item removed."

I looked the agents in the eye. I wanted to let them know that their tactics didn't scare me, but it wouldn't have been the truth. I told them what they wanted to know. Teddy had failed to mention the cache of furniture on JSB's property, and I drew them a detailed map, providing them with the gate code, the last ounce of loyalty draining from my body.

I'm Good for One More

A ringing phone in the middle of the night is always bad news, but when Talie's out with her friend Holly, it's always the same bad news. "Charlie," Talie's voice falters on the other end. "Will you pick me up?"

I try to rationalize, try to say it might be something else, too drunk to drive, lost her keys, *anything*.

I wish Talie would've called Dale, but Dale wants to marry Talie and something like this might change his mind, even though Talie has never said she wants to marry Dale.

I'd like to see Dale handle this one.

The scene at Holly's is as predictable as it was in high school, and I get into my old routine: ask Holly how Talie is, how it happened, who this time, where she is now.

For a change, Holly isn't acting groggy, like she doesn't know the details.

"It was this asshole from Texas," she says, crying.

Cowboys. I can't stand them. Many cowboys have seen the inside of Holly's apartment, which looks newly cleaned, each magazine and remote control whisked back to its proper place in anticipation of after-hours company. It's not me she had in mind when she cleaned earlier.

"She didn't do anything," Holly is saying, defending Talie's behavior. I haven't even accused anybody and Holly is spinning the defense—this is how bad it really is.

There's common knowledge between us: I think Holly's a slut, so she can't help but not like me. The first time I was hauled out in the middle of the night, my sophomore year (there was a guy who had Talie's shirt off in the backseat of Holly's car), Holly didn't say anything to me. Instead she stayed in her room while Talie explained very rationally about the four maybe five tequila shots that had poured her into the backseat of Holly's car.

Now I'm listening to what Holly's saying, marking her words, "innocent," "charming," "seemed," "drunk," "outside." The last word I hear makes me wish I *were* outside, listening to the little sounds the night makes when everything is where it should be in the world.

Holly can't force the narrative together and she breaks up, crying to the point of heaving, but I know no matter how bad it is in here, behind that door, inside her bedroom, it's much, much worse.

Talie's on the bed in the dark and I go to her.

When I wrap myself around her, she smells of alcohol and says it feels like she's hurt for real. She doesn't say anything else, doesn't cry. I don't either.

"It's okay," I tell her.

She says my name with a weak voice.

"Yes?"

She's silent, whimpering a little, and I let up on my grip, gathering her around me, waiting for what's next.

It's the first time we involve the police.

I love that Talie isn't embarrassed by the questioning, the photography. Talie answers the questions as they're asked. I listen to the description of the perpetrator, hear his name, how it happened.

I hear the words "not my fault" and I wonder about them, keep hearing them over and over.

I'm asked some questions too. Being in the police station creeps me out.

The officer seems to suspect everything, what we've said, how his desk is arranged, the way the sun starts coming up outside his window, people he works with saying hello.

They want to talk to Holly too.

I give my answers, saying things like "I can't say" or "I don't remember."

I remember coming close to being here once before but don't tell the officer. A friend of Talie's, in from out of town, some guy she knew once from somewhere. He left town before I got a chance to confront him. Talie didn't spare me anything. The way she told it, he was all over her, but not at first. At first, always, everyone is innocent.

We are finally released into the early morning and I drive us home in silence. Talie leans her head against the cold window but doesn't close her eyes. I wish we were on our way to dinner, or to a movie, or to anywhere but Arrowhead.

Thankfully, JSB has left for the office before we get back.

"How can you sit there and take it?" Talie asks, standing in the kitchen.

I ask her what choice I have.

"You can stand up and do something," Talie says. "Are you going to let this happen to me again?"

"I'm not letting anything happen," I tell her. I want to get out of the kitchen and into the living room, but Talie has me trapped. "Why didn't Holly try and stop it?" I ask.

"She did try," Talie says, yells. "She climbed on his fucking back, but he knocked her out." She starts to cry but won't let me comfort her.

"I don't want you to hang out with Holly anymore," I say, half saying it, floating a test balloon.

"What?" she asks.

I don't let her scare me off my point.

"Everything bad happens when you're with Holly," I point out. "I just would rather you didn't—"

"She's my friend," Talie says. "She tried to *help* me."

"I don't believe you," I say, a statement that confuses her, and she backs down.

"I can't believe you won't do something about this," she says. The phone rings and it's Holly, my argument over. Talie recounts our early-morning activity and I'm forgotten in the kitchen. I'm planning my escape when I hear Talie in the other room, "Oh, really?" loud enough to know that it somehow involves me.

"Well, *someone's* going to do *something*," she tells me, hanging up the phone.

"Who? Holly? She's done enough."

Talie shakes her head. "Dale."

"What's he going to do?" I ask.

Talie just shrugs. "He's going to do what any *man* would do," she says.

"Not a *rational* man," I say, getting mine in too.

"Whatever," she says, her key to many victories in our past. The phone rings again but I don't wait to hear who it is, imagining it's Dale, calling to detail his plan of action.

The bar at the County Line is two deep all the way around, and I have to wait a half an hour for a small table in the corner. Several at the bar fit the description Talie gave the police, any or all of them looking capable. The one on the dance floor, some honky-tonk with a halo of sweat from his hatband, becomes the focus of my investigation. For a moment, I fear for the woman he is dancing with, but then he turns, faces me straight on, and his weak jawline and sloping nose exonerate him.

The two women behind the bar, older, late forties and all sex, are making the drinks so efficiently the drinking at the bar seems to increase, heated talk rising up toward the ceiling fans, where it's spun around and forgotten. Two cowboys at the table next to mine rise up suddenly and one's on the other, knocking over their chairs. I'm ready for the riot, the beer and the bad energy flowing through me, when the jukebox quits midway through a Hank Williams tune.

"God damn it," someone yells, a body moving through the crowd. The jukebox is plugged back in and then the brawlers are shown out. I'm ready to leave, satisfied with having made an effort, hoping it brings redemption in Talie's eyes, when I spot the suspect sitting at a table in the opposite corner, quiet and alone.

First off, he's smaller than I pictured. Talie's description made him out to be large and bulky, yet he's nicely wedged in the corner, out of sight. He doesn't seem to be looking around and doesn't look up when someone backs into an empty chair at his table. Someone else asks if they can take it, and he lets them.

I forget what he's done for a moment and understand why he did it. In this place, Talie and Holly very easily would have been the most attractive—if not the only—women around. If I were this guy, and those two let me buy them a drink, let me dance close with them, twirling in the cake-clumped sawdust, I wouldn't have expected them to say no, and I probably wouldn't have believed them when they did.

Keeping an eye on his table, I call the police, who tell me to stay where I am, which is what I plan to do. I'm going to wait ten minutes, giving the police some travel time, and then approach him, maybe push him around some. The other option is to charge at him with a broken bottle, a move I've never made, unsure if I'd be able to actually stab someone, something I'm pretty sure you'd have to be sure about before breaking the end off of a beer bottle.

I'm admiring the different-shaped bottles at the bar, sizing each up for grip, and when I look back at the table in the corner, Dale is leaning into the guy. No one seems to notice, none of the backs at the bar swivel around with interest. Dale hoists the guy out of his seat and drags him toward me.

I'm not happy to see either one of them.

"Charlie, meet Shane," he says. Shane is struggling in Dale's grip and doesn't look at me. It strikes me that Dale isn't surprised to see me.

Shane is dragged to the parking lot, more by Dale than by me, but I get a hand on him too. What exactly Dale has in mind isn't known by me, but whatever it is, it's going to take place in the darkened end of the blue-and-yellow-neoned pavement. Shane is forced to hug a telephone pole while Dale ropes his hands together.

"Do you know this guy?" Dale yells at Shane, pointing at me. Shane sees me for the first time and doesn't recognize me. "Do you?"

"No," Shane says. "Fuck no, I don't."

"You raped his sister," Dale reminds him.

"I didn't rape her," Shane says, which sends Dale off, a few kicks landing in Shane's stomach, landing him on the ground.

I'm bothered that Dale refers to Talie as my sister, which she obviously isn't, instead of as my girlfriend, and it's definitely something to ask him about later, but I'm too impressed by his heroics, and the old feeling of admiration I had for him from Talie's letters returns.

"Charlie, get what's on my seat," Dale says.

I walk slowly to Dale's truck, hoping the police will show up before this goes into real violence. I pick up the baseball bat on Dale's front seat. The aluminum is cold and round and I heft it over my shoulder. I hit a piece of asphalt from the parking lot into the trees. The bat lets out a *ping* when I connect, and the sound travels to distances beyond where we're standing.

Shane cries out as I slam the door. A few guys stumble out of the County Line but make so much noise they don't hear anything.

Shane's in bad shape now, his pants thrown up on the car next to us, a beer bottle wedged mouth-first up his ass. The thought occurs to me that whoever was drinking from that bottle earlier had no idea how it would be repurposed.

"It won't be as bad if you say you're sorry," Dale is telling Shane. I don't think Shane buys it. I don't.

"Man, I'm telling you, I didn't rape her," Shane says, crying, I think.

Dale whips the bat out of my hand, swinging it again and again in the air, warming up. A car pulls up behind us, the headlights shining so that I can see a few swallows of beer left in Shane's glass tail.

Holly and Talie get out and Talie gasps when she sees Shane.

"Dale, don't," Holly says. "Don't do it."

"Why not?" he asks.

"Tell them what happened," Shane pleads, then angrily, "Tell this psychopath what happened."

Before Holly can say anything, Dale brings the bat straight across. I kick the bottle away a moment before Dale connects, but he doesn't seem to notice or care. Shane screams, the only one not afraid to speak. Holly and Talie are silent; Dale just grunts as he hammers away. Shane's shrieks get softer and softer and less insistent as he slumps and slides to the ground.

"I'm going to be good from now on," Talie promises, whispering it in my ear. She reaches for my hand, locking her fingers into mine. Her grip on me tightens. She smiles as the yellow and blue neon gives way to flashing red and blue and we all scramble into vehicles, not turning our headlights on until we're blocks away from the County Line.

Journal #4

My relationship with Jenny began to feel like a separate life, one with a separate set of friends and venues (church dances, cards and board games at her house, or the occasional date now that she was sixteen). The serenity the relationship bred when I was with Jenny convinced me that we belonged together. But the fact that I hardly talked about her when I was with Talie, who still didn't know much about her, or with my friends, who knew her about as well and saw her even less, or with anyone at Buckley Cosmetics— Jenny's mother thought JSB a crook and forbade me to mention his name—drove a wedge in that serenity and I began to be aware of a split personality I had inadvertently developed: the caring and loving husband type I exhibited when I spent time with Jenny, and the adventurous nighthawk that combed the streets late at night with my friends, looking for something interesting to do, like the rave at the Icehouse, an abandoned meatpacking plant in downtown Phoenix, hosted by a former porn star who was embarking on a new career as a DJ. As Jason and I twirled with the crowd of drugged-out teenagers, I wondered what Jenny would say if she could see me.

Or if she could've seen me at the warehouse party Jason and I crashed after a fruitless night of asking adults in 7-Eleven parking lots to buy us beer. The warehouse was in a notoriously bad part of town. A homeless shelter was nearby and even the police seemed to ignore the war zone. The only parking spot I could find for my beloved Pulsar NX, purchased with the help of the Chandlers, who had all but adopted me, was on a dark street around the corner, and so midway through the keg party in the unlit, windowless warehouse I stepped out to move my car closer to the front of the building, skipping quickly through the deserted streets. Upon my return, I noticed a large man standing in the center of the floor without his pants. As my eyes dilated, readjusting to the darkness, I noticed that the woman standing next to him was naked too, and that other guests were in the throes of removing their clothing.

"Time to go," Jason said, grabbing me as we launched out into the night.

I tortured myself over what to do about Jenny. I knew I loved her, and I loved how we complemented each other. I couldn't imagine anyone with finer qualities and I knew it would be a waste and a shame if we didn't end up getting married. Marriage to Jenny was my only road to salvation and redemption, I knew. But the universe was unattuned and just saw us as kids. I allowed myself to indulge in self-pity about having met the perfect mate too soon, the self-pity inducing the feeling that I was the victim of cruel fate. A breakup seemed inevitable, an idea that reduced me to tears when I considered it. I had no idea how to undertake something as emotionally devastating as ending a great relationship without cause. I knew it would come out of the blue, shocking Jenny and our mutual friends, dynamiting a cornerstone of my otherwise fly-by-night life. The best I could do was write Jenny a letter, cowardly sending it to her through the mail, asking her not to contact me for a month but to meet me thirty days later in the courtyard of the Biltmore Fashion Park, an upscale outdoor shopping center where Jenny and

I sometimes had lunch. I hoped the month off would prove to Jenny that she could get on with her life without me, a wish I wanted for myself, too.

I lay awake the night before our reunion. I felt silly for having asked her for a month's worth of silence, and a little surprised and afraid that she'd assented, without so much as a hang-up phone call over those long four weeks. I didn't know any more than I knew a month earlier, and I wondered if Jenny had solved anything. The answer to the latter was quickly apparent as she strode up to me in the deserted Biltmore Fashion Park courtyard, letter in hand, launching into her response to my letter, the bitterness of the response having grown exponentially while it festered for thirty days.

I sat there listening, knowing I deserved every word of it.

Essay #5: Affection

The highest emotion one human being can have for another. There is no greater feeling than showing affection and having that affection reciprocated. It's possible to feel different degrees of affection, depending on the nature of one's relationship to another person. Without a doubt, the most gratifying form of affection exists in a realm of physical and sexual freedom. A realm without judgments.

Most people live in a world of constraint, where affection is merely reciprocated, like a game. I do something nice for you, you do something nice for me. While this existence is placating, there is no real emotion, only prescribed emotion.

Free from constraints, however, a person is allowed to indulge in the kind of affection a relationship can create. A person is allowed to give as much affection as he wants; and more importantly, he is allowed to take as much affection as he needs. Each is totally satisfied.

Take Karine, for instance. A good example. Karine had existed for so long on the crumbs of affection various men in her life had thrown at her that when Karine happened into La Onda that night, she looked like she hadn't eaten in days. Even though I didn't know her, I put myself at her mercy. I pretended that I had the utmost affection for her (I'm sure I would've developed a sense of affection for her, given time) and gave her all the affection I possibly could, replenishing her. It was just that she was so shocked that she didn't know how to react, she wasn't used to the wonderful feeling of unbridled affection. She just couldn't . . .

Maybe Karine's a bad example.

I arrive to find Jane on the couch, naked, watching TV. I sense she is about to be coy, but then I notice (sigh) Jane has been crying. I sit down next to her, blocking the view, and she pulls her feet up so that her heels are in her crotch.

"What's the matter?" I ask.

"Nothing." She looks over my shoulder at the TV.

"Tell me what's wrong." I rub her knees tenderly. "What is it?"

"Nothing." She sniffs quietly, dramatically.

"Something must be wrong, Jane," I sigh.

"I can't decide what to do," she blurts out.

"About what?" I'm massaging her thigh now.

"About anything." She starts to cry.

"Like what?" I'm beginning to be agitated.

"I just can't decide about . . . California or here . . . or you or . . ." Her voice trails off.

"What do you think you should do?" I ask, genuinely trying to help.

"It's just that I know [*sniff*] that I'll [*sniff*] meet someone like you in California and [*sniff*]—"

"What does *that* mean?" I pull away from her.

"That my life [*sniff*] will be the same . . . wherever I go."

"That's probably true," I say coldly.

"I'm fucked up." She really starts to sob, but it's just a ploy because she knows she has upset me, and I go for it, putting my arms around her.

"It's okay." I try to calm her. "You're not fucked up. You're going to be fine."

"You really think so?" she asks, pressing a wet cheek against my neck.

"Sure." I pat the back of her head and right then I hate her more than I've hated anyone in a long time. The way she smells makes me crazy and I jump up off the couch.

She looks up. "What's wrong?"

"Nothing."

"No, really, Charlie." She stands up, fully naked in front of me.

"I just wish you'd make up your mind about us." I try not to look at her.

"I know. I'm sorry," Jane says. "I just don't know what I want."

"Well, you better decide."

I make myself cry, and this moves Jane to put her arms around me. I struggle out of her grip and stand there with my head down. When I look up at her, fake tears sliding down my face, she's looking away, at the TV.

I like hair. All kinds: brown, black, red, blond, long, short, curly, wavy, straight—whatever. And skin. I can't get the feel of skin out of my dreams.

When other guys were showing their prowess at basketball on the playground at recess, Steven Howfield and I were starting clubs and trying to get girls to join: Saturday Afternoon Club (weekly picnics designed to be romantic, like on TV); Very Secret Society (initiation included kissing both Steven and me on the lips for ten seconds—we promised not to tell anyone, hence the name); Daisy-Chain Gang (the main function of this club was to play out a bizarre game Steven and I had concocted, the rules of which I have forgotten); and the Millionaires' Club (we tried to convince cute girls that we were going to be lawyers and that we'd make a lot of money). Once Erica Ryan and I stayed out on the playground after the bell, hiding in the corner where the gymnasium joined the administration building, and we kissed until Ms. Fisher, our fifth-grade teacher, realized we were missing and came looking for us. Erica and I had to stay after school with our heads down on our desks until her parents and my grandparents came for us. I peeked over my hairless arm several times, but Erica would not look back at me.

And at Erica Ryan's birthday party I was the only boy (Steven Howfield was particularly pissed at being snubbed, but losing out to guys who are better than you is something you can never learn too early in life) and my grandmother was hesitant about letting me go. Imagine what it was like to be the only boy at Erica Ryan's eleventh birthday party. Imagine being locked in a closet full of gloriously dirty laundry and Erica opening the door after counting to sixty and yelling "Here!" Imagine Erica Ryan throwing her older sister's bra at you. Imagine her slamming the door shut again and all the girls giggling. I had never smelled anything more wonderful than that bra. Imagine me pressing the cool fabric against my forehead. Imagine me inhaling.

Years later, in San Diego, I babysat for my divorced piano teacher, Ms. Thomas, who gave lessons out of her house. I was her favorite student. She would sit next to the bench and point along to the music with her slender fingers as I tried to keep up. She smoked a lot, but once you were in her house for a while, you hardly noticed it.

One night I babysat her two kids, Harry, eight, and Sidney, six. I put them to bed at nine, like Ms. Thomas had told me, and I knew she wouldn't be home before midnight, so I had plenty of time to myself. I normally don't like to snoop around because I am impatient and don't know what to look for, but something was clearly drawing me to Ms. Thomas's bedroom.

The dark was cool, and after my eyes adjusted, I could make out a dresser, a bed. The room was a mess, clothes thrown everywhere. I stood motionless, breathing in the peculiar scents the room held.

I moved over to the dresser, opening the top drawer and pulling out one of Ms. Thomas's lace bras. The silk and lace sent an electric charge through me, and without even thinking about it, I unzipped my pants and put the left cup over my erection, letting it hang like a lace flag in a stifled wind.

I'm not sure what made me commit the act. I'm not even sure where the idea came from, except that suddenly I was on my knees at the foot of her bed, and the bra with my cock wrapped inside it was wedged between the mattress and the box spring and I began moving back and forth, like I'd seen in cable movies. It felt awkward at first, a little rough even, but then it smoothed out and felt all right and I was really moving. A couple of times it slipped out and I had to readjust the setup. Right when it started to feel the best, I began to sweat. I moved a little faster and then something went wrong. I wanted to scream. I stopped moving but something was happening and it felt like someone was cutting me with a knife. Finally it stopped and I pulled everything out and felt the hot goo puddled in the left cup. I buried the bra in the rest of the dirty clothes and got out of the room as quietly as I could, shaken and exhilarated.

For a Good Time Just Call

Jane and I have a game that we sometimes play where I leave and come back.

I cruise around the block while Jane tucks herself into bed, and when I come back, I pull a ski mask over my face and crawl through the front window of her apartment. The place is dark and I feel my way around the living room to the bedroom. The door badly needs to be oiled, but Jane pretends she doesn't hear it squeak.

I leave the door open and pounce on the bed, startling her awake. I press my hand over her mouth and her eyes get wide, a suitably terrified expression comes across her face, and I growl: "I've seen you . . . I've been watching you." On some nights Jane works up tears, and the wetness on my fingers really makes me violent. "I'm gonna make you really cry and *you'll love it*." Jane nods fearfully.

"I'll bet you've got a pretty pussy," I say, and pull the sheets back. She clamps her knees together and folds them up to her chest, but I slip one hand between them, breaking them apart while unzipping my pants. "Show me your pretty pussy," I say. "Here, pretty, pretty, pretty."

I pin her arms to her chest and put all my weight on top of her so Jane can't flail around. I kick out of my pants and boxers. "Shush now," I say to quiet her sobbing, and I pretend that if she's quiet, I'll pull my hand back. At this point she begins to whimper and this is usually when I enter her. "Oh, yeeeeees," I moan. "You have a pret-ty pus-sy, pret-ty pus-sy," I sing as I hump to the rhythm my words are making.

After I come, I pull out and roll off her. Jane gasps for air. We both grab for each other's hand. We lie still for a moment, not saying anything, and then Jane mounts me until she comes too.

Journal #5

The week Tim was suspended for starting fires in the boys' bathroom, my reputation was revealed to me. Principal Edwards had summoned us for interrogation simultaneously, and everyone was shocked to see me return to my seat so soon. I imagined the others regarded me with an air of caution, wondering what I would do to retaliate against those who had nominated me to the principal's ears. I dreamed of radical terrorism, toilets spouting like fountains, poison ivy on the swing set, ink in the lunch milk, the entire playground on fire. Transferring schools seemed bad enough, but transferring from Rapid City to San Diego in the middle of my freshman year was socially disastrous. Not picked for basketball or football or baseball, Tim was the only other kid no one wanted anything to do with. "Those guys are a bunch of fags, anyway," Tim said. "Humping each other over a little ball. Fuck 'em."

Tim and I spent most of the time hanging out after school at Tim's hideout, a tin construction shack left by the crew who had paved the highway behind my new home. We called it the clubhouse. It could hold up to five people, but only Tim and I ever went there. Weeds sprouted up inside the shack, nourished by the shaft of sunlight the doorless entrance allowed. We collected cans there, rummaged from the Holiday Inn Dumpster down the highway, and cashed them in at the local recycling center. Weekends were our big score. In addition to the cluster of beer cans, we usually came away with a full library of porno magazines discarded by weekend surfers. When the bell rang at the end of the school day, Tim and I raced to the clubhouse and spent the afternoon leafing through the fleshy pages.

Tim learned the delivery schedule at the Texaco next to the Holiday Inn and knew that when a truckload of goods came in, one of the clerks would have to leave a register to check them in. The other clerk was usually overwhelmed with cars pulling in off the freeway.

So we started stealing beer.

First it was six-packs behind our back. Then we started walking out with a twelve-pack each. Olympia. Hamm's. Pabst Blue Ribbon. I selected mine more on the basis of color and design, but Tim always stole Coors.

"My dad drinks Coors," he told me. Tim's father left his mother when Tim was five. Tim never talked about him, except he always told me that his father drank Coors. I wondered if it was the only thing Tim knew about him. A small picture on the hutch in Tim's apartment showed the three of them. Tim was in his mother's thin arms. His father had his arm around his mother. They both had long, thin faces with eyes the size of marbles, and their hair was identically feathered in the style of the times. I never told Tim that my parents died in a gas explosion before I could really know anything about them, back when I lived in Sacramento. That was before I was shipped from relative to relative, first Denver and then Santa Fe and then Rapid City.

We added our empties to the aluminum heaps outside the shack.

"Look at this," I said, fishing a used rubber out of an Old Milwaukee can. The tip was full and it was tied off in the middle.

"Gross," Tim said, coming closer. He knocked it out of my hand and stepped on it. The white fluid leaked into the dirt. "Have you ever used one?" he asked.

I shook my head.

"I have," he said. "On my neighbor."

I looked at him skeptically.

"Really. You can too, if you want. She's about forty," he said. "She's a mental defect, though. She sits on the curb and drools on herself all day."

We really did find Dora on the curb, just like Tim said. I'd seen her before but thought she was just waiting for a friend, or the bus.

"Hi, Dora," Tim said.

"Hi, Tim," Dora said without looking at him.

"This is my friend."

"Hi," Dora said without looking at me. She seemed to be concentrating on something in the distance.

"You want to go inside?" Tim said.

"No," she answered. She shaded her thick-framed glasses and turned her head up to get a look.

"C'mon," Tim said. He pulled Dora by the arm and Dora rose like a genie.

"Let go," she said.

"C'mon, Dora," Tim said, gently turning her toward his apartment. "Let's go inside."

"I don't want to," she said. "I'll call the police."

I grabbed Tim's arm. "Man, don't." I tried not to sound panicked.

"Don't worry," he whispered. "She isn't going to call the cops."

"I am," Dora said. "I called them last time."

"Yeah? And what did they tell you?" Tim asked, smiling.

"They told me not to let you do it again," she said.

"Did the cops really come?" I asked worriedly.

"Yeah, they came. Didn't they, Dora? You called the cops on Timmy, didn't you?"

"Yep, yep," Dora said.

Tim grinned and I looked away, Dora's gaze following mine, trying to see what I was looking at.

Dora began waiting for me on the curb in front of her apartment, three doors down from Tim's. Her last name was Wells. "I think I'm English," she said. Dora would say things like that that would crack me up, without trying to be funny.

What Dora told me about herself wouldn't be more than an hour's conversation no matter what day of the week it was, but she parceled the information out over time. She was born in San Diego and had never left. Dora didn't have any other friends besides me, she'd lived in her apartment for more than twenty years (before I was even born, I thought), and her parents lived "somewhere else." Someone from a special service came and checked on Dora twice a week, bringing her a small amount of marijuana to relieve the shooting pain in her eyes. The only thing Dora loved was bingo, so three nights out of four we'd take the bus to Our Lady of Hope, smoking a plump joint on the way.

Even though the bingo hall was the size of a double-car garage, they somehow managed to pack in more than two dozen people every night. The room was charged with nervous excitement. Dora played faithfully every week but couldn't seem to win. And it didn't appear to bother her. She only ever talked to one other person besides me, one-armed Eva. Eva's husband axed off her left arm in a blind rage. "He was cuckoo," Eva said, laughing like the joke was somehow on her. I liked Eva's sense of humor. She could really work her bingo marker too.

Dora never played for more than a couple of hours. I'd sit in the corner, propped up on the stool with the wobbly third leg, smiling for good luck when Dora turned around in her metal folding chair. I didn't mind waiting; bingo didn't interest me. I liked to sit and picture myself on the stool, like an image from a satellite, and wonder if any of my old friends back in Rapid City would recognize me. I wanted to see the look on Lloyd Inman's face when he saw me with Dora. Man, old Lloyd would've been surprised. The whole gang would've. Zeke and Bruce and Georgie and J.P.

"Okay," Dora would say when she was finished. We'd hold hands while we waited for the return bus. Once or twice Eva took us out for a late dinner at Hardee's or Arctic Circle—the only two places where Eva would eat. But it was usually just me and Dora. We'd spark up down the street from Our Lady of Hope and imagine we could hear the 57 bus before it turned the corner. The bus driver would accelerate on the freeway on-ramp, Dora's face pressed against the window, the yellow freeway lights flashing by like lightning.

I didn't tell Dora about the note someone passed me the morning after Tim's suspension. "I never knew you were a fag," it said. Someone had written "Me neither" in blue, curlicued letters. I turned around in my desk, but everyone was staring at the chalkboard, intently watching Mrs. Riggins explain algebra. Heat flashed across my forehead and I stood up and walked over to the trash can. Mrs. Riggins stopped the chalk and everyone was looking at me. I crumpled the note into a ball and dropped it into the garbage. Mrs. Riggins waited for me to reach my seat before she continued.

"What do you and Tim do up in the shack by the highway?" Tony Richards asked me at lunch. Now that I was infamous, I'd tried sitting at the popular table.

"Suck each other's dicks, probably," John Killspotted said.

Everyone at the table laughed and looked at me. I tried to laugh with them, to take the joke, and Greg Knot pointed and said, "Look, he likes it too."

Tony's sister, Lucy, spit out her mashed potatoes, laughing.

I picked up my tray, my hands and arms shaking.

"Oops. Time to suck a dick," someone said, and the table erupted.

The others started in too. John Killspotted said he'd heard I was in the hospital and asked if it was to get my stomach pumped. Greg Knot told a disgusting story about a gerbil.

I set my tray back down on the table. "Listen, fuckers," I said. Nobody moved. "Tim's the fag, not me. In fact, when he gets back, I'm going to kick the shit out of him." I was shaking as I said it, and when Tim came back a week later, I was even more nervous. The whole school was talking about it and I was worried Tim had heard what I'd said. John Killspotted put his finger in my chest at lunch and said, "We're coming up to your love nest. We expect you're going to do something about Tim."

"Yeah, okay," I said. I felt Tim's eyes on me. John Killspotted walked away and I set my tray of turkey and gravy down across from Tim.

"Why are you talking to that Injun?" Tim asked.

"He asked me if I would do his homework," I lied. "And I told him, 'Fuck no.'"

"Doesn't surprise me," Tim said. "Stupid fuckin' Injun."

It was for reasons like this that I hadn't told Tim about Dora. I had been grounded by my aunt and uncle when report cards came out, and I told him I was still grounded to keep him from calling me up. I always ran to the door at Dora's in case Tim was looking out the window.

"Hey, do you want to meet at the clubhouse after school?" I asked nervously. "You know, drink some beers."

Tim looked across the table and smiled. "You mean you aren't going to visit Dora?" he asked.

Hearing her name in the cafeteria caused me to blush, and I stammered, trying to deny it.

"It's cool," Tim laughed. "I won't tell anyone." He shoveled a forkful of corn into his mouth. "I mean, that pussy's pretty sweet," he said. He smiled as he chewed. "And *easy*."

A sick feeling came over me.

"She can't keep her mouth shut about you," Tim said. He winked. "I think she really likes you."

"Yeah?" I asked weakly.

John Killspotted walked by the table. "After school, then," he said, and walked away.

"What's after school?" Tim asked.

"That's what I meant to tell you," I said. "When I told that fuckin' Injun that I wouldn't help him, he called me and you fags, so I told him to show up at the clubhouse after school. We'll fuckin' show him who's a fag."

Tim put his fork down. "Fuck yeah. I hate that Injun anyway."

"Meet me up there, then," I said, and picked up my tray. I spent the rest of the afternoon in the nurse's office with a sick stomach, sprawled out on a cot, staring at the ceiling.

John Killspotted and Greg Knot met up with me as I climbed the hill toward the shack.

"Hey, fairy," Greg Knot said.

John Killspotted laughed. "Hey, Tinker Bell."

"Shut the fuck up," I said, walking in front of them, as if I was eager to get to where I was going.

"You better beat your boyfriend into the ground," John Killspotted called from behind. "I'm not coming up here to watch you two make out."

We passed a group of sixth graders who had just gotten off the bus. "There he is," one of them called out, and the pack fell in behind me. I saw myself from the satellite again. I saw Zeke and J.P. and the others looking too. This would remind them of Dallas Tucker, the new kid at the high school adjacent to Knollwood Heights whom everyone had heard about, the beating and the disappearance. It occurred to me that I, too, was a member of that phantom class. I never even knew what Dallas Tucker looked like. It galled me to think everyone back in Rapid City would probably remember us both in the same breath.

I thought about the satellite picture and heard what anyone who knew me before would've thought out loud: *Is that really him? Is that where he went? It doesn't even look like the guy we knew. It must be a mistake.*

I didn't see Tim at first, but he poked his head out when he heard the excited voices converging. He glanced at me and then at the crowd behind me, confused. He started to say, "What the—," but I rushed up and shoved him to the ground.

"Shut up, faggot," I said. Tim tried to get up but John Killspotted kicked him hard in the stomach. Tim doubled over and the others started chanting, "Get him, get him." John Killspotted nodded, menacing, and I hauled off and kicked Tim in the crotch, my foot aching. My blood surged, rushing through me, my skin pinpricked. Images of Zeke and Bruce and Georgie and J.P. swirled across my field of vision and I buried my foot again and again into Tim, who curled up on the ground. He wore a quizzical look and I thought of Dora and I kicked him again, tripping and falling over his shaking body. Greg stepped up and kicked Tim and kept kicking and the crowd kept chanting and finally Tim rolled over onto his stomach and quit moving. John Killspotted said, "There you go, faggot," and kicked Tim hard again and Tim groaned.

I pushed through the crowd and ran. I could hear Tim's groans all the way back to my house.

After bingo, Dora asked if I wanted to stay awhile, but I said I should probably go. Tim's window was dark. The temperature had dropped suddenly and the wind cut through my jean jacket. I hugged myself as I waited for Dora to put her key in the lock. All the apartments resembled one another from the outside, each unrecognizable from the next. Once Dora was inside, I kissed her good night. She waved to me from the window, but I was distracted by the large chunk of siding still missing from the corner apartment building. Tim and I had blown it away with a shotgun Tim's uncle had left behind. I guess I was surprised no one had fixed it. I felt the jagged groove. Tim was gone. I felt it right then. The next morning I would hear about how someone had called an ambulance, about Tim pissing blood. By lunch it would be confirmed that Tim's mother had transferred him to another school. Dora wouldn't know anything about Tim and Tim's mother moving out, a young couple with an infant moving into their old apartment. Dora wouldn't have any idea about her having to move apartments either. Less than a month later, I would be standing in front of Dora's, peering through the ghostly curtains at an empty apartment.

The houses across the street were strung with lighted candy canes and Santas, but the apartment buildings remained dark. The holiday season had begun across the street and on the street over and block after block throughout the city. I can't remember what I got for Christmas that year. By then I had moved again, to Phoenix, where there aren't any seasons.

I Take Jane on a Hot-Air Balloon Ride

Here's the key to any relationship: surprise.

Surprise breaks the repetition that is the death knell of all contemporary unions. That's why for Jane's birthday I surprise her with a sunrise hot-air balloon ride/champagne brunch.

There is nothing more magnificent than watching the sun rising over the desert (except maybe watching the sun *setting* over the desert). Jane loves it. We stand holding hands and look out at the eastern horizon, spellbound. Looking down, we watch the shadow over the desert floor slowly pull back, revealing its harsh landscape, awakening wildlife.

Our pilot pours us champagne and we eat fresh fruit with our fingers, ignoring the handsome pastry display.

"Happy birthday." I kiss Jane on the cheek.

"Thank you." Jane smiles.

We hardly speak the rest of the ride. I can tell she is totally enraptured and this makes me feel good. It's a good feeling to treat people the way they deserve to be treated, according to Dr. Hatch, and he's right.

In need of money, I took a part-time job at Pete's Fish & Chips. Over the first few weeks, the regular set of customers slowly became known to me. One customer in particular, a comely woman in her late twenties with a young daughter, ate at Pete's with a frequency that shamed the other regulars. I soon learned that the woman and her daughter lived in one of the three low-income houses that shared Pete's asphalt parking lot, housing that was clearly from another era and was one development phase away from being leveled. The woman's daughter liked to ride the mechanical pony under the awning out front, and I began slipping the girl quarters as I chatted with her mother while they waited for their order. We talked about my situation with Jenny, me couching the demise of the relationship more in terms of my not being Mormon, which I'd come to blame as the truth.

"That's a tough one," she said. She told me how her husband had deserted her and her daughter, an idea I obsessed over between her visits. I wondered what kind of person could do such a thing, disappear on purpose.

A loneliness descended upon me as Christmas neared, and an innocuous conversation with the woman about the holiday deepened the feeling.

"Buy your tree yet?" I asked as she hung around the front window.

She shook her head no. "It's either buy the tree, or buy something to put under the tree," she said. The answered floored me; having a Christmas tree ranked up there with the other inalienable rights Americans enjoyed. Determined to right this enormous wrong, I borrowed my friend's truck and bought one of the last Christmas trees available from a corner stand, stopping at Target to purchase a bag full of bulbs, lights, and tinsel. I enlisted the help of a coworker to help me drag the tree to the woman's front door, the coworker happy to be excused from work. The woman answered my knock, perplexed.

"Merry Christmas," I said, smiling.

She arched her eyebrows. "You playing Santa?" she asked. An awkwardness descended as my coworker and I stood supporting the wilting tree.

"Thought you might like to have a tree for that present," I said.

The woman smiled awkwardly and stepped aside, admitting us into her tiny living room. That the tree was too big for the living room didn't diminish my enthusiasm, and my coworker and I quickly strung the lights and hung the bulbs. The woman's daughter peered around the corner, scared at the sight of the monstrous tree.

"It's a Christmas tree," I said, plugging in the lights. The room was aglow in red and green.

"Want to see our Christmas tree?" the girl asked. "I made it."

"Sure," I said, caught up in the holiday spirit.

The woman folded her arms and leaned against the wall as her daughter led me around behind the tree I'd brought to show me a tiny tree she'd fashioned out of empty toilet paper rolls. The girl and her mother had glued cotton snow onto the tree, sprinkling glitter over the whole creation to give it the appearance of having lights. I stood grinning at the tiny tree, embarrassed as the girl excitedly ran through the various steps involved in making your own Christmas tree.

Friday

Cunt, cunt, cunt, cunt, cunt, cunt, cunt. Bitch cunt. It's fucking hilarious how women always say, "I want you to tell me what you're thinking about," and then they pull out of your life without so much as a "Had a good time!" or "Thanks for the cock!" Jesus, why?

I call in sick to Aztecka and then call back in ten minutes and tell them I'm quitting. Later I'm dressed up, leaning against the bar, and Jason is so pissed off at me he pretends not to hear my drink order. I wave down Miles and he brings me a vodka but doesn't take my money, and this gesture of kindness renders me mute.

It isn't long before I spot another one, alone at the table in the corner, but there is a revulsion within me, remnants of my loyalties to Jane, a revulsion I've felt many times before, the final pull of the last one's personality and the arrival of the next. The vodka clears the slate and I saunter through the crowd to her table and I can tell that she wants me to give her one good time in the vacuum of her life, and when I smile, she invites me to sit down and I do.

Essay #7: The End of Utopia

The end of Utopia comes in a poorly lit room, a wooden chair at the foot of a hospital bed. Outside the window a city carries on, ceaselessly. At the end of Utopia, I am sitting in a wooden chair, smoking a cigarette for the first time in my life, desperate for pleasure. My skin is a chemise that has been left out in the sun for too long. I want to get up and look out the window and see what's happening on the street below, but I don't have any strength. At the end of Utopia, I look over at a telephone on the nightstand next to the hospital bed and my mind is blank. At the end of Utopia, all I can wonder is what I had for dinner the night before. I draw on the cigarette and gag and it occurs to me that if I die, it could be days before anyone notices.

Jason's in his office at Aztecka after the place has closed for the night.

"Bitch," Jason says when I tell him about Jane. "What a bitch."

He looks up at me and says, "You're not gonna fuckin' believe this, but Sara's gone too."

I'm shocked by this but can't feel anything resembling an emotion beyond despair. "What a bitch," I say.

Jason looks back at his receipts, entering some numbers into the computer, the green glow of the screen painting his angry face.

Journal #7

My decision to join the Mormon Church was borne not out of religious zeal but out of romantic sacrifice. I wanted to prove to Jenny that taking me back hadn't been a mistake, that I could commit to our future. The anxiety induced by our separation drove me into a depression, the idea that I'd thrown away something of value plaguing my daily thoughts.

I kept my plan to be baptized Mormon a secret at first; Jenny was wary when I asked to start attending church with her and her family, sensing my motive. "You don't have to," she said, though I knew she was thrilled about having me in the pews on Sunday.

As far as I could discern, the Mormon religion seemed as harmless as any of the others, with the added advantage of securing the ribbon around my relationship with Jenny, whom I began to think of as my wife. We complemented each other nicely, and I noticed that the other Mormon couples did too, the women hanging on the men's every word, gazing upwardly at them lovingly, laughing at their jokes.

The first step to becoming Mormon was an interview with the bishop. While I knew the interview was a formality and that the bishop couldn't thwart my intentions, I considered the audition seriously; my preemptive loathing for the bishop as a potential obstacle powered an authentic performance that persuaded him away from his specu'ation that I was simply joining for Jenny, and I convinced him that my intentions were true and well considered.

The next step was a consultation with the missionaries. The elders like to convene with you in your home, but because I knew my first cousin twice removed wouldn't want Mormons in his living room, I arranged to meet them at Jenny's cousin's house. The missionaries took the regular-guy tack with me right away, a shtick they no doubt devised to play up their regional differences: one was from Alaska and one was from Texas. Elder Alaska was the quieter of the two, the foil to many of Elder Texas's jokes. Once we established that we were just three regular dudes, we proceeded with the business at hand.

"What do you know about the Church?" Elder Alaska asked.

I told them what little I'd gleaned from my limited exposure to the Church.

"We're ahead of the game," Elder Texas joked. "We normally spend the first interview correcting mistruths and rumors." A smile spread across his meaty face.

Elder Alaska produced a video and we settled onto the couch, Jenny's cousin and her cousin's family artfully dodging the front room as they moved silently through the house. The video dramatized the finding of the Book of Mormon, the lost addendum to the Bible, by Joseph Smith in upstate New York, the actor playing Smith effectively portraying piousness. Next the Mormon belief system was detailed: God as the Heavenly Father; Jesus Christ, his son; how Mormons can return to live with God through the atonement of Jesus Christ; the function of the Holy Ghost as a guide to help recognize truth; that the Church of Jesus Christ has been restored on Earth through the Latter-day Saints; how God reveals his wishes through modern prophets (as he did in his own time); and, most appealingly, that by leading an exemplary Mormon life of sacrifice and service, families can be together forever in eternity.

The elders asked if I had any questions and I shook my head, still absorbing everything I'd learned, connecting the dots between the ideas I'd heard uttered at dances and on Sundays and among the Mormons I'd known, the key to their secret language finally revealed. The question the elders were really asking was if I believed what I'd just seen—I imagined they were on the hook if they let a nonbeliever join for nefarious purposes, like wanting to marry another Mormon—but the question of belief didn't enter my mind. Sure, some of the LDS principles were hokey, but I weighed losing Jenny against having to pretend to believe in an afterlife and decided that the latter was nothing matched against the sorrow of the former. And so I accepted the pamphlets filled with supporting information and signed up for the conversion process, which consisted of a set number of meetings with the elders to prepare myself for baptism. Jenny's cousin was gracious to offer up her living room for these sessions so that I could continue my study in secret. By then, I was less concerned about my first cousin twice removed than I was about Talie finding out. For her part, Jenny continued to prod me with questions meant to ensure that I was acting of my own free will, my answers becoming more and more demonstrative as I pretended to embrace the Church.

The day of my baptism finally arrived. I'd chosen Jenny's father to perform the baptism, which involved full immersion into a tub of water. Arriving early Sunday morning, I sat in my car in the parking lot, the gravity of what I was about to do occurring to me for the first time. The absence of any family or close friends would not be a signal to the other members of the congregation, but I felt their absence and wondered if there was a tenable exit strategy. The fall from trying to convince Jenny that I was committed to our future to standing on the doorstep of conversion had been fast, and I looked around, a little shaken by what I'd done. Jenny's family arrived and I switched on the autopilot, smiling and shaking her father's hand. The parking lot soon filled with well-wishers and those brothers and sisters who made a sport of attending baptisms.

I waited in a small room attached to the baptism chamber, whose front opened out into the chapel. Jenny's father entered with our baptism suits, a one-piece long-underwear type garment that left little to the imagination. We both suited up and Jenny's father stepped into the knee-deep lukewarm water in the baptismal tub. He asked me if I was ready and I nodded that I was, wanting to be over and done with the embarrassing ceremony. The shield on the baptism chamber went up, revealing a gallery of smiling faces, ready to accept me into their fold. I looked away, not wanting them to be able to read my face or that I was preoccupied with how exactly my frame was going to fit into a tub the size of a small whirlpool. My concerns proved to be real when, during the ceremony, Jenny's father leaned me back for submersion and we both toppled into the water, his small arms unable to hold me as I fell backward. The crowd didn't react, and Jenny's father and I bounced up, drenched, the first part of the ceremony over.

The second stage of the baptism involved me ascending the pulpit to deliver my conversion speech, a talk I hadn't worked out in advance. I began by listing the litany of nice things I knew about Mormons, naming the Mormons I personally knew, breezing through Jenny's name so as not to give rise to speculation. I knew the crowd was anticipating my humbling, an act I understood from the missionaries (who were in attendance as the two required witnesses) was as much a part of the baptism process as the submersion. My eyes teared as a surprise homily about the importance of family and friends issued forth. The ghosts of everyone I'd ever known and would never know again floated through me as I completely broke down, sobbing, gasping phrases about how nice it was to be among so many caring people.

I Give a Handout

Some women don't know how well they've been treated. When Jane comes back, she's going to owe me a truckload of apology. If she tries to start up with another guy, she is going to see right away how superior utopian love is. Most men are only out to get. Take, take, take. Taking is a natural behavior, like for instance the guy with his sign, standing on the median across the intersection, clean shirt, blue jeans, worn tennis shoes. He walks along the median, pausing at the driver's side of each car for a three count before moving on to the next. The left-hand turn lane holds six cars at a time. The third car and fifth car give him money. The sixth car rolls up the window.

The sign says, FATHER OF 3, GOING TO BE EVICTED TOMORROW A.M. I see it when he swivels around and walks back toward his duffel bag, which is planted at the base of the traffic light. The car behind honks for me to make the right turn, and I almost go, but I see the girl in the seventh car, which is now the first, roll down her window.

The car honks again, and I switch on my hazards, letting traffic go around. The girl in the car is classically beautiful, the sort of vision of perfection you'd see on TV, and the guy with the sign doesn't move on after the girl shakes her head no. The guy goes into some kind of rap and the girl just stares straight, praying for the green light. I think I'm going to jump out of my car and maybe tackle this guy if I have to. The girl finally rolls her window up, pissing this guy off, and he smacks her window with his hand, yelling "Bitch!" just as the light changes and she speeds off.

I change lanes, drifting left, and flip a U to enter the left-hand turn lane.

"Spare any change?" the guys asks me.

"How much do you need?" I ask.

He says, "Whatever you can spare, man," without missing a beat.

"I can spare lots," I tell him.

He's never heard this and lowers his sign a little, looking me over. "A couple bucks would be good."

"I can give you more than that," I say. "Climb in, we'll drive to the ATM."

"I'll just take the change in your ashtray," he says.

"Look, the light is going to change and I'm going to drive away," I say. "Get in and we'll go to the bank and I'll give you a couple hundred bucks."

The light changes and he says, "Wait, man," and grabs his duffel bag.

The first thing I notice is that he doesn't smell like he's been standing outside all day. His hands are rough and he has the fingertips of a smoker.

"I'm Robert," he says, a little nervous.

I couldn't care less.

He starts his rap about how he lost his job (a lie, most likely) and then his wife left him (who would even consider marrying this guy?) and his children, oh, his children (they're better off).

"The world is a cruel place," I say in my best patronizing tone.

"You said it, man."

Robert stares at the mirrored bank building as if he is looking at heaven, turning in his seat when I pull around back.

Thankfully, there are no cars at the ATM.

"Wait right here," I say, and, just for sport, I leave the car running.

After moseying to the machine, I thumb through the cards in my wallet, standing out of range of the camera watching from behind the tinted glass. I look up and wave for Robert to come here.

He jumps out of the car, leaving the door open. "Yeah?"

"You're pathetic," I say.

"What?" He cups his hand to his ear, still walking toward me.

"Is two hundred enough?" I ask.

"Oh man, that'd be great," Robert says, putting his hands together like an altar boy.

"How about three hundred?"

"Oh, no." Robert shakes his head. "That'd be too much."

"Two hundred might not be enough, though."

"It's plenty."

"I think five hundred would be better," I say, nodding my head to make the decision final. "Yeah, five hundred."

We stand, looking at each other. "Man, you're jerkin' me around," Robert says, realizing something.

"No, really, it's right here," I say, opening my wallet. "Just take it."

Robert approaches me slowly, peering ahead as if afraid of stepping off a high cliff, his feet dragging loudly against the pavement.

"Just take my wallet," I say, folding it up and holding it out.

In the instant Robert reaches out, I grab his arm and whirl him around, slamming him into the side of my car. Too stunned to say anything, Robert tries to get his balance, but I kick him in the stomach and he quietly falls over.

"You shouldn't . . . *take* . . . *money* . . . *from* . . . *strangers*." I get in his face. "You fuck."

Robert looks like he's sorry, that he'll never do it again, but this in no way satisfies me, and I prove myself to Jane and the world as a Great Defender by kicking wildly, and I keep kicking and kicking and just as Robert starts to scream, I hear a car pulling around to the side of the bank and I stand up straight, smoothing out the front of my shirt, feeling the sweat underneath, thinking, *Oh, God, Jesus, it's a cop*; but instead it's a white limo, idling. For a moment the whole earth is quiet. I can't jump in my car and drive away, since I'm blocked by the limo. Robert is writhing on the asphalt on the driver's side.

A chauffeur gets out and opens one of the limo's doors. A guy dressed in Bermuda shorts and a Duran Duran concert T-shirt steps out, looks over at us, looks away, steps up to the ATM. When Robert doesn't yell for help, I look down at him and see how badly I've fucked him up.

Another door opens and another guy gets out, dressed in a tailored suit—I can't tell if it's blue or black—and he looks so impressive I have to wave and smile.

"What's this?" he asks.

The guy at the ATM looks over at us.

I feel like this guy could really understand my anger, so I explain, pointing at Robert, "This guy was taking money by the freeway." I'm gasping, and the guy is trying to understand me. "He was slapping this girl around who wouldn't give him money."

"No, I didn't," Robert protests, crumpled in the fetal position.

"Yes, you fucking *did*," I yell. I'm so freaked out by the limo, the limo driver, the guy at the ATM, and the guy who is practically standing on my shoulders that I can't remember if that's exactly what happened, even though I'm pretty sure it is.

"Scumbag," the guy says, spitting on Robert.

"Let's go," the guy at the ATM calls out, and just as I'm about to say something polite like "Thanks for stopping by" or "Nice to meet you," the guy standing next to me kicks Robert in the head, once, twice, until Robert is unconscious.

All I can think is, *This guy isn't even sweating*, and his grin makes me step back.

The limo pulls away slowly, flowing through the outside teller channels. I jump in my car, maneuvering around Robert, trying to follow the limo, but the limo gets lost in traffic.

Best Man

Slowly I start toward JSB's office, the walls of the hallway lined with framed posters of past ad campaigns for Buckley Cosmetics, twenty years' worth. Sunlight wafts in from the rectangular windows above me. I stop in front of Talie's mother's layout, the one introducing her as the 1971 spokesmodel, her face peeking out from behind her long brown hair. She is dressed up like a mermaid, submerged in very blue water, her hair floating behind her, the words "World Gone Water" in black print floating around her. I'm staring into her eyes, wondering about the exact moment JSB decided that she was the most beautiful woman he'd ever seen. I begin to move away from the poster, watching Talie's mother's eyes as they follow me down the hall until I am out of sight.

"He left a message he wanted to see me," I tell JSB's secretary, and she nods that he's in and smiles. The double doors to the office are open and I feel the air become cooler as I step forward, the Oriental rug muffling my footsteps, the light from the picture windows causing me to squint. When my eyes adjust, I see the back of JSB's head, his hair trimmed tight. He is staring intently at the desert-landscaped inner courtyard, watching two speckled birds just outside the window. Boxes stacked in the corner lean pathetically

and I feel myself begin to pity him. I stick my hand in my pocket
and jingle my keys, warning him that I am coming up behind him.

"Hello, JSB," I say.

"How are you?" he finally says, swiveling around in his chair,
looking me over, up and down.

"I'm fine," I say, not smiling.

A grin spreads across his face and he jumps to his feet. "I've got
some news for you," he says. "I'm getting married."

"Really?" An automatic response. I get that familiar feeling that
I'm misunderstanding something. "When?"

"Next month," he says. He's actually beaming.

"But I thought . . . ," I start. "The other day . . ."

"We're really in love," he assures me. "Will you stand in my
line? Be my best man?"

"Of course," I say.

"And I want you to initiate a promotional contest for the new
line of cosmetics," he says. "You can handle it. Just organize a party
and make sure we get a winner. I'm going to fight this bankruptcy.
I'm not giving up."

"Okay," I say, and it's a long time after I've left his office before
I can even comprehend what any of this means.

Saving Room for Dessert

The dinner Talie has prepared is laid out on a small table in the corner of the formal dining room at Arrowhead. Penne pasta steams from a porcelain bowl; the single candle is reflected in the oval faces of the two china plates and silverware. "This is fabulous," I say.

"We're having a date," Talie says breezily, which explains her request that I wear a suit. She spins playfully, showing off her strapless black gown.

For the first time since Jane left, I sense that I won't go to bed with a gray feeling pulsating through me.

Talie tells me I look fabulous too and kisses me on the cheek. "A couple of us from the cotillion have been doing these mock dates," she tells me. "You know, to learn how to weed out bad men. I told you I joined the Phoenix Cotillion, right?"

I nod, vaguely recalling her telling me about joining what sounded like a girls' finishing school held on weekends at the Phoenix Cultural Center. "What's the sign of a bad man?" I ask, pouring a dark cabernet into her glass.

"There isn't one sign," she says. "It's an accumulation."

"What kinds of things do you talk about on these mock dates?" The pasta sears the roof of my mouth and I wince, flush it down with wine.

"The gentleman is supposed to lead the conversation. A lady punctuates with witty interludes and thoughtful asides," she says, quoting something. The echo created by the vast darkness of the dining room forces us to calibrate our words to low humming.

I tell her about Jane, lying that I don't really care that she's gone. I consider telling Talie about utopian love, about how Jane and I were a model couple, but her newfound stock in the conventional keeps me silent.

"Did you think you might marry her?" Talie asks, pointing up her beliefs.

I shake my head no. "Do you think you'll marry Dale?" I ask.

"No," she answers. "There's something bad about him. But he'll do until someone wonderful like you comes along."

"I'm not so wonderful," I say.

"You're a gentleman," Talie says, embarrassing me. "You're gentle and giving and, most importantly, considerate. Everything good stems from consideration," she points out.

"You're the only one who thinks so," I say.

"Actually, I did sort of meet someone like you," Talie says, giving up on her pasta. She pours us both another glass of wine.

"Really?" I ask.

Talie's secret lover's name is Frank, and Frank is a corporate attorney, which sounds like the cat's meow, and I get very excited for Talie, until I find out he's married, has two children, and lives in Scottsdale. Frank didn't call Talie like he was supposed to when his wife went out of town, which is why I was invited to dinner.

"You should see his little girl," Talie says. "She is so adorable."

"Are you sleeping with him here?" I ask.

"No, only when his wife is out of town," she says. "At his house."

We sit, not drinking, not eating, sharing our frustrations like we did when we were sophomores together at Leone Cooper High, before I transferred to Randolph.

"Is Frank a great guy?"

"Yeah." She nods, smiling. "Frank's a gentleman, too. He makes me feel at ease, you know?"

Talie's always given me great tips about how to treat a woman, and I log this one in. "Where does he take you?" I ask.

"Take me?" she repeats.

"You know, what do you do?"

"We generally just meet at his place," she says.

"Oh."

"Oh what?" she asks, anger in her voice.

"Nothing."

She closes her eyes. I surprise myself by reaching out and touching her face. Her skin is warm and smooth, and as I stroke the tiny invisible hairs on her cheek, she smiles. Her smile disappears and she opens her eyes. "I know Frank's just another user," she says.

"But you're in love with him," I say.

"I don't understand why he stays with his wife," she says absently. "I mean, can you?"

Wax spindles hang from the candle, which has been steadily melting between us.

"He's just having his cake," I tell her. "Forget this guy."

Talie looks away and I start to pull my hand away from her face, but she grabs my wrist, holding it steady while rubbing her cheek against my outstretched fingers. She stands suddenly, pressing her fingertips on the tablecloth for balance. I stand too, a reflex. She slips her arms under my jacket, clasping her hands at the small of my back, resting her head on my chest. She sighs dramatically, like Jane used to, and I embrace her, stroking her hair like I would Jane's when Jane was suffering.

"I should probably go," I say.

"I need you to stay," Talie says, pleading. She kisses me, tracing my lips with her warm tongue. I close my eyes, knowing if I stay, I'll be that much farther back on tomorrow, but Talie has always been stronger than me and I feel her hand inside my now unzipped pants. Talie reaches over and pinches out the candle with her fingers and she leads us out of the darkness, toward her bedroom, where tomorrow is farther away than the past.

Sylphs

Jon, a photographer for *Stylish* magazine who is in town to shoot the print ad for the new line of cosmetics, forgets to give me the password to get into Sylphs. Consequently, I get into a fight with the doorman, almost knocking him on his ass before Chandra Moses, one of the models hired for the campaign, arrives with another model I recognize from the head shots JSB approved, and I push my way inside behind them. I touch the photo of Talie inside my jacket that I want to show Jon.

We spot Jon at a table on the upper deck with two other models, Belinda and Alisha, and as we climb the wrought-iron stairs, I look down on the dance floor, watching the bodies swirling below me on the black concrete floor, the yellow lights cascading down on them. A free-fall sensation overtakes me as a woman passes behind me. The scent of her perfume is pungent enough to draw me away from the railing.

Introductions are made. The model with Chandra is named Kyle and has gorgeous black locks that bounce whenever she shakes her head. I have a difficult time not staring at all the cleavage that surrounds me, unlike the panting beasts who are circling our table three and four and five times to get a glimpse.

"I tried to get the whole balcony," Jon yells unnecessarily, and we wait for the end of this statement, but Jon just shrugs.

Alisha is listening to the conversation between Belinda and Kyle, of which I can make out only the names of perfumes, and I watch Alisha's eyes, childlike and empty as they drift out of the conversation and her gaze floats around the balcony, sizing everything up. I smile when Alisha glances over at me, trying to create some kind of conspiracy between us, unsure if Alisha even knows who I am, but she doesn't smile and simply looks away.

Chandra excuses herself and the men in her wake follow her exit.

"Did you hear about the place that does cosmetic cloning?" Belinda asks.

"That place outside the city?" Kyle asks.

"Yeah, at the Clinique de Hollywood," Belinda says. "They can make you look like someone else. All you have to do is bring in a picture . . . like getting a haircut, you know?"

"Is that legal?" I ask.

"It's just *plastic surgery*," Kyle says.

"The woman I saw on TV looks like Marilyn Monroe now," Belinda says.

"God, who would want *that*?" Alisha asks.

"Who would you be, then?" Belinda asks.

"I wouldn't even do it," Alisha says. "I think I look just fine."

"You do," Jon agrees. Belinda and Kyle look around, making eye contact with the men who are by now two deep. They flash winning smiles and Kyle even goes so far as to pout, giggling about it with Belinda. The guys nudge one another when Kyle looks away.

Jon puts his arm on the back of Alisha's chair and Alisha is visibly uncomfortable. I reach for the envelope in my pocket as a way to distract Jon, to stop his assault, but Alisha doesn't look to me for help, and I am confused as to whether or not she wants any.

I pull out the photo of Talie and slide it across the table to Jon. "What's this?" he asks.

"A local girl," I say. "I thought we might consider her."

"We've got enough models for the ad," Jon tells me. "Besides, I'm not allowed to use unagented girls."

Belinda and Alisha glance at the envelope, at me, and then back toward the crowding men.

"You should at least take a look," I say. Jon drinks his vodka tonic down to the ice and looks at me. "JSB wants you to consider her," I say. I know if I can get her this one thing, it might project her in another direction, away from Dale and Frank and even me.

Alisha catches the photo as it falls from Jon's indifferent grasp. "She looks nice."

"Her features are too far apart on her face," Belinda says. "Who is she?"

"I suppose your features are perfect," I snap.

"Well . . . ," Belinda says.

"Give it back," I say, reaching for the photo.

"Excuse me," a voice says. We all turn.

The guy Kyle pouted at stands in front of our table, trying not to lose his nerve.

"What?" Jon scowls.

The guy looks at Jon and then leans in over Kyle's shoulder, whispering something in her ear.

Kyle puts her hand on his cheek, turning his head, and whispers something back.

The guy smiles faintly and leaves.

Belinda laughs. "What did he want?"

"He wanted to dance," Kyle says.

"Why didn't you?" I ask, everyone turning to look at me.

Kyle glares at me and winces. "I don't want his hands all over me."

"Definitely a groper," Belinda says.

"This place is getting crowded," Jon says without looking around.

"Yeah, let's go," Belinda agrees.

"Where to?" Kyle asks, finishing her wine cooler.

"Caveat Emptor has a back room," Jon says, standing up.

"I'll meet you," I say, having no intention of letting this night drag on.

I toss the photo of Talie in the trash can in the men's room, knowing I could never look at it again without hearing Belinda's criticism. The bathroom attendant retrieves the photo as I push out of the bathroom, and I don't look back as I rush through a throng of people coming in the door.

Essay #8: Free Topic—Impropriety

It has only recently occurred to me that I open more doors than are opened for me.

I am keeping count.

Previously, I would hold doors instinctively, a natural reflex. And I believed that this was a form of common courtesy, that it was all about fellowship and kindness. But of course it has to be about much more.

I learned this as I listened to a woman, a peer, someone I don't really know, but someone I have held the door for, vehemently arguing that holding doors is an "undue exertion of influence by men over women." There were others who chimed in, talking in cool, clinical terms about things like "equality" and "empowerment." I could not fathom the implications of this conversation. Was common courtesy really an exertion of influence, a favor to be repaid, a debt? Does this mean that a smile or a look can suggest possibilities, make promises, imply?

There is a clear inequality between the sexes.

I have been privy to the secret conversations of men, the in-between comments, the raised eyebrows that telepathically communicate low whistles. There is nothing in these conversations or in this behavior that makes me think these things will ever change.

But I understand why things need to change.

I am on the side of progress.

To prove this to myself, I laughed out loud at a pair of city workers who slowed their truck as they passed a young woman striding along the sidewalk, yelling "Hey, baby" to her and bravely speeding up before she could respond. I laughed out loud at their pathetic existence. And as they passed me (I was just sitting at a bus stop, drinking a cherry Slurpee), the one in the passenger seat nodded to me as if we had an understanding. He thought I was smiling, approving of his behavior.

And I'm not sure I wasn't.

I mean, I saw the young woman first, before the truck came rolling down the street, before the catcall. I looked up and there she was in front of me. I did not say, "Hey, baby," either out loud or to myself, but I did make note of her appearance. That's all: I simply registered whether or not I liked how she was dressed.

But I know not to tell a woman that she looks nice, even though I am thinking that she does.

I've learned my lesson on this one.

I shouldn't even be thinking it, I know.

Because I know that by evaluating her appearance, I am objectifying her, making her an art piece in a museum of other women, and everyone knows that the objectification of women is the cornerstone of pornography and all this leads to the fact that I am considering her, rating her, telling her that I am willing to have sex with her. And I know that if a woman tells me that I look nice, that she likes my new haircut, that she likes the color of my eyes, she is really, subtly, telling me that she would like to sleep with me.

Of course Dr. Hatch disagrees.

I'm learning not to look directly at women I don't know. I understand that this is an invasion of their right to walk down the street unmolested. By looking at them, by trying to catch their attention with a smile or a look, I am frightening them, making them feel uncomfortable, demanding something in return.

Like a smile.

Or a hello.

Or a look.

I understand this completely.

I mean, I really do understand this. I understand that living among an enormously anonymous population can bring out the worst in people. It is very easy to hurt someone. Women have cause to be afraid. But most people are kind and treat people with the kindness and respect they deserve.

There are aberrations, of course.

The two girls we find in a club in Tempe—whose names neither of us can remember—promise they'll do a good job. Jason asks them several times if they've ever done a bachelor party and it's the blonde who says, "Of course not."

I am unamused by this blonde's cuteness, but Jason's panic at not reconfirming with the call girls we finally decided on after a night of endless interviews and evaluations is just now starting to subside. I give Jason the look I've been giving him all night, and he says, "I know, dude, I know."

The gathering of men in the suite at the Pointe South Mountain Resort hushes when the girls walk in. I think the blonde is named Tammy. The girls get back to back in the middle of the tightly mowed tan carpet. Ross MacDonald and Steve Speerman from the accounting department at Buckley jump out of the hot tub on the patio and come inside.

JSB is at the little bar in the corner with his back turned, but Peters from legal turns him around and they both fill their eyes with the two girls.

Everyone is waiting for someone to put the girls in motion, and I tell Jason, "Make them work."

Jason introduces the girls to everyone.

"This is Kiki and Cherry," Jason says.

"Hi, Kiki. Hi, Cherry," a unison chorus greets them.

The girls, whose real names aren't Kiki and Cherry, ask if there's any music, and Jason produces a boom box, which thumps to life. A couple lamps are switched off as the curtains sweep across the wall of windows looking out onto west Phoenix.

The couches and love seat are pushed back into a crooked circle, and any chair available fills the gaps until everyone is seated, JSB on the couch in the middle.

Kiki and Cherry dance the entire song without taking any of their clothes off. Their feeling that suggestive grinding and head rolling will put everyone in the mood fails to take into account that everyone was in the mood when they heard there would be a bachelor party.

Sensing the room's impatience, Jason yells, "Take it off, for chrissake."

Kiki and Cherry try to hide their panic as they lift their shirts off over their heads, buying them another thirty to sixty seconds of dancing before the crowd will want another sacrifice.

There's a knock at the door that no one hears but me. A fat man—two men, it seems—in matching Arizona State University sweatpants and sweatshirt shifts his weight in his maroon and gold flip-flops. The two call girls from the night before are behind him, leaning on the rail.

I step out into the hot night air and close the door.

"You didn't call, so we just came over," one of the girls says. She was the driver of the Lexus in the parking lot of the Circle K where we'd conducted our interview.

"You booked these girls," the man says. "I don't know what you've got going on in there now, but you'll have to pay for these girls." He nods in the girls' direction and his unshaven chin multiplies.

"Look," I say. "Somebody fucked up."

Everyone waits for further explanation, but I cross my arms and the four of us just stand there, waiting.

"We don't have to go in, but we have to get paid," the man says.

The master thespian would be good at this point and I tell everyone to stay where they are.

Inside, the music has stopped and Kiki and Cherry are on their knees naked in the middle of the circle, which has now collapsed in around them. Peters and MacDonald have their shirts off and JSB is on the couch in his boxers.

"Can I have my clothes back?" Kiki asks.

"We want to go," Cherry says, looking up at me.

"If you want to go, you can go," I say. A groan travels around the room. "The *real* girls are here," I tell the room, smirking at Jason.

A chorus of hurrahs chases Kiki and Cherry into the bedroom, their clothes thrown after them. The master thespian lets himself into the bedroom where they're changing, and I bring on the call girls, who you immediately know are going to give you your money's worth when they strip down and start fisting each other in the center of a newly formed circle.

"I'll let you know when we're finished," I tell the fat man, who stands post outside.

I look around to see if JSB is having a good time, wanting to see the satisfaction on his face, a look I single-handedly deserve for saving the fucking day here, but JSB has for the moment disappeared.

I check the bedroom and find Kiki and Cherry sobbing, half clothed, the trauma preventing them from getting fully dressed. The master thespian is sitting between them on the bed, and I'm about to say, "You're still going to get paid," when JSB comes out of the bathroom, still in his boxers, and walks past me without acknowledging me, then sits down on the other side of Kiki.

The master thespian looks up at me, smiles, and turns his attention back to Cherry, whose sobs are becoming less insistent. JSB puts his hand on Kiki's leg and she doesn't push it away. JSB says something in Kiki's ear and she laughs, two tears dripping from her chin onto his hand.

Cherry nuzzles Jason and he looks up at me and winks in a way that sends me to the moon.

"Never let another man take anything from you," JSB used to tell me.

"You have to reach out and take what you want," he'd say.

"Remember that you're the better man," he'd say.

"You'd be surprised who gets what they want," he'd say. "It isn't the one with the most talent or the most brains, but the one who perseveres. You have to be the last man standing," he'd say.

"Excuse me," I say, going into the bathroom, shutting the door. I sit on the closed toilet and consider.

They were here first, it isn't that big of a deal, probably nothing's going to happen. You have to be the last man standing.

You're the better man.

None of them looks up when I open the bathroom door.

"Listen," I say.

Kiki and Cherry look up at me again.

"I'm sorry about tonight," I begin. "We really appreciate you making the effort you did—"

"It's okay, dude," the master thespian says, holding up his hand. "Everything's cool now."

MacDonald opens the door and I can clearly hear Peters's whooping. "JSB, you've got to see this," MacDonald says.

JSB, who I notice for the first time is drunk, slides off the bed, and MacDonald pulls him into the front room.

I close the door behind him and twist the lock. Kiki is staring blankly at the white light coming from the bathroom, and I slip in next to her. She may not even know what has just happened.

I overhear the master thespian say something about a shower and he and Cherry are gone just like that.

How to get from here to there: "Are you okay?" I ask.

It's the wrong thing to say.

"I'm fine," Kiki says.

"Wild night, right?" I ask.

She doesn't even look at me.

I can feel myself blowing it with Kiki. What I learned is that you have to just reach out and take something if you want it. Whether or not Kiki wants it is, for now, at this moment, a lost point. There is no indication that she *doesn't* want it.

There's a knock at the door and I hear JSB's voice.

"Charlie. Unlock the door."

The shower in the bathroom is running and I hear giggling.

Kiki looks at me, at the door, back at me, and I put my hand on her leg and decide what I'm going to do.

Journal #8

The last ice cube free-falls into the watery ice bucket. The ice machine rumbles angrily and then sighs, sputtering the last of anything it has, a spray of water coating the miniature glacier at the bottom of the bucket. I touch my wet fingertips to the corners of my dry eyes, blinking until the Aztec-patterned carpet comes into focus, my bare feet blending with the browns and greens, so that I'm convinced my toes are disappearing. I blink again and put one foot in front of the other.

Our limo driver, Happy something or other, rushes me when I push open the door. "Too stiff," he says, digging his tree-trunk fingers into the ice bucket, fishing for a chunk of ice. Behind Happy I see my new Jenny, her prom dress shucked in the corner in favor of her brother's army fatigue T-shirt and boxers, expertly holding a lit cigarette and a bottle of Budweiser in the same hand, waving from the balcony at someone as he passes underneath. The room's population seems to have doubled since my trip to the ice machine, other prom couples having found their way to the suite I rented for me and Jenny. I recognize the two foreign exchange students from Germany, Johann and Gustav, both with their hair dyed so blond they look albino; in the corner opposite the master race is Quentin, a second-year senior, and his date, Yesenia, who Jenny knows is secretly seeing either Johann or Gustav, I can't remember which. Jenny's friend Zach puts his arm around her on the balcony and they scream down at someone, Jenny losing her beer over the edge. The sound of the bottle crashing sends Jenny into hysterics.

Happy finds a piece of ice that will fit into his glass of vodka and tells me he'll be out in the car. He asks if I still need him, essentially asking if it would be better just to send the limo away, to stop the hemorrhage of cash, and I punch him in the face, my knuckles glancing off his flat nose, skimming his left cheek and ear. Happy drops the glass of vodka and, too stunned to say anything, runs out of the room holding his face.

Jenny pretends not to have seen, not wanting to acknowledge what I'm pretending to be capable of. She locks herself in the bathroom with Zach and the laughing continues, drowned out by the arrival of more prom couples, ones I don't recognize, who ask loudly where Jenny is. Someone turns on the television, which is sitting on the floor, as the credenza has been moved out onto the balcony for use as a makeshift bench from which to gawk at the other prom couples streaming into the hotel.

I'm just a kid. The echo in my ear since dinner, Jenny's justification for breaking up after prom, dulling the shine on the evening I'd spent weeks laying out. All gone with those four words. Where normally those words would've seemed a skip in a record to me, the turntable having been bumped many times before— sometimes my fault, sometimes not—I recognized right there under the white canopy of Octavio's that with the end of the evening, it would be over between us. My ego had conspired with Jenny to set me up for just such a fall: Jenny calling me her old man, whispering her thankfulness at being with someone who was "experienced," praising the maturity of our relationship, expressing her gratefulness at not having to stand around a keg in the desert, groped by novice hands, romanced by the indolent.

It was my idea, the whole thing, it always is, but I always fail to see—or rather, hope against hope that the entire house isn't built upon sand that can slip away with something like "I'm just a kid." My last Jenny had it sneak up on her, waking up one morning with the feeling that she was ready for what's next, not really knowing what next was. The Jenny before that accused me of keeping her eighteen, an accusation easily defended against by the lack of supporting evidence, of the nonexistence of her case, but even after the verdict was rendered in my favor, she left.

Someone in a tuxedo sticks his head in the door and yells that Vic is going to jump off the hotel roof, and while it seems impossible that everyone knows Vic, or cares about his welfare, the room empties, Jenny and Zach bursting out of the bathroom, the smell of marijuana trailing them out the door and down the hall. The TV blares in the sudden silence, a commercial for a compilation of hit music suitable for parties. Couples dance across the nineteen-inch screen, grooving to songs from my past, reminding me of all my Jennies. One song in particular feels overly familiar, and I mumble the lyrics along with the television, marveling that I know the words to a song I haven't heard in maybe fifteen years or more. The words come down from my brain as if I wrote the song, and I continue singing it even after the commercial has ended, am still singing it when a scream pulls me out the sliding glass door just in time to see Vic catch himself atop the building across the courtyard, windmilling to keep his balance. I spot Jenny and Zach, arm in arm, moving through the crowd below like celebrities at a charity event. The door swings open and Happy starts screaming in my direction. The officer puts my hands on the credenza and reads me my rights. The manager starts bitching at me about the state of the hotel room. Happy tries to get at me with a left hook, but the officer pushes him back. Vic teeters again on the hotel roof, the crowd below shouting up at him, Jenny shouting too, her pleas meant for Vic reaching my ears instead. I watch Vic trying to keep his balance. The officer wheels me around, and even though I couldn't pick Vic out of a lineup, I can feel him falling.

Ceremony

When Talie calls me from the cotillion, crying, I'm sure it's because of Dale.

So when I meet her at the Phoenix Country Club, I'm surprised when it isn't. Sure, Dale canceled out on Talie's cotillion at the last minute, but Talie is more upset that Frank wouldn't even consider it when she called him.

"What did you expect?" I say. I know this isn't helping, but it's a way for me to make my point by using someone else as an example.

"He acted like he didn't know me." Talie sobbed. "Do you know what he said?"

"What?"

"I said, 'Frank, it's me,' and do you know what he said?"

I couldn't guess.

"He said, 'We're not interested,' and hung up."

"That's rotten," I say.

"You know what? I heard his wife in the background," Talie says. "He *is* married."

I couldn't say "Of course he is"—if it were anyone else, I would've, I might've thrown a dismissive wave of my hand for good measure. But Talie says it as if she were just learning of the possibility, and when this innocence washes up on the shore of her cheeks, I just want to stand there and wade in it.

"Have you been inside yet?" I ask. Slow, lyricless music plays in the ballroom at the end of the carpeted hall.

"I can't go in without a date," she says, and without asking me, I know what this means.

"It would be my pleasure," I say, holding my arm out in an exaggerated way.

"Tuck in your shirt," Talie says, pointing.

I shove the ends of the collarless shirt I threw on into my jeans.

"That's better," Talie says, and takes up my arm. "Let's do this thing."

If I live to be one million, I know I won't forget how it feels to stroll through the doors of the ballroom into the garden of sound where couples are waltzing elegantly on the shiny marble dance floor. Talie has those little ways of making you want her, like every woman does, the way she might look at you and make you feel like you are extraordinary when you need it, the way she revolves on the outside of group conversations, like she used to do in high school when we were kids, giving me that anxiety where I was afraid the rope would snap and she'd float into a new orbit and out of mine for good.

Talie scowls at anyone who dares to point out my informal dress. We waltz on the outside corner of the dance floor, and Talie stares straight into me as she waltzes us toward the center of the floor, where we turn and turn among the staring.

"Who do you know here?" I ask.

"There are some girls from my cotillion class," Talie says. "I don't want to talk to them, though. I told them all about Dale— showed them a picture, if you can believe that—and they're probably wondering who you are."

"It seems like there are a lot of couples here," I say.

Talie continues to waltz me in time to the music.

"All these chicks have boyfriends," Talie says bitterly. "They think this is the fucking prom or something."

"Why didn't Dale come tonight?" I ask, suddenly curious.

"You know," Talie says. "He had things to do."

The waltz ends and the eager couples wait for the next song as Talie and I exit the dance floor.

Talie slumps down in a chair at a fully set table and I slip into the chair next to her.

"I just wanted to dance one dance," Talie says.

"I'll stay as long as you want," I tell her. "Do you want me to get you anything?"

"There was supposed to be dinner . . . but it looks like we missed it."

"Where's the bar?" I ask, looking around.

Talie laughs. "You and I are probably the only ones of age here."

"Really?"

"Most of the girls in my class are still in high school," Talie says. She sighs. "I wish I would've learned at that age what they're learning now. It might've made a difference."

I touch Talie on the knee but self-consciously withdraw my hand when a couple passes our table.

"Which fork is this?" I ask.

"Salad," Talie answers automatically, like a game show contestant.

"I used to think the different sizes were for different-size hands," I admit.

Either Frank tells fantastic tales or Talie translates them through a distorted lens, because the description Talie gave when I asked where Frank lived doesn't match the address we pull in front of. Where Talie said "huge Tudor manor" I would say "ranch house."

"Is this it?" I ask.

"Yep," Talie giggles. "Are we really going to do this?"

The question didn't come up in the grocery store where we bought the toilet paper and gallon of vinegar. The vinegar was my idea, and when I see the speedboat parked in Frank's driveway, I know it was the right choice. "Why not?" I say. Talie giggles again and her smile makes me happy.

"This is *so* juvenile," she says before opening the car door.

Frank's front yard is treeless, so we sneak right up to the house.

"Go around back and I'll toss you one," I tell Talie. She nods and her cotillion dress glows in the night. As she disappears behind the darkened house, I unscrew the vinegar and climb aboard the boat. I unzip the plastic seat covers and soak the seat cushions with vinegar. A sharp odor rises and I stand back, spilling vinegar on my shoes. I roll the plastic bottle along the bow, and it comes to rest against a guardrail, empty.

I hop down and unwrap the toilet paper, launching a roll over the house. A thin white stripe hangs over the front of the house. A few seconds pass and the roll comes back over, bouncing off the slanted roof. I can hear Talie laughing in the backyard, and when we're out of toilet paper, the front of the house looks like a giant face with white bangs in its eyes.

I find Talie in the backyard, staring at a tree swing.

"His daughter is adorable," Talie whispers. She gives the swing a little push. "You should see how cute she is."

"We should go," I tell her. "We made a lot of noise."

I tug on Talie's dress and we walk silently across the lawn. As we pull away, Talie looks back for something and I look up in the rearview mirror, but all I see is a house where Talie wishes she lived. A light comes on for a moment in one of the upper windows and then goes out again. The smell of vinegar from my shoes makes Talie roll down the window, and she leans her seat back, silent as I drive us home in the moonless night.

Essay #9: A Nightmarish Day

Here is the worst possible scenario in my life:

I fall in love, get married, live in bliss, have children, get a job with regular hours, watch my children grow up and drift away, lose interest in my wife, cheat on her with prostitutes who don't satisfy me, lose interest in life altogether, kill myself.

I Give a Lift

The more I am kept waiting by the police, the more comical Dale's phone call seems.

"*Please* hurry up," he begged, as if he were going somewhere. "And don't tell *anyone*." I knew he meant Talie, but the thought that I would hang up the phone and turn to anyone and say, "My best friend's boyfriend just got arrested for soliciting an undercover cop," is like the punch line of a really bad joke.

Curious choice, calling me, is what I'm thinking. Before I even find out the details, I know I will use this to blackmail Dale out of our lives forever.

I don't bother to let Dale tell his story in the car. "How are you going to keep this from Talie?" is all I ask.

"She doesn't know what goes on with me," Dale says with mock bravura, then, gloomily, "They impounded my car. I'll have to tell her it's in the shop."

I'm silent, letting him know I won't help him in any way whatsoever.

"Should I pull up or let you off down the street?" I ask. "Talie left Arrowhead Ranch around four, and I'm sure she's wondering why you're not home."

"Go around the block," Dale instructs, his voice full of alarm. "I've got to get it together."

Dale's suit looks damp, giving the impression that he has just come in from the rain. His tie is gone, probably balled up in his pocket, and his jacket smells distinctly of being somewhere he shouldn't have been. I tell Dale this and he takes his jacket off, folds it over his arm.

"All I want to know is, have you done this before while dating Talie?" I say.

Dale doesn't look at me, doesn't even try to hold me with an honest stare when he says, "No, this is the only time."

I sense true confession and pull over, letting Dale out.

"Okay, thanks," he says, worriedly looking down the street in the direction of his house. "On second thought, could you come in? I'll tell her you gave me a ride from the shop."

I consider my obligations here.

I think of things I'd rather be doing.

"Sure," I agree.

Talie isn't in the lit house and there's no note, but Dale rockets into the bathroom and showers without really calling for her. I snap the TV on and sit on the couch, which is warm and recently abandoned. Something pulls me to the window and I see Talie walking away from a car that takes off in the opposite direction.

"Hi," I greet her at the back door.

"Tell him you found me outside," she says, leading me back to the front room.

We snuggle together on the couch, her excited body vibrating next to me. I put my arm around her and she wilts against me. The perfume of her hair is intoxicating and I'm facedown drunk when the shower stops.

The bathroom door cracks and we break apart.

"There you are, honey," Dale calls out.

"Found her in the backyard," I say.

"Let me get dressed," he says. A door slams.

"Let him get dressed," Talie repeats, smiling at me.

Journal #9

"'Cheese' on three," Jenny's mother says. "One, two, three." The camera snaps and Jenny giggles as we blink away the flash.

"Should we go?" I ask, admiring Jenny's turquoise prom dress.

"Haven't you forgotten something?" Jenny asks.

I'm thinking: hotel room, limo, liquor, two cigarettes, box of condoms, the list completed by the mad scramble to find someone in the parking lot of the 7-Eleven to buy the liter of Franzia. I shrug and Jenny smiles, clears her throat, and touches a strap on her dress.

"Oh," I say. "Yeah, hold on."

Jenny and her mother laugh as I jump down the hall to the kitchen to retrieve Jenny's corsage.

"'Cheese' on three," Jenny's mother says after five minutes of my fumbling with the corsage, before Jenny recognizes that I accidentally bought a wrist corsage.

The flash pops, waving Jenny and me into the final lap of our master plan, a night we've been planning since her mother agreed that Jenny could attend the prom at Randolph. So many late nights on the sectional in front of an unwatched movie ending in "Let's wait," so many aborted gropes in the steamed-up front seat of my car.

The last of the day's sun colors a stripe of orange across Jenny's forehead as I shut the door for her, then skip around to the driver's side. I speed down the freeway toward the parking lot of the Marriott, where our limo awaits—Jenny knew her mother would add two and two if I picked her up in a limo, but I fought for the extravagance and persuaded Jenny to lie to her mother, something she'd never done.

"I still feel guilty," Jenny says.

"It's not too late to call off the limo," I say, a little game we've been playing that up until now has given us some measure of power in the matter. We both know that power is gone now.

"I love you," Jenny says, not as a way to end the conversation, or make it veer, but because it's just something we say, and lately it's the only thing that comes out of my mouth that makes any sense to me: "I love you, too," I say.

"Slow down," Jenny says. "We've got all of our lives. Unless you kill us with your driving." She looks over at me and smiles, remembers my joke about how we're like old people, a sentiment echoed by our friends, and I almost don't look at the road again, caught by the way Jenny looks at me, which makes me feel loved, a look that makes me feel like I'm more than I know I really am.

We exchange my car for the silver stretch in the Marriott parking lot. The chauffeur opens the door for us and we feel like royalty. I point out our hotel room through the moonroof as the limo glides out of the parking lot. A shiver runs through Jenny and she says, "I can't wait." She slides her hand inside my purple paisley cummerbund, teasing.

"We could just skip the dance," I suggest casually.

Jenny pulls back in mock horror. "No we can't!"

"We'll see after a few drinks at Octavio's," I say slyly, kidding.

"I left the fake ID in my other purse," Jenny says, startled. "Oh no, I've ruined it."

I shrug dramatically. She could've told me the limo had sunk to the bottom of the ocean, the driver killed instantly, the windows sealed, and I would've assured her it was no problem, a minor inconvenience, a trifling.

"Actually, Mario got fired," I tell her, almost forgetting. "But he's going to have someone from the kitchen stash the bottle in the limo while we're eating."

"Genius," Jenny says admiringly. "It might've been a little obvious, what with you in a tux, and this." She rotates the corsage on her wrist.

"Yeah," I agree, "and I doubt there'll be any other prommies at Octavio's. So it'll be like eating in a fish bowl."

Jenny smiles deviously. "Got an idea."

I smile back. "Yeah?"

"Let's order in."

That's my Jenny. Bold and daring.

"Can we?"

"Don't know why not," I say.

Plates clank around our feet as the chauffer opens the door. Jenny passes me the bottle of yellow-label brut and I finish it, the bubbles swarming in my head. Our chauffer says he'll return the plates and silverware to Octavio's, and I reach into my wallet and pull out a twenty. "Here," I say. "Give this to the guy in the kitchen, would ya?" The chauffer looks at the bill with disdain and then snaps it up. Jenny laughs and we both know the guy in the kitchen will never see the Jackson.

Stepping through the Randolph gymnasium doors, our names ringing in our ears, is like stepping through a portal in time: The walls are papered black, and silver foil streamers float magically through the air, colliding now and again with the silver, white, and black helium balloons hammering away at the ceiling of the illuminated tent anchored in the middle of the floor, the basketball hoops at either end of the floor hoisted up toward the ceiling to make way.

A slow song starts and I grab Jenny up, pressing her dangerously close, a violation surely to bring one of the chaperones. Jenny wriggles some space between us and I spot Jason and his girlfriend, Sally, twirling under a silver banner.

"My head feels like one of those balloons," Jenny says. We sway in time to the song we've made out to many times before, the saccharine words carrying a tinge of weight on this particular night. "Did I thank you for dinner?" Jenny asks.

"Yes, you did," I say.

"Well, thank you again."

"You're welcome again," I say, spinning her. Our forward progress stops and we twirl slowly in a circle, my rented shoes scuffing arcs in the polished floor.

"Are you ready to leave?" Jenny asks.

"I don't know. Are you?"

"I think I am."

A nervous excitement grips me. Earlier, in front of the mirror, there was still the limo to pick up, the hotel key to get, dinner, the dance itself. A song Jenny and I agree we don't like starts up and I say, "I'm ready if you are."

"Think the limo is back?" Jenny asks.

I look at Jenny to see if she's stalling, and see that she's looking back at me in the same way, to see if I'll use the excuse of waiting for the limo to put it off a little longer, which I almost do, reminiscing about the last dance, knowing that once we leave the gymnasium, the prom will be just a memory, but I don't want to send the wrong signal, so I say, "I'll have a friend drop us off."

It isn't until Jenny and I stumble out of Jason's car—the object of Jason and Sally's jokes all the way to the hotel—that we realize we weren't ready to leave. We realize it after we've opened the box of Franzia and kissed drunken kisses, doing everything we've done before, just up and until, our prom outfits laid out neatly, a stall we didn't recognize. Jenny comes back from the bathroom and we laugh at our naked selves, telling each other it's okay, that we've got all our lives.

A Friend of the Groom's

The grass JSB has rolled across the desert landscaping gives the grounds a lush, fertile feel. Everything seems to be growing and alive. Wedding guests mill around the pool, up near the house, next to the bar set up on the patio of the guesthouse. Talie is standing near JSB's rose garden, talking to Peters from legal. I wave and they wave back.

The caterers are clanging around in the kitchen, stacking trays of food in tall metal containers to keep it warm until the ceremony ends. I run my finger into a cream-filled pastry and no one sees me.

The door to JSB's room is closed, so I knock before letting myself in.

"Charlie," he says when he sees me. His shirt is unbuttoned and he's collapsed on the couch at the foot of his bed. "Come in."

He offers me a drink and I say no thanks.

Erin comes out of the bathroom in her wedding gown, and she's so beautiful I forget who I am. "You look fantastic," I say, kissing her on the cheek.

"Thanks," she says. She models the dress.

"That was Talie's mother's wedding dress," JSB says from the couch.

The image of JSB in the bedroom at the suite at the Pointe South Mountain Resort flickers suddenly and I say, "What?"

"Her mother wore that dress on her wedding day," he says. He gestures toward Erin like a tour guide and my eyes follow, tracing the white silk down the curves of Erin's body—Erin, who wasn't even born when Talie's mother married JSB. I want to burn the dress while Erin's wearing it. I want to splash a bucket of acid on her and watch the dress and her skin melt away.

I can't spit out any words.

"Charlie, I know we don't really know each other," Erin starts. I think she's actually going to reach out and put her arm around me, so I take a step backward. "But we're like a family now, and—"

"We *are* a family," JSB says, standing. He poses the three of us together in the full-length mirror, him in the middle, his right hand—the one he probably used either to hold down or to guide himself into Kiki—hangs over my shoulder. "One big, happy family," he says.

Erin giggles.

"I should find Talie," I say, loosening myself from the weight of JSB's arm. "It's your happy day," I say as I walk out. "It's your hap-hap-happy day."

A woman with chocolaty brown hair is admiring the hand-carved antique grandfather clock in the hall when I slam the door to JSB's bedroom.

"God, you scared me," she says, putting her hand across her chest.

I'm not even going to say sorry, I think, but the sight of her seems to calm me and I introduce myself.

"Caitlin," she says. "I work for JSB."

"Oh," I say.

Caitlin, it turns out, is twenty-eight and is the new salesperson hired specifically to champion the new line of cosmetics.

"That's a big deal," I say. Caitlin leans toward me aggressively, and I lean forward, meeting her gaze. She talks about her upcoming trip—New York, Boston, and Montreal—and about how the new products are going to make Buckley a leader in the industry. She uses phrases like "leader in the industry."

I tell her I'm in charge of the promotional contest. I tell her I've named the contest World Gone Water.

"Oh," she says, nodding in a way that suggests she's heard of me, or knows who I am, and I begin to panic. The walls of JSB's estate feel like prison, and the feeling of being stared at and recognized comes over me. I take Caitlin out a sliding glass door on the side of the house and we pass Talie on the walkway. I introduce them. I notice a faint bruise on Talie's neck.

"Where's Dale?" I ask.

"He's here," she says. "Somewhere."

Talie winks and waltzes off.

Caitlin and I walk to the front lawn, where most of the wedding party has assembled. JSB motions for me to come stand next to him.

"Save me a dance," Caitlin says, smiling.

I take my place next to JSB, across from Talie, who is in Erin's line (at JSB's insistence), and Talie rolls her eyes at me.

The organist under the white canopy begins and everyone rises, and Caitlin stands last, making sure I am watching. As Erin passes down the aisle, my gaze lifts from the veiled stranger to Caitlin, whose smile reaches all the way to the back of me.

"It was lovely," everyone says at one point or another during the reception.

Caitlin dances with other men to make me jealous, so I take Gayle Witherspoon, a secretary from legal, and waltz her around the dance floor. A noxious force field of perfume prevents me from really holding Gayle tight, but Caitlin gets the message and rubs up against me after the song ends. I release Gayle and she stumbles awkwardly off the dance floor.

"Does the best man have to stay all night?" Caitlin asks.

A Romantic Interlude

Caitlin brings me back to her room at the Arizona Biltmore Hotel, a cabana near the main pool. The light coming from the pool is webbed on the walls of the cabanas, and the waves from a couple splashing each other in the shallow end send the light into motion, creating the effect of weak lightning. I have trouble keeping my balance when I stare straight down into the pool.

"Come on," Caitlin says from behind me. She's hiding behind the windowed double doors and I can see her nude body through the white curtains. As I reach the door, the pool light goes out and the splashing in the pool quiets. In the absence of the pool light, the moon switches on and Caitlin's skin glows under my fingers.

Unbelievably, there isn't a test to pass before I'm allowed to touch Caitlin.

"We have what no one else does," I'd have to say to Jane.

Caitlin makes me forget about Jane.

And everyone that's ever come before her.

Curiosity overtakes me when we're lying in bed. I can't stop looking at her. I have to kiss her every five minutes. I touch her body with my lips to make sure she is real.

"You're doing something strange to me," Caitlin says, putting her hand over her heart.

"Do you feel it too?" I ask, placing my hand on hers.

"I'll have to be careful you don't capture my heart," she says, giggling. She rolls on top of me and the warm press of her skin undoes me.

Under her spell, I play a game of nude chess with her on the giant lawn chess board on the hotel grounds. Caitlin knocks one of the rooks down and lies on the grassy square. "Come capture it," she says, sprawling out.

In the morning, robed and having breakfast at the tiny table outside her cabana, she looks at me and asks, "How long have I known you?"

"It feels like forever," I say, getting up to kiss her.

Caitlin decides she wants me to come along on her sales trip, and I decide I can get away with saying I'm doing work for the contest, so I leave a message on Talie's machine and meet Caitlin at the airport for the flight to New York City. One of those chiseled-jaw guys is across the aisle from us in first class, and Caitlin makes a comment about him, purring a little, and I'm surprised at how much it burns me, how much it makes me want to pop the window with this guy's head, exposing the whole cabin to a loss of pressure, everyone being sucked out over Kansas. "Oh yeah?" I say, and, sensing I am upset, Caitlin says, "It doesn't mean he has my heart."

"Who has it?" I ask, wanting to hear it. Caitlin touches her finger to my chest and I kiss her in front of the chiseled-jaw guy to let him know what he'll never have.

What we see of New York: We start at the zoo in Central Park, as it's right outside the Plaza Hotel, our digs (we don't pay to go in the zoo, just look over the fence while the sea lions are being fed). I ride my hand up Caitlin's dress when she's leaned over the zoo fence. People are cramming on all sides but no one sees me, and I slip my finger inside her and I think maybe the guy next to us hears her gasp.

We retrace our steps to the Plaza, and once we're clear of the chandeliers and lunch crowd, she pushes me against the inside of the elevator and rips my shirt clean open, the tiny white plastic buttons scattering around us.

Later, I ask if I can take her out to dinner. I'd like to get dressed up, see her across a candlelit table. The fantasy is ruined, though, when Caitlin says, "Dinner's right here"—a line from a thousand porno movies—and puts her hand between my legs. She takes me in her mouth and I remember when Jason and I used to call each other by our porno names. We followed the rule of taking the name of the street where you lived as your last name. I was Charlie Olive and he was Jason Greenwich.

We used our porno names once, I almost forgot, when we met these two sisters in Las Vegas:

"Let's go inside," the tall, blond, big-nosed girl said as she stood up.

"Help me up," I said. I had about twenty gallons of alcohol inside me and I looked down her inclined driveway at the gate, which was just closing.

"Hey," Jason greeted us. He was sitting next to our good friend who'd moved to Las Vegas for the luck, and with them was the tall, blond, big-nosed girl's sister.

"Wanna hit?" Jason asked.

I pushed the joint away.

"Let's all climb in your bed," the tall, blond, big-nosed girl suggested to her sister.

"Great idea," her sister agreed.

Suddenly the five of us were underneath the covers, passing around a chilled bottle of Southern Comfort. (The sister claimed it tasted better cold.) I looked over at my good friend who'd moved to Las Vegas for the luck and saw him kissing the tall, blond, big-nosed girl's sister.

"Go get it, girl," the blond big-nose whooped.

"Shh!" the sister warned. "The housekeeper is sleeping."

"The housekeeper?" I asked.

"Don't worry, she's old," the blond big-nose muttered.

"When are your parents coming back?" Jason asked.

"End of the week," the blond big-nose answered as she took a swig from the now half-empty bottle. "Fuck!"

"What?" I asked.

"I forgot to turn the lights off in the driveway," she said, and sprang off the mattress.

"I'll go with you," I called out after her, and stumbled from the bed.

The hallway was dark and I heard her flicking light switches off. Then she came back up the hall.

"Wait," I said, and pulled her up against me. We started kissing and I put my hand up her shirt and massaged her breasts. She started getting into it, so I reached down her underwear.

"We can't now," she whispered as she pulled my hand out from between her legs.

"I want you now," I said, and lunged at her.

"Hold on." She stopped me.

"Till when?"

"Later," she whispered loudly. "In my room."

"Okay," I agreed, following her back into the bedroom, where the others were still lounging.

"How often do you guys come to Vegas?" the tall, blond, big-nosed girl's sister asked us.

"Not enough," Jason said. A real cheese machine.

I reached under the covers, hoping to get my hands in the tall, blond, big-nosed girl's crotch again, but when I felt down there, I found Jason had beaten me to the prize.

"Go with me to the fridge," the blond big-nose said to him, and the two of them leaped out of bed.

By the time I stumbled after them, they'd already gone into her bedroom. I crept up to the door and listened.

"Let me get a rubber," I heard her say.

"I brought one," Jason said.

"Oh?"

"Never can tell what you're going to run into in Sin City," the cheese machine said.

Oh my God, I was thinking.

He started giving it to her, because she moaned a few low moans and then squealed a little.

"Hey," I said as I walked in.

Suddenly everything was silent. It was so dark I couldn't even make out the bed. I stood there for a minute, hoping to be invited into a threesome, but no one said anything. I quietly closed the door behind me.

I walked back to the sister's bedroom and opened the door. Our good friend from Las Vegas had the sister spread out naked on the bed and was licking between her legs. She looked over and smiled at me and I closed the door.

I was starting to sober up and I didn't like what was going on. I felt what it was like to lose out on something because I wasn't man enough to just take it. I went out into the front room and sulked on the couch, trying to explain to the housekeeper who I was.

In the morning, while Caitlin is with a client, I skip down Fifth Avenue to a bagel cart for some breakfast. A swell of people come out from the subway under the Plaza, everyone in a business suit or dark clothes. I skip back up the Plaza's steps, palming a warm cinnamon raisin bagel, skip past a limousine with its door opening and past a family of tourists gawking at the chandeliers.

**

In Boston, Caitlin and I have a terrible fight on Lansdowne Street. The fight starts in Axis, where we came to dance. "I'm too tired to dance," Caitlin says. "Let's go somewhere else."

Thinking she really wants a good time, I take the lead and force her on the dance floor. She gyrates lethargically in place to the bass beat of an unrecognizable song before turning and walking off the dance floor.

The fight continues in Jillian's, a pool hall down the street.

"You are *insensitive*," she says. "It's amazing what you can find out about a person."

"Let's just go back to the hotel, okay?" I say. Her insults are mortally wounding me.

I sleep fitfully on the floor, dreaming a dream where Caitlin is riding in a horse-drawn carriage through Central Park while I am running after her on foot. I am calling out to her, but when she looks back, her carriage takes off into the air, gliding over the park and into the clouds. When I try to show someone a picture of Caitlin to find out where she's gone, I realize I don't have any. When I try to pronounce her name to the police, it's untranslatable by the cop.

In the morning I wake when Caitlin crawls down on the floor too. "I'm sorry," I say, hoping today is a new day.

"I'm the one that's sorry," she says.

Our breath is foul when we kiss, but neither of us flinches, and Caitlin says, "I have the weekend off. Let's take a car trip."

"I asked the guy at the counter for a romantic place, and he said there's something called the Colonial Inn in Concord. I guess it's supposed to be historic," I say.

"Well, well," Caitlin says, chuckling. "Aren't we a little Romeo?"

"It sounded like a place that might be haunted, though," I say, ignoring her.

"We could go there," she says, kissing my neck. "Or we could go to Cape Cod."

"Why did you say that just now? The Romeo thing," I ask, pulling away.

"I don't know," she answers, shrugging. "I just thought it was cute that you were, you know . . . doing *research*."

"You were being condescending," I say. I know what kind of reaction this'll get.

Caitlin is silent, then says in a quiet voice, "I'm sorry."

I'm surprised that I have her on the fence. I feel like pushing her further. "Are you a condescending person?" I ask.

Caitlin sits back and closes her eyes. She begins to tremble.

"Look, I was only joking," I say, not surprised at how quickly I back off. "I know you're a good person."

My words have no visible effect on her and I'm stuck for what to say next.

Instead, Caitlin says, "I have this terrible feeling that I'm in love with you."

"Why is that such a terrible thing?"

Caitlin stands, not looking at me, and says, "It really feels great, but I have to guard against it. You're not going to be around forever."

The last words sear me completely.

"I *will* be here forever," I want to say. And even though I *think* it's true, it would sound corny and melodramatic after knowing her for only a few days, so I don't say anything, and we move silently to pack our bag for the weekend.

Things are as they were, though, once we're driving toward the Cape. Caitlin touches the inside of my thigh while I drive, and I glance over and catch her smile.

A giant yellow wreath hangs on the bridge over the canal we cross to get onto the Cape, marking the spot where a woman drove head-on into a metal pole, killed on impact. It was on the news the night before in the hotel, and what occurs to me is that forty-eight hours ago at this time, that person was alive and making plans to drive to the Cape, along with whatever else she was doing that day, picking up laundry, paying her electric bill, calling her friends to say she was on her way.

There was a girl who got killed when I first moved to Phoenix, a foreign exchange student from Russia who stepped out in front of a city bus while looking the wrong way. They put her picture in the newspaper, along with one of a makeshift memorial featuring flowers and a teddy bear that sprang up at the site of the accident. I couldn't look away from the picture. I somehow knew the confusion from that morning, the chaos of running late and the nanosecond that was nothing more than a mistake that cost this girl her life.

The windows on the rental car are manual, so Caitlin climbs in the backseat to unroll them. The wind coming off the ocean scrubs everything clean, and you get a new life.

"I'm just going to sit back here," Caitlin says.

"But I want you up here," I say, patting the seat next to me, looking in the rearview mirror.

"Nope." She smiles. "I'm going to sit back here."

"What'll you do by yourself back there?" I ask.

I love to be coy with her.

"I'm going to put my feet up on your shoulders and masturbate. Will you keep the speed above sixty?"

I eye her in the mirror. "Someone will see," I say, even though I wouldn't care if someone did. It simply seems to me that we could have a nice drive on Cape Cod, squeezed on all sides by ocean and sand, and enjoy ourselves in this pacific freedom without starring in a porn movie. "Come back up front," I say, more telling her than asking.

Caitlin puts on a pout and climbs over the front seat. She turns the radio on and a moment of total division passes between us.

"I wasn't going to do that anyway," she says apologetically. "I was only joking."

"It's a nice day, isn't it?" I ask.

Caitlin rests her head on my lap and closes her eyes. "It *is* a nice day," she says.

An old drive-in movie sign in Wellfleet makes me think of a hundred things from high school.

The Cape narrows, and soon there's beach and ocean visible in every direction. The wind becomes fierce, and Caitlin, sensing something, sits up.

"We've driven to the end," I say. "I didn't even notice."

Caitlin points out the sign for Race Point Beach and I pull off. THIS BEACH CLOSES AT DARK, the sign says. Except for a family wading down the shore, the beach is deserted. The showers in the changing room drip synchronically, and the sandy slope down to the water is one of the walks you know is going to be harder on the way back up.

"Bury me in the sand," Caitlin says.

I kick away the dry sand and scoop handfuls of thick, wet sand onto her body, packing it on tight. Caitlin giggles as I do, and I shape two giant breasts out of sand and put a large tangle of seaweed between her legs.

"Is that what you really want?" Caitlin asks, looking down at her mountainous breasts.

"I want what's inside," I tell her.

Caitlin smiles. "I'm trapped here."

"Yes, you are."

The rest of the afternoon floats away on the open water. The sun takes a last breath and goes under, darkening the water until the ocean is heard more than it is seen.

"I love you," I say to Caitlin.

"You are making me crazy," she says, and the way she looks at me, everything inside her collapsing at once, lets me know that that was the reason I was put on this earth and that she's glad she finally found me.

"I can't believe I finally found someone like you," I say.

We kiss until a spotlight lights us up and we're told to leave.

"Do you want to drive into Provincetown for dinner?" I ask.

"We should probably check into a motel first," she says.

I know once we get to the motel, we probably won't leave, that Caitlin will order room service, or order a pizza, and sure enough, she plops onto the blue floral bedspread in a way that lets me know she's in for the night.

"Come over here," she says, lifting her arms.

"Let me take you out tonight," I say. "There's probably a ton of great places to eat right off the beach."

The minute the words leave my mouth, I want to get them all back.

"There's a great place to eat right here," she says, spreading her legs wide. There's a second where I can turn it into something funny, where I can make a joke or a retort, but while my hope that she will quit saying things like that in favor of something sexier and more romantic is being dashed, I miss it.

I do not what I want to do, but what I feel like I am required to do, until the ugly confidence comes back into Caitlin and she rolls away and turns out the light. Outside, the ocean could be a million miles away.

Caitlin's meeting in Montreal is off Sainte-Catherine, so I wait across the street in a café where no one is smoking but everyone seems to want to. Montreal is our last destination and things between me and Caitlin are shifting. She's holding back now, not telling me she loves me, not holding my hand. "Decompressing" is what she calls it.

I try to picture Phoenix again, and it's such a former life that I won't be able to name things I see once we land. My grand plan (the new one) is to put my offer on the table: I'll do anything to be with her. We could live the way we've been living, hotels and new cities. I think Caitlin just needs someone to make the move, and the idea thrills me.

I'm still pretty jacked up about it later at dinner and it's all I can do to keep from spitting it out.

Outside the restaurant window, Notre-Dame lights up dramatically and Caitlin turns to see it.

"That's beautiful," she says.

"I don't care much for churches," I tell her.

"Me neither," she says. "But it looks impressive."

"You don't have a religion?" I ask.

She shakes her head no. "Don't need it."

I jump up and reach for her hand. She looks around wildly and then looks at me, pulling back. "I think we should be together," I say.

"We are together," she says, straightening her napkin in her lap.

"No, I mean I think we should try and . . ." I'm at a loss for what to call it. "You know, I love you and—"

"Charlie, stop," she says.

The whole moment is flushed away just like that. The waiter comes to take our order and Caitlin waves him away.

The jet lag from Phoenix to New York to Boston to Montreal kicks in, and all the organs inside me collapse, my veins narrowing until the air burns in my lungs. "Do you love me?" I ask.

Caitlin looks away, wanting the waiter to come back. "It doesn't matter," she says.

"Doesn't matter how?"

"Please don't do this," she begs. "This is our last weekend together and we've been having a great time."

"*You've* been having a great time," I correct her. "It really isn't a great time having your heart broken." The words "heart broken" hit her like an oncoming truck.

"What do you want me to do?" she asks, crying a little, which pacifies me in some way. "I can't give myself completely over. I've done that too many times and it never works out."

"It can work out with us," I say.

"That's the first thing all of them said too," she says, composing herself.

"Yeah, but this time will be different."

"That's the next thing they said," she says coldly.

"I'm starting to see your point," I say. I throw my napkin on the table. I play my last card: "Maybe it's *not* worth it."

Caitlin wants to disagree, I can physically feel the pull inside of her, see it in her expression. But she wins out over it and looks right into me and says, "I just can't."

The restaurant in Montreal feels like an outpost on a dream map and I wish I could close my eyes and transport myself.

"Where's the waiter?" Caitlin asks.

"You sent him away, remember? You think he's going to rush right back?"

"Don't get that way," she warns. "Let's try to have a nice meal."

"I'm not hungry," I say. "I'll see you back at the hotel."

I walk out, passing the waiter on his way to the kitchen, and the two of us take a few steps in the same direction, walking like Siamese twins. "She knows what she wants," I tell him.

Paroled into the cold night, I head in the direction of Notre-Dame. The shadows vibrate on the pavement and I start to think about how Caitlin is right. Why give yourself up to someone fully?

I was sitting there trying to deny what I knew was true. Months from now I'd be tired of her, or she'd be tired of me, the excitement of newness worn and forgotten.

I tell her she's right when she gets back to the hotel. "You were totally right," I say. "I don't know what I was thinking."

"Who's she?" Caitlin asks, pointing at the redheaded hooker in the bed next to me, who is rolling a joint.

"It's Diedre, right?" I ask the hooker. Diedre nods. "This is Diedre," I tell Caitlin.

"Nice to meet you," Diedre says without looking away from the joint.

If I hear what I think I hear—Caitlin crying in the hallway, stomping down to the elevator—it doesn't faze me one iota, and Caitlin can take her traveling act to California, for all I care.

Dr. Hatch,

Remember what you said about how the thing that affects your life the most—death—doesn't hardly involve you in any way? Remember I said how it affects other people's lives and we talked about my parents, about the vacuum of nothing I was sucked into when they died? I'm writing to you from there again.

The love of my life is dead. You never met Talie, but she came to see me a couple of times at SRC. It was her slut friend, Holly, who got her killed. I don't think I've ever mentioned Holly to you and I'm not going to start now. Talie was always getting into trouble with Holly, and this time it wasn't trouble I could get her out of. The police found them both in a Dumpster with their clothes torn off.

The funeral was at Saint Francis Xavier, the church adjacent to my old school, Randolph College Prep. The only people who came to the funeral were her foster parents, her biological father, me, and the boyfriend I'm sure she was going to leave.

I stayed after everyone was gone to be alone with Talie one last time. I wanted to open the casket and see her again, have her pop up and say, "Let's go." I feel completely untethered without her. You never know how much you need someone until, well, you know.

I used to tell Talie I was going to go to Europe, that I was going to fly away and shed everything anyone ever knew about me and everything that was in my past. Whenever I told her about moving to Europe, she would say, "The unknown is more frightening than what you know, no matter how shitty what you know is." The unknown is what there is to fear, she would say, and the future is definitely unknown. I told her I feared my *past*. But it isn't so much that I fear what I have done, but I fear I am missing some vital component—the gene that makes you walk on green and stop on red, the thing that tells what the difference between red and green even is. My fear isn't of my future; it's that my past lives there, happily, shimmering in the warmth it creates, perpetuating the voice that assures me, *It's all right, it's okay.*

I'm feeling the same sense of loss I felt when I told Karine I was sorry. She came to see me before she disappeared (I know you're dying to hear me talk about this, so here it is), and we sat and did a crossword puzzle. I used a blue pen and she used pink so that when the puzzle was solved, we'd know who did what.

I told Karine I was sorry and she looked across the metal table at me and said, "I forgive you."

Right there, at the metal table, a half-finished crossword puzzle between us, I realized how much I'd lost in life. When I said I was sorry, it started in my mind as a casual thing to say. But when Karine looked at me like she did and said she forgave me, I knew she had been waiting to hear me say it, and I realized that what I had done to her was the biggest loss in her life.

It made me think about my own loss and I saw myself as something small and stupid, with a grin of infinite hope on my face.

Some people just don't get the chance to live in the world.

Talie never got a start, and everyone I know—including me—is to blame.

After the hearse became a black dot on the road, me promising to catch up, I crossed the lawn to Randolph Prep. William Randolph, the school's founder, died at sea. I used to stare at the portrait of him in the main hall, standing on the bow of a ship, maybe the one he went down on, straining to peer so far into the distance, maybe looking for what sailing would lead him to next.

"A banker by profession, Randolph was an avid sailor, captaining many voyages around the world," read the engraving under the portrait.

Details of his death weren't dramatic enough to reach the status of legend. Simply put, he was hit in the head when a sudden wind swung the sail into him. Randolph and his crew were one full day of sailing away from the shore. The banker/sailor never regained consciousness, and the exact moment of his death went unmarked by a dying word or wish for the world.

What a shock it must have been, the initial blow to Randolph's head, coming from his blind side. He probably never imagined he'd die while sailing, a sport at which he had become accomplished.

In my mind I tried to trace it back, not a straight line between Randolph's death in the water and his birth, but I wondered at the steps between the two events. Fate is too easily made the usual suspect. William Randolph could've been killed in any number of ways: an automobile crash (at high speed, or by a careless driver), an airplane wreck, a gunshot (self-inflicted, or random, accidental fire), a heart attack (in his sleep, or while shopping for chocolate bars in the local grocery store)—all could be uselessly labeled fate.

What are probably the facts: Someone introduced William Randolph to sailing, he enjoyed it, and he was killed, accidentally.

But what I really used to wonder about when I stood in the main hall, and what I often think about, was how easily the chain could've been broken. William Randolph might not have met someone who could introduce him to sailing; he might not have enjoyed it, it might have made him so sick he swore never to leave land; sailing might have proven too difficult for Randolph to master. None of the steps that led to Randolph's death was a conscious decision to do this over that, but if just one thing had gone the other way, his story—his life—might have had a different ending.

World Gone Water

I find Dale at Max Maxwell's, the bar at the Phoenician
supplying the beverage service for the World Gone Water party.
An hour early and standing around the Mojave Ballroom, its
taupe-colored walls producing their own kind of nauseating light,
I decided a drink would calm my nervous stomach. I knew one
drink might lead to two, three, or four, but the caterers, with their
suspicious eyes, forced me out of the ballroom and down to Max
Maxwell's.

Dale looks like he's been at the bar since Talie's funeral.

"Are you coming to the party?" I ask.

Dale sips weakly from a glass of bourbon. He looks at me
through the mirror behind the bar and sips again. He closes his
eyes, as if he's trying to circle the wagons around a thought, but
when he looks up again, this time directly at me, his face is blank.
"You should come," I say. "Talie was a part of Buckley and she'd
want you to come."

My capacity to say things that may or may not be true has
reached the level of artistry, and I feel the full force of this statement's design.

"Did I see you at her grave this morning?" Dale asks.

Suddenly I notice the grass stains on his knees, dirty green swatches painted on his suit pants.

"I am not particularly fond of you," I want to say to Dale. "Talie didn't love you," I want to say. "Talie was in love with someone else," I want to say. "I don't want you hanging out at Talie's grave," I want to say.

"I just got back from picking up the winner and her husband," I say.

"The winner?" Dale asks.

Just mentioning it to Dale brings my anxiety full circle, the anxiety I felt waiting in the ballroom for Carol Bandes, our winner, and her husband, Martin, to arrive, the result of what happened when I made the official gesture of picking her and her husband up at their house in Flagstaff by limo, taking them to a private jet, and flying them to Phoenix for her makeover and the party.

I want to tell Dale what happened, but then again I don't, and I let Dale's question float off into space. I decide to skip the drink. I want to skip the party, too. I'm not even sure that I'm *required* to show. I was only to be the agent who brought everything to a conclusion (as little as I had to do with that), but nothing was ever said of me seeing it through to the end.

When I emerge from Max Maxwell's, the sky is black. There is no trace of the sunset I missed, and the moon makes ghosts of the saguaros on Camelback Mountain.

As I walk back toward the ballroom, I can see where the resort backs into the mountain, where the cement ends and the rock begins. A rash of stars suddenly appears in the sky and everything glows for a moment, until my eyes adjust and all I see again is cement and rock.

A caravan of black limousines rolls past me to the chandeliered entrance of the Phoenician. Flashbulbs explode around the limos, making the night blacker. I feel like I'm hiding in the bushes as

I watch Belinda and Kyle and Alisha each step out of their own limousine. Jon isn't among the photographers but is at Alisha's side, holding her hand, waving at the camera like a movie star.

The Bandeses' limousine lumbers up the driveway toward the entrance. Dale suddenly appears, carelessly wandering in the flower beds. He trips and falls to his knees and I move to help him up, but when he sees me, he pulls a dirty pistol from his jacket pocket. The possibilities of just how badly this could end unfold and multiply.

"Dale, don't," I say, but even I am unconvinced by my words, and I'm thinking no matter how it does turn out, all I'll be reading about in tomorrow's paper is Dale. What won't be in the paper, though—the story worth telling—is what happened when I arrived at the Bandeses'.

The contest was rigged so that someone from Arizona would win, and Carol Bandes was the first name we drew from the mailed entries that qualified. I made the half-hour flight up from Phoenix in the Buckley Cosmetics private jet to pick up Carol and Martin. From the airfield, a limousine shuttled me into the trees, in the direction of the Grand Canyon. The San Francisco Peaks loomed in the sky above. The snowcaps reminded you that even though you could see them, they were somewhere else, in a different place than where you were.

At a certain point traffic thinned, so that the only cars on the highway were those loaded down with families and crammed floor-to-ceiling with camping gear and luggage. The limo driver, a thin, dark-haired man, announced the address as he turned at the wooden sign bearing the number of the Bandeses' house.

I presented a dozen roses to Mrs. Bandes when I told her she had won the Buckley Cosmetics World Gone Water contest. JSB had stressed the importance of surprising the contest winner, if only to prevent the winner from declining, which would be bad publicity.

"The what?" she asked, leaning forward, squinting. Her close-cropped blond hair hugged her small features, and her smallish frame seemed to be swallowed by the open space behind her.

"Your name was drawn as the winner," I repeated.

"But I didn't—" Just then a tall, severe-looking man covered the distance in the sparse front room to the front door in two or three steps.

"Can I help you?" he asked. He stood behind his wife, and the two of them made for an impressive couple.

I explained myself again, the look on Carol's face growing increasingly confused, until her husband said, "Oh, I entered you in the contest, honey. It seemed like a lark."

Carol's confusion was replaced by an uncomfortable look, and she peered over my shoulder at the silent limo in her driveway. Finally they invited me inside.

The wooden floor creaked a minuet as the three of us made our way to the couch. Carol took the roses from me and I explained the day's plan to her.

"I don't know if I'm up for the trip today," Carol said. "I had some things I was going to do. As a matter of fact, if you were thirty minutes later, you would've missed us entirely."

Carol shifted on the couch. The silence inside brought every noise from outside right into the amphitheater of their living room.

"If you don't want to go," her husband said, "you don't have to go. I just thought you might like it."

Carol shot him an incredulous look and he glanced down at his shoes.

"I'm sure they have an alternate," he said, looking at me.

"I think you might enjoy yourself," I said. There was no alternate and I could feel this whole thing slipping into disaster. The idea that winning the contest would be an imposition in someone's life hadn't occurred to me, and I was unprepared to make a persuasive argument against it. "A limo ride, a short flight to Phoenix, a party at the Phoenician. Not a bad way to spend a day."

"I don't fly at night," Carol said.

"We'll put you up at the Phoenician for the night," I said. "We want you to enjoy yourselves."

Carol looked at Martin. Martin smiled, and Carol shrugged and said, "Okay, let me change and we'll go."

"There'll be a makeover in Phoenix," I said, which came out sounding more offensive than a litany of profanity, but Carol understood my meaning and reappeared unchanged, a small bag in her hand.

Once we were riding back toward the Flagstaff airport, Carol and Martin relaxed and they seemed to become one person. They laughed about a neighbor who had cut a tree down onto his house, and Martin talked a little bit about his part-time job at Snowbowl, the ski resort nearby. Martin was retired from the railroad—he used to run the logging routes from Washington State to Montana—a business he said was "dying out." His hands were large and powerful, and I felt myself hiding my own under my legs on the seat.

Suddenly the limousine sputtered and lost power. The hum of the engine choked off and we glided slower and slower until the driver pulled off the road and we stopped.

Carol and Martin looked at me, and we waited for the driver to appear at our door.

"She quit," the driver said. "Could be the high altitude."

Martin looked skeptical. "It sounded like the alternator quit." He jumped out, and I felt inclined to follow him even though I knew nothing about engines and how they made a car run.

Martin lifted the hood and peered into the massive gray intestines underneath. He jiggled a few hoses and touched the metal of the engine. You got the sense you were watching a doctor diagnosing a patient. "It's not the alternator," Martin said. "I wonder how old the battery is."

We both looked up to hear the driver's response, but he was leaning on the passenger door, his head tucked away inside the limousine, talking to Carol. Martin scowled and suddenly it was like I wasn't there.

"Excuse me," Martin said.

The driver's head popped up.

"How old is this battery?" Martin asked.

The driver laughed. "I don't work on them. I just drive them." He grinned at his own cleverness.

Martin's voice lowered a full octave. "Do you have tools in the trunk?"

The driver unlocked the trunk and handed Martin a small, red plastic toolbox. The tools inside clanged against one another. The sound carried up the vacant highway.

I stood back to watch Martin operate, but the sound of the limo driver's voice chatting up Carol distracted us both, and the fact that the driver wasn't right there under the hood with us seemed like a fist that just kept pounding and pounding. The driver's voice grew louder as he laughed at something he'd said. His voice took the high, nervous tone of bar talk, and Martin started tapping a wrench against the metal engine housing. The tapping started intermittently and grew louder until the driver looked over in our direction.

I could sense an impending explosion and I feared what Martin might do, so I said, "We could use a hand over here," but before I could finish the sentence, Martin had thrown the wrench to the pavement and was on the driver, asking, "What's the idea here?"

"Nothing." The driver shrugged, unintimidated. "Just chatting."

"That's my wife you're chatting to," Martin said.

"Yeah, she told me," the driver said, defiant. "So?"

The driver stepped back from the car and Martin pushed him into the road.

"Martin," Carol said, emerging from the limousine. She appeared relieved in a way that made her look like she'd come back from a year's vacation on a tropical island where the only real concern she'd had was whether to eat coconuts or bananas for breakfast.

A sound like a clap of thunder echoed and the driver was on the ground, writhing in the middle of the two-lane highway. A look of complete concentration overtook Martin as he kicked the driver in the chest. Carol froze where she stood and then a curious thing happened. Martin's face changed to real anguish, a deep hurt flashed in his eyes, a look in sharp contrast to the look on Dale's face when he had Shane right where he wanted him in the parking lot of the County Line. Dale's look was that of a champion, someone who was enjoying another's defeat at his hands. Martin, though, seemed truly pained as he continued to hammer his foot into the driver, who was by now curled up like a caterpillar on the road.

One of the Bandeses' neighbors happened by, picking us up, and the remainder of the trip was made in silence. I came to believe that Carol and Martin despised me in some way that I could understand and agree with. I parted company with them after we landed in Phoenix, excusing myself on some errand for the company but promising to see them at the Phoenician later that night.

But the look on Martin's face haunted me. When the hurt came across his face, you knew that everything his life was about was wrapped up in his life with Carol. He was protecting the source of his happiness, and you had the immediate feeling, watching him, that he understood that that happiness couldn't be found anywhere else and any threat or challenge to it would be met and extinguished.

As I watched Martin and his warrior-like battle with the driver, I was transported into the dreams of my youth, dreams where I used to see myself way into the future, married to someone who loved me. I dreamed those dreams as a way of comforting myself, I suppose. Talie had told me she'd had the same dreams. We both dreamed of a house, and a car, and a neighborhood where children would play under the afternoon shadows of elm trees. We could easily see ourselves in the windows of these homes on these tree-lined streets, in these phantom neighborhoods. Talie's dreams included enough children to people an entire elementary school, and my dream included similar scenarios. I'd imagine myself coming home from a good job, walking up the driveway, anticipating the warmth just inside the front door, where small coats hung on hooks and lunch pails with half-eaten sandwiches had been dropped next to unlaced shoes. Before anyone knew I was home, I could sense my family, anticipate their excitement when they saw me, an excitement matched in pitch only by my own. And inside our home, everything else in the world remained locked out, strange and foreign in the light of family.

The dream comes back to me with a clarity that is startling, mined from the darkness where dreams stir. Even if the details are the fantasies of youth, buried and forgotten in time, the truth of the dream remains. Dusted off, it gleams anew, and I'm embarrassed at how much I want to believe in it now, how much I want to believe it is something still worth trying for.

Garden Lakes

Praise for GARDEN LAKES

"It takes some nerve to revisit a bulletproof classic, but Jaime Clarke does so, with elegance and a cool contemporary eye, in this cunningly crafted homage to *Lord of the Flies*. He understands all too well the complex psychology of boyhood, how easily the insecurities and power plays slide into mayhem when adults look the other way."

–JULIA GLASS, National Book Award-winning author of *Three Junes*

"As tense and tight and pitch-perfect as Clarke's narrative of the harrowing events at *Garden Lakes* is, and as fine a meditation it is on Golding's novel, what deepens this book to another level of insight and artfulness is the parallel portrait of Charlie Martens as an adult, years after his fateful role that summer, still tyrannized, paralyzed, tangled in lies, wishing for redemption, maybe fated never to get it. Complicated and feral, *Garden Lakes* is thrilling, literary, and smart as hell."

–PAUL HARDING, Pulitzer Prize-winning author of *Tinkers*

"Jaime Clarke reminds us that if the banality of evil is indeed a viable truth, its seeds are most likely sewn among adolescent boys."

–BRAD WATSON, author of *Aliens in the Prime of Their Lives*

"In the flawlessly imagined *Garden Lakes*, Jaime Clarke pays homage to *Lord of the Flies* and creates his own vivid, inadvertently isolated community. As summer tightens its grip, and adult authority recedes, his boys gradually reveal themselves to scary and exhilarating effect. In the hands of this master of suspense and psychological detail, the result is a compulsively readable novel."

–MARGOT LIVESEY, author of *The Flight of Gemma Hardy*

"Smart, seductive, and suggestively sinister, *Garden Lakes* is a disturbingly honest look at how our lies shape our lives and destroy our communities. Read it: Part three in one of the best literary trilogies we have."

—SCOTT CHESHIRE, author of *High as the Horses' Bridles*

It would be the hottest day of the year. The temperature would climb steadily toward a new page in the record book, some one hundred and twenty five degrees by two o'clock, obliterating all previous records. We wouldn't learn of the devastating effects until our return from Garden Lakes—Sky Harbor International being shut down because of melting runways, the body count among the elderly whose air conditioners had failed—and by then the story would be mythic, a legend we would hear over and over as we grew older.

Our concerns that morning were not of the weather. We were weary not only from having risen with the sun, but from having spent the preceding month sauntering by the bulletin board outside of Principal Breen's office, anxiously awaiting the posting of the roster of those select juniors who had been chosen for a fellowship at Garden Lakes. Historically, Garden Lakes Fellows had gone on to good colleges, or to celebrated careers, and while to some the opportunity was merely a jewel in the crown, for others it was an academic life jacket, keeping them afloat until the fall semester of their senior year, the one last chance to bring up the old GPA.

The delay in posting the list was due to vandalism to the statue of St. Francis Xavier in the chapel courtyard. Someone had spray-painted the head lime green and a rumor reached the administration that the vandals were juniors. Principal Breen threatened to cancel the summer leadership program if the responsible parties didn't come forward. We juniors let our displeasure be known and were relieved when a pair of freshman took responsibility (though they would later claim they were pressured into accepting the blame) and the roster was published the last Monday of classes.

And so as we boarded the red and white school bus, *Randolph College Preparatory* stenciled unevenly on the sides, the relief we'd felt the previous Monday had been replaced by sheer amazement. Simply, those of us who had been selected for Garden Lakes still had the feeling that the whole thing was an illusion, that we'd be prohibited from realizing the honor; but once we glimpsed the school bus, looming like a time machine in the parking lot, we believed. Even if we'd had a crystal ball, we couldn't have guessed what lay in front of us. Before that morning, we didn't know how to flatter or cajole or threaten; or how to use suppression, silence, or misdirection in the service of motive. We did not believe in altruism (as far as we understood it)—self-sacrifice was for those who had cashed in their ambition; our understanding was that personal achievement would lead to success in all facets of life, and that this personal achievement could be obtained through hard work and dedication. But our fellowship at Garden Lakes would change that, poisoning us, widening our arsenal for achieving objectives and forcing our will. The story of our fellowship would be as legendary as the heat that summer, the two stories told in the same breath. But as we took our seats, all we had on our minds was privilege and the chance for distinction.

Duane Handley jumped on the bus first. Hands, who would one day lead his family's sixth generation brewery to ruin, was the star guard on our basketball team. Even as an underclassman, he stood out among everyone else in our class. He was taller, more muscular, and always smiling, which didn't go unnoticed by the students at our sister school, Xavier College Prep. He even seemed smarter than the rest of us: Hands had discovered that if you took British Literature instead of American Literature you could cross the street to Xavier, since Randolph only offered American Lit. (Crossing the street only in the figurative sense as a cement walkway with fencing had been erected over Central Ave., which we all took to calling the Bridge of Sighs, named for our reaction to the hordes of blue and green plaid skirts coming and going.) Xavierites figured this out, too, and soon American Lit classes at Randolph were filled with pleasant smells rather than odors, and you learned to pre-register rather than risk getting wait-listed.

Dave Figueroa sat next to Hands. Figs and Hands had been best friends since Lincoln Elementary, where they'd teamed to win the annual talent show with their air band, Phantasm. Figs lip-synched the lyrics to Journey tunes while Hands pounded out the back-up music on an unplugged keyboard borrowed from the nearest high school band department. The two seventh graders tapped to play air guitar lead and bass would ride their talent show glory to the end of their days at Lincoln.

Figs, who would later in life succeed in covering up an embezzlement at the firm where he worked, was renowned for another reason: the sophomore class trip to Mazatlán, Mexico over spring break, a trip sanctioned by Randolph as a way to throw students into the fire together, to make sure that they thought of themselves as a unit, a measurement of loyalty to their alma mater. For reasons that no one could point to, the sophomores didn't have the cohesion that classes before had, but as Figs and Hands and the others blazed through Mazatlán over spring break, working their way down Del Mar, to Gus Gus Bar, to Mundo Bananas, to Mr. Tony's, their bond grew.

How they got from there to a nondescript house brimming with girls named Rosa in the Naval Zone was the subject of much debate. Some thought they were going to a house party, others thought the ranch house was a roadhouse. A party of young men, some they recognized and some they didn't, shuffled around the dirt front yard. They were eventually shuttled into the backyard where the breeze from the Canal de Navigacion picked up, blowing a typhoon of plastic cups and blue plastic bags in circles around them. Everyone except Figs went inside.

Some assumed Figs had reconsidered, though, when they heard him in the musty hallway. A sound like thunder shook the walls, which no one noticed, breaking from their business only when the doors to their rooms flew open, Figs standing breathless and wide-eyed. "Federales," he tried to scream. A panic gripped the house, the Rosas heading for a door leading to the basement, grabbing their camisoles and lace panties. Figs led a charge out a window in a back bedroom, jumping through the screen head first, landing miraculously on his feet. The sophomores laughed about "that night at Rosa's" from thereon after. But while they laughed vigorously at what happened in Mazatlan, they were secretly horrified by what would've happened if they'd been rung up by the Mexican police. They imagined they'd still be in jail, or worse. Needless to say, everyone was grateful to Figs for standing look out, and it wasn't a coincidence that he was elected junior class president the following year, a unanimous vote.

The sole rift between Figs and Hands, which, had we known about it, might've provided the frame of reference that would've saved the fellowship that summer, occurred two months before the end of their eighth grade year, on the graduation trip to Disneyland. As Figs and Hands attended school in a district with a dismal high school graduation rate, the feeder elementary schools felt compelled to treat graduation from the eighth grade with the pomp and circumstance of a high school graduation, renting a room at the Phoenix Convention Center and decking it out with ribbons in the school's colors to give that statistical percentage of students who wouldn't graduate from high school the look and feel of a real graduation. And prior to gradu-ation, the "senior" class went on a bus trip to Anaheim for a weekend at the Magic Kingdom, all paid for by sponsors.

Figs was lucky to make the trip. Two weeks earlier, he'd been busted selling lunch tickets to underclassmen, having lifted a box when the print shop delivery driver asked Figs to keep an eye on his van, which the driver kept running for the air conditioning. Unbeknownst to Figs, the school had called the print shop to report the missing tickets, which were numbered with red ink, in order to get credit on the next shipment. So when students began presenting the same missing numbered tickets in the cafeteria, it didn't take long for the lunch lady to shake down a fifth grader for information.

The principal expressed his disappointment in Figs, but Figs didn't feel it. While he affected contrition, he felt a certain invincibility—his eighth grade head had swelled to the point that he believed his and Hands's presence at Lincoln made people *want* to come to school. This overestimation didn't manifest in arrogance—Figs had time for you no matter who you were or what grade you were in—but as an endeavor he aimed to excel at. His popularity at school was a job that he loved, a job he hated to leave when the bell rang at three-thirty and one he couldn't wait for when his alarm rang at seven a.m. He did understand what he'd done wrong—not in financial terms, but in terms of jeopardizing his status. The lunch ticket stunt was to him victimless and had provided some much needed pocket money, and he knew the principal would let him off. Which the principal did. The principal would, however, have to notify Figs's parents, which was okay with Figs as his parents, who loved him and whom he loved, were so devoted to their jobs that the only communiqué from Lincoln that would've garnered any attention was if Figs was flunking out. His parents had witnessed Figs's self-discipline grow elementary school after elementary school, town after town; and so they never worried over him, offering their advice only when it was solicited, which was next to never.

The principal knew this, too, and flirted with holding Figs back from the Disneyland trip, but Figs lobbied a number of his teachers, who intervened on his behalf, citing an otherwise stellar academic and social record. So Figs was permitted to go, which was a relief as Figs had been keeping secret his knowledge that Hands's girlfriend, Julie Roseman, was breaking up with Hands to go out with him. This bit of treachery had developed innocently. Julie and Hands had been an item since the first of the year; it was reputed (and true) that Julie had been dating a freshman at the high school where her older sister went. Hands and Julie started to fool around at her parent's house after school, though, and soon Julie had called it off with the freshman, inaugurating the trifecta of her, Hands and Figs.

Figs welcomed Julie as a part of his friendship with Hands. On the days that Hands didn't have basketball practice, the three would end up in Julie's pool, engineering the trampoline so they could jump from the roof and bounce into the deep end. Sometimes they'd invite others from Lincoln, but most times it was just the three musketeers.

Julie tried to interest Figs in some of her friends, and Figs was interested in a peripheral way. But he had a girlfriend in Seattle that he met on a family camping trip to the Grand Canyon and to whom he'd continued to sign letters "Love, Figs," and so he forced himself to stay within reasonable limits, imagining that his girlfriend was doing the same.

But the letters from Seattle were fewer and fewer until they stopped all together. A succession of panic-induced phone calls yielded no return call. Figs revealed to Hands his plan to move to Seattle after high school with his parents' consent. The silence from Seattle, however, shattered those plans and he consoled himself by showing up unannounced at Julie's, raiding her father's liquor cabinet and chugging from a half-drank bottle of Jack Daniel's, taking long gulps, letting the amber liquid fill his cheeks, flushing it down his throat while his mouth filled again with the smoky flavor.

Julie cleaned up the vomit in the bathroom while Figs lay comatose on the white leather couch in the living room. She called Hands and said he should come right away, but between Julie's call and Hands's arrival, it happened. It had probably happened before, or the seed had been planted, but before Figs had puked and passed out, Julie was touched by the look of loss in Figs's eyes. She'd never seen anyone so undone by love—not even her parents, the only model of love that she knew. And so when Hands pushed open the front door to find Julie sitting cross-legged on the loveseat, staring at Figs's lifeless form, he had no way of knowing Julie had fallen in love with Figs.

Figs was to find out some weeks later, when he showed up at Julie's for what he thought was a pool party. He found Julie poolside, alone. The clear pool water was still. *Last one in*, Julie said and they scrambled out of their clothes. The pool light cast a shimmering light and before Julie's sister and her boyfriend appeared, Figs realized that Julie loved him. The three had spent so much time together that they had a sort of telepathy. They'd also established boundaries, albeit unspoken, and Figs thought it strange when Julie brushed up against him on the underwater bench in the shallow end. She had never breached his space in that way, and he shrugged it off as having something to do with the fluid dynamics of swimming. But when she brushed him again, this time on her way out of the pool, Figs couldn't help read the signal, confirmed days later on an afternoon at Julie's parent's house when Hands had to practice.

Figs reasoned that just kissing wasn't cheating; anyone can kiss anyone, he thought. Then he imagined Hands, his best friend, kissing Julie and it took several hours to beat back the rage that built inside him. Figs wondered if he had been in love with Julie the whole time, revisiting his argument with Hands when Hands broke up with his ex-girlfriend Kristina on her birthday. Figs tried to convince Hands that breaking up with Kristina for Julie was a mistake, a bad decision guided by only one principle: Kristina wouldn't let Hands go any further than taking off her shirt, and Hands was ready to try more.

Figs knew Hands would remember that exchange, gentle as it was—Hands prevailing without further protest from Figs—when he found out about Figs and Julie. Figs had a trump, but he didn't want to have to use it. A couple of weeks before, when Julie was at a doctor's appointment, Hands had convinced Figs to go with him to Kristina's house. Hands was vague about who would be there, and what they were going to do. It ended up just being the three of them, with Hands and Kristina disappearing into one of the back bedrooms when Figs went to the kitchen for another Dr. Pepper. Figs watched an hour or so of cable and then left. Hands called him later that night, asking what happened, saying he and Kristina weren't gone but a minute, that Kristina had wanted to show him something in her parent's room, which Figs knew was the official version should a version ever be needed. But it didn't come up the next day at school, and Hands and Kristina passed in the hall like strangers.

Figs and Julie fixed on her house as the venue for admitting their relationship to Hands. Figs had expected some shouting, possibly a fistfight. As music filtered from her sister's room, Julie spoke. The tone in her voice belied her nervousness, and she explained the matter straight through. Hands was puzzled at first, looking over at Figs now and again. When Julie wound down, Hands looked at her and said, "Thanks for being honest" before walking away without acknowledging Figs.

In the week or two after, nothing but graduation and a long, hot summer ahead, Figs and Julie managed to avoid Hands. His excision from their routine was easy and the ease was disconcerting.

The day of graduation, Figs met Hands outside the auditorium (he never knew if it had been arranged by Julie or merely an accident) and after an awkward moment where Figs asked about his parents, Hands looked him in square in the eye and said, without hurt or malice, *I would have never guessed at your disloyalty.* He offered his hand, and Figs shook it, Hands's words haunting him all through graduation, through the long summer, through Julie's family's surprise departure for Texas. He parsed that phrase out loud when alone and silently when in the company of others. He researched his past for any history of disloyalty and came up with nothing. He didn't see it at first, his reflexivity keeping his spirit buoyant, but on a particular late summer afternoon, on a walk past Julie's old house on Garfield Avenue, its windows shaded with the blinds and drapes of the new owners, Figs felt the full force of his betrayal, innocent as it had come about, and its lonely wake devastated him.

He knew what he had to do and the week before school started, he circled Hands's house, working up the courage to ring the doorbell. Hands answered the door, his face creased by a tan he'd acquired at his uncle's place in Ranchos Palos Verde, outside

L.A., where Hands liked to spend part or all of his summer. Months of anxiety poured out and Figs halted a rambling explanation as it wavered into defense and simply said, "I'm sorry."

"I'm over it," Hands said, welcoming him inside. Hands's parents said *hello we haven't seen much of you this summer* and Figs blushed, appreciative that Hands hadn't poisoned his parents against him. They spent the afternoon plotting their course schedule and, like the rest of the incoming frosh, speculating about their chances with the girls at St. Xavier.

....

Roger Dixon was the most eager to board the bus. Some of us kidded Roger about how he sat ramrod straight during mass, or about his symmetrical crew cut, but we always kidded gently because once Roger stopped taking the kidding, or if he thought you weren't kidding but poking fun at him, a beating was doubtlessly in your future. There were a lot of beatings in Roger's past. His father, Colonel Dixon, lived his life by a strict set of guidelines and he expected Roger, who would later go AWOL in Iraq, to subscribe to the same joyless guidelines.

Mike Quinn was the most reluctant to go. Q preferred to spend his summers in San Diego, at his family's condo on Catalina Island. But his father, Senator Quinn, thought Garden Lakes was an excellent idea for young men, and Q never had any say in the matter. Q, who would show-up to the twenty year reunion married to a swimsuit model, had long gotten used to everyone kowtowing to his father's every wish, so he wasn't surprised when he discovered he'd been named a Fellow. He had learned to bargain with his father, though, and his stint at Garden Lakes was worth a senior trip to Europe, so Q decided he would try his hand at deferring the customary gratification summer brought.

Phillip Sprague wasn't as keen to get away from his parents as he was pleased to have been chosen as a Fellow. Sprocket's parents had wheeled him up to the bus, dropping his bag next to his chair, telling him to have a good time. He was a lithe kid, sallow from never spending any time outside, and while his parents didn't consider him a burden, they were overwhelmed with his care. They'd politicked intensely to get Sprocket, who would one day sell his fledgling software company for millions, on the roster, even going so far as to donate a set of the Oxford English Dictionary to the Randolph Library. For his part, Sprocket was good-natured, and there were those of us who genuinely liked him and didn't treat him any differently than anyone else.

Casey Murfin, the chronic ditcher, helped load Sprocket onto the bus, his small frame struggling behind the wheelchair. Some of us balked when we saw Smurf's name on the roster, but there was no denying that his father was a powerful businessman whose philanthropy was famous. The Murfin Group controlled the majority of real estate in the Valley of the Sun, the family name minted on signage all over town, which would still be true when Smurf would one day successfully slander a female colleague with whom he'd cheated on his wife.

Warren James fidgeted with his glasses, a new prescription with tinted frames so he wouldn't have to carry two sets. Warren, who later would unwittingly be implicated in an internet Ponzi scheme, was the most well-liked of our class, though our affinity for Warren was born more out of admiration for his contemplative nature than camaraderie. In fact, Warren was regarded as the forward thinker among us. True, conversation with Warren was an exercise in patience, the furious replication of questions with a dearth of answers following, but he was not aggressively opinionated and if you started one that you wanted to break away from, that was your own fault.

Vince Glassburn hung back, reclining against his father's cinnamon-colored BMW. He ran his hands through his long black hair, which he wore within millimeters of Randolph's policy about hair not exceeding shoulder-length. Assburn, who would die plunging into a frozen lake somewhere between Canada and Detroit, had transferred to Randolph from Minnesota his sophomore year and it was well known that he burgled houses in his upscale neighborhood and stole whatever he could grab, selling the loot out of the back of his Ford Bronco in the parking lot after school. Most of us had radar detectors whose former owners lived on Assburn's street—or on the next street over—and some of us had expensive neckwear that we'd flaunt at mass or any other affair that mandated a tie. None of us questioned where Assburn's stuff came from—we didn't want to know. But while we were happy to acquire contraband at bargain prices, Assburn never got what he most wanted: to fit in. There was never an outright edict against him, but for one reason or another he remained an outsider.

Father Matthews conferred with Mr. Hancock and Mr. Malagon, the faculty who administered Garden Lakes. Mr. Malagon, junior to Mr. Hancock by some thirty years and himself a Randolph alum, listened dutifully with his arms crossed, nodding. This was to be Mr. Malagon's first year at Garden Lakes, and he appeared to the rest of us to be taking his duty more seriously than he did the instruction of his history class. Which isn't to say that Mr. Malagon was a bad teacher—students tried to transfer into his class when word spread about how much fun it was. Also, Mr. Malagon's reluctance to put too much emphasis on test scores made him very popular.

Mr. Malagon, whose mysterious exit from Garden Lakes we could never forgive, was popular with the students on the other side of the Bridge of Sighs, too. His classroom was situated inside the breezeway in Regis Hall that led to the bridge, and we gawked at the sidewalk outside his window. And Mr. Malagon encouraged us to gawk. He'd gawk, too, cracking the window on any Xavierites who were dawdling, telling them that they were a major disturbance, sending them on their way in titters. The administration would be particularly interested in these details once their inquiry into that summer began, details we wrongly assumed to be harmless, though we could not have saved Mr. Malagon.

Mr. Hancock, on the other hand, was a sixty-year-old divorcee who was also the school's most-feared disciplinarian. There were those of us who became flushed with terror upon seeing Mr. Hancock's shaved dome towering over other students in the hall. Legend had it that Mr. Hancock, whose excused absence from Garden Lakes would doom us all, had never cracked a smile in his thirty-five years at Randolph, and none of us could dispute it.

The fellows's fathers shook hands with each other (except those who were professional adversaries, either lawyers on opposing sides of a case, or businessmen toiling in competing industries). Some of the Jesuits spilled out onto the steps for a cigarette, concealing their smokes in the palms of their hands. Several of the priests collected around Brian Lindstrum. Lindy's father and older brother were killed in a boating accident his freshman year. Where the stigma of tragedy could've led to ostracization, the school rallied around Lindy, members of all classes adopting a feeling of protectiveness toward him. For his own part, rather than becoming sullen and withdrawn, Lindy immersed himself in his studies, cultivating such a strong love for astronomy that the school's astronomy club asked him to be their new president, an honor reserved for seniors. The Jesuits watched Lindy, who would one day die in his sleep, leaving a bereaved wife and two small children, board the bus.

"Just like camping," Mr. Malagon said, slapping me on the back as I plopped down in my seat.

Father Vidoni blew the horn and Assburn and the group of sophomores volunteering as staff in the hopes of being chosen as a Fellow the following year climbed aboard, the bus still reeking from the basketball team's final away game against St. Mary's (a loss). Smurf dredged an old bloodied bandage from between the seats and flung it at Assburn. Mr. Hancock strode through the aisle, making sure everyone was wearing a seatbelt, while Mr. Malagon called roll.

Hands?

Here!

Figs?

Here!

Q?

Here.

Smurf?

Here, Here!

Lindy?

Here.

Sprocket?

Yes, here.

Roger?

Yes, sir.

Warren?

Here.

Assburn?

Here!

Martens?

Mr. Hancock protested as I answered, the official roster in his hands, unfamiliar with our nicknames. Mr. Malagon reached for it, but Mr. Hancock pulled back. He called roll for the sophomores and all answered accordingly. The two teachers took their seats, Mr. Malagon up front, Mr. Hancock in the back next to Figs and Hands.

The bus pulled out onto Central Avenue, braking at the light at Indian School Road in front of the First National Bank. We felt like Christopher Columbus, serenaded at court, about to set sail for a new world. To look at us was to remark on our similarities: our white Polo shirts, khaki shorts, some wearing socks, some not. But while we might've appeared interchangeable to outsiders, we knew the uniformity of our dress was just a mask for our disparate personalities, though the ambitions that seethed within us remained secret as the bus idled at the light.

The bank sign flashed the time and temperature, which flitted between one hundred and ninety-nine. The light turned green as the sign flashed one hundred and one.

Charlie stirred cream into his coffee, the rhythm of the spoon against the insides of the cup soothing his seared nerves. He'd spent an anxious afternoon refraining from the impulse to search the internet for people he'd known in all the places he'd lived. The same impulse visited him in moments of crisis and each time he vanquished it with the truth that knowing that life had gone on for friends he'd known in Denver and Santa Fe and Rapid City and San Diego and New York City would puncture his precious memories of his time in those places. A small but vain corner of his soul wondered if anyone ever thought of him, wondering what became of the boy who was there and then wasn't.

Outside, cars raced up and down Central Avenue as the sun descended, setting the interior of the coffee shop aflame. The restaurant had been the scene of many late night bull sessions after making deadline, which is why he chose it as a venue for reconciliation with Charlotte. Also, he knew his colleagues at the *Arizona Sun* would be at the Christmas party at Mary Elizabeth's, the swank bar at the Phoenician resort the paper rented for its cozy nooks where office romances that wouldn't last through the winter were kindled.

He longed for Charlotte to clatter through the front door, the diaphanous sunset at her back, her tanned skin ablaze with a warmth he needed to feel. Their last moment together, filled with screaming and the cold touch of her hands shoving him toward the door of her condo on Camelback Road had filled him with a dread he couldn't shake. The scene replayed in his waking hours and menaced his sleep. He thought of a thousand things he could've said, or maybe one true thing. He knew it would make a difference, that Charlotte would reinstate their engagement before their mutual friends and families could learn of the rupture, though he could bridge any personal embarrassment. Closure and final decree worried him constantly and if his job taught him anything it was that any dialogue could extend indefinitely if there was affinity between the speaker and the listener. He aimed to reestablish that rapport with Charlotte and anticipated her arrival with a zeal bordering on lust.

But the gloaming settled over the desert and Charlie's hope faded as his reflection took shape in the coffee shop window, a solitary figure at the end of another long year, taking sips from a never-ending two dollar cup of coffee. He smiled at the waitress, whose curiosity about him had dimmed. He'd delayed an urgent need to urinate out of fear of missing Charlotte's entrance and quickly washed his hands in the cramped, yellow-lit restroom off the kitchen, the air heavy with the smell of greasy meats.

Upon his return, a thin man in his early forties inhabited the space in his booth where he'd hoped Charlotte would sit. Charlie stutter-stepped, the man unfamiliar to him. The waitress, assuming the man was Charlie's long-awaited companion, served him a cup of coffee, refilling Charlie's idle cup as well.

"Excuse me," Charlie said as he approached. Any other day, he would've guessed the stranger to be an anonymous source for a story that the source would plead him to write or, as had happened every so often, the angry subject of one of his columns, though those complaints usually took the form of email or hang-up phone calls.

"Hello, Charlie," the man said, smirking. "I hope you don't mind."

"I'm expecting someone, actually," Charlie replied.

"This'll take a minute," the man said. He extended his hand. "I'm Robert Richter."

"Do we know each other?" Charlie asked. He let Robert Richter's hand fall unshaken.

"I work for Tom Gabbard," Richter said, his voice lowering needlessly as the coffee shop had emptied of everyone including the waitress.

Charlie searched his mind for any unsavory insinuation he'd made about the County Attorney in any of his recent columns but couldn't recall any. "This is my personal time," he said. "If you could email me—"

"Why didn't you go to the Christmas party tonight?" Richter asked, his face lit with curiosity. Charlie noticed that Richter hadn't shaved in a number of days and he began to doubt that Richter worked for Gabbard. "I thought for sure you'd go to the Christmas party."

"Do you have some identification?" Charlie asked. Had Richter actually shown up at the Christmas party? Or had he been following him since he left the office? Richter's casual demeanor suggested the latter, but Charlie couldn't be sure.

Richter comically touched the lapels of his charcoal suit and shrugged.

"How do I know you work for the County Attorney?" Charlie asked. Anyone could say they were anyone, he knew.

Richter shook his head. "I work for Tom Gabbard," he said, his grey eyes slitting above a quick smile. "There's a subtle difference, if you catch me."

Charlie didn't but the freight of Robert Richter's abrupt appearance dashed what small hopes he had that Charlotte would assent to his plea to meet. He'd left specific instructions on her answering machine, calling once and hanging up just to hear her voice. Leaving a message was a bad idea, he knew, but he'd run out of options.

"I'd like to ask you a couple of questions," Richter said, raising his coffee cup to his chapped lips. He reminded Charlie more of a surfer than a...what was he? An investigator?

Charlie waved at the waitress to bring his check, an indicator Richter mistook as his acceding to the request.

"How important would you say integrity is to what you do?" Richter asked as nonchalant as asking him the time.

Charlie blinked rapidly, remembering a piece from last Friday's edition about how liars tend to blink more rapidly than those professing the truth. He remembered the piece was not about rapid eye movement's relation to the truth, but a profile of an outgoing Arizona State University psychology professor beloved by his students for the past twenty years. "The answer seems self-evident," he said.

Richter smiled. "Agreed," he said, nodding. "What's more important, eh? Everything springs from integrity, right?"

The double rhetorical relaxed Charlie; here was no professional, just a hired hack—possibly hired by Tom Gabbard, but possibly not—fishing for...what?

"The world is lousy with people who can't understand that concept, though," Richter added. "Your paper is full of them."

Charlie wasn't sure if Richter meant the content of the paper, or his colleagues, an uncomfortable thought aggravated by Richter's pulling out a pack of cigarettes.

"You can't smoke in restaurants," Charlie warned him more stridently than was called for.

Richter shook free a cigarette and lit it with a fat silver lighter. The waitress materialized and Charlie braced for rebuke, but to his surprise she left the check and ambled back into oblivion.

"I know the owner," Richter said.

Charlie reached into his pocket, wondering if he could still make the Christmas party at Mary Elizabeth's. His colleagues would've outpaced him at the open bar, but their mirth would be a welcome salve to the raw wound of both being stood up by Charlotte and haunted by Richter, who posed two or three more questions that were variables of the first before stubbing his cigarette out in his coffee cup. Charlie tapped the twenty he'd laid across the check and considering leaving without his change, a gesture he was sure would mean something more to Richter than his just wanting to flee the scene.

"You must think you're the cat's ass," Richter said.

Charlie felt his back straightened. "Excuse me?"

"The youngest columnist in the *Sun's* history," Richter said. He let out a whistle. "You got something on old Darrell Torrence, something you're holdin' over his fat head?"

Charlie hadn't heard the *Sun's* publisher's given name spoken since his days at the *Phoenix Tab*, the weekly where he'd started on the west side of Phoenix after his brief foray into the New York literary scene, the only remnant of which was a stack of *Shout Magazine*, featuring his only published short story, and a box of copies of *Last Wish*, his novelization of the movie of the same name, which he'd written for money under the pseudonym J.D. Martens. In the end, he didn't possess the fortitude to continually ruminate on human weakness and desire, to catalogue life's ambiguities in the hope of suggesting meaning, and so ended his career as a fiction writer. He settled for the notion that his columns would be his legacy, however small, an archive of his thoughts and feelings, proof that he'd lived.

To everyone at the *Sun*, as well as his admirers and foes, Darrell Seymour Torrence, Jr. was known as Duke. Duke the renegade publisher. Duke the decorated World War II pilot. Duke the philanthropist, appearing in the pages of the *Sun* every other week at this charity ball or that, flashing his famously toothy grin.

"Look, I don't—"

"I'm joshing you," Richter said. "I know you earned it. When Mr. Gabbard asked me to talk to you, I remembered your name from the *Tab*."

"Why did Mr. Gabbard ask you to talk to me?"

Richter didn't hear the question, or ignored it. "It isn't every day that someone changes the world, right?"

"No one can change the world," Charlie retorted

"But they can change the laws, right?"

Charlie nodded involuntary. There was no sense in arguing over what had been the defining moment in his career, Heather's Law, named for Heather Lambert, the girl who had been killed in a hit and run accident out in Tolleson, the small, predominantly Hispanic

community west of Phoenix, by an illegal alien working as a day la-
borer on a nearby farm. The *Tab* had sent Charlie to talk to Heather's
high school teachers and, preferably, to get an exclusive with the
girl's parents. Just six months back from New York by way of a road
trip to Los Angeles, Charlie had no connections in the local police
or in any city hall in any town in the metro Phoenix area, so verifying
even the basic facts of the incident required a level of sleuthing that
he hadn't yet acquired. It was apparent the real story was that the
farmer who had employed the illegal alien was a Tolleson kingpin
and that the wheels of justice would turn slowly, if it all, in tracking down the illegal alien, who had fled back across the border after
running the red light and plowing into sixteen year-old Heather
Lambert, sending her flying, her body deposited hard against the
oil-stained blacktop at the gas station adjacent to the intersection.
Charlie had proposed a piece to his editor at the *Tab* implying that
if Heather Lambert had been from Tolsun Farms, the gated community on the outskirts of Tolleson, the farmer would already be
arrested, an article his editor promised to fire him over if he wrote it.

Charlie surrendered to his assignment and attacked the story
not from the human interest angle—he canceled his scheduled fol-
low-ups with Heather's teachers and classmates and gave up trying
to contact her parents—but in pursuit of the truth. Heather Lambert
should've been dreaming of endless summer days at the community
pool, splashing in the tepid water with her friends, dreading the return
to school as the calendar turned from June to July to August. Instead,
a wealthy farmer's greed enjoyed the protection of lax prosecution of
ambiguous immigration laws, the precise words he was able to extract
from a prosecutor downtown and ran as a pull quote in his first piece
on the Lambert case. Charlie hammered away at the farmer, who engaged a law firm to bother the *Tab* with threatening letters alleging
libel, but the *Tab*'s circulation had increased as a result of Charlie's
investigation, giving him implicit carte blanche to carry on.

Soon, the farmer began to lose accounts and his lawyers
squawked to the other papers and the local television stations that a

junior reporter at a local newspaper was ruining a man's livelihood. The same lawyers protested that the illegal alien had been captured and was being extradited, that justice had been served which, true or not, didn't quell the outrage toward the farmer who stood in front of the tv cameras and sheepishly declared that the accused had never worked for him, in any capacity and, further, that the accused had stolen the vehicle from the fleet of cars he kept on the farm. The farmer's admission gave Charlie another angle to pursue and he uncovered that many of the day laborers at the farm were illegal aliens paid in cash. Worse, the illegals were part of a network of laborers whose availability was brokered by a set of individuals who had infiltrated the Hispanic populations around Phoenix. Charlie spent a fruitless few weeks trying to unmask the identities of these brokers, but his editor bestowed him the opinion page in lieu of his possessing all the facts and by the time his name was known around town, the farmer had been forced into bankruptcy and Heather's Law making the hiring of illegal aliens punishable by jail for each offence had been swiftly enacted. And not long after that the receptionist at the *Tab* called out that Darrell Torrence was on the phone for him.

"How did they catch Derek Green?" Richter asked.

"I don't know," Charlie said, waving the twenty at the waitress. "Before my time."

"They dealt harshly with him," Richter said.

"Yeah, they don't like it when you falsify your sources," Charlie said.

The waitress finally confiscated the check and the twenty.

"Rumor has it old Duke was so mad he called every paper within a four state radius and told them not to hire Green."

"Doubt it," Charlie said. A smear of white glinted under the arc lights outside the window and Charlie leapt out of the booth, breezing past that waitress and out into the crisp evening air. What he had hoped was Charlotte's Volkswagen Passat was in reality a Honda Civic. It made a U-turn in the coffee shop parking lot and cut into the flow of traffic streaming down Central Avenue.

Though few students would become Garden Lakes fellows, most would pass through its gates as freshmen during the Freshmen Retreat. Garden Lakes itself was in the town of Maricopa, which was far enough south of Phoenix to be in another county, Pinal, which confused the average Phoenician since the metro Phoenix area was known cartographically as Maricopa County. The gates were the only enhancement to the property paid for by the school, the result of some minor vandalism by marauding boondockers committed during the interim between the stall of the development's building phase and the donation of the land to Randolph by Mr. McCloud, a Randolph graduate and Federally-indicted land developer whose business had been seized by the government. The bus charged through the gates, opened earlier for the Randolph Mothers' Guild, who were putting the finishing touches on the dining hall for that night's dinner, whizzing past the only green grass in the whole development, fed by an underground sprinkler system, the palm-tree studded median separating the channels that allowed cars in and out. The development beyond the palms lay before us like a desert playground. Father Vidoni turned right on to Garden Lakes Parkway, the circular drive that traversed the development, the red and white shell crawling toward the encampment at the western edge of Garden Lakes.

The eastern portion of the development lay unfinished. From above, Garden Lakes appeared like a sophisticated crop circle, comprised of two paved roads, an outer and inner loop, a wide river of dirt flowing between the loops, the brick community center bracketing the two loops at their southernmost convex. The manmade lake at the center of the development yawned like an open maw with only its top teeth—the twelve houses that constituted Garden Lakes to date, six on either side of the community center.

A dust devil kicked up and danced along the dry lakebed, petering out near the plug of dirt and rock left of center, the island meant for residents to swim out to, which occurred exactly once, during a Family Day for the homebuilder's employees. Garden Lake brimmed shore to shore with sparkling water that afternoon. Afterwards, the ever-evaporating pool reminded everyone involved with the project of the promises a master planned community could offer, among them safety in an insecure and increasingly violent world, but also an oasis away from the demands the world could make and that eventually condemned Garden Lakes to abandonment and despair, the liquid heart of Mr. McCloud's dream drying up permanently under the blistering sun.

Mr. McCloud was steadfast in the face of prison time, which he served after a year and a half of raging against what he came to recognize was the only mortal battle that couldn't be won: arbitrariness with unlimited reserves of cash and power. He had, however, made a provision for his most cherished property. Anticipating the crush of the government's fist, he'd deeded Garden Lakes to Randolph as a charitable gift, to be used by the school as it deemed appropriate.

When the livid government trustee took steps to reacquire the property he argued rightfully belonged to taxpayers, Randolph announced the Garden Lakes Fellows program, a leadership camp for juniors who would be sequestered at Garden Lakes with two faculty members and a supporting cast of sophomores, who would work in the dining hall and assist the faculty members while Fellows worked their project: the drywalling of a house framed by a local homebuilding company, the labor and framing materials gifted by the homebuilder. Even though the Garden Lakes program featured academic instruction—a philosophy seminar and a class on grammar and written communication—skeptics argued Garden Lakes was institutionalized slave labor, that Randolph had designs on selling the development for a profit upon its completion—or worse, give the development back to Mr. McCloud, who would in turn sell it; but over the years, Garden Lakes had become a model for similar programs whose output was in the way of low income housing in poor neighborhoods consigned by the government to poverty and crime. (Word reached Randolph that the program had a papal blessing.) In addition, college recruiters who washed up on Randolph's academic shores were curious about which boys were Garden Lakes Fellows, causing the sophomore subscription rate to double, each sophomore hoping their volunteered labor would win them a fellowship as a junior.

Father Vidoni honked the horn to announce their arrival. Two eager sophomores whose mothers had brought them directly saluted the bus from the shade of the palm tree waving like a flag from the island, which over the years had been weathered into a dirt cone. A yellow spray of desert dandelion had grown over a squiggle of desert lily, giving the dry lake's lip a mustard-colored mustache. The sophomores jumped over the flowers, dust stirring in their footprints as they made their way to the bus.

To the left lay the sophomore housing; the Fellow housing ran in the other direction, a football field's length west from the sophomores. The housing was separated by a state-of-the art dining hall slash classroom slash auditorium slash chapel (slash dance hall for the Singles' Retreat), the building originally constructed as an elementary school for the someday students of Garden Lakes. As the new owners of the development, Randolph gutted the elementary school, customizing it to the meet the needs of a desert renewal center. A blanket of prickly pear and barrel cactus, fit snug around a stand of saguaro, formed a ring around the community center designed to keep out desert predators.

Though no street signs were posted in the development—the reflective green and white totem marking Garden Lake Parkway stolen by the boondockers who, by now, were in their early thirties— the plans filed with the city called for streets named Palomino Drive, Rockridge Way, Whispering Wind, Evening Glow, and Lakeland Avenue. The Fellows however, had, over the years, rechristened the streets of Garden Lakes: High St. (juniors), Low St. (sophomores); Upper Parkway, Lower Parkway; East Street and West Street. Randolph finally chose Regis and Loyola, an easy identification correlating to the buildings back on campus where the juniors and sophomores kept their lockers. Each house at Garden Lakes had been numbered in honor of a previous class. We numbered our remodel 1959 Regis Street as a tribute to Kevin Randolph, the last Randolph descendant to graduate. Word was Kevin Randolph himself would be attending Open House, the ribbon-cutting ceremony at the end of our fellowship.

Out the window, beyond the community center and past the outer loop, we saw The Grove, the mountain range of dirt and gravel dumped long ago for the landscaping to be done at Garden Lakes, mounds of limestone, pitchstone, basalt, quartzite, sandstone, dolomite, slate, and shale now overgrown with weeds and desert critter tracks.

Hands, who would one day lead his family's sixth generation brewery to ruin, and Figs, who would later succeed in covering up an embezzlement at his firm, had started the rumor that they'd occupy the first house on Regis Street. While this house was the oldest house in the development, it was also the model home built to lure in potential homeowners and had been outfitted with the extras that the other houses lacked: wallpaper, designer faucets, dark-stained wood cabinets (as opposed to the plywood cabinets painted white in the houses by the Fellows), wood slat blinds (not white or crème aluminum), Mexican Saltillo tile (the other houses had thin, playroom-style carpet, linoleum in the kitchen) and a working electric garage door. All of the houses were furnished by Furniture America, whose president was a Randolph alum. Hands and Figs knew they would be booted down to one of the other houses, the model homes restricted to faculty, but this being Mr. Malagon's first year, and Mr. Malagon being an iconoclast, they thought they had a shot of nonchalantly moving in, bumping Malagon, whose mysterious exit from Garden Lakes no one would ever be able to forgive, down the street. It was this arrogance masked as innocence that galled the rest of us. Hands and Figs knew it profited more times than not (though Mr. Malagon wouldn't be suckered out of the model home).

The bus gasped as Father Vidoni brought the vehicle to a stop in front of the junior abodes. The ride from Randolph had been a long one—not mileage-wise, but encapsulated-in-sweat-and-farts-and-b.o.-wise. Mr. Hancock, whose excused absence from Garden Lakes would send us to our doom, refused to let the windows down during freeway travel, citing the noise level as his reason, *reminding us that he didn't need to have a reason.*

The floorboards were warmed from travel and we did our best to form a single file line and disembark patiently, Mr. Hancock stationed at the back of the bus with Mr. Malagon near the finish line, low-fiving us as our duffel bags pulled us out the glass accordion bus doors. We gathered in a semi-circle in the street. The sun blasted light through the windows of the framed and stuccoed house that stood along the avenue. The supply shed that housed all the necessary implements rose out of the cul-de-sac, a mistress of hard labors to come.

"Okay you boys," Mr. Hancock said, "you know the drill. Sleeping arrangements are of your own choosing. There will be no switching houses, so choose prudently. Mr. Malagon and I will take up in the faculty residences."—a glimpse between them implied they'd worked out in advance who would live on which side—"Dinner with Mr. McCloud is at five P.M. Mr. Malagon?"

Mr. Hancock had evidently meant to call Mr. Malagon to step back onto the bus, but Mr. Malagon took the question to mean did he have anything to say and told us, "No fucking around now," a phrase of endearment he'd uttered many times in his class, permitting us to use the same type of language as long as we used it in a clever fashion, never out of anger and never toward one another, and Mr. Hancock's face drained of color.

Mr. Malagon re-boarded the bus, standing in the stairwell as the bus pulled forward a short distance, stopping to let off the sophomores, who milled about tentatively. Mr. Hancock and Mr. Malagon's arrival on Loyola Street was hailed by the sophomores who had not been allowed to ride the bus but had been brought by their mothers, who were unwilling to let their sons off until Mr. Hancock and Mr. Malagon arrived; these mothers who, for either personal or political or financial reasons were not part of the Mothers' Guild, waited with the agenda of introducing themselves to the faculty members for the express purposes of Making An Impression on behalf of their sons, who would soon be eligible to be considered for the fellowship.

Mr. Hancock and Mr. Malagon greeted the eager mothers, Mr. Malagon subjecting their sons to random bag checks before allowing them to settle into any one of the houses they desired, the houses farthest from the faculty residence filling up first.

The juniors quickly lost interest in the Loyola Street goings on. The memory of having stood on that side was too fresh for some, who worried about their worthiness for duty on Regis Street. It was one thing, as a sophomore, to work in the kitchen and in the laundry, studying the assigned texts in the afternoon and before bed, thankful not to be charged with the responsibilities of a Fellow, the failure of such endeavor to be known ever after; and even if completed—and they were never not completed—generations of Fellows and alum would submit your contribution to scrutiny, sure to find fault somewhere within the walls of your achievement.

There had been much talk on the bus about possible roommate combinations, incorporating such factors as who was known to be a slob, who was a neatnik, who was most likely to hog the common area, who took long showers, who might spend the bulk of their free time in their room (complete with innuendo as to what they would be doing in their room), and a top to bottom scorecard of everyone's b.o., provided by Hands and Figs, who both scored counter-intuitively low on the scale.

Certain implicit truths had to be factored in once we were faced with the actual decision, the problem much like the problems that confounded those of us who had participated in SAT prep and the mock-SAT taken one temptingly beautiful spring Saturday:

There are five, three-bedroom houses and twelve students who must live (peacefully and harmoniously) in said houses for forty days and forty nights. The following statements, however, apply:

1. Q and Assburn cannot be in the same house
2. Hands and Figs must be in the same house.
3. No one wants to live with Roger.
4. Sprocket must live in the house with wheelchair access.
5. Warren and Lindy don't care which house they live in.
6. Smurf (secretly) does not want to live with Sprocket.

These complications were ingrained in everyone's minds, having lived with the various prejudices for what felt like forever, so we assembled in our respective houses as if we were coming home from a long day of work at the mill. Lindy joined Figs and Hands in the house next to Mr. Malagon; Assburn and Roger and Smurf took up in the house next to them: their neighbors were Warren and Sprocket and me. Q was our lone neighbor for the moment, the final two Fellows—Tony "the Terminator" Watson and Jimbo Jergens would presumably arrive with their mothers and the rest of the Randolph Mothers' Guild.

A tornado of engine noise rumbled as the first of what would be six weekly grocery deliveries arrived, the truck's logo artfully spelling out the last name (in curlicues) of the grocery magnate whose son was a freshman at Randolph, the donation an obvious appeal for consideration for his son's unofficial application to become a Garden Lakes Fellow a couple of years hence. Previously, Garden Lakes had relied on one of the faculty members to make grocery trips into town with one of the Jeeps belonging to the property, towing along a couple of sophomores as cart pushers and bag handlers. This proved a burden on the faculty member who stayed behind, though, since the Fellows and sophomores alike could smell when they had the upper hand, even if they were unsure how to exercise this transitory rise to power. Occasionally, someone would sacrifice himself, generating a distraction while others raided the dining hall, or snuck out into the desert with a bottle they'd succeeded in smuggling into Garden Lakes.

Mr. Hancock advised the driver that the loading dock was best accessed from the outer loop, the driver and his passenger intrigued by the petite, neatly-coiffed mothers and their imported cars. Mr. Malagon yelled that he would meet the truck around, leaving Mr. Hancock to fend for himself among the genuflecting mothers.

One by one the cars on Loyola Street vanished, the bus giving a final honk as it rattled through the gates, the goodbye carrying through the window Q had thrown open to aerate his stale room. He shook out the dark blue comforter donated by Furniture America and folded it, sliding it under his bed.

Smurf, who would one day successfully slander a female colleague at his family's corporation with whom he'd been cheating on his wife, appeared in the doorway, his arm behind his back. "Guess what I found taped under the sink in the bathroom?"

"What?" Q asked, annoyed.

Smurf brandished a tattered copy of *Penthouse* magazine, fanning the worn pages for effect.

"I didn't hear you knock," Q said.

"Roger is in our bathroom, so I used yours," Smurf said. He looked both ways down the hall, a time-honored move known more formally by its nickname, the Randolph Backcheck, and asked Q if he remembered the week Figs was absent from school, his family's impromptu vacation.

"Yeah," Q said, "before finals."

"His family didn't go on vacation," Smurf said. "Figs was in the hospital."

Q, the future husband of a swimsuit model, stopped rifling through his duffel bag and looked at Smurf. Once this tidbit had sunk in, Smurf continued: "Remember that night, the weekend before Figs's absence? Summer Griffith's party in McCormack Ranch Park?"

Q shrugged.

"Well," Smurf started, "remember I went with Assburn? And we turned out to be the only other juniors there besides Hands and Figs? Some sort of senior party. They'd expelled a couple of sophomores with a garden hose before we got there. So anyway, Assburn and I decided to bail and hit The Hump and a couple of other spots. But I forgot my hat—you know the one, the orange fisherman's hat that I got in Mazatlan; some senior chick snatched it, and I let her, thinking I'd get it later. So anyway, Assburn started the car and I went after my hat. I don't find the chick anywhere and started floating between the rooms upstairs and downstairs. No luck. Finally I went out the sliding glass door to the backyard and see the hat bouncing behind this hedge in the back part of the yard, this immense cow-pasture thing. I asked someone on the patio if they knew the name of the girl who was wearing the orange hat, and she said, *What girl?* So I pointed out the spot of orange in the hedges and the girl said, *What orange? Never mind,* I said and moseyed in the direction of my hat. As I stepped closer, I heard some noises, some grunting and some smacking, and so I'm having second thoughts, but I'm caught in this no man's land where everyone who is looking can see me and there's no way to turn around without acting like a complete dufus. So I slowed up, trying to figure an escape, when Hands comes from the hedges. *Hey, Smurf,* he said as he passes me. But it's not the usual

Hands, you know? He's looking at the ground, and walking fast, not cool like he normally does. I said hey back and figured it's cool to go and get my hat, which at this point I don't really care about, but, you know." Q shrugged again. "So guess what I saw when I reached the girl who has my hat?"

"I heard this already," Q said. "Robert Samuels told me. He told me not to say anything, though."

"What did he tell you?"

"It's too stupid to repeat." Q went back to sifting through his duffel.

"Samuels doesn't know shit." Q knew Smurf was dying to tell him, but Q didn't want to be baited into asking. He knew Smurf well enough to know that if he were patient, Smurf would blurt it out. "What did he tell you?"

"He told me what happened. I'm telling you, it's too stupid."

"Yeah, but what did he say? Did he tell you about Figs?"

Samuels had told him the same story he'd told a half dozen of us, that Hands had banged the senior chick while Figs watched, masturbating. Q was sure Smurf knew the story, thereby knowing the real reason Figs took a week off, too embarrassed to face everyone. But the story died in its sails when Hands denied it.

"Did he tell you about Figs?"

"Hands said it didn't happen." Q said.

"Bullshit," Smurf said. "I saw it."

"You saw it?"

"Was standing right there when it started. I walked in and Figs was smoking pot with some of the seniors, maybe seven dudes and a couple of chicks. They thought I was the cops when I busted through the hedge"—Smurf grinned at this—"but Figs said, 'He's cool,' and they went about their business."

"Why are you re-telling me this story?"

"I'm trying to tell you the real story, dude. You're not listening."

"I'm listening."

"So I was talking to this girl about how I needed my hat back when Figs and a couple of the other guys start wrestling around. But I see that they aren't wrestling at all. The seniors are beating the shit out of Figs."

"Why?"

"Don't know."

"What did Hands do?"

"That's what I'm saying."

"What?"

"He didn't do anything. He walked away."

Q looked at Smurf doubtfully.

"Honest injun," Smurf said, crossing himself.

The story agitated Q. "Go to your own house, why don't you?"

A look of resignation came over Smurf and he drifted toward the door.

"Leave the magazine."

He tossed the magazine on Q's bed and made for the front door.

Down the street, Assburn and Roger settled into their rooms. Assburn, who would plunge to his death in a frozen lake somewhere just this side of the Canadian border, was unhappy about living with Roger, but knew there was nothing he could do about it. Recently, Roger had taken to Assburn, inviting him over to his house after school "for some target practice." Roger had ambushed Assburn with the invitation, catching him in front of the gymnasium so that Assburn wasn't ready with an excuse. Truth was, Assburn had nothing to do and nowhere to go. Roger was delighted when he nodded yes.

After an artillery stop at Roger's house, a two-story colonial set behind a fence of oleander ("reinforced with chain link and barbed wire," Roger told him), they made for the shooting range where Roger's father, Colonel Dixon, was well into his rounds. Assburn admitted that he didn't know much about guns—he once shot a Mountain Dew can with a .22 at his uncle's ranch back in Minnesota—but Roger, who would later be Absent Without Leave in Iraq, reassured him that "we've got something for you."

Silence blew through Roger's open-aired Jeep on the long ride to the shooting range. It always amazed Assburn that something like the shooting range could exist right outside of Phoenix and he'd never heard of it. He felt the same way when he learned that the wedding cake structure off the I-17 was a castle with underground passages, dating back to the early 1900s. Phoenix seemed to Assburn to be something of an archeological dig: on the surface it looked like sun and sky and palm trees and glass skyscrapers and desert, bereft of history, like a movie set, but for anyone willing to dig and sift through the sand, odd artifacts and buried history emerged, presenting itself as dramatically as the appearance of the Ben Avery Shooting Range.

"Ever shoot clay?" Roger asked.

Assburn shook his head.

"That's okay, my father's over at the targets, anyway," Roger said, unloading the rifles and a box of pistols.

The Colonel scarcely registered Assburn's presence as he and Roger set up at the aluminum TV trays placed in front of the shooters. The riflemen—there were no women—laid their weapons down on the metal tables as their targets were retrieved and replaced by men in yellow vests. Roger put his hand on Assburn's wrist as Assburn went to unzip the case on the rifle Roger had handed to him in the parking lot. "Wait until it's clear," Roger whispered, looking at his father. The Colonel pretended to be looking off in the distance at his new target.

"All clear!" one of the yellow vests yelled and Roger let up on Assburn's wrist.

In the span of an hour and a half, Assburn shot an artillery of rifles: a Remington Sporting 28, a Beretta 687 Silver Pigeon II, a Browning A-Bolt that knocked him back, almost knocking him over, soliciting the only remark the Colonel made that afternoon: "Should've brought the old Winchester I gave you for your tenth birthday," he said to Roger, chuckling. Assburn's shoulder ached as he tried to hold his arm steady for the box of Ruger Old Army revolvers Roger opened. Conversation among the shooters was rhythmic, fit in the space between the claps and cracks of rifle fire, but Assburn didn't understand what the shooters meant by things like "sporting recoil pad" and "bore size." His targets were consistently cleaner than Roger's or the Colonel's.

By the next morning, Assburn had a hard time believing the previous afternoon had even happened, and Roger passed Assburn wordlessly in the hallway and Assburn mentioned it to no one.

Assburn parted the blinds in his room with his fingers, watching Q as he broached the manmade lake, shielding his eyes while peering out at the landscape. He watched the last of the Randolph Mothers' Guild arrive, parking their cars around the community center. His master plan had been to offer to room with Q if no one else did, but he hadn't counted on the absent Fellows. He almost volunteered anyway, but the prospect of Q protesting in front of everyone kept Assburn silent.

The year leading up to Garden Lakes had not gone the way he had figured. Toward the end of his sophomore year, a scrape he had with a senior he'd sold a radar detector to—the senior accused Assburn of trying to resell him his own radar detector; Assburn didn't know for sure that the senior was mistaken—led Assburn to the realization that everyone on campus thought he was a lowlife criminal. He'd started his B&E exercises out of boredom and, bolstered by the demand side of the equation, out of a sense of fulfillment. As Assburn punched out a panel of glass in an arcadia door or ripped out a bedroom screen, he kept his clients' needs in mind, covetous of the look on their face when he surprised them with just what they were looking for. But after the senior split Assburn's lip in the parking lot of Lenny's Burger Shop while some of his other customers looked on, Assburn desperately wanted to change his image. He knew he could quit thieving; his paranoia about being caught had risen in recent months. He imagined his clients would be able to satisfy their need for discount electronics, jewelry, and guns in the parking lots of any of the public high schools, or any number of other smalltime dealers Assburn had met in his underworldly travels. The more he turned the idea over, the surer he was of his decision. And so when, the first week of junior year, two seniors asked him if he had any women's diamond rings, he announced to them that he was out. The seniors tried to shake him down, accusing him of holding out, but Assburn held fast. He hoped his classmates noticed.

Word did travel that Assburn was out of the game, but it traveled slowly; and the number of Assburn's customers was small compared to the overall student body, so while his customers quit asking him for goods, the perception that Assburn was a juvenile delinquent followed him wherever he went. To his credit, he didn't revert to his old ways. He believed people would come around, if not soon, then by graduation, which was Assburn's personal goal.

A step toward that goal was returning the presidential pen used to sign the Miranda Act into law he'd stolen from Q's father.

Since Randolph formed the outermost boundary of our existence, Assburn didn't consider the (possibly legal) punishment Senator Quinn could've inflicted on him. Assburn's only concern was with Q, and how to return the pen without encouraging Q's wrath, or exposure to his peers, or to the administration.

Various plans had developed during Assburn's guardianship of the pen. The first and most obvious solution was to break back into Q's house during school and replace the pen in the senator's study. But Assburn couldn't reconcile getting caught *returning* something. In the past, he'd been prepared to go down if caught in the act of procuring; he knew an arrest would in all likelihood result in some community service and a parole officer and little else, and he relished the idea of the hero or cult status he would achieve if arrested. These thoughts had left him, however, by his junior year, displaced by an aspiration to be thought of as an equal member of his class.

Another plan was to mail the pen back, wearing gloves while assembling the package, careful not to lick the stamp. Assburn had scoped out a mailbox near Biltmore Fashion Park, miles from his house, where he spent one afternoon a month wandering the Sharper

Image while his mother had her hair and nails done. But to mail back the pen would only correct part of the problem; Q would continue to malign Assburn even if the pen magically turned up in the mail.

Assburn knew that he was going to have to return the pen personally. On several occasions, he'd fastened the pen against his leg with a thick rubber band, but the opportunity to approach Q never presented itself. Assburn found himself walking down Q's Street, slowing in front of the gates to his house, hoping Q would see him and call out. But the only one who ever called out to Assburn was the landscaper, an Hispanic who waved at Assburn from his riding lawnmower. Assburn flirted with planting the pen on the landscaper, like they did in the movies, but his multiple trips to Dauphine Street made him reconsider. No doubt one of the neighbors, or their security cameras, could I.D. him, if it came to that.

Finally, the right situation appeared, and Assburn was glad that he'd waited. When he saw his name a few lines under Q's on the roster of Garden Lakes Fellows, his hopes surged. Even if Q made noise about the pen, it would only be in front of a limited audience, and during the summer, which would permit the incident—if there was to be an incident—to cool before the start of their senior year.

Assburn removed the pen from his duffel bag. He'd wrapped it in paper towels, sealing it in a Ziploc freezer bag. He stowed the package under the mattress, bouncing on the bed to be sure the bulge was undetectable. Downstairs, Mr. Hancock's voice boomed about the ten degree savings ceiling fans afforded, cautioning the boys not to be late to dinner.

. . . .

The smells from the kitchen filled the hallway. Roasted chicken and dill-seasoned potatoes, and steamed vegetables, and lemoned tuna steaks, and rice and beans, and pies—blueberry and lemon and hot apple, begging to be topped with a globe of ice cream or sherbet. The double glass doors at either end of the hallway that bisected the community center sealed us in with the olfactory splendor.

One half of the community center was further divided into two equal rooms—a classroom and chapel, the rectangle windows of the classroom overlooking the inner loop. The right side of the center held the cafeteria-grade kitchen and pantry, which took up the back fourth of the building nearest the loading dock. The kitchen was well ventilated by the two screen doors, one off the hallway and one on the south side of the building. In the afternoon, scents permeating from the kitchen were known to bring famished desert vermin.

The kitchen was cleverly segregated by a portable wall easily managed by four to six underclassmen. When positioned properly, the wall left about four feet on either side. Placement was dependent upon the event; for the dances at the Singles' Retreat, it was pressed up against the outer kitchen counter (where breakfast and lunch was served); for dinners such as the Randolph Mothers' Guild Dinner with Mr. McCloud, the dividing wall was angled diagonally so the servers—the Randolph mothers—flashed in a dizzy blur from behind the wall like co-hosts on a game show.

Mr. Hancock and Mr. Malagon accompanied Mr. McCloud at the large, round, white linen-draped table in the center of the room. The remaining places were set and consequently the other tables filled up quickly to avoid having to sit with the faculty and Mr. McCloud, so quickly that disparate dinner parties arose, the diners making furtive glances at the door to mark what luckless soul would wander in not knowing his dinner was to be ruined by the repetition of "Yes, sir," and "No, sir."

We were to be disappointed, though. Mr. Hancock and Mr. Malagon dined with Mr. McCloud, whose arm shook imperceptibly as he brought the tortilla soup to his lips. Some years older than the portrait of his likeness that hung in McCloud Hall, he appeared haggard. It seemed that Mr. Hancock and Mr. Malagon had trouble sustaining him in conversation. We realized that Mr. McCloud was barely cognizant of his surroundings, and so we openly gaped at him. We'd never known anyone who had been to prison and as we scarfed down the delicious entrees ostensibly prepared (everyone knew the dinner was catered) by the mothers of boys who, since they were underclassman, we would never truly know, our youth lent us a superiority toward Mr. McCloud, who we'd joke about later.

The white sun gleamed through the curtained windows, showing no signs of evening. Dessert was served, unleashing a symphony of silver spoons clinking against china plates, such props disappearing with the caterers after the dinner, along with all trace of the opposite sex, their perfumes and hairsprays lingering as some of us took down the dining room and swung the movable wall against its stationary brethren, admitting easy access to the stainless steel counter with its inlays for hot dishes, a board game missing its pieces, awaiting the blitz of the breakfast crowd.

After dinner, we settled into our houses. Mr. Malagon called some of us out on the sidewalk, inviting us to beat him at a game of bean bag, a wastebasket from his residence standing in for the bean bag board with its coffee can crown and slope of polished wood that Mr. Malagon kept in his classroom. "All or nothing," Mr. Malagon said, arcing four bean bags one after another into the wastebasket from thirty feet. Our sweat-stained clothes began to dry as the sun finally dropped behind the horizon. The catering truck roared away from the community center, its cough fading until all of Garden Lakes was still. The streetlights buzzed and a purple pulse of light shone above the street. It would be another few moments before the lights would fully engage and for a moment there was both nothing to see and nothing to hear except the plop of denim squares weighted with navy beans falling into a plastic wastebasket.

Mr. Hancock strolled leisurely down the street toward us and everyone except Mr. Malagon and Roger quit tossing bean bags. Some filtered off toward their residences, feigning tiredness or eagerness to get a fresh start for the day ahead. Mr. Hancock reached the bean baggers, stopping a few feet from the wastebasket as Roger concentrated on his last throw, his first attempts strewn like dead rodents along the sidewalk. Roger moved his arm back and forth, as if weighing his payload, letting the bean bag fly with a flick of this wrist that caused it to sail right of the wastebasket.

"Damn," Roger said, forgetting about Mr. Hancock.

"What's that Mr. Dixon?" Mr. Hancock bellowed.

Roger looked up from the playing field, startled. He narrowed his eyes as Mr. Hancock continued toward him. Mr. Malagon stepped between them and collected the bean bags and wastebasket. The rest of us dispersed, saluting each other good night and joshing each other about checking for rattlesnakes before jumping into bed, a scare that was more effective with the sophomores than the Fellows, since we knew Garden Lakes was fumigated prior to the fellowship program, the perimeter secured with pesticides and herbicides. Most of us had come upon snakes in our lifetime, though, either hiking Squaw Peak or stalking golf balls in the rough, and so we learned at an early age that there was very little that would deter a rattlesnake from going wherever it wanted to go.

Mr. Hancock and Mr. Malagon spoke briefly on the sidewalk. Hands and Figs tried to listen from Figs's open window, but couldn't make out anything other than the sound of Mr. Hancock's low mutters peppered with Mr. Malagon's interjections. We'd know soon enough what they were discussing, though, as rumor spread that Jimbo and the Terminator were no shows, and that the administration was unprepared for such a situation. There'd never been a Fellow that hadn't accepted eagerly—*two* was an historical precedent—and there was no such a thing as alternates.

We cursed Q his good fortune, living alone for the summer. Warren and Smurf gathered in Hands and Figs's living room for a bull session after Mr. Hancock's tour of the thermostats. Smurf guaranteed us that Mr. Hancock would force Q to live with him, or with Mr. Malagon. Smurf said he'd go to Mr. Hancock first thing in the morning and volunteer to move in with Q, secretly relieved at the idea of getting out of the same house as Roger. We knew Mr. Hancock would not accept Smurf's proposal. It may be that extraordinary times demand extraordinary measures, but Mr. Hancock wouldn't allow any fundamental rule to be bent, breached, or broken, regardless of whether or not the violation solved the problem.

The problem was to have an organic resolution. Lindy, who would die in his sleep in his early thirties, leaving a bereaved wife and two small children, knew it first, gazing out his window at the night sky. Lindy watched as Q slipped across the street, his duffel bag slung across his back. He cut across the dry lakebed, retreating into a set of headlights that awoke upon his approach. The headlights dimmed. The sound of tires squealing was drowned by the loud yips of an unseen pack of coyote. The red flare of taillights was the last anyone would see of Q until school started again in the fall.

Charlie listened to the outgoing message. The hum of the newsroom receded as he clung to the consonants uncoiling in the lilt of Charlotte's voice. The message assured the caller she was sorry that she'd missed your call, and was eager to talk with you, which Charlie knew was probably true in every case but his. He'd spent the weekend listening to the message after vainly trying to meet up with the *Sun* Christmas revelers, who had disbanded before he could reach Mary Elizabeth's, leaving him to a lonely drink at the bar while the barbacks waded into the vestiges of what looked like an epic bash. Nursing his drink, Charlie blamed Richter for Charlotte's no show at the coffee shop, though he knew his blame was misplaced. Charlotte was intrepid—Charlie was always joking that she'd make a hard-hitting investigative reporter—and Richter's squirrelly countenance wouldn't have deterred her from approaching.

He set the phone back in its cradle as Brennan, his editor, approached in his trademark blustery fashion. Brennan was famous for appearing breathless, as if he'd just eluded capture. "What's the status on the McCloud column?" he panted, leaning against Charlie's desk.

Charlie nodded. "I'll make deadline."

"That's not what I mean," Brennan said.

"What do you mean?"

"I think you know."

Charlie did know what Brennan meant, that the McCloud family had called in protest when they learned about the column being written to mark McCloud's recent passing. The McCloud family matriarch argued with Brennan to let McCloud rest in peace and Brennan privately agreed. Charlie convinced his editor that as a public figure, and a controversial one, the *Sun* was well within its right to cover the passing of one of Phoenix's more notable citizens.

"I think you'll be surprised," Charlie said.

"I never like being surprised," Brennan said before being pulled away by his secretary, who could be seen at all hours of the day hunting Brennan in the reporters' bullpen.

Charlie began dialing Charlotte's number again, undecided if he would leave a message or just listen to her voice when Billy Gallagher, a lifestyle reporter with a recently coined degree from the Walter Cronkite School of Journalism at Arizona State breezed by his desk and beckoned him to follow. Such theatrics were usually employed to gossip about which reporters were sleeping together, or defecting to another paper, or being canned. Charlie watched Gallagher escape into the stairwell and sauntered after him.

"I think Linda noticed," Gallagher said. Linda Macomb, a fellow lifestyle reporter, had the uncanny ability to take a call, write her piece, and converse with a someone at her desk all at once. Charlie was intimidated by Linda and gave her a wide berth.

"I don't think so," Charlie said. "She was chasing after Brennan, something about a source that had recanted."

Gallagher leaned against the door to the stairwell.

"What is it?" Charlie asked. Gallagher had married into a prominent Phoenix family who had let him know from the get-go that their daughter was marrying beneath her station and Charlie had more than once calmed Gallagher's anxieties by kidding that his wife's family's empire was founded on a beer distributorship. "They're drunks, basically," he'd say, which would momentarily cheer Gallagher up before he'd start worrying all over again.

"I got this private detective on my ass," Gallagher blurted out. "He's asking me questions about the paper. At first I thought it was my prick father-in-law, but this guy, Richter, kept asking about the paper."

Charlie shuddered when he heard Richter's name. "What type of questions?"

"Crazy stuff about what goes on here and about this reporter and that reporter. He even asked about Duke," Gallagher answered. "He asked about you, too. I told him to ask you and he said he already talked to you."

"I don't think so," Charlie said, wrinkling his brow as if he were drawing a blank. He'd used this ploy before, especially when he was caught out giving contradictory information or realized that whomever he was talking to was about to grasp that they'd been lied to.

"He said you were uncooperative," Gallagher said.

Charlie smiled. "That sounds like me."

Gallagher smiled involuntarily, worry contorting his face. "Did you talk to him?"

Charlie shook his head. "I have no idea who this guy is." Later, when he reflected back on it, he couldn't rationalize why he'd lied to Gallagher about talking to Richter. He wished he could say his impulse was to assuage Gallagher's jitters, but in truth his concern was that he was the target of Richter's investigation, though on his life he couldn't guess why. He spent the afternoon in the *Sun* archives, his eyes glancing through past columns for any clue as to why the County Attorney would take an interest in him. Charlie hadn't broken any laws, unlike many others whose conduct could only charitably be called lawful. Since the Heather Lambert episode, the law had become a yardstick against which Charlie measured his own behavior, an easier test to pass or fail than the abyss of what was ethical or moral, a test he'd begun to apply to all that transpired at Garden Lakes. Memories of the high school retreat and Randolph

Prep had been on Charlie's mind since he'd received Father
Matthews's call inviting him to lunch at the rectory. Upon his return
from New York, Charlie had treated his relocation the only way he
knew how: as a move to a new city. He didn't tell the Chandlers,
his neighbors from long ago who had acted as his surrogate family
and who gotten him into Randolph, that he'd come back. It was
easy enough to avoid his old haunts and familiar shadows so that
Phoenix appeared new enough again.

He hadn't kept in touch with anyone from Randolph though
he'd periodically run into someone here and there, most recently
Hands, whose wife was the co-chair of a breast cancer benefit
Charlie attended with Charlotte and her boss, who had sponsored
a table. Charlie didn't recognize Hands at first but the secret they
shared from all those years ago forced them into a shy silence, each
unclear if the other could rightly recall the promises from the past.

Father Matthews had been Charlie's most fervent Randolph cor-
respondent, writing him a note of appreciation if he approved of one of
Charlie's columns, or a gentle but chastising word if he disagreed. His
invitation to lunch threatened to elevate their relationship to a new
level, one that perplexed Charlie. He wasn't a Catholic, nor was he an
alum, having never graduated. And while he passed Randolph twice a
day on his way to and from the *Sun* offices, he was never tempted to
circle the parking lot or retrace his teenage footsteps.

Gallagher took a half-day, grimacing as he brushed past Charlie's
desk. He regretted not asking Gallagher what he'd told Richter, if
anything. He could imagine Gallagher telling Richter everything he
knew or whatever Richter wanted to hear. Charlie knew he couldn't
ask now without arousing Gallagher's suspicions. In a long life there
were always mistakes made, things to lament and at thirty-seven
Charlie was beginning to feel like he'd already lived forever.

The Randolph campus was deserted, the students away on Christmas break, a time Charlie remembered as being filled with trips to Vail or California for others, but was just a fermata in the school year for him as he worked on extra credit projects and wrote papers for independent study in a failed attempt to boost his GPA. His junior year he spent Christmas break in a four-week accelerated algebra class at a private tutoring company in order to repeat College Algebra, having flunked it the semester before. He chuckled as he climbed out of his car at how dire the College Algebra debacle had seemed. He'd had an inkling that life would only be harder after high school, but harder wasn't the right characterization. *Complex* was a better word. But how complex he didn't know then and on his worst days he pined for the order of rectifying a failing grade with its proscribed and delineated remedies.

Charlie had pulled into his former parking spot, the lot repaved and repainted with exacting yellow lines. He crossed the parking lot toward the rectory, circumventing a gold Chevy Impala resembling Brian Velasquez's from back when they were classmates. Beav was a scholarship student from South Phoenix who rode the bus until his junior year when he appeared one morning behind the wheel of the gold Impala, which he'd lowered a couple of inches. The thudding bass from the custom stereo made the car pulse. At night, a violet neon light emanated from underneath the car until the glass tubes were shattered when Randolph installed speed bumps. Beav had taken enormous static about being the only Hispanic at Randolph, everyone calling him *chollo*, sometimes in jest and sometimes not. Kids in the other classes referred to him as The Beaner, though Beav never let it bother him. Charlie remembered Beav as his biology lab partner and wondered if his dreams of moving to Los Angeles ever came to be. He was besieged with guilt as he reminisced about Beav, ashamed at all the anti-immigrant sentiment that his articles about Heather Lambert had engendered. An unexpected repercussion of Heather's Law had been to give teeth to every racist's call for razor wire along the borders and all sorts of other craziness. Worse, lawmakers had tried to piggyback on Heather's Law and a legislative session didn't pass where someone tried to introduce a bill in the guise of Heather's Law but that was really institutional racism looking for legal cover, like the immigrant teachers with thick accents being removed from their teaching posts for what the Arizona Department of Education termed "incorrect pronunciation" of English words. The previous week's *Sun* ran a story about a group of Hispanic fifth graders had green cards thrown at them while they walked to school.

Father Matthews greeted him as a prodigal son and ushered him from the well-lit carpeted foyer of the rectory and into a dark paneled room with an oversized oval table made of oak. A tea set had been strategically placed on the table and Charlie took a chair at Father Matthews's bidding. As his eyes adjusted to the light streaming in from a high window that framed the cloudless winter afternoon, Charlie folded his hands in his lap and answered in the affirmative as Father Matthews asked a series of benevolent questions meant to put him at ease. He said yes to tea, too, which Father Matthews poured with delicate hands. Charlie watched with fascination as Father Matthews worked like a machine to steep and pour tea for two.

"And do you find your work satisfying?" Father Matthews asked at last.

GARDEN LAKES   407

"Yes, Father." He sipped his tea.

"That's excellent," Father Matthews said. He breathed a ripple across the top of his tea cup.

"I was surprised at your invitation," Charlie said.

"Were you?" Father Matthews seemed amused.

"I haven't been back to Randolph in years."

"Perhaps that's why I invited you," Father Matthews said. "Sons of Randolph should not stray so far as that."

"I never actually graduated," Charlie reminded him.

Father Matthews waved him off. His willingness to overlook such an important detail as Charlie's dropping out before his senior year—before he could be called to account for what happened the previous summer at Garden Lakes—was curious.

"I'm normally skeptical of invitations like these," Charlie said. The air in the room had become clotted with orange and cinnamon.

"Skepticism is not a Godly trait," Father Matthews said.

"Occupational hazard," Charlie answered.

"I'm sorry that you must deal with elements that try to mislead you for their own gain," Father Matthews said. "Let me pay you the compliment of direct address." The faint aroma of cigarette smoke stirred as Father Matthews situated himself. "I understand you're working on a column on our dearly departed Brother McCloud."

"I am," Charlie said. It seemed like a hundred years ago that he and the other Fellows had sat with Mr. McCloud at dinner. The idea for the column arose from the memory of Mr. McCloud at Garden Lakes upon Charlie's reading his obituary in the *Sun*.

"His was a colorful life," Father Matthews said. Charlie imagined Father Matthews likely had to label all kinds of misdeeds as "colorful," including Mr. McCloud's indictment and jail term, as well as the string of bankruptcies and allegations of hidden wealth in overseas bank accounts.

Charlie sat silently sipping his tea, a tactic he'd use when a subject was having a hard time coming to the point. The tea had grown surprisingly cold surprisingly fast.

"May I ask what the thesis of your column is to be?" Father Matthews asked.

"It's a reminiscence about Garden Lakes," Charlie said, surprised at how easily he'd given away information he'd intended to keep secret.

Father Matthews scowled. "But that was almost twenty years ago," he said.

"Yes," Charlie said, another tactic he'd learned when someone was angling for answers he didn't want to give. That the program had been quietly shuttered had been a steady drumbeat in Charlie's heart and he realized only then how imperative his need to expose what happened was.

"I wonder if anyone will be interested in a column of that nature," Father Matthews said.

"Oh, I've written about all manner of things that people claim not to be interested in," Charlie said, "judging by my mail."

A veil of frustration fell across Father Matthews's face. "Do you think the timing for such a column is right?" he asked. "Some might think you're exploiting Brother McCloud's death."

"I'm sure some will," Charlie said and, worried that he was being too flip, added, "I can't control what readers think about these things, Father. There's always someone out there anxious to assume the worst about some thing or some situation, wouldn't you agree?"

Father Matthews nodded. "I do, my son," he said. "My worry is that you might be creating a situation where a situation doesn't readily exist."

Charlie swirled the residue of his tea and replaced the cup on the tray. Accepting the invitation had been a mistake and he realized belatedly that he'd only wanted a legitimate reason to visit Randolph.

"Would you like more tea?" Father Matthews asked, his congeniality returning.

"No, thank you, Father," he said.

Father Matthews drank the dregs of his cold tea. "May I inquire into your profession?" he asked.

"Please."

"When you're writing something, a column or what have you,"—Father Matthews gesticulated to indicate that he was out of his depths—"how do you know what information to include and what to exclude?"

Charlie thought. "Instinct, I guess," he answered. "When I was with the *Tab* it was more straight reporting so the facts were the facts. But with my column, there's more room to ruminate"—he regretted inserting this newspaper columnists' joke and covered with "if you know what I mean."

Father Matthews nodded sagely. "Do you ever struggle with the morality of inclusion?" he asked.

Charlie didn't know what Father Matthews meant and said so.

"I'm sorry. My question is: Do you now and then cross lines by including information that is...extraneous."

"Is there something you want to ask me, Father?" Charlie vowed not to let his perturbation show, though Father Matthews was testing his resolve.

"I'm just inquiring," he said. "I'm wondering at your methods."

Father Matthews wasn't the only one questioning his methods, it seemed. If Charlotte could borrow Father Matthews's term "moral inclusion" she would, though it wouldn't bring Charlie any closer to admitting that he'd lied about the illegitimate child he'd fathered at twenty-one. Charlotte had made the discovery by accident, a photo he kept tucked away in an envelope in the back of his sock drawer. He never looked at the photo, but was sure throwing it away would be a sacrilege. But the truth was that he hadn't known of the child's existence until recently and that the girl's mother, a bartender Charlie had briefly known, had kept the pregnancy, birth, and first sixteen years of the girl's life a secret from him. The girl was a stranger to him, someone he could pass on the street without recognizing. Her mother had precluded him from the girl's formative years, the time when the world exercises its influence over you and you become who you become, so in answer to Charlotte's question about why he never mentioned the girl he'd said, "Why would I?" He argued he was only trying not to complicate their relationship, that he was trying to protect her from the footnotes of his past. But Charlotte was beside herself with rage and grief, saying over and over, "I don't know who you are right now, I don't know you." He pleaded that he was the same person she'd fallen in love with, but this gaffe—though he wasn't willing to confess to anything other than chivalric omission, certainly not immoral exclusion—became insurmountable. An admission of wrongdoing was what Charlotte required, it seemed, but Charlie's instinct was to continue to persuade her of his innocence, that as a fact, the sixteen-year-old girl living in Iowa was of no consequence to the Here and Now of them and their engagement, an argument that only enraged Charlotte further.

Sleep came fitfully that first night. The air conditioning was no match for the weeks of pent up heat within our residences, and many of us slid our bedroom windows open, the windows sticking from the dust and dead bugs and spider webs encrusted in the metal tracks. The hot night air proved not to be the ally we'd hoped. Also, the open windows were a speaker tuned to ominous noises—creaks and croaks and rustling—that frightened us and our opened windows closed, walling each of us inside our twelve by twelve tombs.

We woke to the sound of pounding. Mr. Hancock and Mr. Malagon banged on our doors a minute before our alarm clocks could strike four. The thundering of fists made our hearts race, and for a moment we wondered where we were. The blanket of night still hung around Garden Lakes. Fatigued bodies rotated in showers, hurried along by the knock of their housemates. Once out on the street, the sensation of being up at such an early hour thrilling, as if we were the last human beings left after a terrible scourge. Laughter rang out, all of us dressed in our regulation khakis and short-sleeved white Polo shirts, the traditional uniform of a Garden Lakes Fellow, on our way to breakfast, a variety of cold cereal presented by sophomores who had been awake minutes longer than the rest of us.

Mr. Hancock looked oddly refreshed, urged us to eat our cereal, to have two bowls if we could eat them, and to eat something from the gigantic fruit bowl filled with apples and bananas and oranges and pears. Mr. Malagon advised us to stuff a piece of fruit into our pants as a snack for later, the first official break three hours away.

Our initial surge of adrenaline abated as we paraded into the chapel for the daily prayer. The Garden Lakes chapel was barren of anything remotely religious, save for the pews and the hymnals, dissimilar in every way to the chapel back at Randolph. Absent a confessional and high windowed ceilings, the Garden Lakes chapel disguised us from each other religiously. At Randolph, it was too clear who was a practicing Catholic—most were—and who was not. And while we were too young to have to cling to differences in religion as a means of separating ourselves from those around us, the demarcation lingered, highlighted in our conscience only at mass or during chapel.

Mr. Hancock rose. "Let us pray," he began, pausing for the drumming of knees against the carpet as we kneeled, resting our elbows on the pews in front of us. "Our Heavenly Father, bless us this day as we embark on our mission of peace and oneness. Let us value each other and each other's work, for we are all humble servants in Your eyes. Let us strive to work diligently and honestly. Let our minds be open. Let us lead by being led and let Your word guide us. Amen."

The chorus of amen lacked the reverb it did off the domed ceiling of mandatory masses back at St. Frances Xavier, instead evaporating with the noise of us crawling up off our knees. Mr. Hancock called for us to open our hymnals to page one thirty-one, to "Before the Ending of the Day," a melodious, seventh century incantation that Warren had sung repetitiously at St. Peter the Divine, a Catholic church his mother had once favored in Litchfield Park. The words flowed from Warren's tongue like a language learned through vigorous study. *Before the ending of the day/Creator of the world, we pray/That with Thy wonted favor Thou/Wouldst be our Guard and Keeper now*. Warren was suspicious of the rhyme scheme but, like all things church-related, his parents told him it was best not to question the small things. "Make big decisions," his parents said. "Don't spend time on the little questions."

"Before the Ending of the Day" reminded Warren of his uncle, his mother's brother, who had survived a plane crash in his fifties. Walked away from the wreckage as easily as shaking a cold. Up until that day, Warren had sampled many religions. He'd been born and raised in Phoenix, but his parents migrated from suburb to suburb, staggering through various neighborhoods as renters, Warren's mother was never quite content with the street they lived on, or their neighbors. In Glendale, the suburb where Warren was born, a sprawl of farms with livestock, his mother re-joined her native Methodist church. Warren's recollection of the Methodists was their hot chocolate and the giant blue tin of cookies frosted with cubes of sugar the size of diamonds, of which Warren could take as many as he liked.

Across the aisle, Roger, who would go AWOL in Iraq, taking a band of men with him and be subsequently court martialed for killing one of them, mumbled the words to the hymn while flipping through the pages of his hymnal, searching not for words of inspiration but for the page number of the book's natural crease. Prior to Garden Lakes, Roger had no working knowledge about how books were printed, but the Colonel primed him in the rudiments of bindery, about how you could see the individual signatures glued and sewn together if you looked closely at the top of a book. A book's natural crease would fall between signatures; and for the prank to work, the crease had to be avoided.

Roger was unsure of the prank. He wasn't even interested in pulling it, but his father had pulled it in Vietnam, and his grandfather had pulled it in World War II, his great grandfather pulled it during World War I, and it was rumored a relation had pulled it while fighting for the South during the Civil War. Roger thought the prank was lame, but since the plan was for him to go to college and not into the military, his father reasoned that Garden Lakes would be Roger's only chance to service the peculiar family tradition.

The hymnal seemed to Roger to have many creases. He lay the book flat during the third verse of "Before the Ending of the

Day" to examine where it would fall open. The pages fanned like a paper peacock. He thumbed through the signatures feeling for any resistance. He decided on page sixty-seven. Not too close to the front, not too far toward the back. Sixty-seven. Sixteen page signatures. Sixteen times four plus three. Roger felt confident with his choice. The next step was to make sure Mr. Hancock suspected the theft. He planned to thieve gradually—two each fork, knife, and spoon to test the waters. If no one noticed, he'd double the quantity until someone did. He imagined that, like everything other resource at Garden Lakes, silverware was a premium and any draw on the supply would be obvious.

Our voices faltered toward the end of "Before the Ending of the Day," the tune accentuated with a less than hearty "Amen." We resumed our seats and Mr. Malagon and Mr. Hancock ascended to the front of the chapel. We took a collective measured breath, knowing what was next: the official rules and regulations of life at Garden Lakes. Much like the first day of a new school year, we knew what to expect. Senior tales of life at Garden Lakes trickled down through the ranks so even incoming freshmen knew the deal. Our nervousness, however, stemmed not from the official decree, but from the knowledge that with the decree came the end of the ceremonies. Our casual air, tinged with arrogance, dissipated as we wandered through the ever-increasing dimness brought on by the drone of Mr. Hancock's voice.

Schedules run off on colored paper—pink for sophomores and blue for Fellows—were distributed. The schedules were virtually identical—rise at four a.m., breakfast at four-thirty, chapel at five. The blue schedule called for construction from five-thirty until the mid-morning break at seven-thirty; the pink schedule called for lunch prep. After the break, Fellows returned to construction and the sophomores to the kitchen, this time for dinner prep. Lunch was served to the Fellows at eleven by the sophomores, who ate at noon while the Fellows were in class. The sophomores cleaned up after lunch and made final dinner preparations until two, when the schedules converged on the playing field for Sports until four, when the Fellows, again served by the sophomores, took dinner. The sophomores ate their dinner at five, after the Fellows retreated to their housing for the Reading Hour. Once the kitchen closed for the night, the sophomores reported to their pod leaders' housing for tutoring and study from *American Democracy*, the spiral bound book prepared by Mr. Hancock, a collection of the documents integral to the founding of America and the birth and maintenance of democracy. Free Time was slotted for eight, curfew and lights out at nine.

"I don't have to tell you boys deviation from the schedule will not be tolerated," Mr. Hancock said. He commanded the sophomores to pick up their copies of *American Democracy* at his house. Each copy was marked with a street number corresponding to the house numbers on Regis Street, indicating the sophomores' pod leaders. The Fellows were to verify attendance before tutoring began. "Unfortunately, our numbers work out evenly now," Mr. Hancock said. "Mr. Malagon will now say a few words on that matter."

Mr. Malagon, who had been standing behind Mr. Hancock, stepped forward. "Thank you, Mr. Hancock," he said. "Yes. Undoubtedly you boys know that Mr. Quinn has left us. That was his prerogative. Mr. Hancock and I are not against the exercise of freedom and personal liberty; anyone who doesn't wish to be here, who doesn't feel he can benefit from the Garden Lakes program is free to leave." Mr. Malagon paused, looking around. "If anyone else would like to leave, please say so." He paused again and our heads swiveled, looking for a telltale flinch, or a head hung to mask plans of desertion.

No one came forward.

"Good, men," Mr. Malagon said.

The liturgy ended and we herded into the classroom, the sophomores splintering off for the kitchen to clean the breakfast dishes and prepare, under Mr. Hancock's direction, the meals for lunch and dinner.

A man in his late thirties stood at the front of the classroom, rubbing his face, his stubby fingers mowing the underside of his beard. We grabbed chairs at the four tables that ran the length of the room. Out the window, the stranger's white pickup truck was parked two wheels up on the curb, STATEWIDE CONSTRUCTION emblazoned in silver on the side.

We knew *who* the stranger was; we just didn't know his name. The stranger embodied the nonchalance with which we'd described to anyone who didn't know, or anyone who did but would listen, how it was that a crew of unskilled high school juniors could drywall an entire house. Our fathers listened half-heartedly to our vague talk of sawing and hammering. They knew as little as we did about how a house was built. To them, construction of a house meant deciding on a floor plan, or choosing between lap siding, panel siding, stucco, or brick exteriors. To us, it meant even less. Our confidence was predicated only on the fact that classes before us had done it. We were clueless about what had been done in the weeks and months preceding our arrival at Garden Lakes: the grading of the site; foundation construction; the framing of the house; the installation of the windows and doors; roofing; siding; a roughing of the electrical, plumbing, and HVAC, as well as insulating the house. Any one of those chores sounded to us the same as drywalling. We were just here to complete the task at hand. And while we knew the project was largely a demonstration of our ability to work together, we also knew Mr. Malagon would be there to chaperone, and we knew that Statewide Construction would oversee the project, driving out to Garden Lakes to inspect the house after each phase.

Mr. Malagon introduced Jack Baker, whose kidnapping would later prove to be our downfall, and the room grew silent. Mr. Baker jumped to life like a marionette, seized with nervous energy, which he walked off by pacing in front of the proctor's desk at the head of the room.

"Morning, gentlemen," Mr. Baker began. His voice reached the far corners of the room, but he talked to the floor as he paced. "I guess you know why you're here. This is my first year doing this, though I've been with Statewide for fifteen years. Some of your predecessors worked with my predecessor, Joe Cotton. He's retired, so you got me." Mr. Baker continued pacing and it soon became evident that he was not going to look up at any of us. We looked at Mr. Malagon, hoping to share a laugh with him, but he was engrossed in the pages of a white binder foil stamped with the same silver logo as the truck outside.

"So, here's how it works. You're here for what, roughly forty days?" Mr. Malagon nodded.

"Plenty of time. There are three phases." Mr. Baker flashed three thick fingers at us. "Phase One consists of measuring, cutting, and hanging the drywall. Phase Two is the taping, beading, stapling, and application of compound. Phase Three is sanding, texturing, and painting. Phases One and Two will require separately managed teams working in unison; each component of the third phase will require all hands for each phase. The job will take a minimum of thirty-four days and a maximum of thirty-eight days. Any questions so far?"

Figs, who would later succeed in covering up an embezzlement at his firm, shifting the blame to an innocent department head, resulting in the department head's firing, raised his hand and to our surprise, Mr. Baker locked eyes with him.

"How long will each phase take?"

"Roughly two weeks. I'm scheduled…" Mr. Baker consulted a binder. "I'm scheduled to inspect the site fourteen days from now, with another inspection fourteen days later. The final inspection will be ten days after that, a few days before the event." Mr. Baker's opaque reference to the Open House on the last day of Garden Lakes suggested he was oblivious about what the Open House was, that he didn't know it was the date we were all anticipating when our parents would drive out to pick us up and marvel at the finished product.

Mr. Baker reached into a box hidden behind the desk and continued talking while distributing a stack of small, black notebooks. "These are your job journals. Each man is responsible for his own journal. You should only write in your journal in pencil." He handed out boxes of pencils and tiny red sharpeners stamped with his company's logo in foil. "The job journal is as important to any building job as a hammer, screwdriver, or ladder. I can't stress that enough.

"Now, what goes in a job journal? Page one should be titled 'Living Room.' Skip four pages and name the next one 'Kitchen' and so forth until there's a section for every room in the house. How many bedrooms is this house, anyone know?"

"Three," Smurf, the future slanderer, said. He stuck his tongue out for our amusement, knowing Mr. Baker wouldn't see.

"Three bedrooms," Mr. Baker said, again consulting his binder. "Upstairs bath. No garage."

"The garages are converted into an extra room," Mr. Malagon said.

"There duct work for this room?" Mr. Baker asked, seeking the answer more from his binder than from Mr. Malagon.

"The rooms have windows for cross-ventilation," Warren said. "It's like an Arizona room." Long before he'd be an unwitting accomplice to an Internet scam, Warren had helped his grandparents build an Arizona room onto their house one summer and was familiar with the architectural absurdity.

"So," Mr. Baker said, finding his place again. "A few facts about drywall: a sheet of drywall is composed of hardened gypsum core wrapped in paper—smooth paper on the face of the sheet, folded around the long edges, and a rougher paper as backing. Drywall doesn't only come in four by eight panels. There are different drywall types for different drywall needs. Types of drywall include moisture-resistant drywall, called greenboard or blueboard because of the coloration of its papering. Moisture-resistant drywall can tolerate high humidity and is used primarily in parts of the country where it rains frequently. Here in Arizona we use greenboard for bathrooms, the area around kitchen sinks, and laundry or utility rooms. Anywhere you suspect water will collect or areas that will be exposed to moisture for prolonged periods of time. You should write that down."

A rumble filled the room as we reached into our pockets for our pencils and sharpeners. Lindy's red sharpener skidded across the tile floor and Roger kicked it back toward him, the sharpener ricocheting off Lindy's foot before Assburn picked it up and handed it back. We turned the journal over and scrawled "Types of Drywall" on the back, employing a skill we learned in Father Mason's memorization classes called "listing," the theory being that once you listed a series of things in a relevant order, you could recall the items with ease. Based on the partial information we'd received at that juncture, we spaced down under the heading and penciled in "Moisture-resistant," leaving room above the notation for a description of the standard drywall and enough space below for a description of fire-resistant drywall, a type of drywall we guessed was a specialty, the valuable lesson learned in Mr. Mason's class being that you didn't always get the information in the order of importance.

Mr. Baker continued. "Standard or regular drywall is forty eight inches wide and comes in panels up to sixteen feet. They come in four thicknesses"—Mr. Baker held up two fingers on each hand— "five-eighths of an inch, half an inch, three-eights of an inch, and quarter inch. For our purposes, we will be using the thickest board, which is?"

Smurf's hand shot up first in a forest of arms.

"Five-eighths."

"Very good. I was told you guys were smart," Mr. Baker commented without a hint of irony. He moved on, discoursing about what thicknesses provide what kind of fire protection absent the use of fire-resistant drywall.

"What color is fire-resistant drywall?" Sprocket asked, checking over his notes. His immersion in detail would be the wellspring of his success as a software entrepreneur.

Mr. Baker wrinkled his nose. "It's the same color as regular drywall. The only difference is its fire rating."

"And are there variances within the fire-resistant drywall that are similar to the variance of regular drywall?" Sprocket asked.

The rest of us rolled our eyes, used to Sprocket's constant over self-education.

Mr. Baker rubbed his forehead. "Sure. But we're not going to be using any fire-resistant board so I don't see—"

"Out of curiosity, then," Sprocket said.

"Okay, sure. Fire-resistant drywall is rated in time intervals—forty-five minutes, sixty minutes, and one hundred and twenty minutes—which is how long the board will resist fire," Mr. Baker answered as he continued to pace the front of the room.

No one but Sprocket entered this information into their job journals.

We adjourned to the site as the sun pitched over the horizon, vanquishing the weak morning light that had spread across Garden Lakes. Armed with our job journals and pencils, and with the tutorial from Mr. Baker, we were able to focus on the framed house for the first time as we stood in the moonscaped front yard among the empty pallets and discarded cement bags. A portable outhouse stood sentry near the front door. The drywall was stacked like a gypsum butte along the side of the house. Inside, incandescent rectangles burned across the floors and through the slats of the framing. The smell of wood was overpowering.

With Mr. Baker as a guide, we began the most crucial step: measuring the rooms for drywall. He asked for groups, two groups to make the initial measurements and two groups to re-check the measurements. Our hesitation was born out of our fear that, once formed, we'd be stuck in the group for the rest of the summer. We stared blankly, some of us standing in shadow, some in sunlight. A couple of us shuffled toward our housemates. Mr. Baker split the group into four, his mind accounting for Sprocket's inability to navigate the stairs.

Tape measures were doled out to each team. At the last minute—sensing something, perhaps—Mr. Baker made an addendum: the measurements would be made twice, the first two sets of Fellows doing the measuring and dictating the results to the other two, then the reverse. Mr. Malagon supervised the upstairs measurements. Downstairs, we could hear Mr. Baker's instructions to Assburn about which way to measure a wall. Some of us pulled out the store we'd stashed at breakfast, munching fruit and torn pieces of bagel as we measured.

. . . .

Measurements in hand, checked and rechecked, we reconvened in the kitchen. Mr. Baker, never guessing he was among those who would plot his kidnapping, freed a set of blueprints from a plastic tube he'd retrieved from his truck and bid us to call out the measurements room by room. We drew together in a circle, our job journals open like hymnals, and sang out the measurements as Mr. Baker called for them.

Across the development, sophomores who couldn't boil water were engaged in a crash course in cooking. They learned the distinction between diced and minced, how a tablespoon was not equal to a teaspoon, and that under no circumstances was a teaspoon a pinch. Mr. Hancock distributed photocopies of the same handout he'd been giving out for over a decade: One fourth cup plus one fourth cup equals _____? One third plus one half is _____? There are _____ ounces in a quart? In a gallon? Sophomores who, on the advice of the previous class had taken an unusual interest in kitchen work at home in the weeks leading up to Garden Lakes, passed with ease. Those who remained baffled by how to double the measurements for any given recipe were relegated to the cutting boards and reminded that the kitchen's first aid supplies were limited.

In addition to meals, the sophs made the Daily Soup from scratch, soups they'd never heard of like spicy red bean soup or roasted bell pepper soup or Moroccan potato bean. Mr. Hancock fervently believed that all that life had to teach was represented in soup making. Lessons about action and consequence (a teaspoon of thyme when the recipe called for an eighth of a teaspoon would render the soup inedible) as well as lessons about how certain ingredients complement each other while others, when brought together, ruin the taste of a particular soup. The critical lesson, Mr. Hancock believed, was the notion that digression from the recipe invalidated it. Mr. Hancock's tenure at Randolph had taught him that boys' impoverished kitchen skills—however feminine and unmanly such skills were regarded by society at large—extended itself to practical matters outside of how to bring a hammer down on a nail, or how to tell a Phillips screwdriver from a flathead. He posited that while the boys may not be headed toward the exacting science of construction—he was sure that none of the boys who had passed through Randolph's hallowed halls would ever be a foreman much less an invaluable member of a construction crew—they would need to feed themselves (juvenilia about their wives or, god forbid, their mothers taking care of their cooking aside) and so Mr. Hancock took the occasion to inculcate the same precision required to calculate how many sheets of drywall each room in the framed house would require. Under Mr. Baker's guidance, we scratched calculations into our job journals amid sighs and feverish erasing. Re-measuring of the electrical boxes was called for; strategies for drywalling the bathrooms were advanced and rejected. Pencil shading turned our job journals into coloring books.

Mr. Malagon interrupted Mr. Baker as he was explaining about how corner beads bridged any gap between juxtaposed drywall. "The boys have their seven-thirty break," Mr. Malagon said.

We tucked our job journals into our khakis and trooped to the dining hall for the muffins and juices laid out by the sophs, who also indulged in the feast.

Sprocket and a couple Fellows huddled at one table, poring over their job journals. Sprocket could be heard muttering, "I think the light switch goes here," or "the outlet is too low." Hands and Figs approached Mr. Baker, who was provided with a cup of Mr. Hancock's black coffee, lobbing questions about taping sequences, the number of coats of joint compound needed, etc. Mr. Baker checked his watch during a dissertation on skim coating and Level 5 finishes. Mr. Malagon slipped into the kitchen and Roger stole closer to the basket of silverware, palming two knives in one hand and a batch of spoons in the other. The sophomores shook out their wrists, stretching their cramped fingers.

Assburn, who would die plunging into a frozen lake somewhere outside Detroit, driving across the ice, smuggling counterfeit game systems into the country, sat by himself, the realization that neither Mr. Hancock nor Mr. Malagon was going to demand Q's return hitting him hard. The first full day of Garden Lakes held so many promises for each of us, but Assburn knew that Q would not return, that he would therefore not be able to return the pen to Q, that the first bead in a long chain of apologies and forgiveness would not be threaded. The rest of us could see Assburn's disappointment, though we hadn't any idea of his dreams of contrition. The day when an accusation could be answered with, *Yes, I'm sorry,* or, *It's true, but I regret it,* slipped from Assburn's reach the instant Q disappeared into the darkness.

As the mid-morning break expired, Figs squeezed past the dividing wall, which had been pulled parallel with the east wall. A perfume of fruit and spices and warm muffins filled his nose. The Randolph faculty had granted Figs license to areas inaccessible by other students—the photocopier in the principal's office, the sports equipment locker in the gym—and the kitchen at Garden Lakes was just another area Figs felt comfortable broaching. His intention was to propose to Mr. Hancock that a soda and juice break be added between the mid-morning break and lunch—a proposal Figs felt sure would be endorsed by the other Fellows—but he changed his mind (and direction) when he overheard Mr. Hancock's baritone voice and saw him point a finger in Mr. Malagon's chest: "I said no. And I'm not discussing it."

Figs drew back, clearing the serving counter as Mr. Malagon reappeared, flushed.

The space between the mid-morning break and lunch was filled with Mr. Baker's instruction on the proper methods for cutting drywall, whether you were using a jigsaw, handheld saw, or a box knife. A tour of the supply shed familiarized us with the implements we'd be married to for the coming weeks. Sprocket inventoried the shed in his job journal, assigning each item its own page, counting the framing edges, chalklines, drywall routers, saws, rasps, panel lifters, stilts, hammers, tape measures, screwdrivers, screws, nails, rubber mallets, hawks, taping knives, trowels, paint brushes, and electrical cords (which could be run to the nearest finished house for electricity) as well as the gallons of joint compound and egg-white latex paint (Cottage White, officially), which he tallied on the back cover. The cataloguing comforted Sprocket. Until after the mid-morning break, he'd suffered from a gnawing suspicion that his selection for Garden Lakes was just charity. Sprocket's parents had raised him to endure his disability without bitterness and he'd come to accept his situation as just one of those things. In that way, Sprocket's thinking was more evolved than our own. At that point, we still believed that life could be regulated at our bidding. We knew nothing of luck or chance or fate—we disdained those words as excuses for failure, a poor apology for an absence of will. As far as we knew, desire and stamina was all that counted.

Mr. Baker rushed through his last twenty minutes with us, peppering his instructions with, "Don't forget to jot it in your job journal!" Our morale couldn't have been higher as Mr. Baker's truck sailed through the waves of afternoon heat rising from the asphalt and out the front gates, a confidence born from the assumption that each of us was paying closer attention to Mr. Baker than the other. But we had until the next day before we'd be tested, and nothing seals a sense of confidence tighter than the promise of the future.

The sophomores broke in shifts from dinner prep to serve lunch, ladling pasta dishes (including macaroni and cheese) from trays heated by an elaborate steam system built into the serving counter. Lunch at Garden Lakes was traditionally traditional—the closest to cafeteria-style food we would encounter, dinner being an elaboration of Mr. Hancock's moods, which ran the gamut between rich and creamy to spicy and healthful. Dinner was our reward for a long day of labor fueled by carbohydrates and was served to us at our tables by sophomore waiters.

The only wait service afforded us at lunch was beverage service, furnished more in an effort to keep the aisle leading to the kitchen clear than for reasons of decorum. Sophomores fluttered in the background, roaming, waiting to be pressed into service. If the Fellow ordered soda, he was also to indicate the brand of soda he wanted. Predictably, Smurf sent his waiter for Pepsi and to his table's hilarity, spit the Pepsi out and insisted that he'd ordered Coke.

Those at Roger's table thought he was following Smurf's lead when the waiter asked Roger if he wanted more to drink and Roger ignored him. The sophomore asked again and Roger started a discourse about drywalling with Figs, who was sitting to Roger's right. The waiter, Dennis Reedy, moved along, asking Figs if he'd like more soda. Roger slurped the last drops from his glass and slammed it against the table, inducing a Pavlovian glance from all the other waiters. Reedy asked Roger again if he wanted more soda and again Roger ignored him.

Roger's tablemates shifted in their seats, sensing that Roger was invoking a shun against Reedy. Everyone at the table knew the shun was as likely as not without merit, much like the shun he'd invoked against Rebecca Clement, the Xavierite who had spurned Roger's invitation to the Winter Formal. The first day of classes after the Winter Recess Roger and two frosh—Donnelly and Hendrickson—were camped out around the courtyard fountain before the first bell. Rebecca Clement and her friends strolled by on their way to first hour Spanish. "Hiya, Roger," Rebecca called out. Roger pretended like he didn't hear. Rebecca called out again and again Roger didn't acknowledge her. Rebecca kept up with her companions, continuing on toward Spanish class, confused by Roger's insolence. Roger gave no standing order, but the next time Donnelly saw Rebecca, he was with two other freshmen, Cooley and Bricketts, and when Rebecca called out to Donnelly, he aped Roger, ignoring her salutation. Cooley did the same in the presence of Fitzsimmons and Anderson, who did the same when Rebecca called out to them in a crowd of freshmen. By spring, half the student body was carrying He-Man Becky Haters' Club cards, printed on a dot matrix printer and laminated at the print shop down Central Avenue from Randolph, flashing the cards between classes and in the parking lot after school. Some Xavierites carried the cards as well, and by the Easter break, Rebecca Clement had transferred out of Xavier. Neither Roger nor anyone else spoke her name, but the He-Man Becky Haters' Club cards kept surfacing around campus, brandished as a punch line or as a threat.

"Roger, dude, do you want more soda?" Figs asked while Reedy shied from the table.

Roger carried on with his purported fascination with sheetrock without pause and everyone—including Figs—made like Figs had never asked the question. Reedy moved on to another table, terror in his eyes, and Roger rattled the ice in his glass. Another waiter who had witnessed the shun against Reedy quickly reached over and snatched Roger's glass without asking him if he wanted more. Roger called out after the waiter, "Pepsi, please," and the waiter returned with a full glass of soda. None of his tablemates spoke as Roger took a long drink and then continued his train of thought about what would happen if you karate-chopped a piece of sheetrock.

Reedy stepped in Roger's direction, intimating that he wanted to clear up any misunderstanding, but Mr. Hancock appeared from the kitchen with Mr. Malagon, the two not so deep in conversation about the upcoming class that they wouldn't have seen a row had one occurred. Reedy reversed, heading for the kitchen. Mr. Hancock and Mr. Malagon continued their conference at a table vacated by Fellows who had trotted down the hall early to the classroom to get the seats in the back row. Sophomores serving themselves lunch repopulated the table as we decamped for class, some of us walking near Mr. Hancock and Mr. Malagon, hoping to catch a sliver of their conversation or to overhear what looked to us like supplication from Mr. Malagon.

We could guess the nature of this conversation. Mr. Hancock was an enemy of change, so when Mr. Malagon, upon being chosen for duty at Garden Lakes, suggested the academic curriculum be switched from English and Philosophy classes (Mr. Malagon successfully argued that, as one of the state's premiere schools, Randolph students were inordinately well versed in English grammar and the fundamentals of classical philosophy) to a discussion about the Great Leaders and Their Decisions in Twentieth Century America, Mr. Hancock balked at the idea. Mr. Hancock's syllabus for American Literature had exactly zero amendments or additions to it over the years and he saw no reason to alter a program of learning so successfully implemented.

But the administration had heard Mr. Malagon's proposal. Mr. Malagon contended a close examination of the great leaders, not just presidents but men and women of substance, was vital to any true leadership program. Without making known his feelings about the legitimacy of arming Fellows with confusing philosophical hypotheses and the keen written ability to express their confusion, Mr. Malagon argued a point the administration held dear: effective academia. Every year the administration combed scores of reports filled with colorful charts and graphs to assess and reassess the school's curriculum, spelunking for ways to improve the relevance of a Randolph education. Mr. Malagon pled his proposal along these lines.

Mr. Hancock rallied the rest of the faculty on the platform of tradition, pointing up the success rate of past Garden Lakes Fellows. His colleagues privately framed the debate as a threat to the more senior, established faculty. Rhetorical questions permeated the teachers' lounge and in the halls after school. If the administration disregarded their position, what would stop students from exhibiting the same lack of respect? What message would it send to students to have a proven, successful curriculum undermined by pop academe? And, more importantly, would a vote for the proposal of a junior faculty member signal an end to the administration's confidence in the advice and judgment of senior faculty members?

The questions would remain rhetorical, however. The administration embraced Mr. Malagon's proposition, paving the way for a new course of study at Garden Lakes. The debate, while internal and secret, was leaked to the rest of us through Figs, who worked as an administrative aid during seventh hour. And without knowing whether the scrapped English and philosophy classes would have been beneficial, the new course—or rather the manner in which the new course came into being—whet our appetite.

As we took our seats in the classroom, we observed an expression Mr. Malagon had never before exhibited: nervousness. Mr. Malagon chafed under the promulgation of historical inaccuracies like the fairytale that Betsy Ross sewed the American Flag, or that Paul Revere ever uttered "The British are coming! The British are coming!" He rankled a few colleagues by crafting a class on Hitler aimed at humanizing the Fuhrer rather than portraying him as a one-dimensional black hat. Could Hitler tell you a joke so funny that you'd wet yourself? was the opening line of the unit. "It's easy to recognize evil once it has manifested," Mr. Malagon would say. "A thinking person should be trained to spot the warning signs." Thanks to Figs and his eavesdropping, we knew the proposed class at Garden Lakes was grooved in the same controversial vein, all of which was confirmed when Mr. Malagon launched into a prepared lecture on FDR's administration, fending off a volley from Mr. Hancock, who added helpfully that many of the New Deal programs didn't survive a court challenge, by emphasizing the New Deal's legacy. We watched the interplay like fascinated children.

The sounds of sophomores shuffling in the hallway broke Mr. Malagon's concentration, a sound that meant it was time for Sports. "More about Mr. Roosevelt and the New Deal tomorrow," Mr. Malagon intoned. "Be sure to read the handout carefully. Did I mention each unit will have a short quiz at the end?" He laughed through our groans. "See you in ten minutes."

Ten minutes later, we met up on the dry lakebed, having raced to our houses and changed for Sports, meaning soccer, which, after cooking, was Mr. Hancock's other passion. The sophomores were waiting for us on the makeshift field, their punctuality presumably the result of a harangue some minutes earlier. Mr. Hancock himself appeared in his usual attire, as did Mr. Malagon, who meandered out to the field from class. Mr. Malagon had lobbied unsuccessfully for baseball instead of soccer but, having lost his treasured Philosophy class, Mr. Hancock would not be defeated on this score. He roused fear in the heart of every administrator with the image of teenage boys wielding baseball bats and throwing fastballs through windowed strike zones. Mr. Hancock took the further step of itemizing a list of equipment needed for baseball, complete with slightly inflated prices. He presented this list with a soccer ball tucked under his arm, the only equipment needed for a soccer match. The administration rebuffed Mr. Malagon's idea of substituting baseball for soccer; the decision came to him via the same route as his suggestion—in passing—so Mr. Malagon was unaware of Mr. Hancock's rigorous campaign.

The sun blazed down on us. Mr. Hancock passed around tubes of sun block and we spread it over our arms, legs, faces, and backs of our necks and ears. We massaged sun block in our hair like shampoo, as we'd been doing since we were old enough to play outside. The lakebed was polluted with the smell of coconut.

Mr. Hancock, whose excused absence from Garden Lakes would set off a chain reaction from which we'd hardly recover, divided us into two random teams, mixing Fellows and sophomores. Sprocket would be the goal judge, a specialized referee needed for the Garden Lakes brand of soccer: the game would be played half-court due to the scarcity of goal equipment. Mr. Malagon, who turned out not to be what we'd all built him up to be, helped Sprocket maneuver down the slope and he rode past us carrying two orange pylons from the supply shed on his lap. He placed them an equal distance apart at Mr. Hancock's instruction. The pylons and the palm tree sprouting from the small dirt island would function as a goal. Sprocket would call balls in and out. Another position not found in Major League Soccer was the Ball Spotter, a position of importance stationed behind the goal whose job it was to track down goals and errant kicks so play was not suspended while someone chased the ball down Garden Lakes Parkway. Mr. Malagon and Mr. Hancock would each referee one side of the field, calling out each team's captain's name to indicate which team would corner kick or throw in. The remaining four players stood as substitutions, two on each sideline. Since the half-field made play immediate, the goalies were to step out of the box when their teams were on offense.

Figs was the natural choice for captain of his team; so too was Hands. Figs designated Lindy as the goalkeeper for his team; Hands chose himself. Sprocket wheeled himself near the goal line as Mr. Hancock flipped a coin to determine play. Hands, who would one day lead his family's sixth generation brewery to ruin by distrusting the CFO, whom he considered a rival for his wife's affections, called "Heads." The quarter bounced on the dirt field and it was a moment before the dust shrouding the coin settled. Tails. Mr. Malagon and Mr. Hancock withdrew to the sidelines, their breaths rattling the tiny wooden ball inside their whistles. Mr. Hancock bounce-passed the ball to Figs, who raised his arms and called, "Ball In," passing it to Smurf, who caught the ball with the side of his foot, the muted thud sounding as if it might have hurt. Smurf, whose expert slander would end his future female colleague's real estate career, showed no sign of pain, though, and crisscrossed the ball away from charging defenders. Smurf passed the ball cross field to Assburn and he advanced it toward the goal by faking out Warren. Hands danced inside the goal, his palms sweaty. Each of his athletic feats—buzzer beaters on the basketball court, long balls on the baseball diamond, touchdowns on the gridiron—was prefaced with the same rush, the same sick feeling inside. Hands jogged in place as the soccer ball whizzed side to side across the playing field, negotiating its way toward the goal. Roger ran alongside Smurf, who was trying to corral the ball on a wayward pass from one of the sophomores. The defenders converged when they saw Smurf make a move for the goal. Hands positioned himself with his legs spread wide, ready to pounce. Roger poked the ball away from Smurf, but Smurf leaped over the runaway ball, stopping it with his heel. Mr. Hancock and Mr. Malagon squared off across the field, moving with the action. Smurf passed the ball to Figs right as he charged ahead of the defenders. Figs stutter-stepped and punted the ball at the goal. Hands put his body in the ball's path and the ball arced off his left arm.

"Out!" Mr. Hancock called.

Mr. Malagon had scarcely put the ball back into play when a scrum broke out. Mr. Hancock's whistle fell from his mouth as he ran toward mid-field. Mr. Malagon was bent over Lindy, who was rolling in the dirt, cradling his left arm.

Lindy's screams increased in pitch as Mr. Malagon and Mr. Hancock sorted out what happened. Defenders closest to the play claimed Roger had deliberately collided with Lindy when it was clear that Lindy had stolen the ball cleanly from Roger. Other players were less sure of the play. Some alleged to have seen Roger flailing his arms, indicating that he was out of control when he smashed into Lindy, who by now was lying prostrate with his eyes closed, he left arm immobile. Roger did not testify in his own defense. He listened coolly as the different versions were re-played, taking count of who was saying what. As Mr. Malagon tended to Lindy, who would one day in his thirties die in his sleep, leaving behind a devastated family, testing the flexibility of Lindy's left arm, Mr. Hancock pulled Roger aside and asked him what happened.

"It was an accident," Roger said.

Mr. Hancock did not pursue the question and instead turned to Mr. Malagon and Lindy.

"He needs medical attention," Mr. Malagon said.

"More than a sling?" Mr. Hancock asked.

Mr. Malagon nodded.

Figs volunteered to pull one of the two Jeeps around, but Mr.

Hancock assured us that only he and Mr. Malagon would ever get behind the wheel of either vehicle. Mr. Malagon pointed out that it was close to the dinner hour, which meant Mr. Hancock was needed elsewhere. "Why don't we have everyone shower up and I'll run Brian to the emergency room," Mr. Malagon said.

Mr. Hancock hesitated. He knew what Mr. Malagon said made sense, but he speculated as to the seriousness of Lindy's injury (though the distressed look on Lindy's face authenticated the necessity for the trip to the hospital). "We'll set a place for Mr. Lindstrum at the dinner table," Mr. Hancock said, though the remark was directed more at Mr. Malagon than at Lindy.

....

The half an hour of free time added to the schedule by the abrupt end of Sports left us disoriented. Some went to their rooms; others began their showers early, opting to use the time to relax before dinner. Mr. Hancock prescribed ten minute showers for the sophomores, then herded their wet heads into the kitchen to undertake the evening meal: coq au vin. The sophomores had spent their afternoon cleaving poultry hindquarters and while the rest of us played cards, or grabbed a nap, the kitchen was busied with shellacking chicken legs with Mr. Hancock's magical red-wine sauce, a sauce made with one less bottle of wine, said bottle residing in Adam Kerr's bottom dresser drawer. Kerr was generally regarded as one of the more audacious sophomores. He once climbed onto the roof of Randolph to spy an accident that had stopped traffic on Central Avenue (and received a three day suspension because of it).

Smurf joined Figs and Hands in a quick game of five card draw. "Everyone's in their rooms," Smurf said about his own residence. He looked at Figs. "Roger's going to get you, you know that, right?"

Figs shrugged and asked for two cards. "I don't see how."

Hands glanced at Figs and then looked away at his cards. "Yeah," he said.

Smurf folded. "Fuckin' guy bulldozed Lindy. Won't be surprised if Lindy's arm is busted to pieces."

There was a knock and the front door opened.

"Never guess what Assburn has," Warren said, pulling up a chair.

"Whatever it is, I'm sure he's not the original owner," Figs said. "You in?"

Warren rapped on the table and Figs dealt him in.

"He's got a mobile phone," Warren said, picking up his cards.

"What—did he steal Hancock's?" Figs asked. The school alleviated parental anxiety by providing Mr. Hancock with a mobile phone, which he kept in a locked box under his bed.

"Guess all that talk about him not being a klepto is bullshit," Hands said. "Figured it was."

"Does it work?" Smurf asked.

"Yeah, he turned it on," Warren said, discarding. "One."

Hands folded.

"Did he let you use it?" Smurf wanted to know.

"Didn't ask," Warren said, uninterested in the story. "You guys see the way Roger knocked out Lindy?"

"I was right next to him," Figs said. "Roger got this look."

Smurf excused himself and the front door opened and closed, but the exchange about Lindy and Roger continued without a beat, and without consensus. Further down Regis Street, Assburn denied to Smurf that he had a mobile phone. Smurf called him a liar, but Assburn stuck to his story. "Damn liar," Smurf said again.

The move to the dining hall was less a shuffle toward a meal than it was a rush to keep an important appointment. Fellows walk-skipped to dinner and we all fell into formation as the waiters brought steaming plates of coq au vin and garlic mashed potatoes.

As promised, a place for Lindy had been set at Figs and Hands's table. The place setting brought stares from the other tables and from the sophomore waiters, who no doubt knew something big was at stake. Roger glided to his table without paying tribute to Lindy's empty chair. He hunkered over his plate and tore into the juicy meat, ravenous.

Mr. Hancock took his seat at the center table, sophomores flanking him. As the meal progressed—seconds on mashed potatoes, more chicken ("It's not chicken, boys. Coke-a-veen.")—Lindy's ultimate disfigurement grew in our minds. We imagined him in a body cast, or worst. Out the windows the sun continued its tyranny of the sky, but we anticipated the pink light that always preceded sundown ("It's all the crap in the air," Lindy had told us) and collectively worried about the ramifications of Lindy's and Mr. Malagon's absence after dark.

We held our breaths as the sound of talking echoed through the outer hall. Mr. Hancock did not look up from his slice of crushed pineapple sour cream pie, the delectable concoction we weren't enjoying as we might. Mr. Malagon's frame filled the doorway, blocking out Lindy, who seemed to be struggling in the background, his left arm in a plaster cast up to his elbow. He *was* struggling, but not because of his useless appendage. His right arm was rendered useless, too, by a cylindrical package wrapped in butcher paper. The package caught Mr. Hancock's attention. Mr. Malagon leaned in and whispered something to Mr. Hancock, causing Mr. Hancock to grimace.

"It's a telescope," Lindy said, taking his seat. A waiter brought a plate of coq au vin and mashed potatoes while another set down a plate of baked apples sprinkled with cinnamon.

"How did you get a telescope?" Hands asked.

"Mr. Malagon bought it for me," Lindy said between bites.

"Does your arm hurt?" Figs asked.

The whole room was listening to the conversation.

Lindy shook a tumor the size of a roll of quarters in his pocket, the bottle of painkillers rattling like a baby's toy. "Can't feel a thing," he said, smiling.

Mr. Hancock spoke to Mr. Malagon gravely, referencing the package at Lindy's feet, obviously aggrieved. Mr. Malagon concentrated on his dinner, looking up only to take a drink.

Lindy described the hospital, how his mother raced to the

emergency room thinking that his injuries were life-threatening. Lindy became animated when he told the part about the telescope. "Mr. Malagon says we can look at the stars during free time," Lindy said. "Bet they look pretty good out here at night."

"If we're still awake when the sun goes down," Hands said. "Christ, I could use a nap."

At the table over, Roger was avidly *not* listening to Lindy's tale. He rattled the ice in his glass, unnerving Reedy. Some of us noticed Reedy's unnatural circumnavigation of the dining hall—taking the long way around to the soda machine, hoping to stay out of the willful rotation that threatened to bring him into Roger's airspace.

Adam Kerr brought Roger another drink, staring down at him after he delivered the too-full glass, which slopped over, a dark stain spreading across the tablecloth.

"What are you looking at?" Roger asked in a way that froze everyone within earshot.

"Not sure," Kerr said bravely. "Trying to figure it out."

Roger stamped the top of Kerr's foot with as much weight as he could bring while sitting down. Kerr yelped and hopped on one foot.

"What's going on over there?" Mr. Hancock asked.

"Dixon—"Kerr began, but Hands jumped in: "Nothing, sir. He tripped over Roger's chair. That's all."

Satisfied with Hands's explanation (though perhaps not believing it), Mr. Hancock returned to his conversation with Mr. Malagon, who was forking a piece of pie cut from the reserve kept for the sophomores into his mouth.

Roger glared at Kerr, who in turn glared at Hands. Hands raised his eyebrows, communicating to Kerr that he was not taking Roger's side, but that Kerr should not cross a Fellow. Kerr heard the message and limped away.

The Fellows adjourned in groups to Regis Street for the Reading Hour, the hour after dinner but before tutoring allowed for us to read over Mr. Malagon's handout. While the Reading Hour was unpoliced, we all honored the rules—each Fellow must read in his room; no talking; no congregation in any room—not out of respect for each other's space and time, but because the Reading Hour was a chance to get forty winks before the sophomores arrived for tutoring.

. . . .

As the hands on the kitchen clocks reached for eight, the tutoring groups dissolved into informal salons, topics covered including the food at Garden Lakes, disbelief that we'd only been at Garden Lakes for one day, and that it would be weeks before we could contemplate the Open House. Fellows rubbed their tired eyes and yawned symphonically. Word was passed that Lindy had set the telescope up in the dry lakebed and while most of us were fatigued into near muteness, we ventured out, our footprints from the ill-fated soccer game earlier that day transforming the lakebed into the scene of a possible lunar landing, or alien invasion, or so we liked to imagine.

Lindy extended the cheap tripod that came with the telescope. Figs helped him raise it until the telescope rested near eye level, the smooth cylinder bobbing precariously on the tripod's crossbar. Lindy adjusted the eyepiece, tapping the telescope up or down, dialing into the sky's frenetic designs. He located the moon, the reddish glimmer of Mercury deep in the moon's backyard. He called out the constellations as he found them: Gemini, Canis Minor, Cancer, Hydra, the stars undulating as if the sky were an immense lake, the depths of its black waters limitless. Lindy believed his father and brother floated in the wake of these constellations, watching over him and his mother. He didn't believe in heaven; the concept was too obviously man-made, constructed out of human desire and fear, but he believed in the longevity of a person's essence and the belief gave him comfort as he searched the skies, his father's tremulous laugh and his brother's endless kidding alive in the stellar oceanography.

Others jostled for a look and Lindy aimed the telescope at Hydra, narrating our view with the tale of how Hercules slew the Hydra as his second labor. "Which was difficult because whenever Hercules chopped off one of the Hydra's heads, two more grew in its place." Those of us who had Mrs. Haberman for Latin knew the narrative and also knew about how Hercules had instructed his nephew Iolaus to cauterize the stumps as Hercules decapitated the Hydra, but we enjoyed Lindy's retelling. There wasn't anyone among us who didn't like Lindy save for Roger, apparently, and there were those of us who admired him. While we possessed fertile imaginations, we were without the facility to imagine Lindy's reality. We couldn't any of us imagine what it would be like to lose a family member, let alone more.

Lindy had long abandoned the search for answers to why his father and brother were struck head on by another boat, thrown into Lake Pleasant. Lindy was to have made the trip with them, but had been laid up by a summer cold. His mother hated the water and was instead home tending to her sick son when the sheriff's department knocked on their front door. For a time, the details obsessed Lindy: the inebriated pilots of the other craft (who were also killed instantly), his father and brother hitting the water head first. Did it look to bystanders that they'd dove out of harm's way? The thought of their mouths and noses filling with water, their lungs distended and shapeless like water balloons, slowed Lindy's own breathing. For weeks after the accident, he labored under the torment of what he guessed was an unusually potent virus, but his mother had been stricken with the same disease that prohibited Lindy from waking before noon, and from falling asleep before the sun started to rise. Junior year brought an audience of eager ears, but no one approached Lindy about the story. To Lindy, the deaths had become part of his heritage, a personal history too intimate to share with strangers. He and his mother had sworn a pact to carry on, to not let the sudden emptiness in their lives overtake them.

Staring through the telescope a summer later, Lindy felt like he'd kept a promise, the halos and coronas glowing overhead comforting him, affirming that he was a small but valuable part of something larger. Lindy didn't realize he'd expressed this sentiment aloud, an

awkward silence descending on the group of stargazers. Even Smurf
and Assburn, who had been arguing in whispers about whether or
not Assburn did indeed have a mobile phone, quieted.

Warren peered through the telescope. "So what you're saying is
that the sky is full of gods," he said.

Realizing that we thought he was talking about the heavens
in the abstract, Lindy expounded on Warren's comment. "They're
all up there," he said. "Venus, Mars, Saturn, Cupid, Juno, Neptune,
Jupiter—depending on where you're standing, they're all hovering,
ruling the sky."

"Neptune was Poseidon in Greek mythology," Sprocket added.
"All of the Roman gods had Greek names." Sprocket was one of the
few students handpicked by Mrs. Haberman for Advanced Latin.
"Venus is Aphrodite, Mars is Ares, Saturn is Cronus, Cupid is Eros,
Jupiter is Zeus…"

"Same god, different name," Warren said, raising his face toward
the moon.

"Yeah," Sprocket said, not sure whether Warren was asking or
reiterating.

"You're looking at Gemini," Lindy said to Hands, who had
swiveled the telescope north-northwest.

"Cool," Hands said. "It looks like two people holding hands." We
lined up behind the eyepiece, all except for Roger, who drifted away
from the crowd. Who wanted to watch two people holding hands?
Girlish behavior, he thought; just like the horoscopes. His mother
liked the horoscopes which was, as his father would say, *case in point*.
"Now Roger," she'd say, smoothing the paper on the table in front of
her, affecting the tone of a sideshow mystic, "You must avoid reckless
moves today, which only serve to embolden your critics. Stay calm."

"What's yours?" Roger would ask eagerly, tilting his bowl to
spoon out the sugary milk. The horoscopes seemed to young Roger
to be real advice—better than advice: it was as if someone could tell
the future. His mother had taken the time to explain the signs of the
Zodiac, but could not answer Roger's persistent questions about *how*

the astrologers knew what they knew, which amazed Roger as he kept secret count of how many days his horoscope had been dead on.

"Okay, let's see," his mother scanned the page, gathering her terrycloth robe around her neck against a blast of air conditioning. "Here it is. Ohhh, this is a good one: Be frugal. Make the least effort for the most effective gain. Going all out can exhaust you before you're finished. Controlled energy, not wastefulness, will see you through the day."

Roger would hurry home after school to compare notes with his mother, rereading the horoscopes, which his mother had folded and set on top of the refrigerator. They would freak each other out with stories that proved the horoscopes' veracity, Roger often embellishing for effect.

His father put a stop to the horoscopes his first day of retirement. Roger was startled to find his father seated at the kitchen table, unshowered and unshaven. His mother acted strangely, too, busying herself around the kitchen: wiping the counters, rearranging the pea green Tupperware silos that warehoused the family's supply of flour, sugar, and coffee. Was today Saturday? Roger asked himself. A glimpse of the calendar under the giant pineapple magnet on the freezer door confirmed that it was a school day. His father didn't appear sick, though Roger didn't possess the type of bravery required to stare at his father long enough to get an accurate diagnosis.

His father was constantly reminding Roger of his deficiencies. His mother glanced at Roger dolefully when his father was in the room, but rarely said anything against his him. Later, when Roger inquired about his father's early retirement from the Army, the swift end to what had been described not just by his father but by his father's buddies—who frequently came around on Friday and Saturday nights, staying long after he and his mother had gone to bed—as a brilliant military career, the only derogatory thing his mother had to say was that his father's promotion to Brigadier General had been denied because his father lacked the "philosophical qualities" the Army mandated of its high command.

The Colonel's omnipresence—the last person Roger saw before the leaving for school; the first he'd encounter upon his return— relegated his mother's luminous personality to the darkened corners of conversation until she disappeared all together. Roger began tagging along on outings to the shooting range, trips that increased in frequency until the Colonel was ready and waiting in the driveway when the bus let Roger off, leaving his mother longing for the horoscope breakfasts and the long afternoons in the living room where Roger would act out his day, or she would assist in what she could understand of his homework. Those days seemed firmly in the past, and his mother surrendered to the harder, coarser Roger, the Roger who locked himself in his room, the Roger who hardly spoke at meals (when he would take meals in the kitchen and not in his room). She'd ceded all influence in Roger's life to his father, glumly attributing it to Roger's maturation. A boy needed his father if he was to become a man, she told herself.

Roger dodged the light emanating from the classroom window. Peering in, he saw Mr. Malagon and Mr. Hancock deep in conversation. The front door would be open, Roger knew, but what about the kitchen? He had two chances: the door to the dining room and the door at the end of the hall that led to the kitchen.

The hallway was suffused with muted conversation and Roger realized his first piece of luck: either Mr. Malagon or Mr. Hancock had shut the classroom door. His cover story, if caught, would be that he'd dropped in for a drink from the drinking fountain, having gotten thirsty from staring at the stars with everyone else, who he'd point out were right behind him. Assembly was sometimes good cover, he knew.

The lock on the door to the dining room caught as Roger turned the knob, his hopes plummeting. What were the odds that the kitchen door was open, he wondered. He knew without doubt that the exterior kitchen door would be locked shut—it could only be opened from the inside anyway. He padded down the hall, past his alibi the water fountain, knowing he'd need a better story if he was caught wrestling with the kitchen door.

The door was unlocked. The knob turned so quickly Roger held his breath. He checked under the door to make sure he wasn't about to surprise a clutch of sophomores in some last minute breakfast preparation, but the air coming from under the door was cool and dark. He slipped inside, letting the door fall against his fingers, easing the knob's metal tongue back into place.

Roger's eyes adapted to the darkness, the outline of the portable wall visible. He felt the sockets of the silverware caddy. Empty. He felt his way along the stainless steel refrigerator, tempted to pull open the double doors in search of a midnight snack, but he kept his focus. His eyes dilated, he maneuvered through the kitchen by sight, zeroing in on the drying rack, which boasted the day's silverware. Relinquishing his plan for moderation, Roger clutched as many utensils as his hands could carry. A thump reverberated through the kitchen, quickening Roger's pulse. No alibi would exonerate him now, he knew, and he backed against the door opposite the one that had delivered him, pushing against the horizontal bar with his backside. The door admitted him into the night, clicking shut behind him.

Roger breathed shallowly. In the distance, he could make out the voices of the astronomy club. This daring take would be enough to execute the prank and put the whole sordid business behind him. Actually, the prank seemed less onerous once he possessed the silverware. Who knew, it might even be legendary.

Roger took a step and froze. The ground shifted near his feet, the drip drip drip from the air conditioner suddenly audible. What looked like six or eight pigs rooted through the remains of a prickly pear cactus, the swine having taken no notice of Roger. He heard a low grunting and took another step, choosing a course which would allow escape, but the sight of one of the pigs in profile chilled him: its long snout saddled with a pair of down-turned tusks. Javelina.

Roger had seen a pack of fifty or so javelina tear up a wild dog on a cable program (to his then delight). Roger identified the javelina at the moment they identified him. The tines of the bouquet of forks glinted in the moonlight. Roger knew from the cable program that he was in less danger if the herd was not comprised of newborns, or if a newborn was not grazing nearby. Roger couldn't be sure that he was seeing the whole herd; the trajectory he'd mapped out could well land him in the middle of the herd, like the wild dog on television. He pressed against the door, afraid to let his hands fall to his side lest the javelina read this gesture as hostile. He could feel his anger rising. *Fuck this*, he thought. He stomped his foot at the two nearest javelina, whose grizzled black and grey fur bristled. The javelina eyed Roger. The rooting and grunting ceased. A musk, earthy and moldy, spread like dye in water. A chill gave Roger a spasm he punctuated by throwing both fists of silverware at the javelina, sprinting in the other direction. Undaunted, the javelina gave chase at angles manageable only for animals who bore their load so close to the ground.

Roger crossed the outer loop, the click-clack, click-clack of miniature hooves in pursuit. Ahead, the gravel domes of The Grove rose. He imagined himself in some absurd video game, knowing instinctively that he could become surrounded if he were to make the wrong move. He circled the first pillar of gravel, chucking a good-sized rock at the pod of javelina. The rock landed without making contact, dividing the javelina into two flotilla. Roger sprang from his hiding place. A dark stain the shape of an inverted triangle bled through the front of his shirt as he skirted the edge of The Grove, hesitant about committing to entry for fear of being trapped.

The lights of Garden Lakes grew faint as Roger charged passed The Grove, expelled into the raw desert outside the development. The grunting sounds became intermittent woofing, like a dog barking at passing cars. Roger swooped up a rock in each hand, spinning around to face the pack. But the javelina had withdrawn, scurrying off into the desert, alarmed by the yips and howls traveling through the bright sky.

Roger let the rocks fall out of his unsteady hands. He looked back in the direction of Garden Lakes, the shadowy points of The Grove obscuring his view, isolating him from the development. The carbon-copy houses appeared fake, a front meant to shake off the cops. He scoured the perimeter, feeling like he'd been lured by the javelina into a sinister trap. Out of the corner of his eye he saw one of the street lights along the Parkway snap out.

Brennan rearranged the set of prism paperweights on his desk, a nervous habit everyone at the *Sun* had grown used to, even fond of. The shiny pyramids skated across the desktop under Brennan's thin, manicured fingers, gleaming under the fluorescence, sprinkling the walls with teardrop rainbows.

"When can I see a draft?" he asked.

"When have I ever shown a draft to anyone?"

Brennan spun the paperweights counterclockwise, knocking them together like steelies in a playground game of marbles. "I'm asking," he said.

Charlie frowned. "Are *you* asking, or is someone else asking?"

Brennan learned forward. "Wait a minute," he said, "what are you accusing me of?"

"I'm not accusing you of anything," Charlie said.

"It sounds like an accusation," Brennan said.

"Do you blame me?" Charlie asked as Gallagher sailed by Brennan's window, glancing into the office. He nodded to Gallagher who sped out of view. "I know the McCloud family is pressuring you," Charlie said, testing an unsourced rumor Gallagher had passed along. He gauged Brennan's face for a reaction, but nothing.

"My loyalties are to this paper," Brennan said, thumping his desk for emphasis. "Everyone knows that. Christ." Charlie knew Brennan often feigned umbrage and called upon his reputation when he felt threatened.

"That doesn't mean the McCloud family hasn't been crawling up your ass," Charlie said, switching tack, injecting his voice with sympathy. "I've got a stack of messages from up and down that family tree on my desk."

"They think you have an ax to grind," Brennan said.

"I don't," Charlie said flatly.

"Yeah, well, they're convinced you do."

"Where's their proof?"

"They don't have any," he said. "But they've got their suspicions." Brennan's harried and much beleaguered secretary knocked, but he waved her off.

"What suspicions?" Charlie asked. Brennan ticked off a series of seemingly unconnected columns he'd written over the last year or so: the closure of a private swimming club McCloud had funded with monies he may or may not have gained illegally through a complicated shell game with the books of American Community; the misfortune of the Tongan families McCloud had imported as landscapers—so many they resided in a community together south of Phoenix—for his assortment of hotels and master planned communities; the death of McCloud's protégé by a self-inflicted gunshot in the front seat of his Lexus in front of a toy store on Camelback Road. The protégé had broken alliance with McCloud upon McCloud's indictment and begun a new company telemarketing genealogy books to those predisposed to pay for such mementos. The company sank into the red and the protégé became aloof, his suicide effectively ending the company and leaving its employees without pay, the average employee owed in the neighborhood of a thousand dollars each.

"Those are all legitimate, newsworthy items," Charlie said. "Is the *Sun* going to start assigning me topics?"

"Hey!" Brennan nearly catapulted out of his seat. "Don't start saying things like that. No way. Have I ever interfered?"

"Some might call this little tete-a-tete interference," Charlie shot back.

Brennan's secretary rapped again, but Brennan ignored her. "The

point is that we ran a story on the swim club and we covered the
protégé's death in the Metro section, as news—"

"Columns are for comment and opinion," Charlie said. He
folded his arms. "That's what Duke hired me for."

Brennan quieted at the invocation of the publisher's name.
Charlie knew Duke prized him above others at the *Sun* and Charlie
could threaten to move to another paper if Brennan persisted.

The phone buzzed on Brennan's desk. "I told you I didn't want
to be interrupted," he yelled at his secretary through the glass.
She motioned for him to pick up the phone. "What? What is it?"
Brennan's face contorted. "Richter who?" Charlie felt a heat rise in
his chest. Gallagher's paranoia about the county attorney's private
investigator had seemed unfounded until Brennan spoke his name
out loud. "Ok, yeah, whatever," Brennan said. He cupped the phone.
"I have to take this. Promise me you're not going after McCloud."

"I promise," Charlie answered. He stood as Brennan swiveled
away, the phone cord falling into the groove in the back of his
leather chair. Charlie tried to eavesdrop but Brennan's voice lowered
as Richter came on the line. He heard the county attorney's name
mentioned and gently closed the door behind him, the air thinning
as he negotiated the newsroom, desperate for enclosure. He guessed
what Richter was after, idly wondering if the county attorney was
friends with the farmer Charlie had so resolutely forsaken for his
own career. Over the years, Charlie braced for retaliation from the
farmer, whose business had collapsed under the weight of the Heather
Lambert case, and the quiet that followed such a public dust-up
was chilling. Charlie had reasoned away the farmer's objections to
his assertions that the illegal immigrant had without a doubt been
employed by the farmer at the time he plowed into Heather Lambert,
who was the perfect victim to tap into the malcontent Phoenicians
held for illegal aliens. But Charlie hadn't been able to erase from his
mind the interview he'd held with one of the employees of the farm
who confided in him that the illegal alien had been a friend of his
from Mexico and didn't work for the farmer—the employee had spat

the word *friend* in his broken English and Charlie surmised that the illegal alien was a source of turmoil in the employee's life, maybe even a relative—and that he'd conned the employee into lifting the keys to the farmer's truck under the guise of needing to run a quick errand. That this quick errand was to procure a quarter pound of marijuana could've been verified by even a cub reporter.

Charlie half-expected the farmer to produce the employee as a witness in his defense against the maelstrom of bad publicity and innuendo. He had promised not to use the employee's name and the employee must've been baffled by Charlie's silence, another fountain of anxiety in those heady days at the *Phoenix Tab*. Charlie imagined the employee's indignation at the concealment of the truth or, at the very least, at the threat to his employment, an indignation that was left to simmer as the days and weeks rolled on, the papers and airwaves filled with vitriol. Charlie's recklessness grew in the shade of the employee's revelation, Charlie's denunciation of the farmer's practices bordering on libel, but he was driven by self-righteousness, a force not easily overcome by reason.

Charlie had indulged in a bit of self-righteousness at the *Tab* a month or two prior to the Heather Lambert story, too. One of the senior reporters was caught falsifying a source for a puff piece spotlighting the struggles of the local chapter of Mother's Against Drunk Drivers to heighten awareness leading into the Fourth of July holiday. The reporter had credited a compliment about the chapter to a Man on the Street who existed only in the reporter's mind. Charlie had suffered innumerable afternoons subjected to the reporter's unregulated rants about this and that. The managing editor was said to be the reporter's best friend in the world and, worse, the two were neighbors so Charlie's complaints about the workplace went unheard. Not even the reporter's politically incorrect language—ranging from calling one of the interns "doll" to referring to Mexicans as "spics"—warranted as much as a reprimand from the managing editor so when Charlie learned of the journalistic shortcut by chance, when the reporter accidentally attributed the fabricated quote to someone who shared the same name as the bartender at a popular watering hole—who refuted the words were his—Charlie seized the chance to ride the reporter in front of the *Tab* staff, including the managing editor. "Just make it up," became a catchphrase he bandied around the office. The reporter began avoiding him, but Charlie's thirst wasn't quenched and he began taunting both the managing and reporter. He'd tell an outlandish tale and finish with "I don't know why I said that, it's not true" before turning to the reporter and saying, "Maybe you can use that in your next piece." The managing editor pleaded with him to tamp down the sarcasm, but to no avail—the office had been infected and soon everyone was taunting the reporter.

When the fevered pitch of his offensive against the reporter dissipated, Charlie's frustrations emboldened him. What began as a casual lunch with the intern the reporter had flirted with turned dark when Charlie filled the intern's ears with the stories of private lust he claimed the reporter admitted in the intern's absence. He surprised himself with soundbites about deviant sexual behavior he'd only seen in movies, or on the Internet. The intern's giggles transformed into rage toward the reporter between their ordering lunch and Charlie's paying the check.

"You can't say I told you, though," Charlie had said.

"I'm going to say something right when we get back," the intern said, seething.

"They're not going to take your word for it," Charlie said. He coached her on what to say, convincing her that she'd have claim that the reporter had touched her in an inappropriate way that made her uncomfortable. The intern questioned the need to lie, but Charlie pointed out how close the managing editor and the reporter were— they were neighbors for chrissakes—and she reluctantly agreed. "I'll back you up and say I saw him touch you, too," Charlie said. "If it comes to that."

But it didn't. The reporter was fired, and the intern quit shortly after that, maybe buckling under the embarrassment of being the subject of office gossip but probably because she found a better way to spend her free time. That's what Charlie told himself in the quietest moments of the now still afternoons of the *Tab* offices.

And so the cover-up involving the employee that could've absolved the farmer in the Heather Lambert matter was an easy elision. Charlie assumed the employee found work on another farm, maybe in another state, or in another industry. If he were being honest, he worried that the employee was lying, or mistaken. But in Charlie's mind the employee was so far into the distant past he'd become fictive, though he couldn't shake the sickening feeling that Richter had dredged him up for a purpose Charlie's nervous and guilt-ridden conscience was all too ready to supply.

Sprocket proved adept in his position as supply manager. With Warren's help, he re-organized the tool shed by construction phase: hanging tools on one wall, taping tools on another, sanding tools on yet another, and on and on. The tool shed had an open front like the illegal fireworks stands on the Indian reservations, providing Sprocket with enough cover to preserve his albino skin, though he slathered himself in suntan lotion as a precaution, the front and back of his job journal decorated with his oily fingerprints.

Sweating under the tin roof of the supply shed during construction, Sprocket had occasion to do plenty of reading. Over the years, a library had collected on a low bookshelf in the classroom and Sprocket would fill the Randolph book bag he'd affixed to the side of his wheelchair with titles like *The Encyclopedia of Ancient and Forbidden Knowledge*, *The Astrologer's Handbook*, and *A Treasury of Supernatural Phenomena*. The bag also contained a few volumes of *Super Seek-and-Find* from a subscription his parents renewed yearly for his birthday. The puzzles were a throwback to his pre-accident days, before he crashed his BMX on a homemade ramp in the backyard of the twin brothers who ultimately joined the military, and his parents had kept paying the renewal notices as just another household bill, even though the brightly hued covers grew into a skyscraper in the corner of Sprocket's room after he'd returned from his stay in the hospital, the puzzles unworked. Sprocket spent many an afternoon resenting the puzzle books, refusing to even flip through their pages; to do so would be to admit defeat about how his free time could be spent. But then one day he reached for the issue balanced atop the pile and once he started circling words, he couldn't stop.

The rest of us went about the duties of a Garden Lakes Fellow with zeal. A heap of drywall blossomed into a garden of scraps, board cut too small or broken solidly in two by the freight of miscalculation; or by pressure applied in the wrong place; or from navigating a corner too sharply. Regardless, under Mr. Malagon's watchful (but as it turned out, unhelpful, as his math skills were suspect) supervision, 1959 Regis Street started to look habitable, the dust covering us so thoroughly we appeared ghostly to the sophomores at lunch.

Our sleep patterns adjusted; some of us anticipated the doorbell alarm, waking thirty to sixty seconds before the peal of chimes. A shower routine developed, Fellows showing for breakfast in the same order day after day. Mr. Malagon revealed himself not to be an early riser, his eyes still half-hooded as he ambled through the breakfast line, hardly distinguishable from the rest of us. Come class time, though, he was rejuvenated, slapping the back of one hand into another for effect. The unit on FDR and the New Deal transitioned into a unit on the Teapot Dome scandal. Mr. Malagon wasn't entirely successful in impressing upon us the enormity of the country's first political scandal as the news a couple of years earlier was devoted to AzScam, the undercover sting operation that caught Arizona legislators selling their votes for money. In order to shake up our jaded attitudes, Mr. Malagon composed an especially difficult exam for the conclusion of the Teapot Dome scandal, which all of us—including Sprocket—failed.

Assburn continued to ignore Smurf's inquiry about the mobile phone in his possession. Assburn, who would plunge through the ice somewhere between Canada and Detroit, sinking to his death along with a load of counterfeit game systems, led a troop of us to his room (after we pledged solemnly not to breathe a word to anyone) and showed us the phone, which was smaller than the brick-sized phones we'd seen. We passed the phone around as Assburn regaled us with the story of how he'd stolen it from his father's telecom business. "They're like four grand a piece," Assburn said proudly.

When the laws of relay brought news of our secret preview to Smurf, he was irate. He threatened Assburn with a shun and Assburn relented, allowing Smurf to use the phone to call his girlfriend. The shun against Reedy had escalated with the pouring of honey in Adam Kerr's hair while he slept, the penalty for his standing up for Reedy in the dining hall. Kerr was absent during breakfast the next morning, but appeared for chapel with a shaved head. Roger snickered at Kerr and Kerr avoided Roger's glare. Kerr had told Mr. Hancock and Mr. Malagon that he'd shaved his head because of the heat, but by lunchtime we'd all heard the story and knew that Reedy had lost his only ally. By dinner, Reedy's nerves were so fragile every sound brought a momentary state of paralysis, as if his next breath, or any movement at all, would bring swift punishment of a kind Reedy could only guess.

Some of us talked about bailing Reedy out, but no one wanted to approach Roger about the reprieve. We'd never observed a shun in a closed environment (at Randolph the shunee got to go home at the end of the day, and only had to withstand being ignored between bells), and some were fascinated with the experiment, knowing the shun would ultimately be rescinded. Which is exactly what happened.

Roger cornered Reedy after tutoring one night, waiting for him at his residence. Reedy had been walking in a group that included Adam Kerr and some others, but they shot through the front door when Roger materialized from the side of their house. Reedy thought about screaming, but knew even if Mr. Hancock answered his cry for help, Roger would retaliate the following morning (or in the dead of the night, as he had Kerr).

Roger, who would in the future go AWOL in Iraq with a platoon of his men and be court martialed for shooting one of them, laid out the conditions of Reedy's release: Reedy was to secret a predetermined quantity of silverware from the kitchen, in increments proscribed by Roger. (Reedy had been the first to happen upon the silverware strewn outside the kitchen door and had hurried to wash it and replace the spoons, forks, and knives in their proper place for fear of being blamed by Mr. Hancock.) Roger told Reedy to store the pilfered silverware until he called for it. Reedy was also made to understand that if he were caught, he was to take the heat himself, that Roger would deny knowing about it.

"Imagine how stupid you'll sound," Roger said. Reedy got the picture.

The next morning, Reedy moved around the dining hall with his old jauntiness, and we knew the shun had been called off. Hands ceremoniously called out to Reedy at lunch for another soda and Reedy smiled, buzzing for our table, bringing us all more soda, whether we asked for it or not.

Reedy brought his energy to the soccer field, too, though no matter which team he played for—or the make-up of the two squads, for that matter—the score of the soccer matches was inevitably a tie. For the first few days, we thought nothing of the deadlock. Mr. Hancock and Mr. Malagon drew up new rosters daily, no two teams consisting of the same teammates on successive days. If we thought about it—and we didn't—this could've accounted for the scoring anomaly. Closer monitoring would've detected the silent communication between Mr. Hancock and Mr. Malagon before a foul was called, or before Sprocket's goal line calls were overturned, but we were still of the mind to accept things as they appeared.

It was Hands who ferreted out the conspiracy, alerting the rest of us to it during free time as Lindy whirled his telescope around the night sky, hunting for a constellation he was keen to show us.

"Guys need to keep a watch," Hands said. "If you're on the bench, or if you've got a clean view from the field, check for Hancock and Malagon to line up across from each other. They do this right before they call a foul. And they only do it if one team is ahead by two."

We'd never known Hands to exhibit signs of paranoia, but the next day didn't bear out his misgivings. Neither Mr. Hancock nor

Mr. Malagon seemed to be looking to the other for calls. Nor did they appear to be acting in concert. Some wondered if Hands's ultra competitiveness had driven him to delusion, though the even scores piled up. Hands continued to cry conspiracy but the rest of us lost interest in Hands's theory until that Friday's match. A ball that sailed wide of the palm tree—and correctly called out by Sprocket— was ruled a score by Mr. Malagon, bringing Figs's team within one score of Hands's squad. Hands conferred with Figs—who had been standing on the sidelines—at dinner that night.

"Who cares?" Figs said. "It's meant to be exercise. Like in a prison yard, you know?" This brought laughs from the table.

Hands snorted. "Let's run laps around the Parkway if we want exercise. A match is meant to have a winner and a loser. What's the point of keeping it even?"

"Maybe it's some new teaching method," Warren said. "So no one feels badly about losing."

"Don't be dumb," Hands said, eliciting a couple of laughs before we realized he wasn't trying to be funny. "What would you guys say to a competition for Open House? A match in front of our parents. They couldn't fix that." Hands searched the table for the same fervor he felt for the idea, but met only disaffected stares.

"Yeah, sure," we shrugged.

"Good idea," someone threw in.

We watched Hands work the other tables, his idea getting the same reception; but Hands was undeterred. He knew he was popular enough that no one would protest his idea—he didn't need outright frenzy, just compliance.

"Mr. Handley, what's with all of the table jumping?" Mr. Malagon called out.

Hands gave a short oration on "the Fellows' desire for a soccer match at Open House." Mr. Malagon appeared immediately sorry he'd asked. "We'll take your suggestion under advisement," Mr. Hancock said without looking up from his asparagus soup, the day's special. Disenchantment shaded Hands's face; he knew the phrase "we'll take your suggestion under advisement" meant something all together different had it been spoken by Mr. Malagon. Thoughts about the Open House soccer match would dominate Hands's thinking over the next week, but his primary attention was focused on an idea hatched that first Friday: a stilt race through the Grove after curfew.

The race was Figs's idea. Hands had inadvertently provided the inspiration, though, as we finished off a ceiling during construction. Figs and Hands each strapped on a pair of stilts that lifted them about three feet off the ground. The rest of us hung the ceiling by standing on drywall benches, adjustable metal saw horse-like platforms that could hold two drywallers at a time. Sprocket's cataloguing and organizing of the tool shed had unearthed two pairs of stilts and Figs and Hands volunteered to lace them on. The stilts had joints that flexed. "It's like standing on a spring," Figs said, traipsing around the dirt front yard of 1959 Regis Street like a circus performer.

Hands's learning curve was more concave. He took off after Figs, but fell in front of Sprocket, who reached out to help him up. Smurf had witnessed this ignominy and cackled from an upstairs window. Figs waltzed through the house, bounding into rooms, yelling "Just passing through!" as he swept in and out.

Mr. Malagon reined Figs in, though he was enjoying the hijinks. Hands stumbled through the open front door, tripping over a cut two-by-four someone had lain carelessly in the hallway after using it to cinch up a piece of drywall.

"You okay there?" Figs asked.

"I'll race you any time in this get-up," Hands countered.

And then it was forgotten. Hands acclimated to the extensions and strode confidently through the house by the end of the working day, looking away when Figs stepped into a hole punched into the earth by a rock that had taken up residence elsewhere. Our enthusiasm for Figs and Hands's stunt waned as the day progressed;

we'd practically forgotten that it had happened as we congregated for free time, which Figs and Hands had ritualized by inviting the other Fellows to drop in without knocking.

"C'mon, it's Friday night," Smurf begged Assburn. "Let me at least call her and see what she's doing. Hey!"—his eyes widened— "Should I tell her to come out, and bring some friends?"

Those playing stud poker at the kitchen table looked up from their cards.

"Are you nuts?" Hands asked. You could never tell when Smurf was joking and when he wasn't. Hands shook his head no to settle the question, excusing the rest of us from having to weigh in on what we knew was a terrible idea, but an idea that tantalized us nonetheless.

"What then?" Smurf asked. "It's goddam Friday night."

"So?" someone said.

"So?" Smurf echoed. "So we should do something fun. We can't just work, work, work. *Christ.*" Smurf, who would one day successfully slander a female colleague with whom he'd cheated on his wife, spit the curse out in disgust, realizing what he'd said wasn't true: we would in fact work, work, work, and that would be all.

"What about that stilt race?" Figs asked slyly.

Hands glanced over Sprocket's head as Sprocket dealt. "Anytime, tough guy," he said.

Figs stood. "Why not? If we were quiet about it, we could do it away from the houses," he said. "Maybe down at the entrance. The pavement's better there anyway."

"Why not back in The Grove?" Hands asked, anteing up. "A little obstacle course action."

"No way I can give you the keys to the supply shed," Sprocket said without stopping the fourth round of cards. "No way."

"That's true," Hands said. "There really is no way you can give us those keys." He paused. "We could take them," he smiled, "but there's no way you could give them to us."

"You want to get me kicked out?" Sprocket asked.

"No one's going to get kicked out," Figs said. "Has anyone ever gotten kicked out? I don't think so. And with Quinn taking off, and the others not showing, they can't afford to kick anyone out."

Some of us nodded in agreement.

"Sorry," Sprocket said.

"Yes!" Warren said, scooping up the pot of plastic poker chips.

Sprocket passed the deck of cards to his left. Warren picked up the cards and shuffled them liberally. "Who's in?"

"This one is just me and Sprocket," Hands said gamely. "For the keys."

Sprocket eyed Hands. "What?"

"If I win, you set the keys on the table and I take them from you. If we're busted, I tell Hancock and Malagon I stole the keys from your room. Everyone in this room will stick to the same story."

"I'll get in trouble for not keeping the keys safe," Sprocket said.

Hands turned to Warren: "Deal."

Luck seemed not to be on the side of the scheme. Sprocket landed all four aces and quickly won the first hand—prompting a call to reshuffle the deck, which Warren did with exaggerated effect. Skill worked against the endeavor as well. Hands's lack of skill as a poker player, that is. Some of us were taken aback by his poor play— we'd all assumed his talent for winning was inherent; him losing at anything was inconceivable—and felt more than not that his being in on a big pot was mostly bluff, a suspicion borne out by Hands's asking for four new cards before said pot was acquired by the winner (never Hands). Consequently, Sprocket beat Hands two games out of three. Hands lobbied for best of five. Sprocket acquiesced under protest, spurred to accept the challenge by the jeers masquerading around the room as encouragement. Hands evened the game at two apiece, but a pair of jacks delivered Sprocket the fifth and decisive game. Hands looked like he was going to propose a best of ten, but instead said, "Well, you're a mighty fine poker player, Sprocket. But we need those keys."

Sprocket glanced up from his cards, puzzled.

"Same deal," Hands said. "We get caught, we say we stole the keys from you."

"The deal was *if you beat me*, you could have the keys," Sprocket said, waiting for confirmation from the rest of us, glancing around the room when it failed to surface.

"Aw, c'mon, Sprocket," Figs said. "We're not going to get caught. And if we do, you're not going to be in trouble."

Hands saw that Sprocket was unmoved by Figs's appeal. "No one will care about a stupid little race," he added. "We should just ask Hancock and Malagon and they'd let us. Maybe I should run over and ask Mr. Malagon," Hands said, standing. "He'll probably want to take on the winner."

Sprocket knew the social consequences if Mr. Malagon assented to the race—and he believed Hands *would* ask, even at the risk of being told no—and surrendered the keys from a hidden Velcro pocket on the inside of the right armrest of his wheelchair, dropping them with a contemptuous jangle on the Formica kitchen table.

There were those who remained behind with Sprocket, either out of sympathy or out of cowardice; the rest of us walked on the toes and heels of our rubber-soled tennis shoes toward the supply shed, which shone under the phosphorescent moon. The Grove was similarly lit, the symmetric grid of gravel knolls beckoning all comers to test their navigational skills. Figs and Hands suited up first, the vaunted match-up producing cries of "I got next!" from the gallery of faces washed gray by the moonlight.

The ground rules were laid: contestants were to weave through a specified row of rock. Points would be assessed: one if the contestant grazed any rock pile, two for each fall taken by a contestant. The winner was indicated by the contestant with the fewest number of points against him.

"Ready...set...go!" Hands signaled the start of the race with a wave. Figs and Hands darted through the maze, in and out of the shifting piles of limestone and slate and shale, some worn into cones by wind, others leveled off by unknown tracks, some human, most animal. None of us acknowledged the orbital train of paw prints that could only have been made by coyote. The absence of yipping told us coyote were unseen spectators watching from a distance.

Hands vanished momentarily behind the second rock pile from the finish line and Figs called out "Point!" in a voice loud enough to be heard, but quiet enough not to perk the ears of Mr. Malagon or Mr. Hancock. Hands swore through his teeth, knowing he was beat. Figs galloped to the finish line, a full rock pile in front of Hands, and circled back, weaving toward us so as to avoid Hands's bitter disappointment.

"Two out of three," Hands said, his hands on his knees. He rubbed at the smear of dirt on his khakis incurred from his fall.

"No way," Roger said. "It's my shot at the champ."

We each raced once, though there was no clear champion—Figs beat Hands but then Roger beat Figs; Assburn beat Roger, and then beat me, finally falling to Warren, who was promptly beaten by Roger. Hands was still talking about a rematch with Figs when Warren remarked how late it was. We sneaked back onto Garden Lakes Parkway. The still houses along Regis Street seemed to foretell our doom.

Our alarm clocks read nine-thirty, a half an hour beyond curfew, and we each feared being the one to be called on to explain the night's activities. Fantastic improbabilities floated through our minds: *Maybe Hancock and Malagon didn't make a bed check. Maybe they poked their heads inside the door and assumed we were in our beds, exhausted. Maybe we could say we were out stargazing with Lindy.* Some of us set our clocks back a half an hour, creating a digital alibi. We lay awake, though, until we put back those thirty minutes, knowing it wouldn't work.

It was no surprise, then, when Mr. Hancock rang our doorbells angrily, calling out "No showers!" Our blood pumped in our ears, our eyes dry and tired, but we double-timed it to the dining hall, averting our eyes as we entered and took our seats. The kitchen was busy, but no food had been laid out for breakfast.

Mr. Hancock stormed into the room, Mr. Malagon in tow, a sour look on his face, a jury of two called back from deliberations to render their verdict.

Mr. Hancock, on the verge of leaving Garden Lakes with the school's permission, shot Figs a look that stole all of our breaths. He knew. Someone had ratted us out—Figs in particular—and the pool of suspects began and ended with Sprocket. Possibly Lindy, though Lindy had been leading a pod of sophomores on a celestial exploration through his telescope.

Realizing he had been caught, Figs internally ran through the arguments. He could deny it, though he usually eschewed denial because of its stringency: once you started denying, you had to keep on denying, regardless of the evidence brought against you. Figs knew unilateral denials were trouble; he preferred the maneuverability of vagueness. He would calmly wait for the case to be presented against him.

Mr. Hancock's glowering unnerved Figs, though. Another thought, one that visited Figs now and again was that someone—somehow—was on to him about what happened in Mazatlan, that he'd invented the Federale raid to make himself out as a hero. The next day and every day since, Figs knew he'd made a mistake. He'd come close to divulging it to Hands, but he knew the information would make Hands co-guardian of the secret and realized his desire to let Hands in on it was a selfish move to lessen the stressful burden. Each time Rosa's or Mazatlan was mentioned, Figs had to call up the mental note cards etched with the details of that night. He had to remember what he'd said about how he'd heard a car pull up; about the quick footsteps on the dirt driveway; about the excited voices speaking Spanish. He'd memorized the details with the same concentration as he had his social security number and date of birth, and guarded the information with the same care.

As lucid as the manufactured minutiae was the very real cause of said manufacture. Pacing the backyard that night, the ramifications of not going inside to meet one of Rosa's girls weighed on him.

He knew he couldn't let Hands and the others walk out with the distinction of having visited Rosa's between them. The playful taunts weren't what worried Figs. The idea of *not* wanting to visit a prostitute required some sophistication on the part of the mind trying to understand it and, as Figs knew, it was easier to substitute slander and innuendo in the place of understanding.

Panic morphed into desperation. A carload of teenagers arriving at Rosa's prompted the idea of the raid. The sudden absence of the bouncer at the door was the impetus. Figs made up his mind, the strangers in the backyard glancing casually as he charged the door, hollering.

The memory turned Figs's stomach.

But while the occasion of the showerless, foodless breakfast *was* a curfew violation (and it was clear to all of us that Mr. Hancock had been hipped to our derby in The Grove), we wouldn't have guessed in a million years if we were given a million guesses what had steamed Mr. Hancock and chagrined Mr. Malagon so.

"You boys will notice that Mr. Murfin is no longer with us," Mr. Hancock said.

We scanned the tables, acknowledging each other for the first time that morning, and confirmed what Mr. Hancock had said: Smurf was not in attendance.

"Mr. Murfin has been sent home," Mr. Hancock continued, "for violating curfew."

A silence fell across the room. Our empty stomachs rumbled, our hunger muzzled by our rattled nerves. "Boys, Smurf was kicked out for smuggling in his girlfriend," Mr. Malagon said with dispiriting frankness. Clearly he'd fought for Smurf and lost. Mr. Malagon wouldn't have considered the offense expellable; Mr. Hancock, on the other hand, would have argued for capital punishment (in which case Smurf got off easy). "There are some questions about how exactly Mr. Murfin was able to summon his girlfriend to meet him," he said. "So if any of you boys have anything to add, please feel free to speak up."

Assburn's face glowed with sweat, though he refrained from wiping it for fear of drawing attention. But Mr. Hancock appeared oblivious about Assburn's mobile phone. Warren and a few others glanced at Assburn, but Assburn trained his eyes on the clock on the wall behind Mr. Hancock.

The particulars of Smurf's rendezvousing became known over the course of the next two days: Smurf instructed his girlfriend to wait with her car hood up outside the gates of Garden Lakes (this detail was particularly hilarious; Smurf was often the victim of his own imagination: once while his parents were on vacation, he fired his father's .357 through his bedroom door, thinking someone was trying to break in in the dead of night. His parents never fixed the spider webbing on Smurf's door where the bullet exited, lodging in the hallway between portraits of Smurf and of Smurf's grandparents). Smurf waited until ten o'clock and then tiptoed out of his residence on Regis Street, careful not to wake his housemates, padding along Garden Lakes Parkway to the entrance, where his girlfriend was waiting. A perfect plan. Perfect except for Mr. Malagon who, unable to sleep, was out for a walk. He spotted Smurf and, thinking that Smurf had followed Q's lead and deserted, he reported the departure to Mr. Hancock early the next morning. But Mr. Hancock's search turned Smurf up, asleep in his bed. Mr. Hancock questioned Assburn and Roger, who knew nothing about Smurf's nocturnal voyage. Once satisfied in this, Mr. Hancock hauled Smurf to his residence on Loyola, where he made Smurf phone his parents to come pick him up, which they did before Mr. Hancock woke the rest of us.

We feared Mr. Hancock knew about the stilt race, too, but was prevented from prosecuting by Reedy, who rushed into the dining hall, his bloodless face shaped by terror.

"What is it?" Mr. Hancock growled.

"Laird got bit," was all Reedy said.

"Scorpion?" Mr. Malagon asked, but Reedy's pale look told us it was not a scorpion but a rattlesnake.

The dining hall emptied and we crowded around Laird, a sophomore whose first name some of us didn't even know, who was curled up on the smooth kitchen floor, grabbing his right ankle in anguish. The kitchen smelled of pureed tomatoes.

"You boys stand back," Mr. Hancock said. He and Mr. Malagon kneeled around Laird. Mr. Malagon ripped Laird's pant leg and we saw spots of blood coagulated around the puncture marks.

"How did it happen?" Mr. Malagon asked.

"I was taking the garbage out," Laird explained, "and it was outside the back door." Laird twitched. "God, it stings."

Mr. Malagon, who would break all of our hearts, cautiously opened the back door. "It's gone," he said. "I'll take Laird to the emergency room. Maybe I can talk them into a good rate on visits."

Mr. Malagon's attempt at humor brought a titter from the crowd. "I'll take him," Mr. Hancock said automatically. Mr. Malagon appeared as if he might protest, but didn't. Instead, he rounded us all back into the dining hall, calling on the sophomores to serve breakfast. Mr. Hancock and Laird rolled past the windows while we devoured cereal and fruit as if we hadn't eaten in days. Mr. Malagon disappeared into the hall, reappearing a moment later after having cleared the community center of any sign of the snake.

"I'm going to need some volunteers," Mr. Malagon said. "Fellows and sophomores, both. Need teams of three to search the houses and scour the area, beating the brush for this thing. We don't want it sunning on a rock in our vicinity." We looked at each other fearfully. "To be clear," he continued, "I'm not asking you to corner it, trap it, or kill it."

"I'll go," Roger said, hailing Mr. Malagon from a back table. "Count me in."

"Good shoe, Roger," Mr. Malagon said. "Who else? Hands?"

Hands brought his face out of his cereal bowl. "Yeah," he said, reluctantly. "Sure."

"Attaboy."

One by one, we volunteered. Not because we wanted to be snake hunters, but because with each raised hand the moment changed from an opportunity to volunteer into an event that would forever divide us into two camps: Those Who Did and Those Who Didn't.

A few of the sophomores, not yet schooled in the ways of coerced volunteerism, elected to stay behind in the kitchen to decipher Mr. Hancock's instructions for Caldo Verde, a difficult Portuguese green soup whose ingredients included Portuguese sausage and kale. Conscription not being in Mr. Malagon's nature, he did not press the sophomores.

We spread out across Garden Lakes, angst about the day's schedule abetting our search, which we undertook with caution. Under Mr. Malagon's directive, we were to throw open the front door and yell, listening for the clack of the snake's rattle. Cupboards were not to be opened, but were to be banged on; toilets flushed before lifting the lid; each bedroom receiving the door-flown-open treatment, accompanied with yelling. Beds were to be bounced on before anyone scouted beneath with the sawed off ends of two by fours scavenged from the construction site. "Don't stick your kisser under the bed," Mr. Malagon said.

Sophomores trailed Fellows through the front doors of their own houses. The snake hunt momentarily suspended our disbelief that Smurf had been kicked out. His bellowing was plainly absent our screams and yelling as we tried to flush out the rattlesnake, half hoping for a chance at it, half hoping that it was on its way to Mexico.

The houses on Loyola Street seemed unlived in. The pristine kitchens and unused couches in the front room gave the feeling of a model home. A veneer of dust blown in from open windows and open doors had accumulated on the kitchen countertops. Those who had been sophomores at Garden Lakes knew that the downstairs was just a hallway linking the private life spent in the sanctuary of the bedroom to the life of servitude all sophs lived for five of the hottest weeks of the year.

Roger led Reedy (who had become his new best friend, apparently) and Adam Kerr through their residence, violating Mr. Malagon's instructions by boldly opening the kitchen and bathroom cabinets without knocking. Reedy and Kerr stayed back as Roger opened door after door. Being bitten was better than being afraid, he reasoned.

A sweep of Loyola Street turned up nothing. We marched down Regis like a street gang looking for a fight, the air interspersed with tough talk about what would be done if the predator was found. Hands recommended the sophomores be permitted to return to the kitchen and Mr. Malagon agreed. The relieved sophs hastened inside the community center, leaving us to continue the hunt.

We split up into teams, each inspecting their own house. Mr. Malagon tapped Figs and Warren, who were standing nearest him, to help check his residence. "We'll meet at 1959 to check the job site," he said. "But wait for me in the street. No one goes in until I say so." Mr. Malagon's commands fired us up, as if we were war heroes taking back a beachhead, or liberating a village overrun by tyrants.

Our labors to turn up the snake in any of our houses were unsuccessful. Assburn charged ahead to his room, yelling as he pushed open the door, listening nervously for any rattling. He wasn't concerned about the mobile phone—though he still wanted to control the number of people who knew about it (we all knew, at this point)—but worried the package with Q's father's pen would be discovered. He leapt from the doorway to his bed, his head coming within inches of the acoustical ceiling finish. Hopping off the bed, he swabbed underneath with the board he'd snagged from the pile out front of 1959. Nothing. "All clear!" he yelled, double-checking that the bulge between the mattresses could not be seen or felt.

Mr. Malagon called us all out of our houses for a report.

"Negative," Figs said.

"All clear," Warren said.

"Nada," Assburn said.

"What about Smurf's room?" Mr. Malagon asked.

Assburn and Roger exchanged glances. The door to Smurf's room had been closed, slammed by Smurf in protest as Mr. Hancock and Mr. Malagon stood watch earlier that morning. Assburn had opened his door to investigate the commotion, but had been shooed back inside by Mr. Hancock. They'd regarded Smurf's room as quarantined as they swept the house for the snake.

Roger spoke up. "We didn't check."

The sun blasted the rooftops and street with heat. Since none of us wore watches—the schedule our only guide—we would've sworn it was after noon. In reality, it was little past six a.m. We followed Mr. Malagon, who took the steps two at a time, the way men in their thirties do to test their fading athleticism. Hands and Figs and Roger followed through the house and up the stairs, too, others jogging behind.

Mr. Malagon battered the door as he turned the knob. Hands began yodeling until Mr. Malagon told him to shut up. The snake was not in Smurf's room, the sheets still mussed from what little sleep Smurf must've gotten the night before. An empty pack of Camel Lights lay crumpled defiantly on the dresser, but Mr. Malagon made no effort to throw the pack away, his eyes roving the room. "Okay, boys," he said. "There's nothing here."

A deferential silence fell among us. Smurf was a general pain in the ass, but he could cut the tension in any room. He would've goofed on us for thinking a lowly snake was interested in menacing us, we knew, and this much-needed solace made Smurf's expulsion reverberate. Mr. Malagon lingered, opening Smurf's top dresser drawer as he put one hand on the bedroom door. Figs turned in time to notice Mr. Malagon retrieve Smurf's job journal and fold it into his back pocket. "Let's go," he said to Figs, clapping him on the back.

"We're going to get back on schedule," Mr. Malagon said after we'd all reunited in Hands and Figs and Lindy's living room. "We'll make a search of the jobsite and then we'll work until the morning break. Any questions?" There were none. As we let ourselves out, Mr. Malagon pulled Figs aside.

"That was a stupid stunt last night," Mr. Malagon told him. "It would've been you who was thrown out and not Smurf if Smurf hadn't have done you one better. Is that what you want?"

"No, sir," Figs said, eyes downcast. He'd assumed this pose before, but this time felt grateful that he hadn't been tossed out of Garden Lakes.

"Mr. Hancock is going to be keeping an eye on you from now on," Mr. Malagon said. "I can't do on that score other than to alert you to the fact. So watch yourself, okay?"

"Yes, sir."

Mr. Malagon appraised Figs's face and smiled. "Knock that sir shit off," he said. "Everyone else might buy it, but I don't."

Figs smiled back. "Okay."

"Here's a piece of advice, for what it's worth: the only people who like a politician are those who are getting something from him; everyone else hates him. You'll learn that sooner or later, but thought I'd give you a head start on that bit of wisdom."

Figs didn't understand what Mr. Malagon meant, but nodded as if he did. He knew most adults were appeased by nodding in agreement.

. . . .

To alleviate our anxiety over the snake—Laird had been given an antidote and returned with nothing more than a sore ankle and a slight limp—Mr. Hancock announced the screening of a movie at 7PM in the dining hall—refreshments would be served—and so the reading hour and sophomore tutoring passed slowly, our excitement about the movie overmatching our concentration. We hadn't accounted for the truth that neither Mr. Hancock nor Mr. Malagon would have run to the closest video store and would instead be selecting one of the boxless videotapes stored in the locking compartment under the TV/VCR combo mounted on a cart used to show instructional videos at retreats. So we were dismayed when Mr. Hancock revealed the evening's fare: *The Lost Weekend*, a movie none of us had heard of, starring actors we didn't recognize. But none of us complained, glad to be out of our sweltering houses while the air conditioning worked to cool our rooms to temperatures that were livable. We were gladder still to be bunkered in the dining hall, forgetting for a couple of hours about the day's events.

Mr. Hancock watched the first half an hour of the movie with us then slipped out the door. Roger crept to the front door, waiting until Mr. Hancock was safely inside his house. He tapped Reedy on the shoulder, who rose like a soldier and followed Roger into the kitchen. Quickly, they filled a plastic five gallon bucket that had previously been filled with sliced dill pickles with all of the silverware from the silverware bins. Spoons, knives, forks—everything. Those who had seen Roger and Reedy duck into the kitchen pretended not to; the rest of us were too weary to take notice.

By the end of the film, Roger and Reedy had returned, brazenly walking through the front door of the community center. Mr. Hancock reappeared right as the credits rolled, none the wiser. "Half an hour to curfew, boys," he said in the business-like tone. Subconsciously we appreciated his tone as a constant from our life outside of Garden Lakes. Privately, we aped Mr. Hancock, whose nickname among the brave was Handjob, addressing each other in parody of his brusque speech, but we obeyed his every instruction. Not to would have reduced him and would've shattered any semblance of what we'd come to regard as our life together, a life forged from the admonishment we'd collectively endured.

Lindy approached Mr. Hancock as the last of us filtered out of the dining hall. Lindy, whose tragic death in his thirties would traumatize his young family, would rather have asked Mr. Malagon's permission to climb up onto the roof with his telescope, but we hadn't seen Mr. Malagon since dinner and presumed he was busy grading our quizzes. "The lakebed is unsafe," Lindy explained to Mr. Hancock, "what with the snake and all."

"The roof isn't much safer," Mr. Hancock said, spying a glass half-filled with ice and soda that someone had abandoned under the

Coke spigot of the soda machine. "Why not just point that thing out your window?"

"The window faces north," Lindy said, protesting mildly.

"No stars in the north?" Mr. Hancock looked at Lindy dubiously. He sensed that a scheme was afoot, having been ambushed by Smurf's late night dalliance. Never in his tenure had Mr. Hancock experienced such a flaunting of the strictures of Garden Lakes. Outwardly he blamed modern youth; inwardly he worried his age made him vulnerable to the agitations of the young.

"I'm tracking the Hydra," Lindy said. "We've been plotting it on the back of our job journals and—"

"We?" Mr. Hancock asked, hoping to ascertain the conspirators in this unnamed conspiracy.

"Some of the sophomores are interested in astronomy, sir," Lindy said, adding the "sir" in a transparent bid for consent which, astonishingly, persuaded Mr. Hancock.

The rooftop view was spectacular as Lindy could lie on his back and probe the sky without worry that the telescope would slide from the tripod. He entertained himself watching the itinerant stars shoot against the black sky. Sensing it was near curfew, Lindy dusted himself off. For his amusement, he surveyed Garden Lakes from his new vantage point—the supply shed, the construction site, the empty playing field. A movement in the telescope caught his attention. He focused the lens, startled to see Smurf's face fill up the telescope. He followed Smurf as Smurf hunched behind creosote bushes on the eastern edge of the development, his eyes on the lights in the windows of the houses along Regis Street.

. . . .

Hands and Figs came upon Warren pacing in front of the locked dining hall door, a hastily markered sign bearing the announcement BREAKFAST CANCELLED DUE TO SILVERWARE THEFT taped crookedly above the square window in the door.

"In here," Mr. Hancock said, appearing at the end of the hall.

"Goddamn Roger," Hands murmured.

We were herded into the chapel and directed to sit in the pews. Mr. Hancock promised to send home the first person who spoke without permission. Mr. Malagon watched anxiously from his seat on a folding chair at the front of the room.

"You boys know why you're here," Mr. Hancock said. He was deceptively calm, but Mr. Malagon's countenance evinced the danger we faced. "And since asking which of you is responsible for the kitchen theft is surely a waste of your time and mine, Mr. Malagon is going to search each room in each house while you wait here with me. This will afford the guilty party or parties a few moments before they are exposed, oh"—Mr. Hancock looked at his watch—"about thirty minutes from now."

Mr. Malagon obviously did not approve of Mr. Hancock's theatrics, but restrained himself, instead leaning over and putting his chin in his hands.

"What do you think, Mr. Malagon?" Mr. Hancock said. "Should we give the guilty party a chance for confession?" A dull dread settled over the pews. Mr. Hancock continued without losing the thread of his performance. "I guess it wouldn't hurt to ask," he said.

No one flinched.

Mr. Hancock turned to Mr. Malagon, who stood awkwardly. "It might prove interesting to interview these boys separately," Mr. Hancock said, wrapping up the final act. "I'm certain we'd have the answer to our question, then." He turned back toward us. "But we haven't the time." He gave one last look through the pews.

Nothing.

Mr. Hancock nodded at Mr. Malagon, who didn't make eye contact as he passed on his way out.

We found Roger's poise remarkable. Miscellaneous theories ran through our minds. Maybe Roger dumped the silverware out in The Grove. Or behind the supply shed. Maybe he buried it in the sand. Each solution would be unsatisfying to Mr. Hancock, we knew, and we secretly hoped Roger had left the silverware under his bed where

Mr. Malagon could easily find it.

Which is what we thought had happened when Mr. Malagon returned with Roger's bag, the clank of silverware proceeded his entrance. Consternation replaced the bemused look with which Mr. Hancock had held us during Mr. Malagon's absence, as if he was disappointed that the silverware had been found, confirming its theft and thereby identifying a thief in our midst.

Mr. Hancock waited for Mr. Malagon to disclose the hiding place of the stolen utensils.

"Found it in Casey Murfin's closet," Mr. Malagon said.

The Smurf! A new respect flared up for Roger, who none of us had considered very clever. Roger's face betrayed little as Mr. Malagon handed the bag to Mr. Hancock, who squinted into the sack. His face clouded with anger. "Mr. Malagon will hold you here until the guilty party steps forward," he said. "You'll make the time up out of your meals." He summoned his kitchen staff and led the sophomores across the hall, discarding the silverware loudly into the stainless steel sink.

Mr. Malagon closed the chapel door. The first glimmer of dawn rose though the window as he spoke. "Let me tell you why this prank is not only unfunny," he said, "but also why it was incredibly stupid." He crossed his arms. "You may not know about the power of cohesion yet, but let me tell you that it is essential to a working environment like this. We enjoy cohesion on campus—we're not walking arm in arm and whistling zip-a-dee-do-dah, but I think you'll agree that Randolph Eagles are a tight unit. You may be surprised to know that this is not the norm. Life in public school is more scattershot. It's hard to know who to count on. Believe me, I've taught public high school and, for better or worse, there's a difference in the social fabric.

"And, as you can guess, cohesive communities experience a better quality of life. That would've been the case before today, but now Mr. Hancock is angry and an angry Mr. Hancock is anathema to cohesion. Why? Because the only thing more important than cohesion is discipline. And now Mr. Hancock must punish someone for this…this idiotic exhibition."

Mr. Malagon's face reddened at having to appear before us as a disciplinarian. Mr. Malagon had a perfect record for never sending anyone from his classroom down to Principal Breen's office, but this record was kept perfect only by the tacit understanding that while fear of punishment had been diminished (if not obliterated), this alleviation brought a measure of responsibility on our part: we had to know how far to take things.

Roger stood.

Mr. Malagon glanced at Roger. "Yes?"

"I know who is responsible," Roger said.

We couldn't guess what Roger was up to. That he would confess in open court was too incredulous even for Mr. Malagon, who looked skeptically at Roger.

Mr. Malagon waited patiently, a clamor from the kitchen piercing the air. "Well?"

"I'd rather tell you in private," Roger said.

Mr. Malagon narrowed his eyes. "Very well," he said. "Step out into the hall."

Roger stepped out of his row, pushing past Warren and Assburn, and fell in behind Mr. Malagon, both sidestepping Sprocket, who was dozing in his wheelchair.

None of us wanted to break the silence, afraid of what was going to happen next. We didn't care if Roger was kicked out of Garden Lakes. We would've gladly doubled up to cover his contribution if the labor would've guaranteed his removal, a plot that Figs said he would float in secret after we learned that Roger wasn't going to be censured after all. Roger hadn't even copped to the theft, instead ratting out Reedy, who willingly admitted that he'd taken the silverware as a joke.

The missing silverware was the penultimate crime, as Mr. Hancock and Mr. Malagon discovered when the sophomores were brought back in for chapel. (Breakfast had been cancelled as a penalty, but also because the sun was rising rapidly and we all knew we were about a day behind on the construction.) Mr. Hancock bade us to open our hymnals and the cacophonous sound of butter knives falling against the tile floor rang in our ears. Reedy appeared close to passing out as Mr. Hancock lunged for him amid a torrent of curses. Some of us noticed Roger's contentment and pleasure at seeing Mr. Hancock explode. And he chortled when later we learned of Reedy's fate: Mr. Hancock forced him to move into his house, doubling Reedy's reading assignments and conscripting him to be his manservant. The slump in Reedy's posture and the lag in his step affirmed the severity of this discipline.

Mr. Hancock did not return and chapel was abbreviated by the weekly grocery delivery. Mr. Malagon took command of the sophomores while they checked in the groceries, allowing the rest of us to pass through the kitchen, grabbing an orange or banana or a bagel of muffin on our way out to the construction site.

"I need four volunteers for garbage," Mr. Malagon called out. We weren't clear if he meant us or the sophomores—the garbage detail was normally handled by the sophs, who collected the refuge from the community center and from each residence, riding with Mr. Hancock to the front gates where the plastic bags were heaped like a black igloo along the side of the road for the early Monday pick-up. As could be expected, Figs and Hands volunteered directly, commandeering two sophomores as aide-de-camps. Their mission was interrupted by the exodus of the grocery truck, however. The truck revved and soldiered away from the loading dock, lightened of its load. As the truck gained its footing on the paved outer loop, we all saw it at once: the head of the rattlesnake crushed into one of the encrusted tracks, its tail and rattle swaying hypnotically in its final throes. We stood waiting for its scaly body to lunge, to make one last attack, sure that it was feigning weakness to draw us closer, wanting us to play a hand in our own misfortune.

. . . .

No one was happier than Reedy when Mr. Malagon announced Mr. Hancock's departure two days later. Rather than calling everyone together, which may have caused confusion and upset, Mr. Hancock excused himself to attend a family funeral after curfew. Some of us heard the Jeep's engine and parted the slats in our blinds on a pair of headlights, followed by a set of receding taillights. We had no way of knowing about the conversation preceding Mr. Hancock's exit— Mr. Hancock's proposal for bringing in a substitute; Mr. Malagon assuring Mr. Hancock that he could hold down the fort until Mr. Hancock's return the following Monday. We imagined Mr. Malagon relished the opportunity. He may have even had inklings of heroism, how he'd run Garden Lakes solo for four days.

"Mr. Hancock's leave of absence is not without precedent," Mr. Malagon explained to us at breakfast the next morning. Apparently Mr. Hancock had once been hospitalized with an allergic reaction to a bee sting sustained during Sports, though in that instance he'd only been gone overnight. To cope with Mr. Hancock's vacancy, revolving teams of Fellows would alternate between kitchen duty and construction. "I'll float between the groups," Mr. Malagon said. "We'll keep to the schedule the best we can, though the sophomores will have to join us for class." We groaned, not really caring. "Oh, and you may have to get accustomed to grilled cheese and tomato soup." Mr. Malagon clapped his hands together and grinned.

We welcomed the change in routine. While it had only been a week and a half since we'd left the civilized world, the monotony of the schedule had slowed time to an unbearable pace. A minute was an hour, just as it was when were in class, or serving Saturday detention. Not knowing which team we'd be working on each day added the necessary mystery to pry our eyes open, our alarms shrieking from our bedside. We were also eager for the chance to prove that our selection as Fellows wasn't a mistake, that we were worthy of the honor.

Splitting shifts in the kitchen wasn't the only emendation. To the delight of all, Mr. Malagon announced the lifting of curfew. "I'll trust you to know when you should call it a night," he said. "However, I retain the right to reverse this policy should it be abused." The sophomores enjoyed the changing of the guard, however ephemeral the new regime might be. Banter around the kitchen increased during meal prep, Fellows teasing sophomores and vice versa.

Mr. Malagon accepted the sophomores' offer to aid us in construction, too. We agreed to temporarily suspend the soup program (the soups to date were rotting in their containers in our refrigerators anyway) so the sophs would be free to lend a hand, mainly on clean-up but also to make uniform our various fastening techniques, some of us hammering a nail every foot or so, others spacing them even farther apart. And while the surplus workers underfoot created an element of bedlam, we were glad for the help.

Mr. Malagon rewarded our cooperation by sending out for pizzas that night, retrieving the mobile phone from Mr. Hancock's residence to place the order. The girl who delivered the pizzas was a blonde angel draped in red and blue, her baseball hat sporting the pizza company's log pulled down over her eyes. The dining hall fell silent as Mr. Malagon signed the credit card receipt. "I thought it was a prank," the delivery girl said, her voice transporting us back to the real world, reminding us of our mothers and sisters and girlfriends.

"Well?" Mr. Malagon said.

We'd forgotten about the pizza. Those of us closest to the door scrambled after the delivery girl to help with the boxes. We could still smell her perfume as she pulled away, leaving us in her fragrant wake. We munched, relaxing for the first time since we'd arrived. Mr. Malagon joined us in telling dirty jokes (though he drew the line at Roger's racist sprinkler joke), later excusing himself to work on the next day's lecture. He advised the sophomores to keep up with their reading, but without the threat of quizzes, tutoring turned into bull sessions about the Randolph faculty, or boasting about Xavierites we knew, most of which we knew was bullshit, though the sophomores ate it up.

The tutoring pods broke up early and Hands suggested a game of poker, but Figs quashed the suggestion as too boring. Warren, whose unwitting accomplice in an Internet scam would bilk millions from the elderly, volunteered to get the bean bags from Mr. Malagon, who had disappeared for the night, but Figs demurred. Roger challenged everyone to some Indian wrestling and we cleared the furniture out of the front room and played several matches, Roger's powerful thighs beating each of us handily. Warren gave Roger the most trouble, his long legs making it difficult for Roger to flip him over.

Sprocket watched from the sidelines, initially cheering on Roger's opponents, but ultimately bored by their predictable outcome. It was barely eight o'clock when we tired of wrestling.

"Let's drop in on Mr. Malagon," Hands said. "Maybe he has some booze." The idea of sharing a beer with Mr. Malagon didn't sound as far-fetched as it probably was, but we would never know since the idea never moved past debate.

It was well after one in the morning when we finally crawled into our beds. The four-thirty alarm hectored us from our nightstands. Assburn slept less than any of us, though. He fought the onslaught of sleep, making sure his residence was still before creeping out the front door, the package with Senator Quinn's pen tucked in his pocket. He hurried across the lakebed and through the heart of East Garden Lakes. Assburn located an outcrop of rock and dug with his hands until he'd hollowed out a space big enough to fit the package. Packing the dirt over the pen, he heard a shuffling noise in the darkness. He called out Roger's name instinctively, but no one answered. He listened for the sound again, but the quiet spooked him further and he ran back to his room, swallowing his heavy breathing as he neared Regis Street.

Smurf, that unparalleled future slanderer and adulterer, waited until Assburn had faded into the night and then pulled on the corner of the freshly buried package until the earth let go, sand and silt caving around the hollow as the package came free of its hiding place. He turned it over in his hands, wondering what it contained.

....

Assburn woke relieved. Even the realization that he'd missed breakfast and would have to rush to catch up with the rest of us in chapel did not ruin his exaltation. Burying the pen in the desert was like undergoing a successful operation to remove an invisible tumor, one Assburn saw every time he looked in the mirror.

Mr. Malagon acknowledged Assburn's tardiness with a nod but, under Mr. Malagon's reign of self-government, hunger would be Assburn's only punishment. The rest of us took note and wondered what would happened if, say, Assburn had missed chapel. Or class. We valued our newfound freedom too much to test Mr. Malagon, though. We'd be back on the old schedule soon enough, the days grinding away under the burden of Mr. Hancock's omnipresence.

We labored to stay awake during chapel. Mr. Malagon, whose betrayal we'd never forgive, refrained from asking us what had kept us up so late. His response to our tiredness was to sing louder, his surge of energy underscoring our lethargy.

The day wouldn't get any easier. Mr. Malagon reminded us that Mr. Baker, who would be our hostage before it was all over, was set to return that Sunday, to inspect the first phase of construction and give us guidance about the next phase. With the aid of the sophomores, we were able to bring ourselves back on schedule; but the walls of 1959 Regis Street, pocked as they were with openings needing drywall, lashed us to a day's work. We moved in a delirium, each minute warmer than the last as the sun rose.

Mr. Malagon was chastising Sprocket for napping in the supply shed when Roger's fist glanced off Warren's jaw in one of the upstairs bedrooms. As a testament to how exhausted Roger was, the blow hardly fazed Warren, who in turn collared Roger, dragging him to the ground. The wrestling match overturned a pair of drywall bench-es, a tape measure resting on one skittering into the corner. The combatants rolled into a drywall lift holding an unfastened panel against the ceiling and a few of us rushed over to steady the brace, which wobbled and then came to rest.

Mr. Malagon burst through the crowd as Roger had regained his composure, standing and delivering two successive punches to Warren's midsection. "Cool it, Roger," he yelled, but Roger was deaf to the instructions and continued to go after Warren, who was no less committed.

Mr. Malagon instructed Figs and Hands to remove Warren from the room. Without hesitation, they locked their arms around Warren and whisked him down the stairs as he screamed epithets at Roger. Roger headed for the stairs but Mr. Malagon detained him, pushing him into a corner. Some of us slunk away as Mr. Malagon shouted for Roger to calm down. The fight had stirred the dust and a gray haze floated through the room.

The subsequent minutes were spent interrogating both Roger and Warren, but Mr. Malagon learned only that the fight had started over Roger's co-opting Warren's tape measure. We found this explanation implausible (as did Mr. Malagon), though none of us knew of a beef that existed between Roger and Warren. The lameness of the fight's impetus infuriated Mr. Malagon. He strode through the house, knocking a cut piece of drywall to the ground, calling out "Any boy who is not inside his residence within five minutes will find their parents here to pick them up."

We milled around for a minute, bewildered. Was he serious? There was work to be done before Mr. Baker's arrival. Any deviation from the schedule jeopardized the Open House. We'd witnessed Mr. Malagon's ire only once before, the time Garth Atlon made bird calls from the back of the classroom every time Mr. Malagon mentioned Lady Bird Johnson during a lesson about LBJ and The Great Society. The first bird call soared under our laughter—Mr. Malagon's too—as did the second and third time Garth put his hands to his mouth; by the fourth time, we were completely distracted from the lesson. Mr. Malagon called for Garth to quit, giving Garth his famous stare that meant it was all right to goof off but now it was time to work. But Garth was dialed in, the bird calls tickling his fancy, and Mr. Malagon's stare couldn't reach him. Mr. Malagon beaned Garth with an eraser from the grease board, an impressive throw that silenced us all. Garth snapped to and the lesson continued, though Mr. Malagon was visibly shaken.

Sprocket was the first to accede. He wheeled up the ramp and inside his residence. The rest of us pretended to drift toward our houses, though we were mindful of Mr. Malagon's clock. Five minutes later, the streets were vacant, our tools scattered throughout the rooms of 1959, abandoned mid-use.

Our residences were flushed with a foreign light, everything bathed in a paleness we never had cause to witness. The way the light fell across the kitchen counters, against the backs of sofas and inched up the stairs lent the houses a new demeanor reminiscent of our own houses on a Sunday afternoon, thoughts of school on Monday held at bay for a few hours longer. Through the window we saw first Roger and then Warren released from custody, Roger breezing out of Mr. Malagon's front door, stomping into his own house. Warren appeared with Mr. Malagon at his side. The two spoke calmly for a minute or two before Mr. Malagon slapped Warren on the back, sending him back to his residence. We watched Warren until he was inside, curious about what would happen next.

Mr. Malagon vanished inside his house for close to fifteen minutes. When he reappeared, he walked purposefully toward the house next door where Figs and Hands and Lindy were pretending to relax in the living room, saying little as the drama unfolded out the window.

Mr. Malagon gave a blunt rap before letting himself in.

"How's the arm?" Mr. Malagon asked Lindy.

Lindy stared dumbly at his cast, yellowed from the dust blowing through Garden Lakes, black where his fingers folded into his palm. "Okay, I guess."

Mr. Malagon rocked up on his toes. "Figs. Hands. I'd like to see you boys next door," he said. He turned and left as swiftly as he'd arrived. A surprised Figs and Hands followed in his wake, closing the door on Lindy, who bore under his cast to reach an itch.

As Figs and Hands would later say, Mr. Malagon's house had an uncharacteristic chaos about it, one that hinted that our confinement was related to something other than the fight between Roger and Warren. In fact, Mr. Malagon did not allude to the fight in his instructions to Figs and Hands.

"I'm canceling the rest of the day," Mr. Malagon told them. There was to be no lunch, no class, no sports, no dinner, no tutoring, no free time. "All privileges are suspended and tomorrow's privileges are subject to how well everyone behaves today." Mr. Malagon spoke in a measured tone, asking Figs and Hands's help in maintaining the quarantine. A siege of questions raced simultaneously through Figs's and Hands's minds, paramount among them the question about Mr. Baker's impending arrival that Sunday. A second question, and one of even more concern, was Mr. Hancock's return on Monday. He would doubtlessly be displeased about the sophomores' tutoring being in arrears.

But Figs and Hands raised none of these questions; instead they nodded and accepted their charge. Hands would patrol Loyola Street and Figs would marshal Mr. Malagon's rules to the Fellows. Hands was grateful for his luck of the draw. He knew the sophomores would rejoice in a day spent lounging around their houses (even the cancellation of lunch and dinner would be cause for celebration along Loyola St.). The Fellows, on the other hand, would see Mr. Malagon's edict as an attempt to submarine their fellowship, the exceptional nature of the lockdown surely to bring derision from generations of classes of Fellows to come, not to mention the perversion of the construction schedule, risking our showing at Open House.

We didn't believe it when Figs first told us. Assburn ravenously downed a quart of gazpacho the moment he heard, gulping the soup from its plastic container, searching the cupboards for filched fruit or stale bagels. Roger remained in his room, not even coming out to use the bathroom or to raid the refrigerator.

Sprocket staved off boredom by working seek-and-finds. Warren had sequestered himself in his room, traipsing down for a glass of water wearing a glum look. He regretted losing his temper with Roger, though he had no intention of apologizing, as Mr. Malagon had urged. Roger was a bully and bullies get what they give from time to time Warren told Mr. Malagon, who didn't disagree. "Some situations are better than others for reprisal, though," Mr. Malagon had said. "You want to be careful you don't do as much damage to yourself—or more—by striking back in a setting like this. And now you've both put me in a bad spot. One fight leads to another if it goes unpunished. That's not my rule, that's just the way it is." Warren appreciated Mr. Malagon's position and said so, slinking away to await Mr. Malagon's verdict.

. . . .

Night fell without word from Mr. Malagon. The light pulsing from behind the blinds implied he was slaving over appropriate sanctions. Roger and Warren came out of their rooms and joined their housemates, who had congregated in the living room to pass the time playing cards or telling stories.

Figs and Hands made the rounds, checking that thermostats were correctly set, the windows in all the houses sliding shut, the air conditioning vents exhaling cold air into our cages. Empty soup containers were piled high in our sinks, crusted with lip prints in drying shades of green and red and brown. We'd rummaged every cupboard and drawer in the kitchen in the search for food. Some brought out the fare they'd squirreled away in their dressers, bagel halves and oranges and biscuits formerly fresh and buttery but now so hard they had to be moistened before they could be eaten.

The sophomores had less sustenance, having been too afraid of Mr. Hancock to pilfer any food. They complained to Hands about their hunger and Hands said he'd see what he could do, knowing there would be nothing he could do short of sneaking them food, which he wasn't prepared to do.

"Let's go to Mr. Malagon," Figs said when Hands mentioned the sophomores' plea in passing.

Hands argued against the idea. He hadn't been in class the day Mr. Malagon had whipped the eraser at Garth Atlon and was surprised by the quarantine. Nothing suggested Mr. Malagon was even capable of such drastic measures. Hands secretly coveted Mr. Malagon's reputation, always striving to inculcate the same loyalty and casual deference that the student body showed Mr. Malagon. Unflappable, they would say—the word Hands had heard Principal Breen use to describe Mr. Malagon. (A trip to the Randolph library gave Hands the definition of unflappable.) The letdown Hands felt over the end of Mr. Malagon's streak of imperturbability shattered his practiced art of cool.

Typically, Figs was ready to lead the charge on an idea that wasn't his. Figs's intimate rapport with the staff in Principal Breen's office made him a conduit for the groundswell of ideas generated by other students. Some approached him looking for an indication on how the administration would respond. If Figs was enthusiastic, he would talk the idea up among the principal's staff so when it was presented, the administration felt as if the idea filled a need left void until that very moment. If, however, Figs was not enthusiastic, the student was spared presenting a proposal that would hurt his credibility. In this way it appeared to us that Figs was serving us, looking out for us the way he had in Mazatlán and a hundred times since, from advocating for a better menu in the cafeteria to lobbying the administration to allow students in academic clubs to be excused from class to meet during school instead of after.

Hands knew Figs's M.O., though he didn't mind Figs's constantly ingratiating himself with the administration and with his peers. Hands recognized Figs's savvy and on more than one occasion he had been the direct beneficiary of Figs's ability to form a field of goodwill around himself and anything he deemed worthy. What irked Hands was Figs taking undue credit for a particular idea, or shifting a disproportionate load of the blame onto someone else in the face of failure.

Phantasm was a good example. The air band at Lincoln Elementary had technically been Hands's idea. He couldn't deny that Figs had done the legwork in recruiting the other members and arranging with Mr. Butcher, the Lincoln music teacher, for the band to borrow the needed instruments (keyboard, drum set, amps for show) from another music department in the school district. And Figs had called practice, helping choreograph the lead guitar's movements around him while he lip-synched. He also came up with flourishes for the drummer and the bassist, and positioned the stage lights to shine on Hands in a flattering way.

Still, Hands couldn't help feel slighted. He could've made a play for another instrument, or even to be the lead singer, but he didn't. He understood Figs's powers of persuasion. What did it matter whose idea it was? Phantasm raised everyone's profile, even with their teachers. So what if Figs received a smidge more attention for an idea that wasn't his? And what did Hands care if Figs offended a pair of seniors at Summer Griffith's party that resulted in an ass-whipping Figs like as not didn't deserve but Hands did nothing to stop? Hands watched long enough to have his thirst for equality in his friendship with Figs quenched and then slipped away from the crowd. At first he'd been ashamed of resisting his instinct to jump into the fray, but he realized that he was sick of Figs prancing through life unscathed. He'd never paid any real price for stealing Julie Roseman away from him, though at the point at which Figs and Julie confessed, Hands had covertly been seeing his old girlfriend Kristina for months, so it hardly mattered. But still Hands liked lording it over Figs, calling him out at graduation, avoiding him for the summer, not thinking of either Figs or Julie while he and Kristina holed up in his older brother's apartment in Florida to live like husband and wife, if only for a couple of weeks. He was over it, and even missed Figs's friendship when Figs showed up on his doorstep, his apology spurred by his admission to Randolph. Hands viewed the beating as a corrective, and restored his conviction in the natural order.

And so it wasn't a surprise when Figs, the expert field commander, led a delegation consisting of him and Hands to appeal to Mr. Malagon to excuse us from the quarantine for dinner. We half-believed that Figs and Hands would return triumphant, the dining hall opened up for a buffet of anything we could scrounge from the refrigerator. Some of us could taste the salty meats and the sweet desserts, could imagine washing them down with ice cold soda, fantasies dashed by Figs's and Hands's hunched shoulders as they reported back from Mr. Malagon that the quarantine was in strict effect until the morning. Figs and Hands plopped on their couches, agitated, not speaking or looking at each other. They shifted restlessly while Lindy busied himself pointing the telescope out the living room window, finally agreeing to an early curfew check, Figs complaining he was tired, Hands echoing the sentiment, grumbling about having to do Mr. Malagon's job for him.

. . . .

We woke before our alarms, our stomachs baying with hunger. We scarcely spoke during breakfast. Our banishment had cowed us so that we felt thankful rather than angry toward Mr. Malagon, who seemed lively as ever, encouraging us to eat up. "We've got a long day in front of us," he said. A morning prayer after breakfast substituted for chapel so we could train our fresh attentions finishing the first construction phase.

Mr. Baker's truck parked in the littered driveway of 1959 distressed us.

"Didn't realize tomorrow was the Fourth of July," he explained. "So thought I'd come out a day early."

Mr. Malagon led Mr. Baker inside, soliciting Mr. Baker about his plans for the Fourth. Mr. Baker chatted amicably about a family picnic and fireworks show up in Flagstaff.

We knew Mr. Malagon's conversational ploy wouldn't last forever and feared Mr. Baker's opinion about the job we'd done hanging the drywall. To our surprise, Mr. Baker's appraisal of our work was favorable. He pulled a mini T square from his back pocket and took spot measurements in every room, clicking his tongue as he hummed a tuneless number none of us recognized. Our confidence skyrocketed as we followed Mr. Baker from room to room. The upstairs bedroom, the scene of the previous day's title fight between Roger and Warren, remained cluttered with tools and overturned drywall benches. Mr. Malagon stooped to retrieve the tape measure from the corner as Mr. Baker stood back from the far wall and shook his head.

"Too many butted seams here," he said.

We followed Mr. Baker and with his help saw what he saw: two ten foot panels nailed horizontally along the top of the wall, and five foot panels on either side of a ten foot panel nailed along the bottom of the wall. Mr. Baker tapped his finger on the butted seam running down the top half of the wall. "Remember what I said about butted seams," he said. "If you have to have them, put them on the outside, like you did down here." He indicated the two butted seams on either side of the ten foot panel below. "But this wall has too many."

Mr. Malagon spoke up in our defense. "This was the last room we hung and we didn't have any sixteen foot panels left, so the boys had to improvise. And we thought it would be better to stagger the butted seams, rather than align them on either side of ten foot panels."

"Well," Mr. Baker said, staring at the wall the way you had to stare at the poster on the back of the door in Mr. Malagon's classroom to make the figure of the naked lady appear. "We'll have to patch the problem with some superior taping."

Mr. Baker checked off all of the electrical boxes, making sure we hadn't walled over any outlets. He identified gaps between panels that would need to be filled in with compound before taping as well as a corner in the kitchen where the drywall had been damaged by an incriminating indentation the shape of a hammerhead punched wide of a nail head.

We gathered in the living room for Mr. Baker's Phase Two instructions, each of us taking a space along the walls to copy down taping sequences, recipes for mixing joint compound, and the hazards of corner beading in our job journals. "If Phase One was the most physically demanding, Phase Two will require patience. Phase Three—sanding, texturing, and painting—will be a walk in the park unless you rush through Phase Two. It's near impossible to fix mistakes made in Phase Two once you've started Phase Three. If you remember that, and do not cheat when it comes to taping and applying the three coats of compound required to stabilize the seams and make them part of the wall, which in turn makes the house one solid unit, you will have finished the job before actually completing the work."

Some of us stopped scribbling when we realized Mr. Baker was indulging in the poetics of construction. Our focus was so intent on proper construction technique—which is to say we did not want to build a lasting monument to our ineptitude—that only the practical interested us. Sensing this, Mr. Baker veered from the philosophical and continued. As he began an aside on the difficulty of taping inside corners without roughing up adjacent corners, Mr. Malagon excused himself, summoning Figs and Hands to follow. Their excusal was an irritant, though, floating through the dust and heat, working its way into us with each chalky breath. The stress and lack of sleep wrought by the quarantine elicited a smattering of vulgar remarks directed toward Figs and Hands. We were used to Figs's (and to some degree, Hands's) insinuating himself in the good graces of the faculty and administration and we'd welcomed their initiative on campus; but at Garden Lakes the advantage was an affront to the uniformity of our existence. Simply, their elevation by Mr. Malagon subjugated the rest of us, and it burned us up. We blinked momentarily in their absence, drawn back to our job journals by the resumption of Mr. Baker's voice.

The salve, of course, was that Mr. Hancock's return Monday would put right again the pecking order at Garden Lakes and Figs and Hands would be taping and beading right next to the rest of us, wiping their brows and griping about the heat. Unbelievably, some of us found ourselves daydreaming of Mr. Hancock's return during the last of Mr. Baker's instructions. But that day seemed far away as Mr. Malagon put Hands and Figs in charge so he could run to town to buy binoculars for us to watch the fireworks, his Jeep rocketing through the front gates. We'd been programmed too completely to realize that, for the moment, we were without supervision, and even Mr. Malagon was pleased to learn that all was well upon his return a few hours later.

....

Hands and Figs were disputing a call when Mr. Malagon called us together to watch fireworks the following evening, instructing us to bring bath towels to sit on. The palm trees standing guard to the entrance of Garden Lakes were lit yellow and orange, the last of the sunlight burning furiously. Finally the sun was slain, the red sky dissolved into a pale lake that gave way to the bluish purple of night. We wiped sweat with the backs of our hands. The dirt we stirred caught in our lungs, powdered our shoes.

A cannonade of color flared against the sky as Mr. Malagon passed the binoculars. Lindy angled his telescope at the concentric circles erupting from the show being put on at South Mountain. The muffled *crack crack crack* of someone shooting their gun in the air died in the wind.

Mr. Malagon leaned back on his elbows. Some mimicked his pose while others of us lay flat for a panoramic view.

Outside the front gate, Smurf lay on the roof of his car, his smiling face reflecting the same colors as our own. He could hear odd strains of our conversation—our kidding Warren about bullets fired into the air landing near us, our asking Lindy if we could look through his telescope, Mr. Malagon making a run to the dining hall for soda, taking Figs and Hands with him (and the foul joke Roger told in Mr. Malagon's absence); and as the fireworks were spent, Smurf awaited the silence that signaled the beginning of his plan to rejoin our ranks. We trudged wearily toward slumber, for what would turn out to be our last night of peaceful sleep.

The arrest happened at home, saving a shamefaced walk through the newsroom. Charlie had been dialing Charlotte's number again when Gallagher pulled him into the stairwell to tell him what that day's headline would be, that Darrell "Duke" Torrence, Jr. was resigning as publisher of the *Sun*. Gallagher couldn't say what Duke had been arrested for, but it came to light that Duke had not been arrested but had resigned, which only piqued everyone's curiosity. Duke, after all, had a court-appointed driver to keep him from behind the wheel after a string of DUI arrests. The newsroom quieted as the managing editor huddled with Brennan and other editors in the conference room, the blinds turned. Charlie absentmindedly tidied his desk. A series of messages from Richter he'd left unreturned, as well as his to Charlotte that she wouldn't return, had sent his mind into overdrive and Duke's resignation cinched the idea that he'd spun in the sleepless early hours that everyone was gunning for him, a lifetime of misdeeds revisiting him until he fled his airless apartment for the friendly confines of a noisy all-night diner near the *Sun* offices. He'd successfully managed to appear at work propped up by caffeine, a high that evaporated as the conference room door shut behind Brennan, who cast a disappointed glance in his direction. He reached for a half-torn roll of mints in his top drawer as Gallagher slipped out a far exit. Charlie resisted a similar urge until caffeine withdrawal caused him to stand on shaky legs.

He popped a mint and sauntered toward the elevator, running to his car in the underground parking lot, the echo of his squealing tires resounding as the guard at the gate saluted him with two fingers.

The horror of Duke's downfall being a consequence of his hiring Charlie away from the *Tab* was a humiliation that would dog him to the end of his days, he knew. He'd spent countless hours at Duke's feet, in his office and his home, both decorated with the trophies of Duke's many accomplishments: his early days as a runner for one of Arizona's most notorious post-Prohibition liquor distributors; his season as a catcher for the Seattle Rainiers, where he wound up after serving as a fighter pilot in WWII; his subsequent rise through a resume stocked with stints at papers weekly and daily before marrying the daughter of the owner of Desert Newspapers, Inc. His offices included photos of Duke with political personages of note, both local and national. Duke's laissez-faire administration of the *Sun* was lauded by some and mocked by others but everyone at the paper respected Duke and his career.

But the voices coming through Charlie's car stereo as he drove aimlessly from Phoenix to Tempe to Mesa, coursing the freeways, alighting at gas stations to refuel or use the restroom, shredded what respect Duke had held. Charlie's attention divided between the traffic and the volume of information filling his ears about Duke Tully and his fictional military background, endless updates about the carefully crafted war stories Duke had apparently spent decades constructing. Charlie fought lightheadedness as revelation after revelation spilled forth, the fake war plaques, the closetful of tailored military uniforms bearing the rank of colonel, the new information that Duke's youngest brother was killed in action and the news commentators' speculation that this tragic childhood fact might account for Duke's deceptions. Charlie tuned out the amateur psychoanalysis, as well as the purported detail of Duke smashing his war trophies, but was interested in the innuendo that the investigation was fueled by the *Sun*'s pursuing a story about questionable expenditures in the county attorney's office.

Charlie's disbelief was overridden by the blow that Duke was the target of Richter's investigation and not him. He'd anticipated a humbling and craved the penance and redemption that was to be Duke's alone. He envied Duke his chance to ask for forgiveness. He'd been prepared to confess to every lie he'd ever told in exchange for forgiveness. Charlie had even convinced himself that religion—the popular curative he loathed the most—was a viable salve and found himself struggling with the handles to the Randolph Chapel after midnight, after cruising past Charlotte's darkened windows. The chapel doors had been open to him all the time he'd been a student at Randolph, but he'd only graced them parochially, sitting for the requisite masses while his mind wandered.

But the doors were shut against the pews he'd so freely accessed in his youth. To kneel where he'd previously kicked up his heels in defiance of his Catholic brethren would be sweet relief. He contemplated waking Father Matthews, wondering if anyone in the rectory had heard him wrenching on the chapel doors. He bemoaned his flip answer to Father Matthews's question about whether or not Mr. McCloud deserved forgiveness for the sins he'd committed.

"That's between him and his God, I suppose," Charlie had said. He hadn't been in the mood to parse the subtleties of posthumous forgiveness; but if Father Matthews would answer his midnight calling, Charlie would gladly continue the conversation. He'd admit peremptorily that his columns about McCloud and Garden Lakes were retribution for what happened that summer, what he'd been exposed to, validating Father Matthews's suspicions. Charlie understood that McCloud was just a symbol of his misery, that at some point long ago he'd been unable to keep his head above the tide of his experiences. He'd taken to journalism as a dare, to see if he could tell unembellished truths, but his emotional reaction to every story more suited the temperament of a columnist. It's what Duke must've seen in him. But there were too many Heather Lamberts in the world and not enough chroniclers to herald their stories. Worse, the number of people like those that contributed to

Heather Lambert's death seemed exponential. How did so many find it so easy to live with so much selfishness? It was laughable to him that the customs and laws he'd come to think of as absolute were anything more than ceremonial, talking points when referring to the behavior of others.

Maybe it was inevitable that Charlie had succumbed—his promising Father Matthews that access to Randolph's Garden Lakes files would end his investigation into the past his most recent transgression—but like anyone, convenient blame and excuses easily defeated the notion of personal responsibility and he realized then, holding onto the chapel doors, what he didn't realize that day in Father Matthews's office: he wasn't a strong enough person to overcome the malice in his heart.

Katie Sullivan was a name that didn't mean anything to any of us, though Katie Sullivan was the axis on which the plot at Garden Lakes turned that summer. That she was Mr. Malagon's lover, and that she was a freshman at Xavier, became known to us much later when the story was laid bare, after Mr. Malagon was fired. The story as it was told to us then was remarkable not just for its spectacular nature, but also because once we worked back through it our own unwitting complicity in Mr. Malagon's lusty schemes thrilled us.

No one could attest to Mr. Malagon and Katie Sullivan's first meeting. As a freshman, she would not have had any classes at Randolph; and her older sister graduated before Mr. Malagon began teaching at Randolph. Still, we all knew that freshman girls would travel in packs across the Bridge of Sighs to torment us and to activate our super-charged hormones. So while there was no official link between Mr. Malagon and Katie Sullivan, it was easy for us to imagine a superficial one based on Mr. Malagon's charismatic ribbing of any blue and green plaid skirt he saw bounce in front of his classroom window.

In the administration's version, the relationship began toward the end of the school year, in either April or May. The stone-faced administration did not provide any scurrilous details but only reported that the relationship included "inappropriate behavior against the moral code of Randolph College Preparatory." Some whispered that the inappropriate behavior featured weekend jaunts to Mexico, as well as all-day quote unquote tutoring sessions at Mr. Malagon's condominium. Unconfirmed stories placed Mr. Malagon at Katie Sullivan's house after school, before her parents returned from work.

The chief witness against Mr. Malagon was Mr. Hancock, who happily related the incident whereby he discovered Mr. Malagon using the mobile phone to call Katie Sullivan from Garden Lakes. Then Mr. Hancock hauled Lindy, who had suffered unimaginably and who would tragically die young, before the administration and compelled him to recall the events that occasioned his visit to the emergency room. Lindy reluctantly recounted how Mr. Malagon disappeared for hours while he waited in the emergency room lobby, his arm slung in a cast (which is why Mr. Hancock insisted on driving Laird to the ER for his snakebite). Katie Sullivan would tearfully admit that she had met up with Mr. Malagon on that afternoon after he had called her from the hospital. She would also accidentally divulge that she was the one who gave Mr. Malagon the telescope—an unopened Christmas present from a faraway aunt and uncle—so Mr. Malagon would have an excuse for his absence. Katie also volunteered that she'd met Mr. Malagon in the mall food court the day Mr. Malagon bought the binoculars for us to watch fireworks.

The most damning testimony came not from Mr. Hancock or Katie Sullivan, but from Figs and Hands. Their testimony concerned the night of the quarantine. Several gave supporting testimony that Figs and Hands had gone to solicit Mr. Malagon's permission to free us from the quarantine for dinner. That we were denied food was a fact in heavy rotation among the administration in the first days of the inquiry, the truth about our houses being stockpiled with soups—enough to get us through the night—exorcized as a matter of convenience.

Hands's testimony, given separately, mirrored Figs's: that Figs and Hands had approached Mr. Malagon's house on Regis Street with the intention of securing Mr. Malagon's consent for the Fellows and sophomores to eat dinner; that upon knocking on Mr. Malagon's door, Mr. Malagon could be heard talking to someone whose voice neither Figs nor Hands recognized; that the conversation halted and a period of no less than one minute elapsed before Mr. Malagon answered the door.

Figs and Hands described Mr. Malagon's demeanor as impatient as he replied to their request. One or the other—Figs accused Hands; Hands said it was Figs—wore a suspicious look that caused Mr. Malagon to bark at them, telling them that their stretch as monitors was over and that they were to report to their house until morning. Figs and Hands started down the walkway when they heard a girl laughing. The two wended their way around the house and peered in the windows, spotting Katie Sullivan (though they did not know her name) and Mr. Malagon bounding from room to room in amorous chase.

Figs, who would later successfully cover up an embezzlement at his firm, shifting the blame to an innocent department head, resulting in the department head's firing at the insistence of his father-in-law, who also happened to be his boss, testified that Hands was particularly incensed and that it was he who led them through the unlocked front door, frightening Katie Sullivan, who screamed and scampered up the stairs. Figs and Hands watched the backs of her tanned legs disappear and then demanded to know what was going on. Mr. Malagon threatened to expel them both from Garden Lakes if they did not leave, but Figs and Hands repeated their question. Mr. Malagon reached for his shirt, which lay strewn across the back of the couch and buttoned it up, saying that if they knew what was good for them they would leave without uttering a word to anyone. Mr. Malagon then threatened to engineer Figs and Hands's expulsion from Randolph if they told, Katie Sullivan peering surreptitiously from the top of the stairs. Mr. Malagon's even tone was more menacing than his threat.

It was at this point, according to Figs's and Hands's testimony, that Katie Sullivan called Mr. Malagon upstairs. Mr. Malagon told

Figs and Hands to have a seat. While neither could remember precisely how long Mr. Malagon spent upstairs, it seemed to them both that he was back in a flash, wearing a less combative expression.

"This is no one's business," Mr. Malagon said. "It doesn't have anything to do with anything." He searched their faces as he spoke, hoping for affirmation, but Figs and Hands were too stunned to speak, which Mr. Malagon read as insolence. His face colored like it did the day he threw the eraser at Garth Atlon, but the redness drained and he pleaded for discretion. "It's important that this not get around," he said.

Mr. Malagon's supplication ended when Katie Sullivan reappeared at the top of the stairway. Her red and yellow floral sundress was like seeing color again for the first time and Figs caught himself before he could say hello and ask her name. Hands stood, staring Mr. Malagon down. "You should get her out of here before someone sees," he said indignantly. Figs stood, too, with the purpose of raising the idea of dinner again, but Hands's exit pulled Figs toward the door.

Figs was startled by the intensity of Hands's anger. "He's going to ruin it for all of us," Hands said, pointing back toward Mr. Malagon's residence.

"Are you going to say anything?" Figs asked.

Hands breathed deeply through his nose and exhaled, his nostrils flaring. "If I see her around here again, I will," he said.

"I was going to use it to get us dinner," Figs said.

Hands wheeled around. "Fuck *dinner*," he said. "Don't you get what's going on? Don't you see how he's trying to sabotage everything, wasting our summer and shit canning our fellowship?"

Figs didn't answer. While he agreed that Mr. Malagon was acting recklessly, he didn't see how it would jeopardize all of our fellowships, especially since he believed that Mr. Malagon would make sure that Katie Sullivan exited the premises quietly and without a long goodbye. Figs would later say that Hands's hostilities were partly a result of the whispers of favoritism that they'd both heard but ignored. Favoritism was an asset as long as the person showing you favor was not a lecherous soon-to-be fired teacher and interim leader of your summer leadership program. Hands fumed about Mr. Malagon's duplicity, accusing Mr. Malagon of setting him and Figs up for a cover story from the beginning. "He must've known he would need someone to protect him if he were caught," Hands said, spitting the words out. They sulked back to their residence, not letting on what they knew. Only the sound of Mr. Malagon firing up the Jeep to drive Katie Sullivan home later that night brought Hands peace and he fell asleep, fatigued by bitterness.

Mr. Malagon did not recognize Smurf's car as the Jeep's headlights swept across the blue Toyota parked on the side of the road outside the gates of Garden Lakes. Smurf was not in the vehicle; he had snuck up to Mr. Malagon's residence when he heard the murky stew of raised voices. Smurf kept hidden as he strained to hear the conversation, making out enough bits to piece together what was happening. He'd overheard Figs and Hands on the sidewalk in front of the house, too, and the whole picture came into focus when he saw Katie Sullivan in the passenger side of the Jeep. She appeared to look right at Smurf, but he realized she was seeing her reflection, checking her tear-stained face for smudges.

What Smurf said to Katie Sullivan that weekend he would never say. Some of us speculated that Smurf had threatened to tell the administration about her affair with Mr. Malagon if she did not do his bidding, but blackmail was not Smurf's M.O. It was more likely that Smurf, before he successfully slandered the woman at work with whom he was cheating on his wife, falsely colluded with Katie Sullivan, coaching her on what to do to make Mr. Malagon hers forever. Smurf learned what the rest of us would later: that Katie Sullivan was so sick in love with Mr. Malagon that she had once physically harmed herself when she believed that Mr. Malagon was seeing the Spanish teacher at Central High. What Smurf didn't know was that Katie Sullivan had a plan of her own, one that involved her running away to live with her college-aged friend in North Carolina, a scenario we had to believe Mr. Malagon would've found juvenile. The plan as Smurf had designed it in his mind was simple: Katie Sullivan would keep Mr. Malagon away while Smurf snuck back into Garden Lakes before Mr. Hancock's return. He would skip breakfast, as would Mr. Malagon, owing to the eye drops Katie would mix into a vodka tonic for Mr. Malagon the night before. Smurf would catch Mr. Hancock outside of chapel. Mr. Hancock would be surprised and Smurf would explain that Mr. Malagon had accepted Smurf's apology and that he'd worked out the punishment with Mr. Malagon, which would be executed once school commenced. He would then pay a visit to Mr. Malagon, who would be recuperating from his stomach trauma, hinting that he knew about Katie Sullivan without having to threaten to use the information—he still admired Mr. Malagon and did not want to embarrass or demean him in the presence of others—and voila!, his re-enrollment at Garden Lakes would be complete.

Smurf's plan went awry immediately, however, as Roger discovered him in the bathroom in the middle of the night. "I'm back!" Smurf was surprised into saying, to which Roger grunted. Smurf lay awake in his room, adjusting his plan accordingly as the sun's yoke appeared on the horizon. He would let Assburn and Roger be the messengers of his return; it would lessen Mr. Hancock's shock. The key would be to show at breakfast after it had started, long enough for Mr. Hancock to hear the rumor of his return, but not long enough for him to go to Mr. Malagon. Smurf recognized the delicate timing this amendment required and crept downstairs to lie on the couch, where his housemates found him the next morning.

As the rest of us headed to breakfast, Smurf panicked, changing his plan, which he knew was dangerous. He decided to approach Mr. Malagon first, to cement their story. There was a good chance Mr. Malagon would see him anyway, as he had to pass in front of Mr. Malagon's house on his way to breakfast and it wouldn't do to have him come screaming out of his house, in plain view of the dining hall windows, drawing Mr. Hancock's attention.

Smurf knocked lightly on Mr. Malagon's door. He knocked again using his knuckles. The house was silent. Smurf pounded on the front door and the door broke open, pieces of the door frame scattering at his feet. The living room and kitchen were dark and Smurf called out Mr. Malagon's name. Fearing that Mr. Malagon had been made sicker than Smurf had intended, he thundered up the stairs, sure Mr. Malagon was hunched over the toilet, or retching over the side of his bed into a garbage can. Instead, he found cool darkness. He backtracked out of the house, closing Mr. Malagon's door as best he could, though it wouldn't close properly. He did what he could to stifle the panic that somehow his and Katie's plan had been botched. He imagined Mr. Malagon in the hospital, hipped to the plot by an emergency room doctor in a long, white coat.

We noticed Smurf in waves, the murmur of those who looked up from their bowls of cereal provoking the rest of us until we all saw Smurf standing tentatively in the doorway, his eyes roaming the tables for Mr. Hancock. The sophomores steered clear of Smurf, avoiding him as they would a predator. Finally, Assburn, who would later die plunging into a frozen lake somewhere between Canada and Detroit, driving across the ice, smuggling counterfeit game systems in order to raise bail money for his best friend, called out to Smurf and Smurf took a seat at Assburn's table. What we didn't know then but would find out later was the Assburn was providing Smurf with a day-to-day summary of life at Garden Lakes in Smurf's absence, a duty he performed religiously after Smurf lured Assburn out into The Grove with a note placed under Assburn's pillow, along with Senator Quinn's pen.

We were astounded by Smurf's redemption. Those of us who doubted Smurf's story were the first to realize that neither Mr. Hancock nor Mr. Malagon had made it to breakfast.

The blunder that left Mr. Hancock's absence unrectified was purely administrative—Principal Breen, distracted by surprise divorce proceedings, misunderstood Mr. Hancock's petition to be replaced at Garden Lakes due to his family emergency, thinking that

Mr. Hancock would let him know *if* a replacement was needed. Mr. Hancock believed a substitute had been sent and was frankly glad to be relieved of his duties with respect to Garden Lakes. The rest of the summer was spent contemplating whether to appeal to Principal Breen about finding a permanent replacement. The leadership program sapped too much of his energies, leaving him spent come the fall. The admission left him feeling elderly, but he could not deny the joy he felt at having the remainder of his summer to entertain any fancy he could dream up, and to be free from a student body that became increasingly foreign each year.

Mr. Malagon, we would later learn, had driven Katie Sullivan to North Carolina—with her parent's permission—using the occasion of trip to try to change her mind about leaving. Mr. Malagon would later claim that he believed Mr. Hancock had returned and that, while he regretted abandoning his responsibilities at Garden Lakes, he wouldn't have endangered us had he known that the administration had failed to send a replacement for Mr. Hancock. (This form of apology/finger-pointing was not enough to save Mr. Malagon's job, however.)

The confusion surrounding both Mr. Hancock's non-return and Mr. Malagon's disappearance was quickly muted by Figs and Hands, who called us together in the chapel to suggest that Mr. Hancock and Mr. Malagon were testing us, relying on a campus rumor about just that, though we never thought it was anything more than legend.

"It's in our interest to keep the schedule," Figs said convincingly. "If it is a test and Mr. Hancock and Mr. Malagon show up at lunchtime, or at dinner, and find us off the schedule, we'll have failed."

Hands concurred. "They'll probably be back by lunch."

"Bullshit," Roger said.

Figs and Hands winced. Figs beat a tattoo on the carpet with his right foot and then looked Roger straight in the eye. "No one is being forced," he said. "Anyone can do whatever they want."

A hush descended. We could not fathom either Mr. Hancock's or Mr. Malagon's absence, nevermind both, and so we complied. The sophomores fell into order in the kitchen, Hands volunteering to manage them; the rest of us took up the taping and beading at 1959 Regis Street. Figs attempted to direct who should work in which room, but Roger, who would one day go AWOL in Iraq with a platoon of men and be court martialed for killing one of them after the soldier had been wounded by enemy fire and begged him for a mercy killing, blatantly ignored the commands, the rest of us busying ourselves with tape guns or mixing joint compound at random.

We rushed to the dining hall for lunch, expecting to be greeted by Mr. Hancock and Mr. Malagon's satisfied smiles, ready to accept our accolades for a Job Well Done. We were disappointed, though, and paraded through the lunch line with a growing anxiety, incited by the worried looks of the sophomores as they dumped macaroni and cheese on our plates, the cheese too runny, the over-boiled macaroni disintegrating in our mouths.

We gave Mr. Hancock and Mr. Malagon the lunch hour to appear, striving for nonchalance, which only reinforced our fear. The lunch hour expired without sign of either teacher. Roger became expansive and voluble, launching into a pointless story about how he helped his father restore a classic automobile one summer. Those who were paying attention to the tale sat restively, aware of their violation of the schedule, but also aware that there was no one to lead the class.

Hands pulled Figs into the kitchen.

"We have to do something," Hands said.

An army of sophomores marched through with dirty dishes. Hands motioned for Figs to follow him into the hall.

"This whole thing is going to fall apart if we don't do something," Hands said.

"Do you think they're coming back?" Figs asked.

"I don't know," Hands said truthfully. "But if they don't, how great will it be if we complete the fellowship anyway? That's never been done before. This is a chance to distinguish ourselves from all the other classes of Fellows."

Figs nodded. "But how?"

Warren and Assburn sauntered into the hallway to have a look at the empty classroom and Figs and Hands ducked back into the kitchen.

"We say we saw Mr. Malagon this morning," Hands said.

"They'll want to know why we didn't mention it earlier," Figs said.

"We'll say Mr. Malagon told us not to," Hands said, inventing the story on the spot. "We won't announce it; we'll tell a few people and let it get around."

"What if people don't believe us?" Figs asked.

Hands reached out and grabbed Freddy Cantu, who nearly spilled the tray of leftover macaroni and cheese he was carrying. "Cantu here will back us up," Hands said.

"Back what up?" Cantu asked.

Hands filled Cantu in on his role in the scheme, how it was for the good of all and how Hands would make sure Mr. Hancock and Mr. Malagon knew of Cantu's role, a distinction Cantu appeared to prize. Figs and Hands had their man, then, and they fanned out across the dining room, Figs telling Warren, Hands telling Sprocket, Cantu telling the sophomores who stood in range of Smurf.

Upon hearing the story, Smurf's worry that his plan had gone askew subsided. Mr. Malagon had come back after all, it seemed, which fit with the narrative he was spinning. "I saw him, too," he said. "He looked sick."

Figs awkwardly acknowledged Smurf's confirmation, grateful for the support. With Cantu and Smurf's independent corroboration, the dining hall emptied, the Fellows crossing the hall to the classroom, leaving the sophomores to their kitchen work under Hands's direction.

Without a particular lesson to study—we'd been pondering Woodrow Wilson's Fourteen Points, discussing their aggregate diplomatic effect on the end of World War I, leading up to an exercise about the creation of the League of Nations—we spent the two hours playing hangman on the grease board, the only rule being that the solution had to be the name of a great leader. We reasoned that if Mr. Hancock or Mr. Malagon walked in on this activity, we could claim it had *some* educational value.

But Mr. Hancock and Mr. Malagon did not come and we shuffled out of the classroom, Figs fetching the soccer ball from Mr. Malagon's house for Sports.

Hands realized that without Mr. Hancock and Mr. Malagon, we had our first shot at a fair match. We took the opportunity to draw up the teams that would compete the day of Open House. Hands designated himself captain and Figs volunteered to captain the opposing team. Hands selected Warren, Smurf, and Roger, filling out his roster with sophomores of varying degrees of skill. Figs chose Assburn, Lindy, and the remaining sophomores. Sprocket would officiate the goal line, as usual.

The first match was a lopsided affair with Hands's team winning four goals to none. We opted to play into the dinner hour, best two out of three, Figs's team taking the next game. Hands complained that Lindy's cast was an unfair advantage, Lindy using it to deflect the ball with ease. "He's not that mobile," Figs said. Hands protested, but his team called for them to play on. The final game was tied into overtime when Smurf passed the ball to Hands and Hands drove at Lindy, who deflected goal after goal with his cast. But Hands used his foot speed and misdirection to clear a path to the goal, the ball sailing near Lindy's head.

"In!" Sprocket called out, leaning forward in his wheelchair.

Dinner was served, though the entrée for that night—Mushroom Meatloaf—was ruined because the recipe was not clear about how long the meatloaves should bake, the mushrooms layered in the middle that lent the dish its juiciness dry and rubbery. The sophomores crumbled the meatloaves into the garbage can while the rest of us feasted on a sloppy smorgasbord from the reach-in refrigerators and cupboards.

After dinner, we swarmed around Lindy and his telescope, set up under the palm tree in the lakebed, Lindy dialing the telescope in on a constellation that we were too preoccupied to care about.

"Look," someone said, pointing out a light in Mr. Malagon's window. The yellow glow quelled our anxiety.

"Bet he's resting," Smurf said. "He seemed really sick."

We were too in awe of the light to challenge Smurf's diagnosis. Figs and Hands testified that at that moment they were only relieved that their lie had turned out not to be a lie. We had no idea that it was Smurf who had turned on the bedroom light when he went to coordinate Mr. Malagon's story to match his own and found the house empty.

"Where was he?" Lindy asked, expressing the question on all our minds.

"He didn't say," Smurf answered.

"I'm going to go knock on the door," Roger said.

"I wouldn't," Smurf said.

"I didn't ask what *you'd* do," Roger said.

"Cool it, Roger," Figs said.

He sneered at Figs and Figs flinched.

"You think you're special." A prickling ran across Figs's back before Figs realized that Roger was talking to Lindy. "Why are you allowed to have that telescope anyway?"

Lindy stood up, the front of the telescope dipping, aimed at the well-worn dirt. "Mr. Malagon bought it for me," he said.

"Mr. Malagon bought it for me," Roger mimicked.

"Knock it off, Roger," Warren said. He snatched the telescope and looked through the eyepiece at nothing in particular.

"Yeah?" Roger said.

Figs looked at Hands, who was staring at Roger, waiting for Roger to react. The sophomores quieted.

"C'mon, Roger," Figs said.

"What makes Captain Astronomy here so special?" Roger asked.

"Wow, check it out." Warren turned the telescope away from Roger, training it on a patch of blackness, hoping to defuse Roger's vitriol.

"Check this out," Roger said. He seized the telescope and threw it to the ground. Warren fell back, rubbing his eye. Roger kicked the telescope in the dirt and it skidded toward Warren.

Warren withdrew as the others gathered around Roger and Lindy.

Lindy resisted the urge to reach for the telescope until Roger had stormed off. Roger gave Mr. Malagon's lighted window the bird as he passed by, shouting something the rest of us could not hear.

....

The next morning, Assburn hurried into the dining hall, startling the few of us who had waked for breakfast. "Warren's gone," he said, wheezing. He steadied himself on Figs and Hands's table, grabbing at his side.

Figs asked him what he was talking about.

"You checked his room?" Figs asked.

"Yeah," Assburn said. His breathing returned to normal and he sat down next to Hands

"And?"

"His bed is made and his stuff is all there," Assburn said, "but he's...gone."

"Has anyone seen him?" Figs asked. Sprocket shook his head, as did Lindy and Smurf.

"Christ," Hands said under his breath.

"We'll have to look for him," Figs said. "Something could've happened to him."

Assburn's eyes widened. "What could've happened to him?"

Figs shrugged. "Nothing. Maybe."

"Should we tell Mr. Malagon?" Assburn asked.

"I'll let him know," Smurf said.

A brief investigation confirmed what Assburn had described. No one had seen Warren since the night before. Figs pressed us for any strange behavior we may have observed, but we hadn't noticed any; Warren was nothing if consistent in both his reserved bearing and his inquisitive nature. Any conversation with Warren invariably ended with you telling more than you learned, Warren's ability to answer a question with a question unmatched in our limited experience.

Not everyone was sympathetic to Warren's disappearance.

"Probably went home to cry to his mommy," Roger said. "Little moody bastard."

Figs and Hands lagged behind the rest of us as we headed toward the construction site, composing the roster of a potential search party to comb the area for any signs of Warren. Hands raised the possibility of dissent among those who would have to stay behind and do the work on 1959 Regis Street, a concern that proved prescient when Roger threw down his trowel and taping knife in protest, arguing that the labor should be borne equally.

"We need a few people to look around for an hour or so," Hands said. "What if it was you who was missing?" he asked us.

"I suppose you and Figs will be two of the chosen ones," Roger said.

"Figs is coordinating the search," Hands said forcefully. "I'm going to stay here and continue with the taping."

Surprised by this declaration, Figs stepped up. "And the search party will rejoin the construction after lunch," he said. "We expect the search won't take long."

"Who's in the search party?" Roger wanted to know.

Figs pointed with confidence, as if the matter had been previously decided: Assburn and Lindy would accompany him on a door-to-door search, as well as a search of the surrounding area.

"Bullshit," Roger said. "I want to go."

Smurf jogged up Regis Street with an urgent look. "Mr. Malagon said we should look for Warren," he said, catching his breath.

A wave of murmuring went up.

"You told him that Warren was missing?" Assburn asked.

Smurf nodded. "He's real sick. He looks bad. But he wants us to try to find Warren. And he wants us—he wants *me*—to keep him updated. He said he'll call Warren's parents if we don't find him. He's got Mr. Hancock's mobile phone."

"Where's Hancock?" Roger asked.

"He's…" Smurf fumbled. "He's still visiting his family. Mr.

Malagon doesn't know when he's coming back."

Smurf's mandate gave Figs's plan weight and Roger backed off.

"Why not supervise the sophomores?" Hands said to Roger, extending a compromise.

Roger accepted the assignment, returning his tools to Sprocket, who logged them back into the supply shed.

The search party ventured from 1959, poking our heads into each of the houses as we made our way toward the community center. Figs made the decision to enter Mr. Hancock's residence. "If he's hiding out," Figs said, "Mr. Hancock's would be a good place to do it."

Heat radiated from inside the house. The box that previously contained the mobile phone provided by the administration lay open and empty on the kitchen counter. The house was still. Figs opened and closed every door while the rest of us moved outside.

"Nothing," Figs said, his hair matted to his wet brow.

As the party moved through the houses on Loyola Street, Figs's demeanor switched from one of pursuit to one of determination. "He's got to be here somewhere," Figs said. He led the search into The Grove and identified what might've been fresh footprints on the ground. "They lead that way," he said, pointing to the desert beyond Garden Lakes.

"What's that way?" Assburn asked.

"The freeway for one," Figs said.

"We should get some sun block if we're going to go out there," Assburn said. "It's almost noon."

Figs shielded his eyes. "Let's go out a ways," he said. "Just to see if these tracks go cold."

We agreed to trek on, though the footprints faded a couple of hundred feet from The Grove. Figs forged ahead with his head bent toward the ground, his eyes roving for signs of life. We snaked along in the sand, led here and there by footprints, none of which looked fresh.

As Assburn renewed his call for a retreat for sun block, we stumbled onto a rock grouping that had seen recent use. Figs examined the prints, circling the rocks. A variety of trash had collected: Styro-foam cups riddled with teeth marks of indeterminate origin, scraps of candy wrappers, a confetti of plastic and rubber and metal ground down by the elements. A pile of discarded apple peels gave away that Warren had been in the vicinity: Warren's aversion to eating the skin of anything—chicken, fruit, pudding, whatever—was famously known.

Figs argued for pressing on, but Lindy said that if they did, "there'd be four more lost." Figs relented and the party hiked back toward the development, arriving as the construction crew was calling it quits for the day.

"Nice timing," Roger said, peeling at a scab of joint compound on his arm.

"We found something," Figs said. He reported what we'd discovered in the desert. "I should let Mr. Malagon know," he said.

"Mr. Malagon wanted me to report back," Smurf said. "I need to get the handout for class, anyway. I'll let him know."

Smurf dashed off before Figs could protest.

"What should we do?" Hands asked.

"Not sure," Figs said. "We'll wait and see what Mr. Malagon says."

"Wonder why Smurf," Hands said. Figs wondered the same. Smurf had somehow supplanted him and he could only reason that it was a lesson Mr. Malagon was trying to impart. He remembered Mr. Malagon accusing Figs of being too much of a politician; it would be like Mr. Malagon to send a subtle message by drafting Smurf over him as a confidant.

Mr. Malagon's decision, rendered through Smurf, was that we should wait until morning. "Mr. Malagon called Warren's parents and they said he sometimes wanders off on his own," Smurf told us.

"His parents weren't freaked out?" Sprocket asked.

"Apparently not," Smurf said.

None of us knew Warren well enough to know whether that statement was true or not, so we followed Mr. Malagon's directive and assembled for class to read through a handout on the First Continental Congress, though we couldn't concentrate on anything other than Warren's disappearance and the pallor that had begun to settle around the development in the wake of Mr. Hancock's continued absence and Mr. Malagon's prolonged illness.

The rest of the day was carried out as per the schedule, the illumination from Mr. Malagon's window spurring us on. Curfew was lifted per Mr. Malagon via Smurf, though none of us took Mr. Malagon up on his offer, instead turning in early to lay awake in our beds, wondering where Warren was and how much longer Mr. Malagon would be bed-ridden.

....

Our anxiety-induced insomnia petered out in the early morning hours and most of us woke well after breakfast, scurrying through the deserted streets to the dining hall, hoping that life at Garden Lakes had regained a modicum of normalcy.

Instead we found the tables in the dining hall rearranged to imitate a command center, Figs and Hands attempting to map the local terrain on the grease board that had been wheeled in from the classroom. The whiff of bacon wafted through the building, awakening our hunger. Over plates loaded with bacon and eggs, we listened as Figs and Hands divided us into teams and assigned each team a quadrant. The search had two phases: the quadrants making up the morning phase falling inside the outer loop, the afternoon phase a grid of quadrants beyond The Grove. One team—Sprocket, Lindy, and Smurf—would remain at the community center to receive updates, Lindy stationing himself on the roof with his telescope for a bird's eye view. Smurf persuaded us the search had the blessing of Mr. Malagon, who wanted hourly reports on our progress.

We stalked out of the dining hall, charged with our duty. Some of the teams were realigned along friendship lines as we scattered to our quadrants—miffing Figs and Hands, though they did not protest.

The morning search produced the same results as the search from the previous day. Warren was not anywhere inside the walls of Garden Lakes. Those whose quadrants did not include any of the residences and were thus quickly searched doubled back to the dining hall, waiting for the others to arrive. Sprocket drew an X through each quadrant on the grease board as the teams returned, transferring the information to a reproduction of the map he'd sketched on the inside back cover of a book of seek-and-finds. He split his time between overseeing the search and setting up for the cold cuts lunch we'd agreed on, determining that all hands were needed in the field.

Lindy encountered Sprocket reaching for a plastic tub of mayonnaise on the pantry shelf.

"Let me get it," Lindy said.

"Thanks," Sprocket said. "Not used to shelves that high."

Lindy offered to lay out the bread and cold cuts, but Sprocket declined his help. "You won't tell on me if I get a sneak preview, will ya?"

Sprocket smiled. "Help yourself."

Lindy made a roast beef sandwich while Sprocket ribbed Lindy's sandwich-making abilities, Lindy laughing along at the primitiveness of his sandwich—bread, meat, cheese, mayo—but shifted into another conversation all together.

"Let me know if you hear another team come back," Sprocket said, sticking his head into the refrigerator to gather condiments. Lindy said he'd keep a lookout. Sprocket wheeled up to the counter carrying half-empty ketchup and mustard bottles in his lap, placing the opened bottles in front of the new, unopened ones from the pantry. "Smurf is giving the reports, but I'm tracking all the information," he said without self-importance. Lindy chewed his sandwich. "I'm going to miss it here," Sprocket said.

Lindy swallowed the last of the sandwich, wishing he had something to wash it down with. "What do you mean?"

Sprocket looked at Lindy, embarrassed. "I mean, it's nice to be useful. People like you when you serve a purpose," he said bashfully.

"People like to take advantage," Lindy said, feeling protective of

Sprocket.

"That's true," he said, "but you can't go around thinking everyone is taking advantage of you. I mean, I don't mind if people want me to do things for them. It's a good feeling." Sprocket caught Lindy staring at his legs and Lindy averted his gaze. "It's okay, I know what you're thinking. I mean, I know. I know that this"—Sprocket swept his hand around the kitchen, but Lindy understood that he meant much more—"is all artificial. Everyone accepts my handicap here and I'm not made to feel grateful for it, which I *am* grateful for."

"Nobody cares about—"

"Do you know that I have *two* personal assistants at home?" Sprocket asked. "I mean they come on different days," Sprocket said, realizing the melodramatic tone in his voice, "but the point is I'm so useless at home that I have to have personal assistants as counterparts to my parents, who are on high alert whenever I'm in the room. They actually sit up in their seats. They would've never let me organize the supply shed, they would've never even let me try. And they surely wouldn't let me be in charge of the search party and laying out lunch." Sprocket's voice cracked and he fell silent, staring shamefully at a mustard stain on his pants.

Lindy grappled for words, not wanting to pity Sprocket, though pity is what Lindy felt through and through. It had been a long time since he felt sorry for someone other than himself. "I'm sure they—"

Sprocket interrupted again, looking up with a smile. "I don't blame my parents," he said. "They're typical of what waits for me after graduation. I have to prepare myself for being pitied." Sprocket fingered the stain thoughtfully. Lindy was too moved by Sprocket's analysis of life after Randolph—a life Lindy hadn't begun to contemplate, but a life he guessed Sprocket thought about all the time—to offer any comfort, though he couldn't think of what to say.

In order to prevent any team from getting lost, the desert beyond Garden Lakes was reimagined into pie-shaped quadrants, each team sweeping the quadrant from side to side, meeting up with alternating neighboring teams every ten to fifteen minutes to exchange intel and head counts. The afternoon search brought with it an extra measure of preparation: we took turns passing suntan lotion around the dining hall, having to raid Mr. Hancock's supply to cover everyone. A squad of sophomores collected and washed the plastic soup containers from our residences, filling them with water so each team member had a quart for the journey.

Smurf escaped to Mr. Malagon's to think. Warren's unexpected vanishing was a monkey wrench in his plan. The secret about Mr. Malagon's disappearance was a pressure that manifested itself physically, his head throbbing. He cradled Mr. Hancock's mobile phone, pressing the ON button. He'd call Randolph and let them know what had happened. Maybe the administration would appreciate hearing it directly, rather than from the police or whoever would get involved with the search for Warren. He tricked himself into thinking this for less than a minute, coming around to the realization that he would undoubtedly be expelled from Randolph unless he was somehow able to sustain the illusion about Mr. Malagon, which would keep order, and which in turn would make everyone campaign for Smurf's getting credit for the fellowship.

He looked at the mobile phone as it gave three quick beeps and expired in his hand, the luminous face going dark. Smurf peered out the window, wondering whether or not Mr. Hancock had a charger (which would be missing from the case upon Smurf's inspection) when Hands appeared on the sidewalk below. Smurf pushed open the window and called down to him. The mobile phone was heavy as a stone in his palm. He could not bear the burden of Mr. Malagon's disappearance alone.

"Come up," Smurf said nervously.

....

By nightfall, the command center in the dining hall was littered with dirty dishes and the remnants of an unsatisfying dinner of our ever-dwindling supply of leftovers. There had been no new evidence to justify a further search of the outlying area. A committee comprised of Figs, Hands, and Smurf revisited Warren's room with the intent of analyzing the room's content, but they returned without a conclusion.

"If he was dead, he'd be stinking by now," Roger said, which was funny to no one but him.

A rattling of the window focused our attention. The fronds of the palm tree embedded in the lakebed stood horizontally, blown by a fierce wind. Sand brushed against the window, giving off a sound like static electricity. The sky was the color of ink.

"Whoa," Assburn said.

A barrage resembling artillery fire sounded behind us. We rushed into the kitchen and found Adam Kerr, Reedy, and Cantu pacing. The sweet smell of butternut squash soup hung in the air.

"What is that?" Kerr asked.

Figs climbed up to peer out of the small, rectangular window that overlooked the loading dock. An immense grayness blew across the outer loop and Figs winced as the building was fired upon again.

"Rocks from The Grove," Figs said. "The wind is really blowing."

The windstorm died down as quickly as it began and we let our curiosity about the storm's aftermath draw us outside, freeing us from the command center without having made a definitive plan for resolving Warren's disappearance. Garden Lakes Parkway was powdered with sand, but Regis and Loyola Street were clear except for a sprinkling of sandstone that had leapt the community center. We snuck off in twos and threes to crawl into bed, too worn out to think.

A few of us stayed behind and helped clean up the mess in the dining hall, avoiding all topics of conversation: what should be done about Warren, and what would happen to the schedule. We moved with a fluidity that suggested clearing the tables and washing and drying the dishes was the utmost important job in the world.

A sonorous honking disrupted our concentration. We recognized the honk as that of the grocery truck and it occurred to us that we had not received any groceries in over a week, the confusion about Mr. Hancock and Mr. Malagon and Warren preoccupying our minds, distracting us from our worry that the previous Sunday had come and gone without a grocery delivery.

"Mix-up because of the holiday," the driver said without apology. "Thought you got the shipment on Monday, but the log said you didn't so we guessed you guys were maybe starving." The driver noted the dirty dishes stacked on the counter. "Looks like you're doing okay, though."

Figs grabbed the clipboard Mr. Hancock used to hold the grocery list and followed the driver outside to check in the groceries.

Adam Kerr and Cantu were finishing up the dishes when Figs asked them to move the groceries from the loading dock into the pantry and refrigerator.

"Where is everybody?" Figs asked.

The kitchen was suddenly empty, as was the dining hall.

"Everyone looked pretty tired," Cantu said.

"You guys look beat, too," Figs said, feeling guilty about asking them to help with the groceries. "Why don't we drag this stuff inside and deal with putting it away tomorrow so you guys can get to bed. I'll take care of the perishables."

"No one's been sleeping," Cantu said. He glanced at Kerr, who nodded. "Some of the guys are talking about leaving."

Figs started. "Leaving to go where?"

"Home," Cantu answered.

Figs put his foot up on a mixed case of pickles, mayonnaise, and ketchup. "Who is thinking about leaving?"

Cantu shrugged. "Some of us."

"*Us?*"

"Not us," Cantu said, pointing at himself and Kerr, "but some of the other guys want to go home."

"You mean some other sophomores," Figs said.

Cantu nodded.

"I don't understand—" Figs began, but Adam Kerr cut him off.

"They think maybe Warren was murdered."

Figs brought his foot back down, rocking back. He'd guessed the sophomores' mutiny was about Mr. Hancock's and Mr. Malagon's flight, not Warren's. Figs forced a laugh. "Warren wasn't murdered," he said. He laughed again for effect. Kerr and Cantu didn't look convinced. In the face of their doubtful stares, Figs spoke as rapidly as his mind spun an answer. "The grocery guys found Warren."

Cantu's eyes grew wide.

"Yeah," Figs said. "They said they would've been here sooner but they ran into Warren wandering around by the freeway and they took him to the hospital."

"What happened to him?" Kerr asked.

"He fell down and hit his head," Figs said. "Dehydration. They said he didn't even know who he was when they found him. But they recognized his outfit." Figs's voice acquired a conspiratorial tone. "We'll let everyone know in the morning."

The story picked up Kerr and Cantu's step as they finished moving the groceries off the loading dock. Figs reminded them again to keep their secret as they parted ways in front of the community center, Figs treading down Regis Street. He knocked on Hands's door to confer and cement the story, but Hands was passed out from exhaustion.

Hands woke early, refreshed. His dream about a flood that had submerged Garden Lakes amused us as he told it over breakfast. "It was like Atlantis," he said, equally amused.

Someone had erased the grease board and rolled it out into the hallway, packaging it for its return to the classroom, an action that leant credibility to the tale of Warren's rescue by the grocery truck, which by breakfast had circulated so that Hands quizzed Figs about the details upon his late arrival to the dining hall, Figs having overslept.

"Where did he fall?" Hands asked.

Figs buttered a bagel. "Not sure."

"Did the driver say Warren was bleeding?"

"He didn't say."

Conversation around the dining hall dropped off so we could hear the story.

"Was he really by the freeway?" Hands asked.

Figs took a bite of his bagel, nodding.

Hands drained a glass of chocolate milk, replacing it on the brown ring that had formed on the tablecloth. "Is he going to come back?" he asked.

"Don't know," Figs said.

"It cheered Mr. Malagon up to hear that Warren was okay," Hands said, looking across the table at Smurf.

"Yeah," Smurf said to bolster Hands's statement.

Figs curbed his feeling of betrayal that Hands had been taken into Mr. Malagon's inner circle, the need to speak confidentially with Hands growing urgent.

"What exactly did the driver say?" Hands asked.

"What I told you," Figs said, dropping his butter knife on the floor. He bent down and retrieved it. "That they found Warren by the freeway and that he had amnesia, or something like that. They didn't say a whole lot about it."

"Maybe we should give him a call and see how he's doing," Assburn said. "You know, to make sure he's okay. We could use Mr. Hancock's mobile phone."

Smurf belched to mask the jolt he felt at the mention of the mobile phone. "Great idea," he said. "I'll ask Mr. Malagon. Though he'll want to make the call himself. You know how he is."

We nodded, knowing what Smurf meant.

A motion proposed by Smurf (which we read as coming from Mr. Malagon) that each would be responsible for making, eating, and cleaning up after their own meals—so all hands could report to 1959 Regis Street—was roundly passed. The motion was put into effect and we all chipped in with the breakfast dishes, working with a precision we didn't know we possessed. Figs made several false attempts to try to isolate Hands, to explain his lie about Warren and to be briefed on the situation with Mr. Malagon, but Hands sensed Figs's anxiety about not being privy to the secret about Mr. Malagon and, for the moment, Hands did not want to share the deception he considered insignificant if it kept order and motivated everyone to move forward with the essential obligations of the leadership program. Also, he knew Figs would ask endless questions about Mr. Malagon, a quiz Hands wanted to avoid. Warren's disappearance was a bigger threat, Hands reasoned, and with the resolution of that situation, there was no reason they couldn't soldier on toward the finish line. The who, what, when, where, why, and hows would sort themselves out after, he told himself, and would pale in comparison to our collective achievement.

We sent up a hurrah as we passed under Mr. Malagon's window, letting him know that we were working in solidarity toward the objective laid out on Day One. We imagined Mr. Malagon smiling to himself, maybe hobbling to the window to get a look at the parade of conviction.

While Sprocket rounded up the tools that had been deserted a day earlier, checking the list of implements against the master list in his job journal, we broke into teams of five, each team incorporating two or three sophomores, the work force swelling noticeably so that we decided on two overall teams: one to tape and bead the upstairs and one to do the same downstairs.

We wouldn't get any further than deciding teams, though, before our intentions were derailed.

"Look who's out of the hospital," Roger said.

We stood still, all of us, as Warren approached, a girl we didn't recognize following a few steps behind him. His clothes had been bleached by the sun, the knees of his pants blackened by dirt. He clearly had not showered in a couple of days. Warren waved hello when he saw us and some of us waved back, the girl waving too. Warren reached back and clutched the girl's hand, pulling her close.

W arren's eyes brimmed with excitement as we fired questions at him, his sour- breathed answers fogging up the dining hall, though we were too entranced to care. The girl sat quietly, her enormous green eyes taking us in. She, too, traveled in a cloud of dust, but her earthen odor wasn't as offensive as Warren's. She swung her bronzed legs under the chair and some of us tried harder than others not to stare. She could've been sixteen or she could've been twenty-six; her weathered skin made judging her age problematic.

Warren's odyssey was triggered by his habitual insomnia, a condition he did not have to delineate for any of us. Though he would not identify the fight between Roger and Lindy as the catalyst, he alluded to it. "My stress level was up here," he said, his hand above his head. He thought a walk might help tire him out, so he stole out of bed and out of his residence, cutting behind the community center and crossing the outer loop. "I was going to walk the loop," he said, "but the moon was so bright that I could see in every direction, so I wandered off toward The Grove."

From The Grove, Warren bounced out into the desert, drawn by the remarkable moonlight. He described meandering in a blinding light, the monotonous landscape drawing him farther and farther away from Garden Lakes.

"Then it got darker," Warren said. He reached into his front pocket and pulled out a homemade gunny sack made of two back pockets from an old pair of Levi's hemmed together, a zipper (presumably from the same pair of Levi's) threaded across the top. He unzipped the primitive pouch and plucked out what looked like a black pill, popping it into his mouth. He extended the open pouch. "They're olive pits," he said.

Hands pinched a pit out of the sack. "Nice and salty," he said, rolling the seed around with his tongue.

We passed the pouch as Warren continued.

"I couldn't see much then," he said, "except for this piece of driftwood about twenty feet in front of me." The driftwood had baffled Warren. "How did it get so far from the water? And what was it before it drifted into the ocean?" The second question held more possibility for Warren, knowing as we all did that arid parts of the earth were once covered by water. But before he could expound on his find, a truly unbelievable occurrence distracted him.

"Right there in front of me," Warren said, hopping out of his seat and tracing an imaginary circle at his feet, "like it was reaching out to me." A thrill ran through us and he paused, setting the scene. "There's a tall cactus over here"—pointing off to his left—"and a wash just past the cactus. On my right are creosote bushes, all dried out with its flowers turned to fuzz. I turn around to see how far I am from the outer loop and realize that I can't see Garden Lakes at all. I can feel myself starting to panic, and I think I'm hallucinating about vanilla ice cream when this…thing"—Warren clasped his hands together and spread them slowly—"starts growing."

Those of us who had had Mr. Bisesto for biology knew what Warren was talking about—the Queen of the Night, a flower that bloomed one night a year, emitting a strong scent of vanilla. Mr. Bisesto annually told the story of how he once spotted the rarely seen night blooming flower on a retreat in California.

"So I see this sign and I keep going," Warren said. He walked farther into the desert that night, trekking onto the Tohono O'odham Indian Reservation, north of Maricopa. He moved unmolested through the reservation, encountering no one, until he reached a dirt road running alongside to the freeway, frustrated by the circuitous route he'd taken. He mapped out the easiest path back to Garden Lakes, using the I-10 as a guide.

"But I decide to walk in the opposite direction," Warren said. "I don't know why. I just do. I look one way and go the other, back into the desert." He walked parallel to the freeway, though he moved to the interior of the land, away from the headlights caroming around him. "I ended up getting lost," he said. "I couldn't hear the freeway or see any headlights, but I kept on going. It all seemed like a mistake. That's when I found Axia." Warren gestured toward the girl, who smiled. We didn't understand her name when Warren said it, but were too shy to ask him to repeat it. Axia was *not* Tohono O'odham; she was not even Native American, a fact we did not know until later. We assumed otherwise as Warren continued with his story, about how he came upon a band of Tohono O'odham—"thirty or forty, a bunch of them kids"—under a ramada. "They had these tools and they were using them to pop the tops off of the cacti," he said. He stood and demonstrated the motion, hoisting an invisible pole in his hands like a shotgun and crooking his elbows.

We foolishly imagined Warren walking into a nest of Indians like the ones we'd seen in Westerns, with scowling faces, their headdresses piercing the air. We only knew two varieties of Native Americans: the kind that wore colorful t-shirts emblazoned with brand names, and the kind from the movies. Warren assured us the group looked "like you and me, except for the color of their skin."

The Native Americans were in reality a family that had come together to harvest the fruit from the Saguaro cacti and pay homage to their ancestors.

"What, like a rain dance?" Hands asked.

Axia laughed, revealing a snaggled top tooth.

"No, not a rain dance," Warren said. "The Tohono O'odham are very informal about their rituals. This was the nearest thing to the wine festival ritual that celebrates the new year. I learned about it from Axia. The family didn't speak English."

Figs could feel Hands staring at him from the next table over. He ran his lie about the grocery truck driver finding Warren frontward and back, parsing his words for the loophole that would set him free from Hands's scorn. If he could just explain everything to Hands, he was sure Hands would've done the same. It was the same as telling everyone that they'd seen Mr. Malagon when they hadn't. Figs would momentarily elude our inquiry, though, as our thoughts were preoccupied with Axia.

Warren continued his tale, how the family brought him back to their olive farm (and how the olive pits we were all sucking on had not been pitted by a machine but had been sucked clean by the olive farmers, causing us to spit the seeds out. "They've been roasted," Warren said.); how he learned Axia was not Native American, but had been traveling around the United States by thumb.

"I left when Axia left," he said.

Our eyes shifted to Axia. We could see the young girl she was through the dirt and grime that clung to her skin and clothes. We imagined her in a blue and green plaid skirt, the uniform of all of the girls in our dreams. Axia's hair hung in clumps and it could've been any color in the world. She began to fidget, her hands adorned with chewed fingernails moving restlessly in her lap.

"She can't stay," Hands said, breaking our trance.

Warren's look cut through Hands.

"I'm sorry, man," Hands said, "but you know the rules. We've got work to do."

We wanted to protest, but knew what Hands said was true. The extraordinary circumstances that brought Axia to Garden Lakes would have to be ignored if we were to accomplish our goal. We would have to classify Axia as the enemy in order to persuade ourselves that turning her out was the correct thing to do.

Some were more easily persuaded than others.

"Why not let her get a shower and some rest?" Figs spoke up.

"I don't understand why she has to leave," Warren said.

Figs held up his hand to quiet Warren. He turned to Hands. "If we can all agree to keep on schedule, there's no reason why she can't stay," he said. "I'm sure we could use her help." He addressed Axia: "Would you be interested in helping us?"

"She's an excellent worker," Warren piped up.

"Wait, wait, wait," Hands said. "The question isn't if she can stay, but when she'll go."

"Can I smoke in here?" Axia asked. She pulled a tarnished gold cigarette case studded with turquoise from her pocket. Her question emboldened Hands.

"There's no smoking in any of the buildings," he said, sounding eerily like Mr. Hancock.

Axia got up and strode through the dining hall, perching outside the window to light one of her hand rolled cigarettes.

The sophomores excused themselves to start lunch prep as the exchange reheated. Figs argued that Axia's arrival was an interesting twist to the program, but Hands viewed it as a clear breach of what Garden Lakes stood for.

"How can you say it's a breach?" Figs asked. "The whole point of being a Fellow is proving yourself. Here's a chance for us to prove ourselves."

"What will it prove?" Hands demanded to know.

"That no matter the circumstances, we know how to make good decisions," Figs said.

We'd never beheld such a disagreement between the two and it was hard to know when to chime in, or whose side to ring in for. Hands garnered Smurf's allegiance, who agreed that allowing Axia to stay would be a violation of the rule against having visitors. "Look at what happened to me," he said, playing his expulsion for laughs. The joke missed its mark, though, and the debate stalled.

"I don't see any harm in her spending the night," Figs said.

"Me neither," Warren said.

Figs's proposal met with a smattering of approval. Hands was about to object, but Figs spoke over the top of him. "I say we let her shower, get something to eat, and rest. Why don't you"—he indicated Hands and Smurf—"go to Mr. Malagon and see how he feels about her staying."

Realizing his advantage, Hands agreed.

"But first," Figs said, "we have to deal with the schedule."

We bolted back plates of sandwiches, stuffing apples and oranges and bananas and bagel halves into our pockets to sustain us through an afternoon shift at 1959 Regis Street. The sophomores were charged with manning a water line to combat the white hot heat billowing through the rooms, filling and refilling any container they could find with cold water for our water breaks. Our minds were not on the job at hand, though, but on Axia, who had been given the keys to the house relinquished by Quinn so she could clean up and rest. We imagined her brown body turning under the water, the days' and weeks' worth of filth falling away to expose the girl she'd been before she took up a life on the road. We willed ourselves to concentrate on applying the first coat of compound in an attempt to cover up the constellation of nails spread across the walls in every room.

The afternoon shift was one of our most successful and we knocked off thirty minutes early as a reward, to allow us to scrub up for dinner. We compared smears of joint compound on our extremities and in our hair to prove that a good shower was warranted, but we secretly wanted to be presentable at dinner.

Hoping to meet up with Hands at their residence, Figs reached over Assburn and handed Sprocket his trowel. "One at a time," Sprocket complained, but Figs persisted, dropping the tools into their corresponding plastic boxes.

Figs was unable to locate Hands, though, Hands's dry towel hanging untouched in the bathroom. He asked Lindy if Hands had come in and Lindy remarked that he saw Hands talking to Smurf in front of Mr. Malagon's house. Figs peered out the window in the direction of Mr. Malagon's, but the sidewalk was empty, Hands and Smurf having moved into the house to continue their discussion.

"It's too dangerous now," Smurf said. "We should tell everyone."

"Tell them what?" Hands asked, aggravated. "Tell them that you lied about Mr. Malagon being sick?"

"What about you? You're in this now."

Hands moved them into the kitchen, away from the broken front door.

"I'll say that I didn't actually *see* Mr. Malagon," Hands said. He smirked. "I'll say that it was all coming from you."

"But you said you saw him."

"Figure of speech," Hands said.

"I don't understand why you don't want anyone to know."

"And I don't understand why you *do*. Do you want everyone to think you're a liar? A lie like this will make Assburn look like a saint. Is that what you want, people laughing at you and calling you names?" Hands never understood why Smurf didn't take more care of his reputation and needed Smurf to focus on just that for his threat to take hold.

Smurf leaned against the dusty kitchen counter. He regretted taking Hands into his confidence, the strain of keeping Mr. Malagon's absence a secret multiplying rather than lessening. "No, I don't," he answered.

"Good," Hands said, softening his tone. "I want the same thing you do: for us to complete our fellowships and then go home. We'll go to Assburn like we discussed and ask to use his mobile phone to call the school to find out what the fuck is going on. That plan is solid. But before we do that, we have to get rid of that chick."— neither Smurf nor Hands could remember her name—"If they come out here and find her here, we're done for."

Smurf took in what Hands was saying.

"Do you agree?" Hands asked.

"Yeah," Smurf said, "but what about letting a few key people know about Mr. Malagon?"

"Good idea," Hands said. "But you know what happens once you let someone know something. Everyone knows. Plus we're not in the position of having to build a consensus. All we have to say is that Mr. Malagon says she has to go and that'll be that. End of argument. Then we can call the school."

Smurf guessed at how tough it would be to keep the secret about Mr. Malagon close once a few people knew. He agreed to go along with Hands's idea and stood next to him as Hands delivered Mr. Malagon's verdict during dinner. Axia's absence had left us dejected—"She's sound asleep," Warren reported after a collective query—and our egos were soothed by the knowledge that Mr. Malagon had ordered that she leave.

"Should we wake her up and tell her," Figs said angrily, "or should we let her sleep?"

"Mr. Malagon said she could stay the night," Hands said without missing a beat.

The idea encouraged various amorous plots, all of which depended on Axia waking from her nap. The gulf in communication between Figs and Hands had jettisoned our studies, but we knew we wouldn't be able to sit in our living rooms poring over ancient texts or handouts while Axia luxuriated in Quinn's old residence. Sensing this, or perhaps as a way to sharpen his skills, Hands suggested an after dinner soccer match. We shouted excitedly when we touched the ball, cheering our teammates, in some cases chanting each other's names.

Hands was the only player who knew the score at the end of the match, taunting the opposing players for another game. We played another three, our muscles aching, some of us bleeding, all of us hoping that Axia would appear to witness our skill and cunning. Even Sprocket was infected with a new enthusiasm, calling "Gooaaaalllll" if we scored, or barking "Out!" if we missed.

We would've played best of five, four out of seven, first one to ten—anything to dawdle long enough for Axia to wake, but she slumbered through the night.

It was nearing midnight when we lay down our disappointed heads.

....

We came to breakfast the next morning, fatigued to the brink of hallucination, to find the sophomores camped around Axia, who was relating an apparently hilarious tale about a truck driver she'd hitched a ride from outside of Albuquerque. Warren sat next to her, punctuating her story with his sharp laughter.

The sophomores took their stations as we shuffled in, serving us an unusually gourmet breakfast consisting of omelets, raisin muffins, hash brown casserole, and handmade sausage patties spiced up with jalapenos and other herbs. The sophomores whispered Axia's name in response to our wonderment at the delicious spread.

Figs sat at Axia's table, introducing himself. He stuck out his hand awkwardly and Axia shook it.

"Figs's sort of the captain of the team," Warren said. The rest of us looked around for Hands or Roger, who might've had something to say about Warren's anointment, but they arrived late, stumbling in as Axia, in answer to Figs's questions, told her story.

After spelling her name for us, she admitted it was not her real name. "I read it in a book," she said. Her given name was Virginia Dare and she was born in Ft. Wayne, Indiana eighteen years earlier, but was raised outside of Lincoln, Nebraska ("in a place that doesn't exist for me anymore") by a couple who adopted her at age two, after her birth parents had been killed when their car collided with a cement embankment. The couple that brought Axia to Nebraska renamed her Heather Grayson as her adopted mother had a bedeviling aunt named Virginia that the mother loathed.

Life in Nebraska was grim and Axia was not permitted to watch television, or play with friends after school, or any of the other activities that we presumed all other kids enjoyed. The household sounded overtly religious, but Axia did not allude to any particular church.

"I didn't find out I was adopted until I was sixteen," she said.

Warren howled. "Can you believe *that*?" he asked us. We helped ourselves to seconds of hash brown casserole, listening all the while.

"The idea that I was adopted set everything in motion," Axia said. Some of us stared at her snaggled tooth, which we thought made her even cuter. "I looked at my adoptive parents like strangers from then on. Every worry that I had about turning out like them vanished."

A turbulent two years followed in which Axia disobeyed every word her parents and teachers said. She suffered through a series of groundings, detentions, and suspensions with a smile, her surroundings suddenly felt fake, a movie set against which her life had played out for the last fourteen years.

"Did you try to find your real family?" Assburn asked, having come in after the part about how her parents had been killed. Someone threw a crumpled napkin at him.

"What?" he asked defensively.

Axia repeated the information and Assburn covered with, "I meant your parents' family. You know, like aunts and uncles."

Axia shook her head. "I could've," she said, "but any life back in Ft. Wayne would've been as strange to me as the one in Nebraska. None of it belonged to me."

She counted the months and weeks and days and hours and minutes until her eighteenth birthday. Axia had asked The Graysons (which is how she referred to them) if she could invite a friend from school over—the only friend Axia had made in four years of high school—but they said no. That simple, one word, two letter answer germinated the resentment and bitterness that Axia had been nurturing since she was sixteen and, rather than eat the fried chicken and mashed potato dinner The Graysons had prepared (fried foods being forbidden in the Grayson residence except on special occasions), Axia scooped up as many of her meager possessions as she could fit into a bag. She walked out to the highway and had a ride south within the hour.

Twelve hours later she was stranded east of Denver, tired from the amphetaminic blather of her first chauffeur, who took her as far as Branson. "The end of the line for me," the driver said, grinning under his greasy baseball hat stitched with the word GAMECOCK in camouflage lettering. The second leg of her journey—she was flirting with an idea that she was bound for Mexico—took her as far as Albuquerque, a good test to judge what life in the desert would be like. She did not have a driver's license and it would be difficult to re-enter the United States once she committed to leaving. She took a job at Five Points Bakery near the Rio Grande. "I would eat my lunch on the riverbank," she said. "It was actually an ugly spot, but I liked to watch the river." She took a furnished room in downtown Albuquerque two months before moving in with a co-worker who wanted someone to share the rent and utilities.

But the morning after she'd verbally agreed to move, Axia took the money she'd been able to save by eating popcorn for lunch and dinner—something like two hundred dollars—and cushioned the soles of her shoes with the bills. She packed her belongings—less in number than at the start—and hit the highway, rolling into Phoenix as the sun set across the valley.

"You came down the I-17," Warren gushed. His subservience around Axia was beginning to grate on all of us and we started to intuit how it was she had come to Garden Lakes.

The sophomores busied themselves around our tables to hear Axia's story, collecting the dirty dishes with an alacrity only curiosity could incite.

Axia told of catching a ride with a carload of Arizona State students on their way to Mexico for spring break. The students treated Axia to so much beef jerky and Miller Lite that she became sick, vomiting out the window to the loud applause from inside the car.

The spring breakers invited Axia to tour the Mexican side of Nogales with them—they were paying a quick visit to someone named Spanky before speeding off to Rocky Point—but she declined, though she accepted their parting gift of a maroon and gold t-shirt depicting a devil with a pitchfork, the school's mascot. She changed into the t-shirt in the bathroom of the McDonalds on the American side where she'd said goodbye to the students, the restaurant overflowing with tourists too afraid to eat across the border.

To quell her stomach, Axia removed a five dollar bill from her shoe and ordered a large Sprite and a small French fries, finding a seat by the window to rest while she ate the skimpy dinner. She would spend the nights wandering the busy streets of Nogales, tempted to cross the border but dubious about what awaited her there. Every experience she'd had—good or bad—was American in nature. The lark of living in Mexico faded as Axia began searching for a way back north, finally grabbing a ride back to Phoenix with an elderly couple who had crossed the border to fill their prescriptions.

"Same as my grandparents," Warren chimed in.

"Woo woo," Roger said, drawing circles in the air with his finger. He pushed back noisily from the table and we heard the front doors close behind him.

We watched Roger pass in front of the dining hall windows while Axia finished her story. "I got as far as Casa Grande and that's where I went into the fields,"—which we took to mean her stint as an olive farmer—"and then I met Warren," she said.

"You've been living with the Indians for *four months?*" Sprocket asked.

Axia shrugged. Hands rustled in his chair as others lobbed questions. Figs sensed confrontation and hoped to deflate it. "Give me a hand in the kitchen?" he asked Hands.

Hands frowned. "What for?" he asked.

"I'll go," Warren volunteered before Hands could answer. Irked, Figs traipsed off to the kitchen with Warren at his heels.

Warren took Figs's arm and pulled him into the hallway.

"I'm on your side," he said.

"What?" Figs asked.

"About Axia staying," Warren said. "She should be allowed to stay. What if you and I go to Mr. Malagon and ask? Maybe we could take her to meet him. I'll bet if he could meet her, he would change his mind."

Figs contemplated Warren's plan. He cared less about Axia than he did about Hands and Smurf's burgeoning importance with Mr.

Malagon. Why should they be the only conduit? Figs understood that if he and Warren took the issue to Mr. Malagon and Mr. Malagon's decision held, he would be at an even greater disadvantage. An alternative plan—one that Figs had been working on overnight—was to reverse his stance on Axia, hoping the recompense for his support for her expulsion would be access to Mr. Malagon. The likelihood that Mr. Malagon would let Axia stay was slight, Figs knew. His inclination was to play the percentages, but if he fought for Axia and won, he would be elevated and not simply part of a triumvirate.

Warren pressed the case for approaching Mr. Malagon on Axia's behalf, but his words were muted by Hands's voice floating into the hallway from the dining hall. "We have to get to work," he said. A bustling followed as we took the cue to stand and collect our dirty dishes. Axia stayed seated, looking passively for Warren, who pushed through us as we filed out of the community center. A shoving match erupted between Smurf and Warren but was quickly broken up by Figs and Hands, each taking their respective fighters to their corners.

"Don't worry," Warren said to Axia. "We're going to Mr. Malagon ourselves."

Hands let loose of Smurf. "What?"

"You heard me," Warren said. A wild, chaotic look possessed him.

"Maybe I don't want to stay," Axia said.

"The choice should at least be yours," Warren said, breaking free of Figs's hold. "If you want to leave, fine. But I'm not going to let them"—he pointed a finger at Hands and Smurf—"throw you out. That's not fair."

Warren walked with purpose out of the dining hall. Hands clambered after him, leaving Figs and Smurf in his wake. Smurf barely spoke—something about Mr. Malagon not being home—when a loud crash rang out. We rushed to the window expecting to find Hands and Warren engaged in hand-to-hand combat, wondering what broke. The view from the window, however, was remarkably serene: Roger standing on the lip of the lakebed, shading his eyes; Assburn and Lindy huddled together on the sidewalk, their conversation interrupted; Hands outside the community center doors, lurking in the shadow of the roof; Warren and Lindy gathered around Sprocket in front of Mr. Malagon's house, their sunlit faces searching Mr. Malagon's bedroom window, smashed out when Roger's kick sent the soccer ball over everyone's head, the faintest trail of the ball's trajectory lingering in the air.

We stood breathless, waiting.

Warren lifted a wedge of decorative concrete from the walkway and heaved it through Mr. Malagon's living room window. Those inside the dining hall couldn't see the window but heard a pop and then a shower of glass. Warren turned to face the others but everyone looked past him, staring in horror at the two broken windows.

....

In testimony before the administration, the amount of time that lapsed between the shattering of Mr. Malagon's windows and the confirmation that Mr. Malagon was not in the house varied widely. Some claimed to know right away, which was the truth for all of us, while others would say they were shocked to learn later that Mr. Malagon was not laid up in bed as had been advertised but had abandoned us. The discrepancy of who knew it and when was due to our reaction to the broken windows, a reaction the administration found incredulous, calling Fellows in individually to substantiate what they deemed an outlandish lie: that everyone reported for work at 1959 Regis Street, honoring the teams we'd drawn up as Warren had reappeared, working with urgency to compensate for the three days of construction that had been missed owing to the search for Warren.

Our focus was acute, driven by the fear of what we suspected about Mr. Malagon, that he had forsaken us for some unexplained reason. We pored over our job journals, comparing notes. Inside corners called out to us to be taped off; we affixed J-trims to the shower stalls and window jambs; outside corners were fitted with bullnose corner beads. We worked with an expertise that had, for any number of reasons, previously eluded us. We worked through lunch. We worked through class time. We worked through Sports.

Some of us lagged behind the rest, joining their teams late; and of course Smurf did not reunite with his team at all, though we did not realize he had left Garden Lakes—this time of his own volition— until dinner, when it was the marquee gossip. Intelligence about the events leading up to Smurf's departure, as well as the whereabouts of those who reached the job site late was not clear to us until the administration made its official report. We knew generally about Figs and Hands and Assburn's tardiness; their lateness was noted by Roger, who commented when the three walked onto the job without offering an excuse or even a flippant response, reporting to Sprocket for their equipment and jumping in.

According to the account put out by the administration, the reason for Figs and Hands and Assburn's tardiness involved two distinct and simultaneous events, both put into play as the rest of us set upon 1959 Regis Street.

First, Smurf demanded to use Assburn's mobile phone. Assburn, stricken with the realization that Mr. Malagon had deserted Garden Lakes, agreed. Smurf must've believed he could salvage the situation with one phone call to Randolph, though looking back this plan seems impossibly naïve. Smurf's testimony after the fact left open for interpretation why he'd wanted Assburn's mobile phone, largely due to the evidence that Assburn's phone had met the same fate as Mr. Hancock's (though it was a sure bet that Mr. Hancock hadn't squandered valuable battery calling 900 numbers as Assburn had) and Smurf himself said he wasn't sure who he was going to call— Randolph or Katie Sullivan. Smurf's failure to contact Randolph after leaving Garden Lakes threw a spotlight of suspicion on him and the administration was never completely convinced that Smurf wasn't working in harmony with Mr. Malagon, or covering for him in some way.

Mr. Malagon's own testimony on the matter was sealed, forever unknown.

A few houses down, Figs followed Hands into their residence. "Did you *ever* see him?" he asked as Hands ascended the stairs.

Hands pivoted on the bottom step. He eyed Figs coldly, assessing whether Figs was reaching out or digging his finger into the wound. Figs began pacing the living room, signaling the latter. "It was all Smurf," Hands said in a rush of inspiration. "He called me up to Mr. Malagon's room. I wanted to tell everyone, but Smurf thought we'd all hang him. So I went along with it."

"I don't get what the plan was," Figs said, bouncing between the living room and the kitchen. "What was Smurf up to?"

Hands shrugged. "He never said."

Figs stopped pacing. "Where *is* Smurf?"

Figs became the first of us to know that Smurf had become the fourth deserter after Quinn and Mr. Hancock and Mr. Malagon, climbing into his car, which he'd kept hidden outside the main gates. Figs brought his hand to his mouth as Hands related Smurf's getaway.

"What will you say?" Figs asked pointedly.

Hands stepped down and took a seat on the loveseat. He knew it would be his word against Smurf's and, even though Smurf was not present to give his side, his silence was as good as him disputing Hands's story, the room for doubt too great to be overcome by repeating that it was all Smurf's idea. Hands knew he needed an ally. He wondered if he could recruit someone cold. Roger? Not likely. Assburn? Possibly. He knew from Smurf that Assburn's famous cry of innocence over the theft of Senator Quinn's pen was phony, but Assburn had probably disposed of the pen for good by now and leaning on Assburn might have negative results. He needed someone who was weak-minded or, at the very least, weak-willed, someone who could be promised something in return for verifying Hands's version of events. He considered Sprocket, but could not think of anything he could promise Sprocket for an alibi.

Hands ran through the possibilities. Warren was the best candidate—he possessed an indefinable credibility that others respected—but Warren was too distracted by Axia to be of any use, witnessed by the fact that Warren had stayed behind to help Axia, who had begun cleaning the kitchen and dining hall as the rest of us rushed out to the sound of breaking glass.

Lindy had a workableness to him, but Lindy wouldn't be as strong an ally as Figs, a fact Hands had known from the start.

"I'll tell them that it was all Smurf," Hands said defiantly.

Figs gave a look of surprise, knowing what Hands had figured out for himself, that he needed Figs. "No one will believe you."

"Everyone believed *you* when you lied about Warren and the delivery driver," Hands said matter-of-factly, regretting the barb immediately.

Figs winced. Hands's alliance with Smurf still smarted and while Figs wanted to help Hands, wanted to realign Hands's loyalties, he wasn't going to offer. Hands would have to ask.

Figs would suffer through another round of haranguing about Warren before Hands would ask. Figs accepted, seizing the moment to secure Axia's place at Garden Lakes.

"You're crazy," Hands said. "Can you imagine what will happen if the school finds out, either now—if Smurf goes and tells them— or at Open House when all of our parents show up?"

"She'll leave the day before Open House," Figs submitted, an olive branch he'd worked out in advance, knowing Hands would raise this particular objection and further knowing the objection was legitimate. The school couldn't know about Axia; that would be Rule Number One.

Hands continued to object, though his position was considerably weakened. Finally he acquiesced. "I'm not responsible, though," Hands said. "If something happens it'll be all you."

"Fine," Figs said, "but if I'm going to be a hundred percent behind your story, you have to be a hundred percent behind Axia staying. That's the deal."

"Yeah, okay," Hands said.

By the time they joined us for construction, they'd worked out all of the details, though we heard the story for the first time that night at dinner, Smurf's tire tracks still fresh in the dirt along the shoulder outside the gates. We heard about how Smurf had roped Hands in, how Hands had gotten all of his information secondhand, through Smurf. We ate in shock; we'd never known Smurf to pull something so devious. We marveled at his duplicity, impressed by it, but our admiration slowly wore away as we realized the gravity of our new situation.

We had only to look to Figs and Hands for guidance, though. As the sophomores cleared the tables, they made their pitch to keep Garden Lakes afloat until Open House, interspersing their speech with "It's a good opportunity" and "What better way to test ourselves?"

It was agreed that, in order to successfully argue for full credit for our fellowships, the schedule would remain intact, as would all of the rules and regulations—including the reinstatement of curfew. We frittered away an hour on a scheme put forward by Hands, who wanted to break us up into pods, each pod rotating duties every day. "That would work," Figs said, "but what if the administration declared us ineligible because we didn't all have a hand in construction?" (The sophomores would quickly see that the emphasis of the coming days would be on the Fellowship; anything not pertaining to kitchen work or laundry would become background noise.) "We've got nineteen days until Open House. We're pretty much on schedule at 1959. We're a bit behind in our class work"—Figs and Hands had located the two paper case boxes in Mr. Malagon's closet filled with the handouts and tests Mr. Malagon used for class—"but it's nothing we can't catch up."

We didn't see any reason why we couldn't do it. The idea of going it alone appealed to us and while we bore no confidence in our abilities, we were driven mainly by our collective desire to prove that it could be done. We felt sure we would employ any means necessary to accomplish the goal and wouldn't they be surprised? We imagined our parents' reaction when they discovered what we'd done, and the reactions of droves of others' parents when they heard. Our determination would be fabled, one for the annals of Garden Lakes, one that would be discussed year after year. And long after, no matter where we were in the world, our immortality would be resurrected every year as spring brought the first whisper of Garden Lakes—who would be nominated, who would be chosen—and if we strained our imagination we just might hear the awed conversations beginning with "Did you hear about the Fellows from the Class of '88?..."

"We all have to agree," Figs said, calling for a vote. Figs and Hands raised their hands. Sprocket raised his hand as fast; he hoped to become the class proctor and planned to lobby Figs and Hands (and anyone else) for the commission. Roger flashed his palm and then let his hand fall back down on his knee. Lindy voted yes, too.

Warren's hand flew up in the company of hands thrown up by the sophomores, who had straggled in from the kitchen. His vote wasn't just for continuation, but also for allowing Axia to stay, a fact that Figs had tipped him off to, Figs guaranteeing Axia could stay as long as Warren would help counter any arguments against Figs and Hands's proposal to maintain the status quo. The zip in Warren's vote was fuelled by his happiness at not having to help Figs twist arms.

"We've got this, boys," Hands said, sealing the pact.

The administration found the incongruous testimony about Axia unbelievable. Some reported that we believed Axia would be asked to leave, that a vote for continuation was a vote for Axia's expulsion. Others thought Axia was to watch over the sophomores and their kitchen duty. What the testimony didn't reveal was our secret longing to have her around, not only because she was a girl, but because we wanted someone to witness our acts of bravery. We wanted someone to cheer us on in success or buoy us after a day of defeat. We liked the idea that there was someone other than us, someone who, for no reason, we felt accountable to. And while we would not have been able to express this feeling in those terms, the Axia issue was dropped once we raised our hands endorsing continuation, and Axia blended into the background.

We were able to abide by the schedule for exactly ten days.

....

We welcomed the structure of the daily schedule back into our lives. Conformity to the schedule brought the sense that we were steadily chipping away stone to uncover sculpture.

Eagerness woke us that first Saturday. Axia joined the sophomores in the kitchen and proved as adept as Mr. Hancock, her nearness motivation enough for the sophomores, who toiled with renewed purpose. She also served as another pair of eyes for Sports, situating herself on the ever-shifting sand of the island in the lakebed to aid Sprocket in close calls. We offered to substitute her in during play, but she demurred. We did what we could to encourage her to join a team, but she would only let us set up goal shots for her before and after games, Hands batting down every ball she kicked.

We did make one amendment to the schedule, one we knew we could justify: rather than breaking the sophomores and Fellows up into pods for tutoring, we congregated in the dining hall, the sophs reading aloud George Washington's Farewell Address, Justice Taney's opinion in *Dred Scott v. Sanford*, *The Emancipation Proclamation*, *The Gettysburg Address*, Samuel Gompers's *Letter on Labor In Industrial Society*, etc., conversation periodically veering wide of the subject at hand, devolving into joke telling or a bull session about what Mr. Hancock intended by including a particular text in *American Democracy*. Our ability to digest and pontificate on the texts sharpened in Axia's presence, her sitting at one of the back tables where she listened quietly.

Construction continued apace. We made strides in beading and moved into the taping phase, careful to adhere to the taping sequence Mr. Baker, the future kidnapping victim, laid out for us: fasteners, tapered-edge seams, butted seams, inside corners, outside corners—the precise order being important to avoid disrupting a flat seam when working the corners. We each slid a bucket of joint compound along as we worked, the rhythmic harrumph of pails scraping above and below marking the hours.

The next day, an impromptu tour sprang up, Hands showing off our progress to Axia, who had asked him about it during lunch. Hands detailed our work, allowing her to labor under the misimpression that we had erected the frame and poured the foundation, a falsehood none of us worked too hard to correct.

Hands's attitude toward Axia improved once we accepted as true his innocence in the matter of Mr. Malagon and Smurf so that four or five days in, Axia was taking her meals at Figs and Hands's table. Hands even developed an avidity for astronomy once Axia coaxed Lindy into showing her the sky from the community center roof. We all became junior astronomers, electing to spend free time night after night huddled around Lindy and Axia, amazed by what amazed them.

Axia sat in on our poker games, too, bluffing with an earnestness that fooled us every time. Had we been playing for real money and not poker chips, she would've bankrupted us all.

That Friday, the smoky fragrance of barbeque drifted through our windows as we changed out of our filthy work clothes for dinner. The source of the smell was not the kitchen but a barbeque pit Axia and the sophomores had dug. Axia and the sophs had moved fast to carve a pit into the lakebed, the idea sparked by an unopened bag of charcoal briquettes in the pantry. We were too enchanted to tell her that the briquettes were for the Open House; that Mr. Hancock would not be present to strike up the celebratory barbeque lessened our guilt. So, too, did the chicken braised with a homemade bbq sauce that lured you in with the sweet taste of honey only to stab you with the heat of jalapeno. "My own recipe," Axia said. We tried to convey its tastiness but our eyes watered and our lips burned if we stopped eating, so we grunted our approval.

"What was your high school like?" Figs asked, chomping on a plump chicken leg.

"It was nothing special," Axia said. "Not like where you guys go." She described her teachers, some good, some bad. "I didn't hate it or anything," she said.

A game of Truth or Dare started up as the coals died out. Roger asked Warren *truth or dare?*, hoping Warren would answer *dare* so Roger would dare him to kiss Axia, but Warren didn't oblige. Roger thought for a minute and then asked, "What's the *real* reason you disappeared?"

Warren laughed. "I already told you."

"The *truth*," Roger reminded him.

A refrain of "Yeah" went around the barbecue pit.

Warren laid his hand across his heart. "I swear I told the truth," he said, loving the attention.

"Tell them what you told me," Axia said.

Warren blushed. "Well, I—"

"Out with it, weasel," Roger said. Warren could take a little ribbing and it felt good to let out a good-natured laugh at his expense.

"Answer me this," Hands said to Axia. "Did he dance naked with the Indians?"

Axia spit up a mouthful of soda, the spray dousing the briquettes, a wisp of smoke rising on contact.

"I just said that I didn't care if I didn't go back," Warren said.

We hoped Warren's admission would be something hysterical, something light-hearted to stoke our good time, but instead what he said sobered us and we stared ruefully into the desert night.

Lindy broke the silence. "Why not?"

"I don't know," Warren said. "I wasn't out there long, but I liked the simple lifestyle. There weren't so many…questions. It seemed to me"—he looked at Axia for reassurance—"that that other life is about labor and not about always trying to figure things out. That's all."

"True, true," Axia said. She nodded herself into a reverie and some of us looked away embarrassedly, as if we were spying on her getting dressed.

"Don't sweat it," Hands said, throwing an empty soda can at Warren. "You'll never figure anything out anyway."

We loved Hands for bringing us back around. In turn, our guffaws brought Axia back and we continued with the game, hoping one of us would choose *dare* until it became another game not to, each of us not wanting to grant another the privilege. Instead, the night was saturated with earnestly-rendered truths and half-truths (as well as some outright lies), each of us trying to impress Axia by telling a tale on ourselves, gauging the success of our stories by how hard she laughed, or by how well we elicited her sympathies.

A smaller game was being played on the outskirts of the circle. Figs was anticipating his turn, glancing furtively at Hands, who sensed something was up. He doubted Figs had the nerve to ask him the truth about Mr. Malagon as a part of the game, but as the right to ask someone *truth or dare?* worked its way back to Figs, Hands announced that he was turning in for the night. Lindy followed, the next casualty in what was a slow drift of tired souls, Figs and Warren trying to outlast each other in a bid to be alone with Axia.

....

The sight of Mr. Baker's truck drawing near inspired a current of panic through 1959 Regis Street; we weren't unprepared for Mr. Baker's inspection—we'd applied the skim coat of compound the day before—but we had not thought through what we would say to Mr. Baker's inevitable questions about Mr. Malagon.

Without flinching, Figs shifted his paper mask down around his chin and met Mr. Baker's truck, hailing him like a long lost relative.

"Howdee," Mr. Baker said, waving back. "How's she lookin'?"

"I think you'll be pleased," Figs said, a master at making someone feel regal. "We've followed your instructions exactly."

Mr. Baker shaded his eyes, looking for Mr. Malagon.

"Oh," Figs said. "Mr. Malagon had to run out for some supplies. He said if he missed you that we should pay extra attention to your instructions for Phase Three."

"What did you run out of?" Mr. Baker asked.

Figs gave a hearty laugh. "Kitchen supplies." He glanced back at the community center as if to prove his point, Mr. Baker looking over his shoulder too. "And toilet supplies."

"Okay," Mr. Baker said. "Let's have a look."

A rare hush fell over the house as Mr. Baker worked his way from room to room, Figs following close behind. After pointing out several crowned seams—the result of too much compound spread over a taped section—that would need sanding, as well as several cracked seams running like lightning down the wall ("Compound dried too fast," Mr. Baker said.) and a cracked corner bead, Mr. Baker lectured us in the art of sanding, texturing, and painting—the finishing touches we would apply before the Open House.

"First," Mr. Baker said, wiping his brow, "is that you must wear paper masks when sanding. I want you to write that down in capital letters." He paused while we took down the warning. "Do you have the telescopic poles for raising a plastic wall?"

Mr. Baker looked to Sprocket for the answer but before Sprocket could reveal that Hands and Roger had commandeered the poles to use in a spontaneous volleyball game the night before, a forceful spike of the soccer ball by Roger buckling one of the poles, Hands said, "Yeah, I saw them in the back of the supply shed."

Sprocket nodded idiotically to corroborate the misinformation.

"Good," Mr. Baker said. "Just make sure the ends of the poles are buried in plastic before you wedge them into the floor and ceiling. Nothing like having a plastic wall come loose and wrap around you while you're working." Mr. Baker laughed as if it had happened to him more than once.

While the previous class had the luxury of electric sanders, an accident resulted in their removal (and the removal of a finger, according to legend), replaced by manual pole sanders. Mr. Baker ran through the different sandpaper grits we'd need—"120 grit for coarse work; 150 for finer work"—showing us how to move our hand along the wall in front of a hand sander to scout out areas needing sanding.

Mr. Baker cautioned us against sanding the face of the drywall and about the dangers of oversanding. "If you oversand, you'll have to reapply the third coat of compound, and another skim coat," he said. We took this advice seriously, promising to defeat any temptation to erase a scratch or dent in the taping completely. "Just enough so it won't show through the texturing and the paint," Mr. Baker said.

Next we listened to the procedure for what sounded like the best part of the job, the knockdown roller finish we'd have to apply to the walls and ceilings before painting the whole shebang. "Most textures are applied with a hopper and an air compressor," Mr. Baker said, "but there are a couple of ways to texture a wall by hand and one is a knockdown roller finish. Its name gives you a clue as to how it's applied. First you roll on a light coat of joint compound with a paint roller, then you take a trowel and follow by applying even pressure"—Mr. Baker pressed the flat of his hand against the wall at an angle and dragged it down the wall—"to knock down the peaks created by the roller. Very simple. The key is not to press too hard, or load the wall up with compound." He looked at his watch and then out the paneless window at the community center. "How long do you figure 'til he gets back?" he asked.

"Not sure," Figs said, stepping up.

"What about the other one?" Mr. Baker asked. "What's his name? Hancock?"

Figs froze. He hadn't accounted for Mr. Hancock's absence as Mr. Baker had hardly said more than hello to him. "He's…sick," Figs said lamely. "He's lying down."

Hands instinctively supported what Figs had said. "Stomach virus," Hands said.

Mr. Baker grimaced. "I thought this project required adult supervision," he said.

"Mr. Malagon really hasn't been gone that long," Figs said.

Mr. Baker looked at his watch again. "I've been here for close to an hour," he said. "Maybe an hour and a half."

"I think I saw him pull around behind the community center," Figs said.

We craned our necks to look but all we saw was Adam Kerr flinging a bucket of dirty mop water out the back door.

"I'm not sure if I need to come back before the Open House," Mr. Baker said. "I need to find out so I can schedule it before—. When is the Open House?"

"The twenty-ninth," Hands said.

"What is that? A Thursday?" Mr. Baker asked.

We guessed that it was.

"Does Mr. Malagon have your phone number?" Figs asked. It took all his will to contain his desperation. "He has a mobile phone. He can call you with the information when he gets back. I'll make sure."

"Yeah, I'll remind him," Hands said.

"Would Mr. Hancock know?" Mr. Baker asked. "I'd like to clear it up before I go."

"He's awfully sick," Figs said, "but, c'mon, I'll take you to him. We'll ask."

None of us dared to breathe, uncertain of what Figs was up to.

"I'll go with," Hands said. "I want to ask him something, too."

The three started out for Mr. Hancock's residence, making it as far as Mr. Baker's truck before a shrieking pierced the air. Mr. Baker raised his sunglasses and squinted at the display on his pager. "Shit," he said, forgetting Figs and Hands for a moment. We watched from the house as Mr. Baker made Figs copy down the phone number decaled across the passenger side door of Mr. Baker's truck, Figs's promise to have Mr. Malagon or Mr. Hancock call him fading as Mr. Baker started the engine.

"Tell you what," Figs yelled. "If they don't call, that means all's well."

It was hard to tell if Mr. Baker was nodding in agreement or if he was shaking his head, insisting someone call. Figs and Hands deliberated on the subtleties of Mr. Baker's head movement all through the dinner hour. Figs was convinced it was fine, that Mr. Baker was surely overwhelmed with more important responsibilities. "So what if he does show up a few days before the Open House?" Figs asked. "By then, it'll be over. We'll be done."

Mr. Baker showing up before Open House was not what worried Hands. "What if he calls Randolph when Mr. Malagon doesn't call, to find out if he is supposed to do an inspection before the Open House?"

Figs suggested they wait a few days and then call themselves, telling Mr. Baker that Mr. Malagon asked them to call, a ruse for our benefit, Figs and Hands not letting on that Mr. Hancock's mobile phone was inoperable. "Or we could call after hours and leave a message," Figs said. Figs did his best to satisfy Hands that they had options, and time, but Hands knew Mr. Baker could single-handedly ruin their chances of completing the fellowship. The idea of having wasted the summer *and* not getting credit for the fellowship drove Hands's fears. He remained unconvinced by Figs's arguments and sought him out during free time to try to convince him otherwise. He checked in on Lindy, who was hosting the nightly sky watching party on the roof of the community center, but Figs was not among the crowd. He stuck his head in on a poker game between me and Assburn and Sprocket, who asked him if he wanted to sit in. We told him that we hadn't seen Figs since dinner. Hands wandered Regis Street to its end, thinking Figs might have gone back to the construction site, though the site was too dark at night to see.

A light in Axia's living room drew Hands's attention. He kicked through a mound of gravel that had been built on the sidewalk by the wind, scattering the pebbles. As he raised his hand to knock on the door, he leaned over and peered through the window. His fist dropped when he saw Figs and Axia on the couch, Axia practically sitting in Figs's lap. Figs's hand bounced on Axia's knee as he spoke and she laughed as Figs finished whatever it was he was saying.

Heat burned across Hands's forehead. He stomped back down the walkway, blinded, a portrait of Axia sitting on Figs's lap projected everywhere he looked. He was on the precipice of homicide when he pulled me out of the poker game, though I put up a small fight—"The best hand I've had all night"—but the bloodthirsty look in Hands's eyes communicated that he was ready to yank me away from the table and so I folded the four aces and king and followed Hands outside. His litany of grievances against Figs had a violent timbre, Hands straining his voice as we strolled along Garden Lakes Parkway.

"Loyalty is the only thing one friend can offer another," he said. "Disloyalty should be treated accordingly."

He'd regained his breathing, his hoarse voice scarcely above a rasp. Our legs ached; we'd walked miles around the lakebed. "Keep it quiet until the morning," was my parting advice. Hands didn't say anything that night, or in the morning, either, instead moving out of his room and into the house next door, Mr. Malagon's old residence.

The sound of hammering woke us, Hands deafened by the pounding as he repaired the door frame of his new house, not hearing our calls as we passed by on our way to breakfast.

We did not curse the sun as a heat wave gripped Garden Lakes, though the heat persisted well after midnight, dropping only a few degrees as the moon waned. The unbearable stifle distracted us from the truth that Hands was not merely repairing the damage done to Mr. Malagon's residence—a notion we commended as prudent, seeing how our parents would be arriving in a week or so and would ask questions—but had moved his belongings into the house, rehanging one of the plywood sheets we'd nailed over the broken windows that had slid to the ground.

There were those of us who guessed at Hands's relocation, but confirmation came only when Hands, who would one day lead his family's sixth generation brewery to ruin by distrusting his chief financial officer, whom he considered a rival for his wife's affections, engaging in endless, meritless litigation against the CFO that ended with a huge judgment against the brewery, circulated a private invitation to a select few for a housewarming of sorts later that night—a Tuesday—after dinner. The invitations were proffered by an unlikely source—Hands had chosen Kerr and Laird to discreetly deliver the announcement—and Roger threatened to punch Laird during breakfast when Laird tried to whisper in his ear. Those of us who had been invited wondered who else had been so privileged. The only certainty was that Figs would not be in attendance, a certainty unwittingly aided by Reedy, who happened upon Figs in his search for someone to take a look at the air conditioner attached to his residence, which had apparently frozen and shut down.

Figs fetched a hammer and a flathead screwdriver from the supply shed and descended on the air conditioner like a paramedic, Reedy right on his heels. Figs's quick reaction was an extension of the mode he'd been in all day, a manner triggered by his lust to impress Axia. Not even Hands's ditching out morning construction could shake Figs's focus. If he had to carry the team himself, he would. And Axia would have a front row seat to his heroics.

The full roster convened in Hands's living room: Roger, Lindy, Sprocket, Assburn, and me. Kerr and Laird hovered near Hands, not realizing that their usefulness had expired.

Hands got right to it. "We've got a problem," he said. "We've all sacrificed our summer to be here and now we have a situation that puts that sacrifice in jeopardy." We knew what Hands was referring to. Hands's tirade continued without mentioning Axia specifically, couching his argument in terms of her residency being a corruption of the rules. "Like Mr. Malagon said, we must have cohesion. And part of being cohesive is following the rules, regardless of what the rules are. If the rules said it was okay to have visitors, we wouldn't have to meet like this."

"It's not right to just turn her out," Laird said, mistakenly presuming he was an equal member of the committee.

Hands continued as if Laird had not spoken. "I'm only inter-ested in what we're all interested in," he said. "I want our parents to roll in here next week, see that we've accomplished what we set out to accomplish, and then go home and enjoy what's left of summer. Is there anyone who disagrees with that idea?"

We did not disagree with Hands's thesis, though the idea seemed to us a reiteration of the case he'd been making since Axia had arrived.

Later testimony would swear that no stratagems were designed that night, no plan of action called upon, a truth that was subverted by the fact that by breakfast the next morning, Garden Lakes was swirling with innuendo that Figs and Axia were a couple and that

Figs was granting Axia haven for wholly personal reasons. Certain of us would not repeat the rumor, but others actively promoted it, Roger and Hands the loudest voices in the choir. Figs's absence from breakfast lent credibility to the accusation.

The heat forced us to retreat to our residences halfway through the morning construction, Roger and Hands calling off work in Figs and Warren's absence. We dropped our sanding equipment where we stood, assuming we would begin again after dinner, racing against the gloaming to finish, not knowing we wouldn't return to our positions until that Friday.

Figs, who would one day cover up an embezzlement at his firm, shifting the blame to an innocent department head at his father-in-law's insistence, resulting in the department head's firing, passed time at Axia's. He'd forgotten about his promise to call Mr. Baker and did not worry about the consequences, firmly believing one of two things: that by not calling, Mr. Baker would have excuse enough to dodge any reprimand or that Mr. Baker's busy schedule would overtake his memory about the final inspection. A third principle guided Figs's confidence: a final inspection the day before Open House would serve only to point up the mistakes—it would be too late to repair any flaws.

Instead, Figs wiled his time in conversation with Axia about how best she could serve the community. He did not want to presuppose that Axia would be content with the kitchen and laundry duties— his parents interchanged these responsibilities in his own house and he knew that it was insensitive to consider kitchen work womanly— and ran down the gamut of our chores so Axia could pick and choose. It became evident, though, that Axia was not interested in helping with the construction ("I don't mind doing errands, but I'm not good with tools") or with the class work ("I wasn't a good student").

"I'm fine in the kitchen," she said.

Figs knew that Axia's contributions would be vital to the un-precedented credit they would receive at Open House. He delighted in the idea of Principal Breen and Father Matthews learning about

Axia, and how Axia pitched in under his leadership. Figs was composing a speech about assimilation in his head, in case the administration tried to level a case against Axia.

Having missed breakfast, Figs was the first to arrive for lunch. The rest of us drifted in whether we were hungry or not, desperate to escape our caged existence. The air in the community center was not as cold as that in our residences and the heat killed our appetite. We sat in front of plates of uneaten sandwiches, opting for liquid lunches, lining up at the soda machine to refill our glasses, which we stocked with ice.

Hands sat at one of the tables positioned under an air conditioning vent, most of the roster from the night before filling the remaining seats. He appeared relaxed, despite the heat. Kerr and Laird were nearby, taking turns holding their hand against the window, one counting until the other drew his hand back, shaking it as if it were on fire.

The whispers that Figs was trying to sabotage our fellowship had reached him via Reedy, who had been recruited by Roger. Reedy promised to follow Roger's instruction to spread the word that Axia was Figs's girlfriend, but he was so curious about the information that he had to confirm it with Figs.

Figs approached Hands's table.

"Can I talk to you for a minute?" he asked.

"Sure," Hands said.

Figs searched the faces at the table. "Privately?"

Hands did not move to get up. "You can say it to me here," he said.

"You sure?" Figs asked. He hid his trembling hands in his pockets.

"I don't see why not."

Figs rocked forward as Sprocket wheeled by behind him. "What is this about Axia being my girlfriend?"

Roger, who would one day be court martialed for taking a platoon of men in Iraq AWOL and killing one of them after the soldier had been wounded by enemy fire, begging him for a mercy killing, couldn't control his snickering.

"Is she?" Hands asked. "I didn't know. Congratulations."

As Figs began to refute the claim, Axia appeared, rubbing the sleep from her eyes.

"Uh oh," Roger said. "The missus."

A sharp laugh went around the table. Figs would later wish that he had called Axia over to dispute the gossip, though what he wouldn't admit to anyone was that he secretly liked the idea and couldn't bear to hear the contrary, especially in front of witnesses.

"It's a lie," Figs said quietly, hoping Axia would not hear.

"The only lie I'm aware of is yours about the grocery truck guys finding Warren," Hands said coolly.

Warren looked up from his ham sandwich at the mention of his name. He grabbed his lunch and corralled Axia, who was looking for a seat under the air conditioning. "Help me in the kitchen," Warren said, leading Axia out of the room.

"Better watch out," Hands said. "Warren's after your girl."

Some of us laughed as Figs turned away. Cantu darted out of the kitchen carrying a jar of pickles and Figs called out to him.

"Yeah?" Cantu set the pickles down cautiously.

"Come over here," Figs said.

As Cantu waded through the room, Figs addressed the crowd. "Many of you no doubt heard the story I made up about Warren's rescue," he said. "I want to apologize to everyone for making that up. Most of you know me well enough to appreciate that I try to do the right thing. Which is what made me come up with that story. I wanted to…" Figs struggled for the words to explain what he'd hoped to accomplish with the lie without exposing the sophomores to ridicule by divulging their fear or their thoughts of desertion. "I wanted to ease everyone's minds." Figs looked down at Hands. "The same reason I went along with the story about seeing Mr. Malagon that first morning," he continued. "I knew it was wrong to lie, but I was persuaded that it would put everyone at ease. So I went along with it."

"*You're* the one who made that story up," Hands scoffed. "Just another lie."

Figs motioned at Cantu, who had been leaning against the wall. "I think Cantu might have something to say about that."

Hands tensed up, realizing that Cantu would corroborate what Figs had said. He regretted not covering this with Cantu, maybe getting Roger to lean on Cantu if he refused. Hands was about to confess that he'd had a hand in the lie about Mr. Malagon when our attention was diverted out the window. We stood as a coyote rambled onto Garden Lakes Parkway, its furry head hung low, tongue wagging. Kerr and Laird stepped back from the window and the coyote registered their movement, raising its head. Its ear twitched uncontrollably and the coyote took a few steps toward the community center and then collapsed, its fur ruffling like grass as an arid desert breath swept over it.

....

Bagging the coyote and hauling it out to the front gates for trash collection was the day's only event, a task Roger handled eagerly. Lunch had left a pall in the air and we languished in our rooms, speculating about if we would finish the work on 1959 Regis Street or not, or if we would receive credit for the fellowship once Randolph realized that Mr. Hancock and Mr. Malagon had left us stranded. The circumstances were so extraordinary we had no way of knowing.

Figs debated disclosing to Axia the rumor circulating about them. It wouldn't be long before she heard it—if she hadn't already—but Figs couldn't decide if it was better for her to hear it as he did, by accident, or if Figs should be the one who would give it voice. He worried that she would believe he was the origin of the rumor, but he also did not want to report the lie only to witness her derision at its ridiculousness. The dilemma tired him and it was when he mounted the stairs to his bedroom that he noticed Hands's empty room, the bed stripped bare, the dresser drawers hanging open like tongues stuck out in scorn.

Figs was awakened later by a knock on his bedroom door by Cantu and Reedy, their backs soaked with sweat. He wondered how long he'd been out. "The air conditioner quit again," they said. With one foot still in slumber, Figs stood on the mattress in Hands's room and shut the air vent, the slats giving a high-pitched whistle. Figs closed the door and followed Cantu and Reedy to their residence.

All of the houses along Loyola Street were shut tight except for Reedy and Cantu's. "We had to open the windows to get a breeze going," Cantu said.

The sun had begun its descent, though the temperature held. Figs stood over the air conditioner without seeing it, wondering what time it was and which part of the schedule was being violated. He hadn't really fixed the air conditioner the time before, he knew, the unit whirring to life when Figs banged it with a hammer. He beat his fist against the metal siding again but this time the air conditioner did not cooperate.

"It's dead," he told Reedy, following Reedy inside where Cantu, Kerr, and Laird lounged shirtless on the couch. "You guys will have to move into Mr. Hancock's place."

The idea bristled the sophs. "No way, man," Reedy said. "If he comes back and finds us living there, he'll freak out."

Figs hadn't considered the idea that Mr. Hancock would return. He wondered when he'd ruled it out as a possibility. That Mr. Hancock would reappear after being gone for weeks was incomprehensible, but not impossible. What *if* others believed Mr. Hancock would return? Would it be enough to keep focus for one more week, until Open House? Figs filed the idea away.

The sophomores continued to refuse to move into Mr. Hancock's residence so Figs told them to bunk in his and Hands's old rooms. "I'll take Mr. Hancock's place," Figs said.

"What will we do about beds?" Cantu asked.

"Can they be moved?" Figs asked.

A short investigation revealed the beds to be too awkward to move down the hall, around the corner, and down the stairs. "What about just bringing your mattresses?" Figs asked.

"Sleep on the *floor*?" Reedy asked.

"Wouldn't it be easier if we moved into Quinn's old place?" Kerr asked.

"Well," Figs said. It wasn't clear if the sophs were suggesting that they should move in *with* Axia, or if Axia should be displaced so they could take possession. He suppressed the surge of jealousy he felt at the idea of the sophomores bunking with Axia. "I'll be right back," he said.

Figs found Axia lounging on the couch in the front room of her residence, flipping through one of his old handouts, the lesson about FDR, using the handout as a fan to whisk away the warm air. "I came by earlier, but you were sleeping," she said. "Hardly anyone came to dinner."

"Was Hands there?" Figs asked, wishing he hadn't.

Axia shook her head.

"How many were there?"

Axia let the handout slip to the floor. She sat up and yawned. "Ten or twenty that I saw," she said. "I sat with Phillip."

"Phillip?"

"The kid in the wheelchair."

Figs convinced himself that Sprocket would not be a host for the gossip infecting Garden Lakes and turned his attention to the matter at hand.

"Listen," Figs said. "I was thinking. There's an empty house down the street that you might be more comfortable in. It used to be a model home and it's a lot…nicer."

"This is good enough," Axia said. "That stuff doesn't matter to me. I'm used to living in a tent, remember?"

"I just thought you'd like it better down the street," Figs said, scrambling. "There's a tub."

"You don't say," Axia said, reclining.

"Yeah," Figs said, sensing he had her on the hook. "The furniture is nicer, too. And the bed is a king, I think."

"Nice furniture. King-sized bed. A tub," Axia said, ticking off the amenities on her fingers. "Sounds like a hotel suite."

"There's other nice things, too," Figs said, though he couldn't remember what.

"I don't know," Axia said coyly. "I'm settled in here."

The last of the sunlight faded and Figs shut the blinds on the living room window, catching a glimpse of Lindy, who was headed out to the lakebed, his telescope tucked under his arm. He held his hand up to the air conditioning vent. "It doesn't feel very cold," he said.

"I just turned it on," Axia answered.

"You should leave it running," Figs said. He went to the thermostat and turned the dial down to seventy. "It'll take a couple of hours before it's cool in here."

Axia shrugged.

"You know," Figs said, struck by inspiration, "the air conditioning has been kept low in the house down the street. You'll sleep better over there."

"Okay, okay," Axia said, exasperated. "I give. Let me get my stuff."

Figs clapped his hands together. "Great. I know you'll like it more. It's the house on the other side of the community center, the first one on Loyola Street. I'll meet you over there in a few."

Figs skipped out of Axia's house, pepped at being able to solve yet another problem. As he broached the walkway leading to the soph's house, ready for the accolades due him for arranging their release from the torrid prison, he heard Reedy yelp. Figs sprinted the final distance, throwing open the front door. Had he been in the company of others, the scene would've been one of hilarity: Cantu poised above Reedy's partially shaved head with an electric razor, a bald Laird jumping around in the background while Kerr looked on. Reedy touched the nick above his ear. "It's nothing," Cantu assured him, continuing. The living room was covered in their hair.

"What's this?" Figs asked, remaining calm. Calmness was the means to managing any situation, he knew.

"It's too hot for hair," Reedy said, keeping his head down.

"Want us to do yours?" Laird asked.

"Whose razor is that?" Figs knew none of the sophomores were old enough to shave.

"Found it at Mr. Hancock's," Laird said.

Figs wondered about this looting, afraid to ask.

"Axia is moving out of Quinn's," Figs said. "You can move in whenever you want."

"She moving in with you?" Cantu asked. He razed the last stripe of hair from Reedy's head.

Figs shook his head. "Make sure you sweep up when you're done. And return the razor. Mr. Hancock's stuff should stay in his house." He shut the door on Laird's question—"Why?"—and turned to find Axia on the sidewalk in front of Mr. Hancock's residence.

"This one?" she asked, pointing.

Figs helped Axia settle in. Mr. Hancock had left his residence impeccably clean; only the mess of ungraded quizzes on the kitchen table (some blown to the floor by the free roaming air conditioning) and a pair of bedroom slippers in the upstairs bathroom suggested Mr. Hancock's absence was accidental. Figs again contemplated whether or not Mr. Hancock would materialize and while he ultimately believed otherwise, he vowed to work on the explanation as to why Axia was living in his house, just in case. Over the years, he'd built a storehouse of unused explanations he'd prepared rather than be caught off guard by anyone over anything.

Yelling brought Figs and Axia to the window. Cantu and Laird and Reedy and Kerr's shaven domes bobbed down the street as they carried their duffel bags stuffed with clothing and bedding. Each had their towel slung over their shoulder so that they appeared like a party headed for the beach.

"What's happening?" Axia asked.

"Not sure," Figs said, hoping that would be the end of it.

"Where are they going?" she asked, peering through the blinds. She watched the sophs as Figs paced behind her. "You know," she said, whirling around, "if you wanted me out so they could move in you should've just asked."

"Their air conditioner broke," Figs said by way of justification.

"Why didn't they want to move in here? Is it *haunted*?" She laughed at her joke, though the smile was only temporary.

"They're afraid of Mr. Hancock," Figs said. "They think he might still come back."

"Could that happen?" she asked.

"No," he said. "I doubt it."

"I still don't understand why you didn't just ask me to move," Axia said.

"I…" Figs started. He didn't know the answer himself.

"All that about the furniture and the air conditioning," she said. "I thought something was funny."

"Listen, I'm sorry," Figs said.

"No you're not," Axia said, a menace creeping over her face.

"What?"

"You're not sorry. You're just saying you are."

Axia crossed her arms.

"No, really," Figs said. "I'm sorry."

"Say it again."

"I'm sorry."

"Again."

"I'm sorry."

"*Again.*"

Figs lowered his head. "I'm sorry," he said softly.

Axia smiled. "See? You meant it that time."

. . . .

Hands and Roger followed on the heels of the sophomores as they entered Quinn's old residence without knocking.

"Fucks going on here?" Roger asked.

"Figs told us we could," Cantu said.

"There are no sophomores allowed on Regis Street," Roger said.

"But Figs said—"

Roger cut Cantu off. "It doesn't matter *what* he said."

"Where is Axia?" Hands asked, bemused.

"She moved into Mr. Hancock's," Reedy said.

"What happened to your heads?" Roger asked.

"Never mind," Hands said. He turned to Roger. "C'mon, we'll clear this up."

Hands and Roger exited in a haste, leaving the sophomores in confusion. Hands halted. "Let's let this go until morning," he said.

"I think we should fix this now," Roger said.

Hands nodded. "I agree with what you're saying," he said, "but it might be to our advantage to let this ride until morning. You'll see."

"I get you," Roger said.

Hands knew that Roger did not *get him*, that Roger didn't have the mental fortitude to know that the sophs on Regis Street could be traded for Axia's expulsion, the larger picture. But he let Roger believe that the morning would bring outrage and that the sophs would be booted back down to Loyola Street. Hands would ride that sentiment, too, though it was not his primary objective.

The morning did not bring outrage, though. Only relief. Overnight, the heat had escaped, rolling on to terrorize another populace and though the temperatures were still in the low seventies when we woke, we rejoiced. The morning brought purpose, too. Figs and Warren led a troupe including Sprocket, Lindy and Axia to the construction site after breakfast, Sprocket outfitting each with the tools necessary for applying the second coat of compound. A hodgepodge of sophomores joined Figs's crew, strapping on paper masks and taking up paint rollers.

Kerr, Cantu, Reedy, and Laird abstained from the sophomore work detail, volunteering for kitchen detail, hoping to avoid the cleave among the Fellows, an unspoken split audible to those sensitive enough to perceive it. The four might've joined Figs's crew, but Roger and Hands had not decamped with the others, Hands holding court in the dining hall.

The conversation at the table swung from talk of the construction site the daily schedule. Hands appeared in a jovial mood, so much so he kidded Roger about Roger needing a haircut. "Maybe Reedy will cut it for you," he joked. The strained frivolity lent itself to Roger's reaction, a smile instead of the expected threat of pummeling Roger extended at such a personal remark.

The mood soured appreciably when Hands railed against Figs's moving Kerr, Cantu, Reedy, and Laird onto Regis Street. "Who gave you that right?" Hands's voice carried into the kitchen, but the four sophs pretended to be oblivious. "What's next?" he asked in mock-exasperation. "We got sophomores living with the Fellows, outsiders living in the faculty housing. Principal Breen is going to shit himself when he finds out." Hands persisted in his argument, testing our reaction to the accusations levelled at Figs. "A total disregard for the rest of us," he kept saying.

Our reaction was sufficient enough for Hands to spread the indictment against Figs globally, Roger and Hands and Assburn servicing the allegation about the sophomores living in Quinn's old residence and Axia camped out at Mr. Hancock's. The slur did not take hold, though, as Figs had leveled the information in a pre-emptive strike during construction, explaining that the whole maneuver was initiated by the sophomores' air conditioner going kaput. The explanation satisfied Figs's crew so that when Hands approached Figs at the mid-morning break, Figs shrugged. "Doubt you could make it without air conditioning," he told Hands.

"That was just a lie," Hands said. "The air conditioner works fine."

Figs and Axia had been tardy to the break, Axia fussing with clots of joint compound that had tangled her hair. Not even Reedy's testimony that the air conditioner was indeed broken assuaged the conspiracy talk. "See for yourself," Reedy said, not looking Roger in the eye when he said it.

"Why don't we," Hands said. He led all interested parties to Reedy's house for an inspection. The investigation would prove inconclusive, though, as the air conditioner lay splintered into pieces, the twisted fan grate sprouting near the unit like a new species of cacti, the inner coil stretched out lengthwise on the ground, the compressor missing.

Figs's crew took up the construction again after the break, Figs boldly inviting Hands and the rest of us to join him. "We could use the help," Figs said disingenuously.

Hands waved Figs off and Figs shrugged, filing out with the rest of his posse in tow. The visit to Reedy's had agitated Hands (who did not know that Roger had destroyed the unit, hoping to pin the blame on Figs) and Hands suggested we take to the lakebed to scrimmage. "We're still having the Open House match, right?" Hands asked.

"You bet your ass," Roger said, standing up from the table.

Practice consisted of little more than kicking the ball back and forth, Hands showing off a couple of new moves he intended to debut at Open House. "Check this out," he said, instructing Roger to pass him the ball. Roger kicked the ball along the ground and Hands pointed his toe at it, the ball rolling up Hands's shin to his knee, Hands using his knee to bounce the ball eye level, whacking it with his forehead. The ball sailed back toward Roger, who caught it with his hands.

"Holy shit," Assburn said. "That was cool."

Hands sent Roger to fetch Kerr, Cantu, Reedy, and Laird, and they joined in.

In the distance, we could hear the cheers from the compound fight that had erupted when Axia playfully slapped a gooey handprint on Lindy's back. The fight spilled into the front yard, Figs trailing, calling for order, which was reestablished when the bucket of compound used for artillery ran dry, most of the grenades landing wide of their mark.

. . . .

Figs and Warren were engrossed in a conversation about how to convert Hands and the others back to the schedule when they were stopped by Roger, who barred the entrance to the classroom. Behind Roger, the rest of the Fellows and sophomores had taken their seats. Sprocket dug into the box of handouts Hands had exhumed from Mr. Malagon's closet, doling out stacks to the first person in each row.

"Problem?" Figs asked.

"Class time," Roger said.

"That's why we're here," Figs said. He stepped in Roger's direction but Roger didn't budge.

"Class is only for those who swear their allegiance to continuation," Roger said. He spread his arms across the doorway.

"That's mental," Warren said.

Figs called out to Hands, but Hands ignored the call. We fidgeted as Roger gave Figs and Warren the same spiel he'd given the rest of us before permitting us to pass: attending class meant voting for continuation and a vote for continuation was a vote to expel Axia. "None of us want your little girlfriend around here," Roger said.

Figs protested weakly that Axia was not his girlfriend, but Roger was unmoved.

"You in or out?" Roger asked.

"This is ridiculous," Figs said. "We agreed she would leave the day before Open House."

"We who?" Roger asked, dropping his arms.

"We," Figs said. "Me and Hands. Hands, tell him."

Roger's arms shot up again. Hands turned and stared at Figs.

"Wrong, wrong, wrong," Roger said. "The only thing we agree on is that your girlfriend must go. We're all about finishing this fellowship and getting credit." He hesitated before shutting the door on Figs and Warren, allowing them one last chance to change their plea; but Figs and Warren would not accede, their eyes searching the class for a friendly face before the door slammed shut.

. . . .

At the start of Sports, Hands was picking through the sophomores as Figs and Warren walked onto the playing field.

"What's going on?" Figs asked. The question was meant for Hands, but Roger answered as he selected Cantu and Laird.

"We're choosing new teams for the Open House match," Roger said, ignoring Figs. "It'll be me, Hands, Assburn, and this group of sophomores. The rest are with you."

"Hey, wait a minute," Figs said. He took a step in Hands's

direction, but Roger stepped in his path. "I need to talk to Hands," he said. Roger refused to move and Figs shoved him in the chest. Roger cocked his fist, but Hands grabbed him from behind.

"What do you want?" Hands asked. "Isn't it enough that you're trying to ruin our fellowship? What else?" Hands's eyes flared.

"No one is ruining anything," Figs said.

A circle formed around Figs and Hands, the unmistakable sign that violence was imminent.

"Everyone here has voted for continuation," Hands said. "You made your choice."

"What the hell are you talking about?" Figs asked. He took another step toward Hands and Roger reflexively stepped toward Figs.

"You know what the hell I'm talking about," Hands said. "Either you're with us or you're against us."

A strong smell of orange blossoms blew across the field.

"Quit wasting our time," Roger said.

"You can do what you want," Hands said, "but she's not part of Garden Lakes, so keep her out of the way. We don't want her in the dining hall or in chapel or in class distracting us from what we've set out to do. And that goes for this"—he gestured at the field—"and the construction site. Those of us who are serious need to focus."

The sound of a horn directed our attention away from Figs and Hands. A burgundy-colored LTD floated along Garden Lakes Parkway, its driver waving madly. The LTD glided to a stop near us.

"Excuse me," the driver said. "Can you tell me how to get back to the freeway? I'm turned around." A heavyset woman sat staring at us from the passenger seat.

"Go through the gate and turn right," Warren said. "You have to go about fifteen miles. Then you come to a fork. Left for Phoenix and right for Tucson. You'll see the freeway soon after that."

"Thanks." The driver pulled on the bill of his cap. "What're you fellas up to anyway?" he asked. "You live out here?"

We waited for someone to answer. Roger telegraphed our punishment if we spoke up about our situation.

"Just a little game of soccer," Figs said, holding his hands out to receive the ball. After a delay, Hands passed him the ball.

"Where's the field?" the driver asked.

Figs pointed a thumb at the lakebed.

"How you play on that?" The heavyset woman shifted to get a better look.

"We make do," Figs said. He leaned in the driver's window. "This is a sharp car," he said. "Is it new?"

"Hell, no," the driver said. "I wish. They quit making these things."

"Man, coulda fooled me," Figs said, masterfully slipping into slang. "This is a beaut."

"Thanks," the driver said. "Thanks for saying so."

"You're welcome," Figs said, pushing off the car. "We better get back to our game. Big stakes!" Figs laughed and the driver laughed, too. The heavyset woman smiled and the car drifted away.

"Good luck!" the driver shouted to us. He swiped the hat off his head and waved it in the air as he screeched the tires around the parkway. The LTD slid through the front gates like a speedboat gliding ashore. We watched the right turn signal blink twice and then the car disappeared.

Figs dropkicked the ball over our heads, staring down Hands and Roger. He turned and walked away, Warren following dutifully. The ball rolled up onto the island and came to rest under the withering palm tree. Hands yelled for Cantu to get the ball, instructing the others to pick a captain in Figs's absence.

We battled well into the dinner hour, Hands driving aggressively toward the goal every time he touched the ball, second only to Roger, who sent fifty percent of his kicks sailing high and wide, Sprocket calling "Out" as one of the sophomores tracked the ball down and threw it back into play.

Our play on the lakebed suspended time, allowing us to suppress our individual feelings about what had transpired between Figs and Hands. More than a few of us disagreed with Hands's hardline stance;

while we agreed that continuation was necessary to validate our commitment to Garden Lakes, we also felt there was room for Axia and thought that any repercussions brought by the administration—*if they even found out about Axia*—could be successfully argued against.

None of us would give voice to these thoughts, though, preferring to mutter them in parties of two and three on the sidelines during play, and later at dinner, employing the Randolph Backcheck before whispering any dissent. Sprocket, however, would act on his conscience, passing Figs and Warren copies of Mr. Malagon's handouts along with the corresponding exams. "I'll file them away with the others," he said. "No one sees them after I grade them anyway."

Figs and Warren would involve themselves in an act of subterfuge, too, sneaking meals from the dining hall with the help of a core of sympathetic sophomores.

"If I have to live like a prisoner, I might as well leave," Axia said, pushing away her plate of goulash and asparagus.

The truth in Axia's statement spooked Figs, who sat on the edge of her bed. "You can't do that," he said. "Then they'll win."

Axia shrugged. "What do I care if they win or not?"

Figs hadn't considered this. Axia had no stake in the outcome. She could blow through Garden Lakes as easily as she'd blown in. "Where will you go from here?" he asked.

The look on Axia's face told Figs he'd called her bluff; she didn't really want to leave and Figs let himself believe that he was part of the reason why, though he knew it could've been anything. He didn't have a clue what it meant to live by your wits and imagined that chancing upon a situation like the one at Garden Lakes was rare.

Axia set the untouched dinner on the nightstand. "Not sure," she said.

An idea popped into Figs's head. "My neighbor has a guest house he might let you live in," he said.

Axia smiled. "You a real estate broker, too?"

"No," Figs said, blushing. "But he's old and needs someone to take care of him." The layout of the guest house flashed through

Figs's mind, he and Hands having spent a week living in it when they house-sat while the neighbor was away. "It's just an idea."

"It's a nice idea," Axia said, yawning. She stared through the slatted blinds at the fading sunset. "I couldn't even tell you what day it is," she said.

"It's Friday," Figs said, realizing Axia's point after he'd spoken.

Axia kicked off the bed. "I'm going for a walk," she announced, intimating that she was going alone.

Be careful, Figs wanted to say as Axia tied her shoes, but he didn't want to frighten her. While he worried about how far Hands and the others would go to intimidate Axia, he knew she could handle them in ones and twos. He also knew that any misbehavior would result in the nullification of the fellowship. Figs would make sure of that.

Figs loitered in Axia's room, too wired for sleep. He'd kill some time with Lindy, who had taken the community center roof as his permanent observatory, animating the night sky with stories, Warren occasionally supplementing the tales with information we'd learned in textbooks but had long forgotten.

Figs's enthusiasm for the idea was brief, however, as he spotted not Lindy but Roger on the roof. He watched as Roger raised a pair of binoculars, sweeping the development in slow arcs. Roger aimed the binoculars in the area where Figs stood and Figs backed further into the shadows.

．．．．．．．．．．．．．．．．

From then on, we manned the daily schedule with clockwork precision, moving in two distinct teams as effortlessly as if the work had been assigned as such. Indeed we ran on two separate but simultaneous schedules—Hands and his team took to the playing field after breakfast to run drills while Figs and his crew took the early shift at 1959 Regis Street, the whole routine swapped after the mid-morning break. Meals were staggered so each team ate in a half-empty dining hall, everyone scavenging the kitchen for themselves, pairs of cooks pooling their expertise to concoct dishes other than peanut butter and jelly sandwiches, or plates of spaghetti dowsed with parmesan sprinkles dumped from the economy size green canisters in the pantry. Figs and Warren continued to refuse classroom instruction—and Sprocket continued to smuggle them the packets and tests—but the rest of us assembled for the vital component of the fellowship, the classroom remaining silent except for whoever was taking a turn reading aloud from the handout. Axia continued to drift behind the scenes, spending the bulk of the day inside her air conditioned room ("catching up on my rest," she called it) and passing the evenings with Figs and Warren and Lindy, the three engaging in various entertainments—most involving cards or dice or the telescope. And while it was true that a disharmonious note rang in the air, it played in the background, and from the vantage of our last weekend at Garden Lakes, it looked like we would make it.

In retrospect, the events of that Sunday night were the seeds from which we would reap out and out failure.

By all accounts, the evening started to ebb until Kerr produced the bottle of cabernet he'd secreted from the case Mr. Hancock had brought. Many times he'd thought to offer it, but was glad he'd waited, sensing the moment was finally right. Kerr and Cantu were passing the bottle when they were paid an after hours visit by Hands and Roger and Assburn, who were looking for Reedy. The search was called off, though, when the Fellows discovered the contraband. Roger requisitioned the bottle from Kerr, who ceded it with a mild complaint. Hands and Roger and Assburn passed the bottle, Hands abstaining because of his allergy, an affliction that astounded Cantu.

A rattling sounded. "Party favors," Assburn said, producing the bottle of Lindy's painkillers Lindy had assumed he'd lost the day after returning from the emergency room. Years later, Assburn's fondness for pharmaceuticals would fuel his decision to smuggle counterfeit gaming systems from Canada, resulting in his icy death as he plunged through the frozen lake somewhere near Detroit trying to raise enough bail money for his best friend.

The living room on Loyola Street grew boisterous and the bottle of wine and pills circled. The pills spread a thick fog through Hands's brain, dulling his senses and draining the stress of the preceding days. In addition to shepherding the Fellows and sophomores through their final days at Garden Lakes, Hands knew he would have to find ways to give Roger some command without giving him too much. He'd made a step in that direction by giving Roger leeway with the soccer team, even looking the other way when Roger screamed at any player that made a foul or a bad shot; but he wanted to make sure Roger understood the leeway had been bestowed upon him, and by whom.

Hands's warning about keeping Axia out of sight had been successful, too. If he thought about Figs and Axia spirited off somewhere, laughing and fucking around, he became so angry his thinking muddled. Whether or not he would be friends again with Figs, he couldn't say. Hands's command of the situation at Garden Lakes—and the recognition he would receive from the faculty and others—would go a long way in equalizing what Hands perceived as a power differential in their relationship.

As he passed the bottle of wine to Roger, he realized that he hadn't imagined hearing Figs's name. He heard it again, this time ferreting out the source: Laird was trying to be heard over the din, asking something about Figs.

"What?" Hands asked, raising his voice. Laird seemed very far away.

"Do you want to know the real story about Figs?" Laird asked.

"What story?" Hands asked.

"About what happened in Mazatlán. At Rosa's," Laird answered.

Hands and Roger and Assburn exchanged looks.

"How do you know about Rosa's?" Roger asked.

Laird glanced around nervously. "Everyone knows."

"Yeah?" Roger asked. "And what does everyone know?"

Hands diffused the atmosphere with a laugh. "Who cares if everyone knows?"

A smile spread across Laird's face. "Yeah, but I know what *really* happened."

Roger coughed. "Tell it or shut up," he said.

Laird settled back, recounting what we all knew by rote about that night at Rosa's.

"What was it like?" Laird asked, making us wait. "Was it cool?"

"Don't get sidetracked," Hands said.

Laird reveled in his station as master storyteller for a moment longer, then said, "There weren't any Federales."

Laird laid out what he knew: that Figs had taken advantage of the heavy at the door leaving his post to run screaming into the house, scattering those inside and those in the backyard, Laird's older brother among them. "He goes to Trevor Browne," Laird said. None of us knew Laird at all, let alone that his older brother went to public school. "He saw everything."

We sat waiting for more details, the truth about that night stirring our hunger, but that was all Laird had to tell. The reality of Figs's elaborate lie sunk in as the bottle was passed around.

"Faggot," Roger exhaled. "I knew it."

Hands stood and bolted for the door. In retelling the story for the administration, he would omit that he'd been high and would declare that he simply needed some fresh air. That Roger mistook Hands's action as an advance on Figs's house would not exonerate those who besieged the residence, dancing and chanting "Federales! Federales!," the chant amplifying, punctuated with the sound of shattering glass. Not even the administrative inquiry could bring to light the identity of the hurler.

....

It was around this time that I began to feel my loyalties shift. I'd fallen in with Hands's bunch instinctually—Hands knew of my dislike of Figs and had invited me to that first meeting with the others. But that meeting seemed to me to be the first step to putting affairs at Garden Lakes back on the right path. I did not sense that Hands wanted to do Figs harm. Conversely, I recognized Hands's ambition to lead the fellowship to its glorious conclusion and, given my choice, I preferred it be Hands rather than Figs who claimed the crown.

I was even willing to overlook the weaknesses in Hands's administration. Certainly he couldn't be held liable for Roger's rough behavior; Hands surrounding himself with lunatics like Roger was a matter of chance. And as far as I was concerned, the fault lay with Roger, whom I considered an asshole. I dreamt lasciviously violent dreams about smashing Roger upside the head during Sports, or leading a gang of vigilantes against him. Roger's heartlessness inspired the kind of cruelty we imagined only the depraved felt.

I had no opinion about Axia. For the most part, Axia kept to herself. Other lusty feelings did not make their way into the official record. And while I was reluctant to say so publicly, I could understand Figs's point about assimilation. Mr. Malagon spoke often of the need for tolerance—no one in his class was permitted to talk over someone else, himself included—and claims Figs made about inclusion struck a chord with me. Still, I was reticent to align with such a risky enterprise. What if, upon learning about Axia, the administration voided our fellowship? Any appeal would be undermined by fraternization. There were others who felt similarly, though we were too cowardly to express it.

The undignified ruckus that Sunday night moved me a step in Figs's direction, though.

I'd looked out my window as Roger led the charge on Figs's residence, Kerr, Reedy, Cantu, and Laird behind him. Roger bade his lieutenants to kick in the door, but as many times as their feet bounced off the front door, the lock held. I imagined Figs cowering inside, fearful of the glazed look in the sophs' eyes. Kerr and Reedy disappeared, Laird and Cantu sticking close to Roger, who was hunting for rocks large enough to hurl at the double paned windows donated by a local glass company. Kerr and Reedy reappeared with a hammer from Sprocket's supply shed—which Sprocket would discover ransacked the next morning. Kerr handed Roger the hammer and he busted out the front room window. Hands looked on as the sophs entertained themselves by tossing rolls of toilet paper up and over the house, the strands billowing in the hot desert breeze.

The chanting began again, but the riot eventually succumbed to thirst, opting for a raid on the dining hall. I sensed that they did not want to confront Figs anyway and was relieved when they dispersed, Roger lingering, glancing at Figs's door as if daring it to open.

My attitude changed, however, when I learned of the smashed telescope at breakfast. A group whose complete membership was never verified set out from the dining hall to spread the word about what had happened in Mazatlan. The group came upon Lindy and his telescope in the lakebed. Lindy would wait until he was securely ensconced in the administration's bosom before he would name those he remembered from the assault. He told about how Roger had knocked the telescope to the ground and how Hands had held Lindy back while Roger stomped the instrument into uselessness. Lindy remembered yelling, hoping someone would hear and come to his aid, but his yells were quieted by Roger's fist, which landed squarely in Lindy's chest, knocking the wind out of him. (It was not this assault but the one on Mr. Baker that led to Roger's expulsion from Randolph.)

While Lindy stayed silent about the attack the next morning, it wasn't hard to piece together that Roger was behind it. And because Hands and Roger moved in tandem, the assumption that they were in on it together was hard to ignore, though it would come out later that Hands hadn't so much as participated as allowed it to happen, turning his back on Lindy as he did Figs at Summer Griffith's party. Not that anyone objected on Lindy's behalf. Instead, we privately assured him that we would take his side of the matter should he choose to pursue the issue. This cowardly turn did not sit well with your faithful columnist and for all of these reasons, I convinced myself to jump ship and throw in with Figs.

I would not get a chance to exercise my decision, though, as my mind would be decidedly changed again the following morning.

To his credit, Figs was able to function as if nothing had happened, though he did skip breakfast, electing instead to get a jumpstart on the knockdown roller finish, the final step toward completion of the work at 1959 Regis Street. He only had to outlast the chiding for four more days. He would work to repair the damage over the summer, first with Hands and then with a few key Fellows that would back him up at the start of senior year. The reclamation of his credibility lay in the fellowship, he knew, a fact Figs could not later reconcile with his actions that Monday morning.

The rest of Figs's crew reported to the construction site and while no one had the courage to challenge Figs about his lie, whispers of "Federales! Federales!" rose with the wind. Whether Figs heard or not no one would ever know, but it was the only rationale for what happened next.

Roger saw it from the playing field, training his binoculars on the construction site. He and Hands had arrived for breakfast with Mr. Malagon's binoculars around their necks and spent the morning zooming in on us, Hands providing commentary on our food's progress as we chewed and swallowed. The binoculars were not as unnerving as Hands and Roger's freshly shorn heads gleaming under the fluorescent lighting, hurrying us through our bowls of cereal.

Through the lens of his binoculars, Roger saw Figs yank a panel of sheetrock from the far wall in the living room.

Lindy and Warren reacted first, racing into the living room.

"What's happening?" Warren asked.

Figs looked at Warren like he wondered who he was. "What?"

Warren pointed at the displaced drywall. The others gathered around the vandalism. Play in the lakebed ceased and Roger and Hands passed their binoculars around so the rest of us could see the commotion in the living room. And while we could not hear what was being said, we understood the look on Warren's face as he chastised Figs.

We raced to the construction site. Figs's explanation—that the piece had been hung improperly—did not convince many. "Why didn't Mr. Baker catch it?" Roger asked when told, quieting Figs.

"I saw it," Warren said, bailing Figs out. "I didn't mention it because I wasn't sure. But it wasn't sturdy. It had a"—Warren chopped his hand through the air—"dent in it."

Warren's corroborative testimony only temporarily mitigated the feelings of sabotage, feelings that intensified when Figs disappeared for the balance of the day, disabusing me of any notion about changing allegiance. Roger's transgressions appeared small when matched against the pettiness Figs had exhibited. Even if I felt strongly about my complaints about Hands and Roger, Figs's ship appeared to be sunk that afternoon.

My renewal of faith in the other side would not last long, however. In hindsight, it is not hard to understand the actions taken by some that afternoon. But I was as baffled as the other Fellows by the second wave of vandalism in the living room of 1959. Hands's convenient evacuation from the vicinity as Roger pulled down a second panel of sheetrock implicated him. Hands knew that he would need plausible deniability, and there were rumors at lunch that Figs had wrecked the entire living room wall. Only those who had observed Roger and his minions, Laird, Reedy, Cantu and Kerr—their bald heads bobbing in unison as they kicked in the walls—knew the truth, though no such witnesses could be found.

The anatomical view of insulation and wiring sprouting from the living room wall brought the application of the finish to a halt.

"End of the line," Warren said. "We need to call Mr. Baker and get some more drywall."

"No can do," Hands said, shaking his head.

"Give me Hancock's mobile phone and I'll do it, then," Warren persisted.

"I can't," Hands said, hoping to leave it at that. But Warren pressed him, following Hands out of the dining hall at lunch. "It's broken, okay? It doesn't work."

"I don't believe you," Warren said.

Hands turned on Warren. "I don't care if you do," he said. "Why don't you ask your buddy," Hands said. "He knows all about it."

Warren did not ask Figs about the phone, though. That Figs was complicit in a conspiracy over Mr. Hancock's mobile phone would've proved too much for even Warren to bear and he persuaded himself that he did not want to know, preferring the impression that Hands was hoarding the device for his own use.

An afternoon spike in temperature drove us indoors, our energy sapped by the heat. It was reasonable to say that we, including yours truly, were overcome by recent events, too. An awful taste developed in my mouth, my mind muddling whenever I tried to get straight what was what. It was impossible to know where virtue lay and I was adrift, overwhelmed by hopelessness, surrendering to the certainty that it didn't much matter what I chose to believe or whom I chose to follow: the fellowship had been consigned to failure, maybe as early as Mr. Hancock's departure—maybe from the beginning—and that inevitably ushered in a flood of indifference that washed over us all.

Under the cover of night, I saw Laird and Reedy and Cantu and Kerr in the community center doorway. They disappeared inside one by one and then reappeared in formation, each carrying sacks of purloined food. Their skin glowed white in the moonlight, their heads floating, is if disembodied from the rest of their bodies that were invisible in the night.

....

Warren wanted to know what the joke was. "I don't get it," he said when Figs told him. "Where'd she go?"

Figs was too angry to repeat what he'd told Warren, that Hands had expelled Axia in the middle of night—he'd been hearing murmurs that Hands was putting Roger up to something and guessed that it was Axia's removal, confirmed when Figs knocked on her door for breakfast to find her gone. The idea that Axia had up and left on her own was inconceivable. That she had no ties to Garden Lakes, or to anything, really, was a concept that Figs couldn't grasp. A concept he *could* grasp was malice. He swore to meet Hands's malice with malice, whatever the cost. Warren bolted for Axia's, blind with rage, wanting to see for himself.

A blast of humidity greeted Figs as he followed in Warren's wake. He gasped when he saw Mr. Baker's truck parked nose first in front of the construction site. He shaded his eyes and watched as Hands and Roger and Mr. Baker stood in front of the exposed living room wall. Hands shrugged several times while Roger pantomimed how the panels of drywall had been pulled down. Figs hoped Hands was negotiating with Mr. Baker for more drywall—there was still time to mend the wall and slap up the finish, but barely—but he refused to join the negotiations. Hands would see how he'd taken him for granted all these years.

Figs scanned the development. Most everyone was at breakfast, he knew. He looked at the sky, the coming cloud cover visible beyond the rooftops on Regis Street, and headed for the dining hall for something to cure his hunger. He passed Warren asking anyone he encountered if they'd seen Axia. No one had.

Eventually Warren changed tack and went after Hands, whom he spotted ducking inside Roger and Assburn's house. Warren kicked in the front door, calling out Hands's name in anger. Roger and Assburn and Hands jumped in surprise, Roger pushing Mr. Baker— whose hands had been amateurishly tied with rope, his mouth sealed with duct tape—quickly up the stairs, Assburn following. Warren exited just as quickly, convincing himself he hadn't seen what he'd seen so when asked, he would say he knew nothing about it.

Roger threw Mr. Baker face down on a bed in an empty room, instructing Assburn to close the blinds. Mr. Baker's initial protest had been reduced to grunts and moans. Assburn watched while Roger wound the tape around Mr. Baker's ankles. Roger had enlisted his help during breakfast. He warned Assburn not to tell Hands and he promised he wouldn't. Everyone in the dining hall had looked out the window in disbelief as Mr. Baker's truck cruised down Regis Street. A beat passed before Hands stood, knowing he had to do something, not wanting Figs to reach Mr. Baker first. Roger followed, pointing at Assburn on his way out the door.

The selection emboldened Assburn, lifting his wilted spirits. He had all but resigned himself to being a pariah at Randolph. His attempts to remake his reputation had failed and he knew that once senior year started, there would be little room for maneuvering. But then Roger anointed him. He followed Roger to 1959 Regis Street, escorted into the upper echelons, or so he imagined. Even Quinn would have to accept him now, he supposed, a relief since Assburn had destroyed Senator Quinn's pen out near The Grove, demolishing the emblem of his shame with a large, flat rock.

Assburn was so enamored of his elevation that he could not impartially judge whether holding Mr. Baker down while Roger tied Mr. Baker's hands behind his back was a building block to respectability or not. The point was he'd been called into action and he'd served. Not even Mr. Baker's screams and calls for help could diminish the merit Assburn was earning.

Hands knocked on the bedroom door and entered, surveying the landscape as Mr. Baker wriggled on the bed. "What's the plan?" he asked.

"You tell me," Roger said.

A moment passed and no one said anything, the three standing around the bed, staring at its occupant. "I have to think," Hands said.

. . . .

The clouds rolled in as Warren straggled out past The Grove. He expected to find Axia hiding out, on the run from Hands and Roger and the others, remembering what she'd said the night before about "wandering some more." He'd been delighted when Axia reappeared downstairs, wanting to go for a walk, the poker game having dissolved into boastful card tricks. The night was muggy and rife with desert insect, but Warren refrained from complaining, influenced by Axia's cool. They'd talked about nothing in particular, mostly about how stressed out everyone seemed. They'd looped around Garden Lakes Parkway, cutting east to tramp through the undeveloped land. Warren asked if Axia was interested in moving to Phoenix, offering up the spare room at his house (he was convinced his parents would not mind). She'd laughed and told him it was the second such offer she'd received. Warren's ears burned when she told him of the guest house next door to Figs.

"It's sweet," she'd said, "but I don't think I'll be moving to Phoenix."

"Why not?"

Axia answered with a shrug and a smile and Warren knew right then that she would not come to Phoenix; or if she did, she would not stay for long. He appreciated her not saying "It's just better..." or "I could never..." His admiration for her tripled. She'd decided to live life a certain way, and with fidelity to that way of life. He was jealous of the clarity he imagined such a decision brought. You would do this, but not that. He imagined there were ups and downs—like anything—but that there wasn't as much uncertainty because you weren't always entertaining all the possibilities, struggling to come out on top. He thought about how unambitious he was before enrolling at Randolph Prep and he shuddered at how he'd been infected.

Warren's anxiety dwindled as they walked well into the early morning hours. Cool air rushed through the quiet development as they retired to their houses and as Warren said good night, he pledged a transformation similar to Axia's. He would ask for her help and guidance and wherever Axia ended up in the world, they would share this bond.

Lightning crackled overhead, thunder booming around Warren as he continued south, fighting the moist air that tried to blow him backwards. He didn't know for sure that he was traveling in a straight line, but he intuited that he was moving in the right direction. He'd seek out the family of olive farmers if need be. Maybe she had returned to them. If not, maybe they knew something about where she might've gone. Warren took refuge behind an outcropping. Sheets of hot rain blew across the desert, the ground wet with puddles deepening until they ran together. He closed his eyes, letting the rain soak through his clothes, imagining a misty curtain parting to reveal Axia.

He opened his eyes, disappointed.

....

Hands crouched on the end of the bed in the room adjoining the one where Mr. Baker was imprisoned, listening to the monsoon as it rapped against the side of the house. The sky outside his window was dark gray, matching his mood. Roger jumping Mr. Baker still seemed unreal. He took no comfort in telling himself that he probably couldn't have stopped it. But he hadn't tried, and he knew it would be his undoing. He replayed the morning in his mind, dreaming of a different outcome.

"What happened here?" Mr. Baker had asked.

Hands could hear his voice, whiny and small, telling Mr. Baker it was an accident.

"Doesn't look like an accident," Mr. Baker had maintained. He'd inspected the precision with which the panels had been ripped out.

"We were hoping to get a little more drywall."

Mr. Baker didn't hear the request, though, instead demanding to know where Mr. Malagon was. Hands had wished for Figs's presence right then, which doubled his regret. On the field or on the court, Hands relied on his instincts, which never failed him. If a defender twice his size bore down on him, or if he sensed he could intercept an errant pass, his mind and body moved at will. But to his chagrin the gift was only physical. Mr. Baker's questions begged for some mental and verbal dexterity he didn't possess. He worshipped this quality in Figs, but confessing this to Figs would not imbue Hands with the gift, so what was the point? Figs had enough people wrapped around his finger; Hands refused to become another. The day before, when Figs was on the ropes, he'd stayed in the shadows during the chanting, hiding behind Roger and Assburn and the others, but the release was as euphoric as if he were leading the barrage. Finally, finally Figs's reputation proved permeable. He didn't really care about Figs's lie, but he knew the ramifications of such a lie and no matter what happened thereafter, Figs's days at Randolph would be humbler.

"Seriously. Where is Mr. Malagon?" Mr. Baker had asked.

Roger had come out of nowhere, lunging. He and Mr. Baker fell to the ground, Roger overpowering his prey with stupefying quickness. Then Assburn appeared and the two strong-armed a dazed Mr. Baker into their house. He would have to convince the others that the abduction was Roger's idea. He could count on Assburn to back up the assertion. Roger had lassoed Assburn as a henchman on his own; it would not be hard for Hands to sell his innocence to Assburn. He would offer Assburn the inclusion that everyone was determined to withhold from him. Assburn had walled himself off by wearing his desires so openly, Hands thought, so that the others made a game of denying Assburn acceptance. Regardless, Hands would make the first offer; he would promise Figs's friendship, too, though Hands knew that some rehabilitation of his own friendship with Figs would be required. The idea repulsed him—he'd never truly be friends with Figs again and he questioned their friendship going all the way back to Julie Roseman. He'd granted Figs absolution, but had he meant it? His boarding the bus to Disneyland so long ago, before he learned about Figs's betrayal, resonated as the last sunny moment of their friendship. And now rather than make a principled stand against Figs, Hands knew he'd have to fall back in line, too, weak to withstand what he knew would be Figs's manipulation of everything that happened at Garden Lakes.

The storm raged as Hands balanced two columns in his mind: Those Who Would Be on His Side and Those Who Wouldn't. Thunder echoed above. The cascade of air conditioning falling on Hands's shoulders trickled to nothing, the electricity flowing through its veins cut off by the storm. The lights flickered and then went dark. He slipped downstairs, braced himself for the deluge, and then dashed from the house.

....

Reedy burst in, a wild look in his eyes, startling Roger from his lookout on the stairs. He had heard Hands leave and expected his quick return, wondering where he went. Rain pooled under Reedy's feet as he stood in the doorway.

"Shut the damn door," Roger said gruffly, still freaked out by the sight of Reedy, his bald head slick with rain.

"Laird's got a snake," Reedy blurted out.

Roger eyed Reedy. "What do you mean he's got a snake?"

Reedy poured it all out about how Laird had been laying down and about how a snake had crawled up in his bed, coiling on his chest. "They do it to get warm," Reedy added. "Laird wanted me to get you. He wants your help to get it off him."

"What does he want me to do about it?" Roger asked, though there was no way he wasn't going to go, flattered that they'd thought of him in their moment of panic.

"I don't know," Reedy said. "He just said to get you. He said to hurry."

Roger glanced up the stairs and thought to make an excuse, but because he didn't yet know what would be done about Mr. Baker, he followed Reedy into the rain, splashing through the loch that had formed along Regis Street.

Assburn watched out the bedroom window as Roger followed Reedy to a house on Loyola Street. He'd heard muffled voices in the living room and wondered what was going on. He suspected he was being set up to take the fall for Mr. Baker, who was struggling face down on the bed, his hands wound behind his back with duct tape, a suspicion that was bred when he saw Hands run out the front door toward the dining hall. It *was* near lunch time, Assburn thought, but why hadn't Hands asked if he wanted anything, or to offer to relieve him of his command? Assburn snuck downstairs. He flicked a light switch on and off. Nothing. He slid open the window above the kitchen sink to admit fresh air into the fetid house, but the steamy air did little to comfort him.

He momentarily mistook a loud bang for thunder, realizing his mistake when Mr. Baker bound down the stairs, his keys in hand, a small piece of duct tape still stuck to his cheek.

. . . .

Roger tapped on Laird's door. He could feel Reedy's breath on his neck, but the sick feeling in his stomach trumped his annoyance. The door was opened cautiously by a soph wearing a look of panic. Roger was surprised to find the room packed with sophomores, a bald circle arranged around Laird, who lay stiffly in bed with his eyes closed. A coiled bulge under the covers rose and fell with Laird's shallow breathing.

"You have to whisper," Kerr said.

Roger tread carefully toward Laird, who opened his eyes. Reedy fell back, blending into the gallery.

"What is it?" Roger whispered. The air in the room was stagnant, fired by the mass of sweaty bodies.

Laird whispered something Roger couldn't hear.

"What?" Roger asked, his voice threatening to rise out of a whisper.

A chorus of "Shh!" went around the room.

Laird rolled his eyes and whispered again.

"I can't hear you," Roger whispered.

"Maybe you should lean in," Kerr whispered.

Roger kept his eye on the coil, listening for the tell tale rattle that signaled the snake's agitation. His breathing became measured, his heartbeat slowing. Roger bent down to Laird's ear but shot upright when Kerr tapped him on the shoulder. "Be careful not to bump him," Kerr whispered. Roger scowled, but Kerr didn't notice. He bent down again, putting his ear next to Laird's lips, the coil eye level now.

"If you rip the covers off, I'll roll the opposite way," Laird whispered in a halting voice.

Roger frowned. "It won't work," he mouthed.

Laird rolled his eyes again and took a deep breath, the snake rising under the sheets. Roger backed away, a look of terror on his face.

"What did he say?" Kerr asked in Roger's ear.

Roger repeated the plan to Kerr in a hushed tone.

"I'll help," Kerr whispered. He went around to the other side of the bed and pantomimed that Roger should take a corner of the sheets.

Roger shook his head. "It won't work!" he whispered loudly.

The room filled with shushes.

"On three," Kerr whispered, grabbing the sheet in one hand. Roger gripped the other side. "One...two..."

Roger clenched the sheet tightly. A rivulet of sweat leapt off his forehead.

"Three!" Kerr yelled, whipping back the sheet. Roger tried to lift his arm, but the room spun away from him as he passed out from fear and stress and the heat, the coil of garden hose on Laird's chest falling to the floor as the room erupted in laughter.

....

Lindy couldn't believe his luck. He realized he'd have more time to operate than he'd ever dreamed as he witnessed first Hands and then Roger bolting out of the house, followed by Mr. Baker running for his truck, Assburn in step behind until Mr. Baker reached his truck and peeled out. Something was up, but he'd have to find out about it later. He knocked for good measure—it was possible someone was loafing in the house, staying out of the rain—but there was no answer. He slipped inside, leaving wet footsteps on the stairs.

The house was in some disarray. All of the doors were blown open as if a tornado had roamed the halls. Panicked that either Hands or Assburn or Mr. Baker would return, Lindy pillaged Roger's room with the efficiency of a burglar. It didn't take him long to locate what he'd come for: the job journal was at sea in a drawer of unrolled socks. He plucked the booklet out and cleared a place on top of the dresser to write. He used the plunger end of his pen to trace over Roger's handwriting. He practiced Roger's disconnected capital printing, lines flaring on the E's and F's, T's that crossed with a dot, R's that looked like P's. He traced over a half page about corner beads and then clicked his pen, ready. He found a space in the margin and wrote *Mr. Morgan is a fag*, the slur matching Roger's handwriting perfectly. The famous episode about Roger transferring out of Mr. Morgan's Advanced English class, complaining to Principal Breen that Mr. Morgan's grading was too harsh, would complement the slur nicely.

Lindy tucked the job journal away in the top of Roger's closet so he could easily find it again during the Open House. He started at what he thought was someone downstairs, but what he really heard was the deafening quiet: the rain had ceased pelting Garden Lakes, the gray clouds concealing sunlight rolling away, the winds blowing their last breath as the monsoon passed.

....

None of us would remember where we were when we first heard the sirens that afternoon. Some of us would remember inspecting the water damage to one of the sophomore houses on Loyola Street, others would remember eating lunch in the dining hall when the first traces of blue and red painted the air. Still others would conveniently forget the answer to the question. Our collective confusion would be a source of consternation for the administration as they spent the fall semester trying to sort out the details.

Your faithful columnist would prove to have the clearest memory of events, becoming invaluable as the police waded through the alibis and plots. Figs fingered Hands as the mastermind of Mr. Baker's kidnapping, having heard about Hands's involvement from Warren, but Hands had a rock-solid alibi. I'll tell it to you as I told it to the cops: Hands was on the roof of the community center with yours truly, watching the storm gather through binoculars when